Abou

Susie Murphy is an Irish historical fiction author. She loves historical fiction so much that she often wishes she had been born two hundred years ago. Still, she remains grateful for many aspects of the modern age, including women's suffrage, electric showers and pizza. A Class Reunited is her fifth published novel.

ISBN-13: 978-1-915770-05-9

www.susiemurphywrites.com

Join the Susie Murphy Readers' Club
for updates and free stories:

https://bit.ly/susie-murphy-readers-club

A Class Reunited

A Matter of Class, Book Five

Susie Murphy

Also by Susie Murphy

A Class Apart
A Class Entwined
A Class Forsaken
A Class Coveted

For my big brother, Declan, whose height is only matched by his immense thoughtfulness and generosity.
And for his incomparable wife, Michelle, who I'm so glad to be able to call my sister.

CHAPTER 1

Emily kept her gaze trained upon the horizon, not even allowing herself to blink, until she could no longer pretend that she could still see the coastline. America was wholly lost to view. At last she blinked, feeling the moisture on her eyelashes. It was only sea spray, she tried to convince herself. She wiped it away surreptitiously before turning to her companion.

'No going back now,' she said, making a valiant effort to keep her tone light.

Rory grunted. She wrinkled her nose. What a joy it would be to spend the next month travelling with him at her side.

No, she would not allow his dreary presence to sour this venture. He could disapprove all he wanted but she had taken her future into her own hands and she intended to mould it into something greater than that which her parents could ever have imagined or provided for her.

Her insides stirred queasily at the thought of her mother and father. Had they discovered her note yet? How furious would they be when they learned what she had done? Would they even welcome her home when she eventually returned to Boston?

Struggling to push her guilt aside, she said, 'Shall we go down below to see what it's like?' She indicated the open hatch in the deck through which many of the other passengers had already disappeared.

Rory shrugged but didn't object, so she picked up her valise and led the way, ignoring her still-queasy stomach. Whereas the June heat had been stifling in the city, here on the ship it was tempered by an invigorating sea breeze which tugged on the golden curls striving to escape from her plain bonnet as she crossed the deck.

A steep set of stairs descended into the gloom of the *Integrity*'s steerage quarters. Emily made her precarious way downwards, grateful that she was still wearing her maid's clothing and could not trip on the hem of her skirt which stopped just short of her ankles. When she reached the bottom of the stairs, she clutched her valise to her chest and stared around.

Men, women and children crowded the space, lurching about as they endeavoured to adapt to the motion of the ship, some cramming their belongings into a storage bay running down the centre between numerous rows of bunks, and others hurrying to claim the berths for themselves or their fellow travellers. Their mix of accents rose in a confused din of bickering and whining and the air was thick with the odour of human bodies.

'Out of the way,' said a gruff voice behind Emily and she sidestepped quickly to let a stocky man pass. Rory followed next, instinctively ducking his head beneath the low ceiling of the steerage area. He carried a canvas bag slung over his shoulder and grasped its strap more tightly as he, too, took in their chaotic surroundings. What were they supposed to do next?

A middle-aged woman stood nearby with her hands on her hips, surveying the mayhem with a weary sort of expression. Her gaze wandered over to Emily and Rory and, evidently identifying them as two lost lambs, she approached them.

'Married?' she asked in an American accent. Spidery red veins criss-crossed her nose and cheeks.

Emily gaped at her. 'N-no,' she said. 'We're brother and sister. Emily and Rory McCarey.' A combination of McGovern and Carey, the invented surname had been the best they could come up with at short notice.

The woman nodded. 'Single men to the bow, single women to the stern,' she said, a slight slur on her 's' words.

Emily baulked. While Rory was very, very far down her list of people she would have chosen to accompany her to England, he was also the only person she knew on this ship. 'Is there a family section?' she tried.

'In the middle, but it's only for husbands and wives and their infants,' said the woman. 'Captain Philips insists upon it for the sake of his passengers' morality. They must live up to the name of his precious vessel.' She rolled her eyes before crooking a languid finger at Emily. 'You come aft with me.'

'Wh-who are you?' Emily asked, smothering her impulse to want an adult to ask the audacious question for her.

'Miss Lovell, the matron. I supervise the women on board and make sure they obey the rules. My private quarters are just over there,' she added, pointing into the shadows past the stairs where Emily could discern a rudimentary compartment partitioned from the main area. 'You come to me if you have any issues.' With a half-hearted pat on Emily's shoulder, Miss Lovell headed towards the back of the ship.

Emily shot an anxious look at Rory. Face impassive, he jerked his chin to indicate that she should follow the matron and he himself turned towards the front of the steerage area. She watched him walk away, unsure whether to feel relieved or abandoned.

The stocky man from before passed by again with a large coil of rope in his arms and she realised he must be a sailor, not a

3

passenger. He caught her staring after Rory and said to her in a slightly less gruff voice, 'Don't worry, Lovell will be drunk for most of the voyage. You'll have your fella back soon enough, unless a prissy broad objects.'

Emily coloured, mumbled something unintelligible and hastened after the matron, the light below decks diminishing as she moved further away from the hatch. When she caught up to Miss Lovell, she found her leaning listlessly against a vertical bedpost joining two bunks and giving instructions to another passenger about the baggage she carried.

'There's no room for it in your berth so you'll have to put it in the storage bay. Make sure it's tied down securely—you don't want it to get dislodged during rough weather.' Miss Lovell glanced around at Emily and pointed at her valise. 'Same goes for you. Space will be tight as it is. The captain was kind enough to take on extra passengers, which means people in steerage need to double up.'

Emily's nausea intensified. She would have to share a bunk with a stranger? Now she was more than glad that men and women were segregated but she still felt uncomfortable at being compelled into such intimate proximity with an unfamiliar woman for a matter of weeks. She tried to recall the circumstances of the last journey she had taken on a ship, eight years ago on the voyage from Ireland to Boston – had she and her family been obliged to share sleeping space with strangers then? No, she had a vague memory that they had occupied a cabin which, though cramped, had still been more spacious than the accommodations presented to her right now. But she and Rory would never have been able to afford the fare for cabin tickets.

'Who should I share with?' she asked Miss Lovell faintly.

The matron gave her a dismissive wave. 'Whoever's willing.'

She drifted away and Emily regarded the rows of berths, petrified.

'You can join me if you like,' said an English-accented voice close at hand.

She spun around. A young woman sat on the bottom bunk nearest her. She was hunching to avoid hitting her head off the bunk above and one of her palms rested on the very large belly protruding in front of her. She caught Emily looking at it.

'No need to be alarmed,' she said. 'I'm a widow, not a harlot.'

Gulping, Emily said, 'O-of course. I didn't think—'

'You did, but I'm not offended. What else are you supposed to assume when you see a pregnant woman in the unmarried section of the ship?' Her lips quirked into a brittle smile. 'I'm Louise Shelby.'

Emily returned the smile, though it drained much of her remaining energy; she was quite fatigued after the upheaval of the day. 'Emily McCarey.' She swallowed nervously. 'You would be willing to share your berth with me?'

'I think it's more a case of whether you would be willing to share with me.' Louise grasped the wooden frame of the bunk above her head and hauled herself to her feet. She had a slender physique which only drew more attention to the considerable size of her bump. 'No one wants to put up with a squalling baby.'

Emily's eyes widened. 'You're expecting to give birth on the voyage?'

Louise patted her belly. 'It's possible. Do you like babies?'

'I do,' said Emily. 'I think.' She hadn't paid the greatest amount of attention to Jack and Gus after they had been born, her interest in them tempered by the fact that she had been denied a little sister on both occasions. However, she had cherished her doll, Mabel, with a deep maternal instinct...until she had started school and callously shut the doll away in a cupboard in an effort to appear more grown up to her classmate, Emmeline. The old guilt resurfaced as she reflected on that abandonment. Had her maternal instinct matured since then? Resolving that it must have because she was now a woman, she said more firmly, 'Yes, I do like babies.'

'Well then, welcome,' said Louise, sweeping her hand towards the bunk.

Emily eyed it dubiously. She supposed it could fit two people lying on their sides but it would be a tight squeeze. Was Rory facing a similar dilemma in the men's quarters? How uncomfortable that would be for him; he didn't communicate well with people he knew, let alone complete strangers. On top of that, he would be too tall to even stretch out fully in the berth's confined space.

She refused to feel guilty on that score. The discomfort would teach him to interfere in her private business. If he hadn't forced his insufferable company upon her for this journey, he could be right at this moment anticipating a good night's sleep in the familiar surroundings of his home on Broad Street instead of contemplating the awkwardness of sharing a berth with a strange man who might snore or have smelly feet or rude manners. At least Emily's partner seemed agreeable, and no doubt the newborn baby would be irresistibly adorable when it arrived.

'Thank y—' she started to say but cut herself off as the ship pitched to the side and she fought to keep her balance.

Louise wobbled too and grabbed onto the bunk's bedpost. 'That was unpleasant,' she said. 'I hope Captain Philips and his crew will make it a smooth voyage on the whole.' She squinted at Emily. 'Is it just the poor light or are you rather green?'

Emily whimpered as she sensed saliva gathering in the back of her mouth. She looked around frantically for a bucket or a pail but saw none. In desperation, she opened her valise, emptied its contents out onto the floorboards, and vomited into it.

CHAPTER 2

Bridget hung the half-finished gown of white muslin inside the cupboard space under the stairs at Acorn House, careful not to disturb any of the pins. Her employer, Madame Roche, had assigned this latest creation to her off the back of her successful completion of the blue silk gown for Miss Halliwell, the daughter of one of Madame Roche's wealthiest customers. Feeling quite proud of the dressmaker's faith in her abilities, Bridget shut the cupboard door as footsteps scampered up behind her.

'Ma, it fell out!'

Jack came to a halt, a bloody tooth glistening in his palm and a gap in his beaming smile.

'That's marvellous!' said Bridget. 'I hope your gum isn't too tender.'

'It isn't,' he said bravely. He stuck his tongue into the gap and probed his other front tooth in the top row. 'When will this one fall out?'

She smoothed back his fair hair affectionately. 'It might take a little while if it's not even loose yet.'

A mop of chestnut curls appeared by Jack's shoulder. 'When will *my* teeth fall out?' Gus demanded.

'Not until you're older,' Bridget said, plucking his plump chin. 'Jack is seven and a half which is the right age to be losing teeth. You are two years younger so you'll have to wait for now.'

Gus huffed in disappointment. 'Where's Da?' he asked petulantly. 'He's not home yet and we've already had supper.'

'I expect he's just been delayed at the workshop,' she said in a light tone, but the same question had been preying upon her mind for the past hour. Cormac never usually came home this late, not even when he used to slip away after a long day's work at the docks to set up his own carpentry business. That new venture was supposed to have been a surprise for Bridget but it had been ruined when Tess had insinuated that Cormac's absences were due to him playing Bridget false with another woman.

Bridget pursed her lips and banished Tess from her thoughts. 'Let's go wash the blood out of your mouth,' she said to Jack, ushering him towards the kitchen.

She set a basin of water in front of him on the kitchen table and he rinsed out his mouth several times, Gus watching in fascination as the bloody spit swirled in the basin.

'Does Jack get a treat?' he asked with the blatant hopefulness of one who expects to be invited to share in said treat.

'Hmm,' said Bridget, turning her back to the boys and rummaging in a cupboard next to the stove. She swivelled back to Jack and Gus with a flourish. 'How about this?'

They both goggled. A bright, round orange sat in the centre of her palm. Jack looked enormously pleased that his accomplishment had brought about such a reward, and Gus licked his lips in anticipation. Bridget carried the orange to the table and began to peel it.

'You may each take every second piece,' she said, 'and if there happens to be one segment left over at the end, then Jack may have it. Do you hear me, Gus?'

Gus nodded without taking his eyes off the juicy treasure. 'Yes, Ma.'

She handed the first segment to Jack. 'It's soft so it should be gentle on your gum,' she said just as the front door banged. 'There's your father now,' she added with relief.

Distracted by their treat, the boys didn't dash from the kitchen as they normally would have; Jack was busy pulping his piece of orange with his back teeth while Gus was reaching out to Bridget beseechingly.

'I'll go greet him then, shall I?' she said with a chuckle, dropping the second orange segment into Gus's chubby, outstretched hand. She placed the remainder of the fruit on the table and, shaking her head, went through the door that separated the kitchen from the front room.

She knew immediately that something was very wrong. Cormac stood just inside the front door, his face ashen and his chest heaving – had he been running? He was clutching a piece of paper in one fist and panic shadowed his blue eyes.

She pulled the kitchen door closed behind her, certain that the boys should not hear whatever terrible news Cormac was about to impart. Crossing the room swiftly, she seized his arms.

'Tell me at once,' she entreated. 'What's happened?'

His gaze connected with hers. 'Emily,' he croaked.

Bridget's heart nearly stopped at the fear in his voice. 'Is she hurt?' she exclaimed. 'Is she ill?'

He shook his head. 'She's...run away.'

Bridget stared at him without comprehension and, wordless, he handed her the slip of paper. She seized it and began to read with a sense of deep foreboding.

Mother, Father,

Please do not be alarmed when you read this. I have boarded a ship bound for England as I wish to accept Garrett's invitation to visit him in London. I believe that his sentiments were sincere in his letter to me and I desire to take advantage of the opportunities he has offered. I reiterate that you must not worry for this is what I dearly want.

I very much hope to see you and my brothers again within the year.

Your loving daughter,
Emily

Horror-struck, Bridget could only gape at the words on the page. She wanted to deny their authenticity but they had definitely been written in Emily's neat hand.

'Oh, dear God,' she said at last, looking up at Cormac's anguished expression. 'Where did you find this?'

'Marlowe House,' he said. 'Emily wasn't there. O'Mali's daughter, Matilda, gave it to me.'

Bridget recalled Emily leaving home that morning with the intention of staying in the servants' quarters at Marlowe House for a number of days while extra guests at the residence placed a greater demand upon the maids' time. She had taken Bridget's valise with her. Had it been a ruse? Was their little girl capable of such deception?

Dismay flooded Bridget as she darted to the stairs and ran up them, still clutching the letter. The eighth step, which Emily had christened Barnabas the day they moved in, squeaked in protest. Bridget reached the landing and rushed into Emily's box room. She fell to her knees in front of the cupboard and opened it. Mabel was there, her limbs splayed and her countenance sombre, but most of Emily's clothes were missing.

Cormac entered the room behind Bridget and made straight for the bed, running his hand underneath the pillow. He retrieved a small note and showed it to Bridget. It contained only two words: 'Ask Matilda'.

'How did you know that was there?' Bridget demanded.

'There was an identical one at Broad Street. I suppose she wanted to cover all options for discovery.' Cormac sighed. 'It was a good delaying tactic, misdirecting whoever found it and giving her more time to get away.'

Bridget pressed her fingers to her mouth. 'She's really gone?'

'She is,' he said heavily. 'Matilda said the ship was scheduled to leave this afternoon. We are mere hours too late.'

A distraught sob escaped Bridget's throat. 'My poor gooseberry. What on earth was she thinking to cross the ocean alone?'

Cormac knelt beside her. 'That's the one ray of light in all this. She's not alone. Rory went with her.'

'Rory *Carey*?' Bridget spluttered, as if there was any other Rory in their acquaintance. 'How can that possibly be?'

'I had a hard time giving credit to the idea too,' said Cormac, 'but all evidence suggests that it's really the case.'

He described how Rory's sister Una had come to the workshop that morning to announce that Rory was unwell and would not be able to carry out his apprenticeship duties that day or the next. Out of concern, Cormac had called to the Careys' rooms on Broad Street after closing up the workshop for the evening, at which point he learned that Una had told Rory's mother, Derval, that Cormac had sent Rory out of town for a couple of days to fetch carpentry supplies. Once the lies had been exposed, all Cormac and Derval could glean from Una was that Rory had made her swear to pass on the false messages and then she had watched him leave Broad Street in the company of Emily, both of them carrying baggage. As soon as Emily's 'Ask Matilda' note had been discovered under Rory's pillow, Cormac had hastened directly to Marlowe House where Matilda had given him Emily's letter and confirmed that its contents were true, admitting that Emily had been planning her departure for the past week.

Ever since Garrett's letter had arrived containing grand promises of a better life for her.

Bridget thought she might be sick. She gazed down at the slip of paper in her hand and imagined Emily writing it with such optimism, believing that Garrett meant to leave her his inheritance as well as arrange for her coming out in London society. How gullible she had been, and how crushed she would be once Garrett's devious nature was laid bare to her. For there was nothing but deceit in his motives, of that Bridget was convinced.

'The scoundrel,' she growled. 'How dare he ensnare an innocent girl in such a way! And what in God's name does he mean to gain from this charade? Is it some sort of spiteful attack against us?'

'I don't know,' said Cormac, his jaw clenched. 'If it is, why wait so long to implement it? It's been eight years since we absconded from London.'

'Perhaps he wanted to exact his revenge when we least expected it, or when he could inflict the most amount of damage.' She worried the tip of her tongue with her teeth. 'Emily would have been too young and sheltered for such a ploy to succeed before now. But she gained independence from us when she began working as a maid.' Bridget gulped. 'And that was when it would have become clear to her precisely what kind of privileged life you and I had taken her from. She must have felt very aggrieved indeed by her situation to act so rashly when Garrett presented her with a prospect for betterment.'

Cormac ran his hand through his fair hair in a swift, exasperated movement. 'But that only raises more questions! How could he have known that she had gone into service or where to send his damn letter for that matter? You've always kept your correspondence these past years strictly related to estate business and all your letters passed to him through Oakleigh, never from this address. How did he ascertain where to contact Emily and also contrive the perfect bait to seduce her?'

Cormac thumped his fist on top of the open cupboard and Mabel's limbs quivered within. Bridget felt like hitting something herself as realisation dawned with startling clarity, as though she had lifted a pair of opera glasses to her eyes.

'He had us followed,' she said with quiet conviction.

Cormac shot her a troubled glance. 'That thought did cross my mind after his letter arrived. Do you think so?'

'I'm certain of it,' she replied.

In a morose tone, she told him about the time she had noticed a man with a high collar trailing after her and Jack on the street. He had been getting closer to them and she had tried to hurry but Jack had tripped and almost fallen, causing his cap and her spools of thread to go flying in all directions. When she had looked back again, the man had disappeared.

'I'm not sure why he fled at that point—perhaps he realised I had become conscious of his presence. It was a frightening incident though and it left an unsettled feeling in my gut.' She shuddered.

'Why didn't you tell me about this after it happened?' asked Cormac in bewilderment.

'We were rather preoccupied with another distressing event at the time,' she said. 'That was the day Derval established that Gus hadn't turned in my womb.'

They were both silent as the traumatic memories of Gus's perilous birth billowed between them.

'In any case,' she carried on softly, 'it didn't happen again, as far as I was aware. Either the man stopped following us or he got better at keeping himself concealed.' She swallowed. 'Who knows, he may have been tracking the movements of our whole family for years.'

'And you suspect that he might have been an agent of Garrett's?' said Cormac, a muscle twitching in his cheek.

'It's very possible. I suppose there's an outside chance that he could have been in the employ of Lord and Lady Bewley, but Garrett is more likely, given recent developments.'

Cormac flinched at the mention of the Bewleys, his guilt over his questionable past never far from the surface. She laid a consoling hand on his thigh and he covered it with his own hand that still held Emily's 'Ask Matilda' note. The rough surface of the paper grazed Bridget's skin.

'I can't believe she did this,' Cormac said with a despairing sigh. 'It's inconceivable that she could be so...' He trailed off, as though he didn't want to say a bad word against their daughter.

'Foolish,' Bridget supplied miserably.

He nodded, looking equally glum.

'She's too naive to recognise what a precarious position she has put herself in,' Bridget went on, lamenting Emily's recklessness with a fresh wave of anguish. 'She thinks Garrett will somehow orchestrate her return to upper class society—and it may well be within his power to do so, if it serves whatever nefarious scheme he has underway—but it probably has not even occurred to her that society might still choose to reject her. Although her birth is technically legitimate because

15

it took place during my marriage to Garrett, she is tainted by the scandal of my running away with you. The gossips of London have long memories. They might not remark upon it to her face but whispers will follow her wherever she goes.'

'What is more, we had her converted to a Catholic when we came to Boston,' Cormac said uneasily. 'And she has occupied a lower class situation for eight years. If those details became known, she could well be openly shunned.'

Bridget slumped. 'And it is under these circumstances that she has thrown herself at the mercy of Garrett. Dear God in heaven, what are we going to do?'

'The first thing I must do is go back to Broad Street,' said Cormac. 'I dashed from there in an almighty hurry earlier to get to Marlowe House. Now that we know what's happened, I need to tell Derval where her son has gone.'

'I'll go with you,' said Bridget. 'I imagine we shall have some explaining to do on several points.' Shame filled her as she reflected that not only Emily's duplicity was about to be exposed. 'We'll bring the boys too. We can't leave them here alone.'

'Are they already in bed?' Cormac asked.

'No, I let them stay up later than usual because Jack lost his tooth. They're in the kitchen sharing an orange.' What an ordinary event that had been in the midst of all this turmoil.

Her knees ached from kneeling on the floorboards. She closed the cupboard door, shutting Mabel into the darkness once more, and got to her feet.

'One thing baffles me,' she said as Cormac stood too. 'How could Emily even contemplate getting on a ship again? She must have forgotten how terribly seasick she was on the voyage from Ireland.'

CHAPTER 3

Gus barged through the Careys' door first, hollering, 'Jack lost his tooth!' and pointing a triumphant finger in his brother's direction.

Although Jack appeared crestfallen at having missed the opportunity to make the announcement himself, he dutifully bared the gap in his front teeth to the Carey children. The two girls, Una and Sorcha, exhibited a distinct lack of interest but ten-year-old Brian said eagerly, 'Was there loads of blood? Did it hurt? Did you swallow it by accident?'

Derval Carey shushed her youngest child and her worried green eyes fixed upon Bridget and Cormac as they followed the two boys into the room. 'D'ye have news?'

Bridget wondered where they would even begin. She glanced at Cormac, who said, 'We do. There's quite a lot to tell. Maybe we should...go upstairs?'

Derval jerked her head. 'Fine. Una, Sorcha, ye two are in charge. Mind the boys 'til we come back down.'

Her daughters looked annoyed that they were to be excluded from the adults' conversation while the boys whooped at being allowed to stay up so late. The three of them clustered together, a hint of devilment lighting up their expressions.

'Be good,' Bridget warned them.

As she, Cormac and Derval left the room, she overheard Una saying to Sorcha in a relieved tone, 'At least it looks like I'm not in trouble anymore.'

They climbed the stairs without speaking and Cormac knocked on the door to the rooms that had been his and Bridget's first home together. His sister Orlaith answered almost at once, concern filling her features.

'Come in,' she said, waving them inside. 'Derval said there's been some sort of commotion with Emily and Rory. What's going on?'

When they entered, Orlaith's husband, Charlie, moved forwards from where he had been standing by the unlit fireplace. Tugging on his misshapen left ear, a reminder of the riot which had occurred between the Yankees and the Irish on the street outside seven years previously, he greeted them all soberly in his American accent.

'Sounds like you've got a tangle on your hands,' he said, throwing Bridget and Cormac a quizzical glance.

Before either of them could respond, Tess emerged from the back bedroom. Bridget had learned to keep her hostility in check when the other woman was present, but her hackles rose now at the flicker of pleasure that crossed Tess's face as her gaze fell upon Cormac. She tamped it down swiftly but Bridget had discerned it. Gritting her teeth, she dismissed it as inconsequential – Tess knew her place and they had greater problems to contend with right now.

Gathering her courage, Bridget said, 'Let's sit down, shall we?'

Derval, Orlaith and Charlie squeezed onto the familiar tattered sofa opposite the hearth while Tess slid the stool over from the kitchen table and perched on it beside them. The bench nestled under the table too; Cormac retrieved it and placed it in front of the fireplace, gesturing to Bridget to sit while he stood alongside. As she lowered herself onto the bench, she felt like she was about to give testimony at an inquisition. It was not dissimilar to the time she had once faced an angry assembly of tenants in Farmer McKinty's barn back in Ireland and tried to convince them that her mother's failings in the management of Oakleigh were not her own. However, on this occasion, she and Cormac had to accept the burden of blame.

Derval eyed them both. 'Where's my Rory?'

'He's safe,' Bridget reassured her, before adding awkwardly, 'That is to say...we think we know where he is.'

Next to her, Cormac cleared his throat. 'We believe he has boarded a ship with Emily.' He hesitated. 'To England.'

Derval gaped at them. 'A ship? *England*? What in heaven's name—' She broke off as incredulity flushed her features. 'They haven't run off to get married, have they?'

'What a notion,' said Orlaith with a laugh. 'They hate each other's guts.' Charlie nudged her and she said defensively, 'Well, they do. They've been at odds for years.'

'No, we don't believe they've eloped,' said Cormac. 'Emily recently received an invitation to visit...an old acquaintance of ours in London. We warned her of the untrustworthy nature of the individual in question and told her to disregard it. Regrettably, she did not heed our advice. We have a note here' – he touched Bridget's shoulder and she produced Emily's letter from her pocket – 'which Emily left for us at Marlowe House, communicating her decision to sail to England in response to the invitation. Judging from Una's account of Emily's departure from Broad Street in the company of Rory, we have to assume that he has travelled with her.'

Four expressions of shock greeted Cormac's summary of the events. Derval found her tongue first.

'Why on earth would he do that?' she said, dumbfounded.

'One of the other maids at Marlowe House was privy to Emily's scheme,' said Cormac. 'She told me that Emily had intended to travel alone and, indeed, there was no mention of Rory in her letter. But the circumstances that Una witnessed leads us to conjecture that Rory learned what Emily was planning to do and elected to accompany her on the journey, perhaps out of a gallant urge to protect her.' He lifted one shoulder in a shrug. 'Unless you can think of any other reason he would wish to go to England?'

Derval shook her head slowly. 'He's never wanted to set foot there. He dislikes the English as much as the Yankees.' She glanced at Charlie. 'Present company excepted.'

Charlie waved a hand to show he had taken no offence. 'Who invited Emily to London?' he asked Cormac curiously.

Bridget shifted on the bench. How she wished she did not have to confess this. 'My husband,' she said.

Charlie's utterly blank countenance suggested that Orlaith had never imparted Bridget and Cormac's scandalous history to him, even after they had married. Though Orlaith and Tess both knew of Bridget's connection to Garrett, they still looked astonished to hear him mentioned now. But it was Derval's reaction that Bridget watched most anxiously – disbelief filled her green eyes, followed rapidly by resentment as the friendly trust that had long existed between them was extinguished.

'Is that so?' she bit out. 'Looks like you've got some explaining to do.'

Bridget nodded, the weight of her shame pressing down upon her. Cormac moved closer to her, his palm brushing her back, reminding her that they shared that heavy load together. She straightened up.

'I'm afraid we have lied to you. Although Cormac is the natural father of our three children, he and I are unmarried.

My lawful husband resides in London. His name is Garrett Lambourne or, to use his official title, Lord Wyndham.'

'"Lord"?' Derval repeated faintly.

'Yes. I am a viscountess by marriage. And a baroness by birth.' She reached out a blind hand for Cormac and he clasped it. 'Cormac and I grew up at Oakleigh, the estate in Ireland owned by my father, Lord Courcey. Cormac's family lived as tenants on the land. We were devoted friends but my mother forced our separation, first as children when our friendship became too steadfast for her to tolerate, and later as adults when I wished to break my engagement to Garrett to marry Cormac instead. My mother could not abide a union between her daughter and a stable hand, even though it was for love. So she banished Cormac from Oakleigh and compelled me to wed Garrett against my will.'

Derval and Charlie could only stare at her, speechless. Orlaith kept casting sidelong glances at her husband to see how he was taking the news, while Tess seemed absorbed in picking dirt from under her fingernails.

Bridget went on, 'Cormac and I endured many years of unhappiness alone before we came back into each other's lives in London. We couldn't bear the thought of losing one another again so we ran away with Emily, returning home to Ireland before journeying on to America with Orlaith and Tess. Although we did conceal our illicit past, I promise that everything we told you about our search for Bronagh was the truth, as has every other aspect of our lives which we have built here in Boston.'

Derval blinked. 'But ye built them on falsehoods.'

'We did,' said Bridget, dropping her gaze to her lap.

The room fell so quiet that Tess's nail-picking became audible. She stopped abruptly. The silence continued until

Orlaith mumbled to Charlie, 'D'you mind that I didn't tell you?'

Bridget peered up in time to see Charlie grimace. 'Yes,' he said. 'I can't help but be honest.'

'Which is more than you can say of me,' said Orlaith glumly.

He pulled on the rim of his ear. 'It's just disconcerting to realise you could keep such a large secret from me.'

'It wasn't my secret to share,' she said, her tone remorseful and her round grey eyes pleading for forgiveness. 'I've been truthful with you in everything else, I swear.'

After a beat, he said, 'We'll say no more about it then.' His voice was a little stiff but he squeezed her hand and she looked relieved.

'Well, I've got more to say.'

Everyone's heads swivelled towards Derval, who crossed her arms and sat forwards on the sofa.

'Damn disappointed, that's what I am,' she said bleakly. 'Not that ye lied or that ye were living in sin all this time. To be honest, I suspected there was something amiss about your situation almost from the start. There was your manner of speech for one thing, and not long after ye moved in Una told me Emily had made some comment about Cormac being her "real papa". I never pried, figuring ye'd bring it up yourselves when ye were ready.' She frowned. 'No, I'm disappointed that you had the opportunity to confide in me and you didn't.' Now she was looking directly at Bridget. 'That day we lost the young lads at Quincy Market, I told you the very worst thing about myself, that Brian Mór had another woman in another port and didn't want me and our children as his wife and family anymore. D'you know how much it hurt to admit that? 'Specially when you and your own fella seemed to have the most loving relationship I'd ever seen?'

Her voice cracked. Orlaith tried to put an arm around her shoulder but she shook her off.

'I felt like a failure of a woman for not being able to keep my man,' she murmured. 'But it was my own fault—I had chosen poorly and must live with the consequences. What a comfort it would've been to know you'd made mistakes too but had still found love afterwards. It would've given me hope when I so badly needed it.'

Tears welled in Derval's eyes. Bridget felt dreadful that her secrecy had borne such a sense of betrayal.

'I am so very sorry, Derval,' she said wretchedly. 'I never meant to hurt you and ought to have offered you solace in that moment by reciprocating your candour. But then we realised that Gus and Brian were missing and—'

'You've had months, *years*, to tell me since that day.'

The accusatory words hung in the air. Orlaith, Charlie and even Tess looked discomfited to be witnesses to what should have been a private altercation.

Bridget bit the tip of her tongue. 'You're right. I have no excuse but that our past ordeals prompted us to exercise caution, even around trusted friends. I beg your forgiveness.'

'We both do,' said Cormac. 'You've been nothing but kind to us and our family, and this was an unjust way to repay you.'

Derval swiped at her tears before they could fall. 'What's done is done. I'm more upset about where my boy is right now. What the hell did this Garrett fella say to Emily in his letter to make her go dashing across the ocean and drag Rory along too?'

'He promised to give her what we could not,' said Cormac despondently. 'A launch into society, which would elevate her status and, in due course, put her in the way of eligible suitors. Such a pledge would turn any fifteen-year-old girl's head, let alone one who had been born into that privilege and had it taken from her. He also claimed that he would leave her his

23

inheritance, and of course his current wealth would be beyond sufficient to fund her artistic dreams. So there would be no more working as a maid to save for tuition fees to attend Brubaker Art Academy.'

Charlie blew out his cheeks and Derval raised her eyebrows, astounded. 'Jaysus, Mary and Joseph,' she said. 'And you reckon these are empty promises?'

'Without a doubt,' said Bridget. 'His foremost quality is manipulation, not benevolence. The problem is that we cannot guess what his true motivation is, apart from attempted retribution for our offences against him. We really don't know what awaits Emily and Rory in London.'

A flash of fear crossed Derval's face. 'Could he do them harm?'

'He's not a violent man,' Bridget hastened to reassure her. 'In all our years of unhappy marriage, he never once lifted a hand to me or Emily.'

The closest he had come to it was the day he had discovered she had been teaching two-year-old Emily Irish words and Catholic prayers. In retaliation, he had burned Cormac's wooden bird carving and had threatened further punishment if she persisted in educating Emily in Ireland's tongue and religion. He had grabbed Bridget's shoulders in anger but he had not struck her. Still, his intimidation had been effective and she had obeyed his command, reluctantly severing her daughter's connection to her homeland.

With that in mind, she now admitted, 'His power lies in exploiting circumstances to his own advantage. He is generally able to achieve what he wants, be it through words or money or influence. We would be lying to you if we said Emily and Rory were not heading into a dangerous situation.'

'And we've had quite enough lying, thanks,' Derval said frostily. This was a side of her that Bridget had never glimpsed before, but then her eldest son had just left his family, his home and his job without any forewarning for what would likely be many months. She had to be terrified for him.

'It's tremendously unfortunate that Rory has become involved in this,' said Bridget, clutching Emily's letter so hard that she crushed the paper. 'We don't hesitate to acknowledge that Emily's actions have been foolhardy in the extreme.'

'And while we regret this dire state of affairs,' Cormac added quietly, 'we thank you for raising a lad who has proved willing to go to extraordinary lengths to protect a vulnerable girl.'

Derval gave a grudging laugh. 'You've got yourself to thank for that,' she said. 'You've been setting Rory a good example since he was ten. It was bound to rub off on him.'

A subdued wave of mirth rippled around the group but it petered out quickly.

Derval rubbed her forehead. 'I just can't get my head 'round what's happening,' she said. 'What're we going to do without Rory? He left me some coins but they won't last long. I suppose Una will have to find employment to replace his earnings in the family.'

'We'll assist you too,' promised Bridget, even though she had no clear idea what lay in their immediate future. 'It's the least we can do.' A thought struck her. 'But that begs yet another question. Where on earth did Emily get the funds to pay for passage on a ship? She's been working at Marlowe House for less than a month. That certainly wouldn't have afforded her enough money for a ticket.'

Her words met with bemused expressions, except for...

'Ah,' said Tess.

Bridget's gaze swung towards her. 'What?' she snapped. 'Do you know something?'

Tess adjusted her position on the stool, looking uneasy. 'Maybe.'

Bridget leapt to her feet, letting go of both Cormac's hand and Emily's letter. The crumpled slip of paper fell to the floor. 'Tell us,' she demanded.

Tess swallowed. 'Emily came to me this morning asking for money.'

Exclamations of surprise burst from the others, but Bridget couldn't make a sound because of the tide of fury that was surging up through her, choking her throat.

'You didn't think to mention this before now?' Cormac said in disbelief.

Tess flushed as red as her hair. 'I was hoping it wouldn't come up. Besides, it makes no difference—she's already gone.'

Bridget finally found her voice. 'It makes all the difference in the world if you equipped her with the means to flee,' she said with deceptive composure. 'Enlighten us on what happened, if you please.'

Tess pressed her lips together. 'Fine,' she said. 'Emily knocked on the door early this morning. Yous were already up and gone' – she jutted her chin at Orlaith and Charlie – 'but I hadn't left for Tremont House yet. She was only here for a few minutes. She asked to borrow some money and swore she'd pay it all back. I know I don't have much of a reputation in this family for doing the right thing, but I asked myself what any of yous would've done. I figured yous would've helped her, so that's what I did. I gave her my coin purse and she left. That's all.'

'That's not all,' said Bridget through gritted teeth. 'Did you ask her what she needed it for? Or why she didn't seek it from us, her parents?'

Tess shrugged. 'She said she couldn't tell me.'

Bridget balled her hands into fists. 'Did she have a valise with her?'

'Yes,' Tess admitted and added defensively, 'but I never dreamed she was leaving the country! I'm raging 'cause I didn't realise it could be so long before she pays me back. That money was supposed to cover my share of the travel costs when we go to Chicago. Charlie's meant to be heading there soon to look for jobs and places for the three of us to stay. What if he comes back with good news but I can't afford to go with him and Orlaith 'cause that little chit hasn't returned yet with my money?'

'Ah, Tess,' Orlaith moaned. 'If only you'd said something earlier, there might've been time to stop her.' Her brow furrowed. 'How had you saved up enough funds for Chicago already? Not from the washing at Tremont House, surely?'

Tess's expression turned shifty. She mumbled her reply in which Bridget could only make out the words 'from before'. Aghast, she stalked over to Tess and glowered down at her. Tess leaned back on her stool, peering up at her warily.

'Do you mean to say,' said Bridget, her blood boiling, 'that my daughter paid for her passage on that ship with earnings obtained in a *brothel*?'

Livid, Tess jumped up, forcing Bridget to take a step back. 'Sure, throw that in my face, why don't you? Jaysus, you're so goddamn high and mighty. You've always thought you're better than me, haven't you? Don't forget that, of the two of us, *I'm* not the adulteress.'

Bridget's hand whipped up and struck Tess's cheek with a stinging slap. The crack seemed to reverberate in her ears as Tess's head snapped sideways.

'You're one to talk,' Bridget seethed, disregarding Orlaith and Derval's shocked gasps. 'Ever kissed a man who wasn't yours, have you?'

Tess whirled back, eyes blazing as she lunged forwards, fingers curled into claws. Her nails would have scratched Bridget's face if she had not ducked to the side. Instead, Tess's fingers caught in Bridget's hair and she yanked hard. Pain seared along Bridget's scalp. She shrieked and seized a handful of Tess's skirt, pulling fiercely to make her lose her balance. Tess toppled and brought Bridget down with her, their elbows and hips thudding painfully on the floorboards. Panting, they both scrabbled to their knees and pounced on each other again.

In the next instant, they were torn apart and Bridget found her arms pinned to her sides by Cormac while Charlie hauled Tess backwards out of reach. Tess flailed, causing Charlie to knock over the stool as he strove to keep his grip on her; it rolled away, thumping against the wall. Orlaith and Derval were both on their feet, mouths covered in shock. A distant exclamation drifted up from the room below but the children didn't come running to investigate the noise overhead, for which Bridget was extremely thankful.

She struggled in Cormac's grasp, loose strands of hair falling into her eyes. 'Let go of me,' she implored. When he didn't slacken his hold, she assured him, 'I have my wits about me again. I won't do anything imprudent.'

With a dubious grunt, he released her and she stood, breathing heavily. She pushed back her dishevelled hair and glared at Tess, who had escaped Charlie's clutches and was hovering by the wall near the stool, her own chest rising and falling rapidly and one cheek scarlet.

'I want to make something very clear,' Bridget said, pointing at Tess. 'For a long time, I have not trusted you, and now I detest you. Knowingly or not, you were instrumental in aiding Emily in this reckless endeavour and I can never forgive you for that. As of this moment, I no longer consider you part of this family.'

Stunned silence fell. Bridget expected Tess to lash out with a caustic rejoinder but her shoulders sagged and humiliation flooded her features. Her gaze flicked to Cormac.

'It would be best if you leave for now,' he said, his tone quiet but firm. 'Our immediate priority concerns Emily and Rory and we can't allow ourselves to be distracted from that.'

She shrank in on herself, as though his gentle rebuke had been a physical blow. She gave a sniff and nodded.

'Perhaps you could visit the Kanes for a little while,' he suggested, 'just until Bridget and I are gone. I know it's late but—'

'I'll head up to Mr Lorenzo,' she said hoarsely. 'He hardly sleeps at all these days. I'll go keep him company.'

She stepped away from the wall and edged past the sofa, avoiding eye contact with everyone. Once she had sidled out of the room, Bridget exhaled, letting the tension seep from her bones.

'I'm sorry that had to happen,' she said to Orlaith, spreading her arms in a helpless gesture. 'I appreciate that she is your longstanding friend and of course I expect that she will remain so—I have no desire to put an end to your own connection with her. However, her behaviour towards me and Cormac has been unpardonable in many respects, and this affair with Emily is the final straw.'

Orlaith bit her lower lip. 'I understand. It's her own fault things have come to this. Even though it does seem like she gave Emily the money in a misguided attempt at goodwill, that doesn't excuse everything else.'

Charlie set the stool upright with a hum of agreement. 'Maybe it's for the best that we're considering the move to Chicago. The number of reasons to leave Boston continues to grow.'

It cut Bridget deeply that her divisive relationship with Tess might accelerate Orlaith and Charlie's departure, for she did not wish to see them go. But they had their own motives for leaving as well, not least among them the attitude of Charlie's parents towards Orlaith. Mr and Mrs Adams had objected to her as a daughter-in-law on the grounds of her being Irish and Catholic, but their alienation had been ensured by Charlie's conversion from Protestantism to Catholicism before he and Orlaith had wed. Relocating to Chicago would free Charlie from the anguish of living in the same city as his estranged mother and father.

'At this rate, there'll be no one left in Boston,' said Derval.

Perhaps she had intended it as a light-hearted quip but the hitch in her voice betrayed her sorrow. Both her husband and her son had vanished on her and very soon her closest friends could be gone too. Orlaith said nothing but she reached for Derval's hand and gripped it tightly. Together, they sank back down onto the sofa.

Charlie nudged the stool towards Cormac. 'Take this,' he said before resuming his seat next to his wife.

Cormac placed the stool beside Bridget's bench and they both sat down. She bent to pick up Emily's crumpled letter and smoothed it out on her knee.

'What are we going to do?' she murmured.

Deep in her heart, she knew what she desperately wanted but she couldn't ask it of Cormac. Time and again through their years together, she had sought the impossible from him – begging him to go into Oakleigh Manor to save her mother when the house had been burning to the ground, insisting that he choose Gus's life over her own when the birth of their baby had been in peril. How could she ask him to do this too?

Next to her, he leaned forwards on the stool, resting his forearms on his thighs and lacing his fingers together.

'I have to go after them,' he said.

She whisked her head around to look directly at him, hardly daring to hope. 'You do?' she breathed.

He blinked. 'Don't you think it's the right course of action?'

'Oh, I *do*, profoundly so. I just—'

'You didn't feel you could demand it of me?' he said astutely.

She lowered her gaze, guilt-ridden. He put a knuckle under her chin and tipped it up.

'You could ask me to do this and I wouldn't hesitate for an instant. I told you before that I would go to the ends of the earth to protect our children.' He glanced over at Derval. 'Rory too. He's as good as a son to me, if it's not too bold of me to say it, and the last thing I would want is for any harm to befall him either.'

Derval's eyes brimmed again. 'You mean it?' she whispered. 'You intend to follow them?'

Her gaze darted uncertainly from him to Bridget and he said decisively, 'Only me. I will go alone.'

A hiccup of unhappiness jolted inside Bridget but she already knew that he was right. The last time they had crossed the Atlantic, they had had only one child. Now they had two more and it would be folly to bring Jack and Gus needlessly on such a lengthy journey when so many unknowns lay ahead. Cormac would be able to spend less and travel faster without three companions impeding his progress. But he would have other causes for concern.

'England is not a safe place for you,' she said weakly, her chest tightening in fear.

'Why not?' Charlie asked with a frown.

Cormac's mouth twisted. 'Are you ready for more revelations?'

As briefly as possible, he described how, in one of the most hopeless periods of his existence, he had assumed the identity of an upper class gentleman called Oliver Davenport and, with that young man's consent, lived for nearly five years as the nephew of Lord and Lady Bewley at Bewley Hall in Bedfordshire. His fraud had been exposed in the midst of his and Bridget's flight from London with Emily, and Lord Bewley had subsequently followed them to Ireland to apprehend him.

It was only when Lord Bewley had believed Cormac's life to be at an end thanks to the appearance of a shady money lender from Cormac's previous time in Dublin ('No need to go into detail on *that* tonight,' said Cormac wryly) that the earl had given up his quest for justice and gone back to England. Though it was likely he had since learned from Garrett that Cormac had escaped to America, he would have had no recourse to act upon that information while Cormac was outside the jurisdiction of the English law enforcement.

'But if Lord Bewley catches wind of your return to London,' Bridget said anxiously, 'won't he renew his efforts to have you captured and imprisoned?'

'I suppose it's possible, if I'm very unlucky,' said Cormac. 'But he'll probably be in Bedfordshire and won't even know I'm there until I've been and gone again. In any case, I'll make sure to remain inconspicuous while I'm in the city. After all, I won't want Garrett to realise I'm there either.'

A snort of laughter burst from the sofa. Everyone looked at Charlie.

'Sorry,' he said as another chuckle leaked from him. 'I know it's not a laughing matter. But I'm just imagining what my parents would say if they knew that the family I'd married into are not just Catholics but lawbreakers and fugitives too.'

This drew a giggle from Orlaith and even a reluctant smile from Derval.

'Well, I feel like 'tis a pair of strangers I'm looking at right now,' she said, 'but if you're going to help get my Rory back, then I'll stomach it.' She arched an eyebrow. 'What d'you plan to do?'

'I'm going to book passage on the next ship to England,' said Cormac. 'I'll see if it's possible to glean any information at the docks about Emily and Rory's port of destination. If I can follow their exact route, I might be able to catch up to them on English soil before they even reach London, depending on weather conditions and the speed of our respective vessels.'

'And what'll you do when you find them?' asked Orlaith.

'Convince Emily that Garrett is using her for some contemptible personal gain. There is no conceivable chance that he intends to publicly claim her as his heir, not when he didn't father her.' Cormac rubbed his jaw. 'I hope to God she sees sense because I don't relish the idea of compelling her to abandon her scheme against her will. But I'm determined that she and Rory will return with me to Boston, and I'll be bringing enough money to cover three tickets.'

A knot of unease was growing in Bridget's belly. 'And what if they get to London before you are able to reach them? She will then be trapped within Garrett's sphere of influence. How will you make contact with her and also avoid detection?'

'I'll have several weeks at sea to figure that out.' He offered her an encouraging grin, though it wilted as lines of worry creased his face.

'Should I come with you?' Charlie said suddenly. 'If this Garrett fellow is as sly as you say he is, wouldn't it be sensible to have some help at your side?'

Bridget cast a hopeful glance at Cormac; Charlie certainly wouldn't slow him down the way a woman and two children would, and it would comfort her to know that he had a capable companion on his long journey.

However, Cormac shook his head. 'I appreciate the offer, but didn't Tess say you're meant to be taking a trip to Chicago in the near future?'

'The day after tomorrow, in fact,' Charlie admitted. 'I sent an enquiry to a fire engine company there and got a response saying they're willing to take on new volunteers if I'll come do a trial with them first. It's a long way to go but I thought I could also scout out nursing and washing opportunities for Orlaith and

Tess, and see about decent places to live before we committed to the move. All of that can wait though—'

'No, it can't,' said Cormac. 'I'm going to be gone for months. It would be unfair to make you put your plans on hold for so long. The three of you have your own lives to live, and Emily is not your crisis to rectify.'

Charlie deferred to this with a nod of reluctant acquiescence. Orlaith patted his hand and whispered something in his ear that made him blush with embarrassed pleasure.

'It's settled then,' Cormac said with an air of finality. 'I'll head to the docks first thing in the morning to find out when the next ship is setting sail for England.'

Bridget leaned into him, hooking her arm through his. He pressed his elbow tight and she understood it to be a gesture of consolation but, as she contemplated their impending separation, she was far from consoled.

Chapter 4

Emily's arms were wrapped around a bucket but she didn't have any notion how it had got there. The only fact she knew for certain was that her entire existence had been reduced to the horrible motion of the ship echoing sickeningly in the depths of her stomach, which she could not seem to prevent from emptying itself even when there was nothing left inside it.

Eyes closed, she was aware that she was horizontal and supposed she must be lying in her berth. Her mouth felt dry and tasted sour. Unpleasant smells filled her nostrils: vomit, sweat, bad breath. Did they all come from her? She gagged but strove to suppress the urge to throw up and the moment passed.

She had never felt so wretched in her life. Then again, was that quite true? Now that she was once more experiencing the ghastly rocking sensation that made her want to moan with misery, she seemed to recollect having suffered through it before. Though she had only been seven at the time and the memories of it were hazy, she could dimly recall that she had been ill on the voyage from Ireland to Boston. How could she have forgotten that until now? Had it been this bad? Had she felt like she was dying then too?

No amount of wealth or status could be worth this torment. What did she care for being presented to high society when her body seemed determined to turn itself inside out? She ought to have stayed on solid ground in Boston. Her situation there had been reasonably promising – she had been earning a wage as a maid at Marlowe House, and her father had gained more commissions at the workshop. If she had just been patient for a little while longer, they would have gathered enough money to pay for Brubaker's fees and her dream of studying to be an artist would have become a reality.

But what of her other dream? A pair of honey brown eyes swam into her mind, deep enough that she could drown in them—

She quivered. No, thinking about drowning was not a wise idea while incarcerated on a ship. Shuddering, she revised the vision: those honey brown eyes were soulful enough to make her soar up to the heavens. And they were complemented by beautiful dark eyelashes, waves of bronze-coloured hair, a well-defined jaw, and an alluring cleft in the chin.

All of these remarkable qualities belonged to Samuel Marlowe, the sixteen-year-old son of the master and mistress of Marlowe House, who was also a thoughtful poet endowed with courtesy, charm and humour. And Emily was deeply in love with him. This journey to England would elevate her social standing and finally make her worthy of him. If this cursed seasickness was the cost, then so be it. He was worth it.

The ship rolled to the side. Although it was not a substantial movement, it was still enough to trigger a detrimental response in her stomach and this time she could not hold it back. She vomited a thin stream of liquid but somehow missed the bucket and got most of it on the sleeve of her dress. Whimpering, she discerned her maid's clothing and realised she had been so sick that she hadn't even changed into her full-length skirts yet.

A concerned face bent over her. 'That's the last sup of water come back up too. She still can't keep anything down.'

The face hovered above a large belly and Emily identified its owner as Louise, the Englishwoman she was supposed to be sharing this bunk with. She didn't have the energy to wonder what Louise was doing about sleeping arrangements with Emily in this state.

Louise's head swivelled around to someone else. 'Should we try to make her drink some more anyway?'

Dismay filled Emily as another face came into view, green-eyed and crowned with shaggy brown hair.

'What are you doing here?' she croaked.

Rory didn't answer her. Instead, he said to Louise, 'I think we should, but maybe just small sips at a time.'

He knelt beside the berth, a cup in his hand. She stared up at him, mortified.

'You're not supposed to be in this part of the ship,' she protested weakly.

Ignoring her, he reached out and put his free hand at the back of her head, urging her to lift it a little. She had no power to resist. He raised the cup to her lips and she took a cautious sip. The water was tepid as it slid down her throat. At least she did not regurgitate it straight away.

'You have to leave,' she tried again. 'What if the matron catches you?'

'Miss Lovell is passed out with drink,' he replied. 'She'll never know I've been here.'

'Doesn't mean you can just break the rules,' said a tetchy voice from a berth beyond Emily's line of sight. 'You shouldn't be in the female section, even if your sister's sick.'

'Oh, I don't know,' said a different voice which sounded far more good-natured. 'I'm enjoying the view, despite his big ears.' The second voice giggled. 'Maybe that suggests he's a good listener. Looks like he's got good hands too, the way he's taking care of her.' Another giggle.

Even in the gloominess of the steerage quarters, Emily could see Rory's cheeks flame red. She thought her own might have done the same, if she were not so green with nausea.

Slumping back onto the bunk, she rasped, 'How much time has passed?'

'This is the third day,' he said.

That didn't surprise her in the slightest; it felt like she had been trapped in this nightmare for a year. But surely she would not be sick for the entire voyage – her body would have to adjust to the motion of the ship sooner or later. She just hoped her guts would still be inside her by that point.

Rory cleared his throat. 'I think you need to change your clothes,' he said awkwardly.

A wave of hot shame engulfed her. How badly did she smell? Had she vomited on herself prior to this occasion? Withering under Rory's scrutiny, she was prepared to make any bargain with God to rescue her from this unspeakable humiliation.

The situation only got worse as Rory added, 'I guess you'll need some help with that.'

She was utterly horror-struck – he didn't mean to help her himself, did he?

But then he turned to Louise and said, 'I'm sorry, would you mind giving her a hand? I doubt she can even stand by herself.'

As Emily sagged with relief, she heard Louise say with a sigh, 'And I thought I'd be the most unwelcome bedfellow on the ship.'

CHAPTER 5

Cormac wanted to bellow with frustration but he said calmly to the ticket seller, 'Thank you for the information,' and walked away from the booth.

Two whole days had passed since Emily and Rory had absconded, and yet Cormac still remained in Boston without passage on a ship. He had purchased a ticket, certainly, but the vessel he was meant to travel on lingered stubbornly in the port.

He felt like kicking himself for the crucial error he had made. Having resolved to pursue Emily and Rory during that fraught conversation at Broad Street, he had gone to the docks the next morning to make enquiries about the forthcoming shipping schedules between Boston and England. The ticket seller had informed him that there was a ship due to depart for Plymouth that afternoon, and another for Liverpool the following day. Wondering which route Emily and Rory might have taken, he had chanced asking the ticket seller if he recollected whether a short, fair-haired girl and a tall, brown-haired young man had purchased tickets together the previous day. By an extraordinary stroke of luck, the man had remembered them.

'The girl caught my eye,' he had said. 'An uncommonly pretty young thing. Nothing stood out about the boy though. Apart from his ears,' he had added with a chortle.

Upon further questioning, the ticket seller hadn't been able to recall their names ('How many folk do you think come to this booth every day?' he had huffed) but he could say with a fair degree of certainty that the pair had been in line to board the *Integrity*, which was the largest vessel scheduled for departure that afternoon.

'Heading for which destination?' Cormac had almost pleaded.

'Liverpool.'

So Cormac had taken a gamble – instead of embarking on the ship to Plymouth, he had decided to wait one more day in order to trace Emily and Rory's steps exactly. The trouble was, the ship to Liverpool, the *Blue Onyx*, had then been delayed because the captain refused to leave port until the hold had been entirely filled with cargo, which had left Cormac stuck in Boston and wishing to God that he had boarded the ship to Plymouth when he'd had the chance. But today, at last, the ticket seller had confirmed that the *Blue Onyx* would be setting sail tomorrow. A full three days behind Emily and Rory.

Hoping that the *Blue Onyx* would prove to be a swift ship, Cormac strode away from the ticket seller's booth along the docks. The inaction of waiting had been excruciating but finally he could make a solid plan. Of course, that brought his imminent separation from Bridget, Jack and Gus ever closer, and an agony of a different kind squeezed his heart.

How difficult it would be to leave Bridget for so long. They had not been parted from one another in eight years – how could he survive the months ahead without her? She grounded him on this earth. No matter where his duties took him by day, she was the compass that guided him home each night. He had forgotten how to fall asleep without her by his side.

But the pain of separation would have to be endured because he could conceive of no alternative but to follow Emily to

England. Losing his daughter in this sinister way had inflicted a critical wound inside him, like he was trying to breathe with one lung or his heart was skipping every fifth beat. He could no more abandon her to this danger than he could sail the *Blue Onyx* single-handedly across the Atlantic. He had to extricate her from Garrett's snare, even if she hated him for it forever.

At least Bridget, Jack and Gus would remain safe while he was gone. It did trouble him that he and Charlie would both be absent at the same time, leaving the women without any male protection for a period, but Charlie's business in Chicago would not keep him away from Boston beyond three or four weeks at most.

In any case, while the falling out between Bridget and Tess seemed irreparable, Bridget would continue to have decent support around her from both Orlaith and Derval. Thankfully, the rift between Bridget and Derval had been somewhat mended – Derval had taken a day to cool down and reflect upon the circumstances which had led to Bridget and Cormac's long-lasting subterfuge and, when they had returned to Broad Street with news of Cormac's intention to take passage on the next ship to Liverpool, she had acknowledged her understanding of their choices, if not her approbation. Her conciliation had been further expedited by the information Cormac had gained at the docks about the ship Emily and Rory had embarked upon the previous day.

'The *Integrity*?' she had repeated. 'You're sure?'

Cormac had nodded morosely. The implication of the ship's name could not be denied.

'Well, that explains a lot,' Derval had said, blowing out her cheeks. 'Emily wasn't the only reason Rory got on board that ship. Jaysus, I hope he doesn't mean to cause trouble.'

'I'm sure he will be sensible,' Bridget had said, trying to reassure her.

Derval had looked doubtful but she had said, 'I hope you're right, Bridget.' Then she had blinked. 'Should I be calling you "m'lady"?'

'Absolutely not,' Bridget had replied emphatically and that had been the end of that.

Now, just as Cormac was passing the open doorway to Robert Smith & Co.'s warehouse, he heard a shout. 'McGovern!'

His old workmate, O'Mali, came marching out of the warehouse, tall and indignant. 'You gonna walk right by without so much as a hello?'

Cormac stopped. 'I was off in my own world,' he said apologetically. 'Good to see you, O'Mali. How are you and the other fellows keeping? And Mr Walker?'

O'Mali's cross expression cracked into a grin. 'All good. The port's getting busy again. Mr Walker says the economy's picking up all around the country so we reckon our jobs are safe for the time being.' He squinted. 'Funny thing. I could've sworn I saw your girl around here a couple of days ago. But she's working at Marlowe House with my Tilly now, isn't she?'

Cormac winced. 'Not exactly.'

Omitting the majority of the facts pertaining to Garrett, he explained that Emily had made a rash decision to go to England without consulting her parents and, believing that she was going to land herself in a troublesome situation, Cormac meant to follow her to ensure her safety. He mentioned how O'Mali's daughter had played a part in the scheme and O'Mali looked shocked.

'Tilly?' he said, bewildered. 'My Tilly helped Emily do this?'

'I think she prefers to go by Matilda now,' said Cormac.

O'Mali blinked. 'She does?'

When at length the two of them parted, it was in agreement that daughters were quite unfathomable beings.

Cormac went by the post office next, where he collected a single letter addressed to him. At the sight of it, he experienced the all-too-familiar jolt of hope that it might contain news of his missing sister, Bronagh. His most recent endeavour in his search for her had been to write to New York, her last known whereabouts, to place a notice in *The Truth Teller*, a Roman Catholic newspaper that was in circulation there – he had even sent one of the portraits Emily had drawn of Bronagh in anticipation that they might print that too. However, this letter wasn't postmarked from New York City, but from Ireland. When he opened it, he discovered that it had been penned by Biddy O'Hara, proprietor of O'Hara's Tobacconist and Lodgings in Dublin and grandaunt of Henrietta, the child of the prostitute Thomasina whom Cormac had once bedded. While he knew Henrietta was not his own offspring, he had still felt responsible for her welfare after becoming the inadvertent cause of her mother's death at the hands of Henry Munroe, Henrietta's father who had subsequently disappeared. With both of Henrietta's parents gone, Cormac had placed the little girl in the care of Mrs O'Hara, her only other kin.

It was a decision he had come to regret several times over the intervening years and yet again today as he read through the letter he held. In it, Mrs O'Hara complained that she still had not received any additional money from Cormac and that the medicines needed to treat the constant ailments afflicting 'poor Henny' were not cheap. Moreover, she expressed her concern that the girl seemed likely to run away again and, should that event transpire, she expected that this time Cormac would provide his immediate assistance in retrieving her.

He stared at the page, shaking his head in disbelief. First Bronagh, then Emily, and now possibly Henrietta too. Well, he couldn't split himself three ways, and Emily had to take precedence. He tucked the letter into his pocket and left the post office, envisaging Mrs O'Hara's displeasure when her demands were met with further silence and praying she would not make her grandniece suffer for it.

A heavy gloom had sunk deep into his bones by the time he reached the workshop. He cast a dispirited glance upwards at the sign that proudly displayed the name 'McGovern' before trudging through the door beneath it. There was not much left to do here; he had already terminated all the projects he and Rory had been working on, making contact with the relevant parties to regretfully inform them that he was obliged to cancel his current commitments. Mr and Mrs Rosemount had been particularly disgruntled by the news and he harboured little hope that they would wait for the reopening of his workshop to complete the refurnishing of their boarding house. They and his other customers would take their patronage elsewhere and his carpentry business would be in tatters whenever he returned to Boston.

Dampening the spark of bitterness that flickered in his gut, he made sure that his tools were clean and tidied away in their cabinet, gathered up a few papers and ledgers, and left the workshop locked and shuttered behind him.

When he got home to Acorn House, Bridget was standing at the open front door and a young boy was skipping down the steps.

'*Pardon, Monsieur*,' he said gaily as he bounced past Cormac and scampered away down the street.

Cormac climbed the steps with a raised eyebrow and Bridget waved a slip of paper in her hand. 'Madame Roche's grandnephew. She sent him with a note to bring the white muslin to the shop in the morning. She wants to check on my progress.' Bridget looked perplexed at this unforeseen inspection, but hastened on, 'What news from the docks?'

'Tomorrow,' he said as he met her on the threshold. 'The ship leaves tomorrow.'

A mixture of relief and dread filled her features. 'At last,' she said tremulously.

'At last,' he agreed with a sigh. He kissed her temple and they went indoors.

Upstairs in their bedroom, he pulled his old valise out from under the bed, although strictly speaking he could not claim ownership of it for he had bought it in London with funds bestowed upon him by Lord Bewley. Nevertheless, the valise had accompanied him throughout his family's travels from England to Ireland and beyond, though he had not had much occasion to use it after they had settled here in America. Now it would be his sole companion on his journey back across the ocean.

He had already packed it two days ago when he had first planned his departure, but he added a few more items now: a couple of extra shirts that Bridget had left out for him freshly laundered, his shaving apparatus, and his pocket knife along with a small block of wood – he would have many hours to while away at sea so he figured his hands might as well be occupied.

'What will you make this time?'

Kneeling on the floor in front of the valise, he glanced up at Bridget who leaned against the bedpost, rubbing her palm over the acorn carved into the top of it. Together, they looked over at the bedside table where the wooden carving of their family sat: a man and woman in the middle and three children clasping their hands. He had gifted it to her upon the opening of his workshop, a day that had been full of joy and hope for the future. What could he make in these fraught circumstances?

'Any requests?' he asked.

'Surprise me,' she replied.

He gave her a lopsided smile and closed the valise, leaving it ready by the side of the bed. As he stood, he said, 'The lease on the workshop is paid up for the next three months. If the landlord finds another tenant after that, he's promised that he'll notify you about clearing out the premises. Go to Donie Kane on Broad Street in that case—he's a joiner so he'll find use for the tools and the wood.'

Her gaze was awash with anguish. 'You mean your livelihood might be decimated before you get back?'

He swallowed. 'Emily is more important.'

'She is,' said Bridget, 'but I'll do my best to set aside money to extend the lease if I can.'

'Don't leave yourself short,' he said. 'I had already paid the three months in advance but it doesn't make sense to hold onto the space after that when it's not being used.'

'I shall keep faith that its proprietor won't be absent for too long,' she said and the stubborn set of her chin told him not to argue the point further.

'You put the money I gave you in a safe place?' he said instead. He had divided his savings for Brubaker between them, taking enough to cover his travel to London and the cost of three ship tickets back, and leaving the rest for Bridget, Jack and Gus.

She nodded. 'And I'll have the income from my sewing too. We'll be fine.'

'You'll need to go to the post office to check for letters while I'm gone,' he said. 'It's more commonly frequented by men so you can ask Charlie to go there for you after he comes back from Chicago. I'll make sure to write from England as soon as I have any news. Depending on the situation I find, a letter might reach you faster than Emily, Rory and I will.'

Before she could respond, Jack and Gus came darting into the bedroom, Gus on Jack's heels with his arms stretched out. Jack dashed past his parents and vaulted up onto the bed but Gus latched onto one of his ankles and bawled, 'Got you! Now it's your turn to catch me!'

He spun around but Bridget halted him before he could sprint out of the room. 'Settle down, the pair of you,' she said. 'You both need to go wash your hands and faces right now. We're heading to Broad Street because you're staying at Auntie Derval's tonight.'

They cheered and ran out the bedroom door to do her bidding.

'Are they?' said Cormac, puckering his brow.

She blushed. 'Derval told me yesterday that she would take the boys on your last night, once we knew when that would be. She...thought we might like to have some time alone before you depart.'

Heat rushed to his own cheeks. 'Well, that was very considerate of her.'

He endeavoured to forget about that tantalising prospect during their visit to Broad Street, where they went upstairs just in time to bid farewell to Charlie before he left to catch his stagecoach on the first leg of his trip to Chicago.

'Safe travels,' he said, shaking Charlie's hand and wondering when, if ever, he might see the young man again. By the time he returned from England, Charlie, Orlaith and Tess might have already moved out west.

The same thought must have been running through Charlie's mind, judging by the firmness of his grip. 'You too,' was all he said.

He and Orlaith shared a touching goodbye, in which she would not physically let go of him until he had reached the landing at the top of the stairs, and then he was gone.

'The next few weeks will pass before you know it,' Bridget said with a comforting pat on Orlaith's arm.

Orlaith looked guilty. 'It's nothing compared to the length of time yous are facing,' she said.

'That's different,' said Cormac. 'You and Charlie are barely married nine months. It's harder to part when the relationship is still so new.'

He didn't really believe that though.

Downstairs, he and Bridget left the boys in Derval's care, with warnings to behave and promises that they would see them in the morning. They had just walked out the front door of the building when Una came bounding up Broad Street towards them. She greeted them with a grin that stretched from ear to ear.

'You look very happy, Una,' Bridget said with a smile of her own. 'Have you got good news to share?'

'I'm officially a working woman!' Una burst out. 'I started at the shirt factory today.'

'Congratulations,' said Bridget. 'Was it very hard work?'

'It was but I don't mind that. 'Tis a great feeling to be earning a wage.' Una beamed. 'Turns out Rory leaving was the best thing that could've happened to me!'

Wincing at the thoughtlessness that came with being fourteen, Cormac said, 'We won't delay you. I'm sure you're looking forward to telling your mother about your day.'

'I'm going up to Mr Lorenzo first,' she said. 'Did ye know he used to be a tailor in Italy? He wants me to describe to him how 'tis all changed now. Although he's gone so forgetful that I'll probably have to tell him again tomorrow.' She skipped past them through the doorway and threw a wave behind her before running up the stairs.

Cormac offered Bridget his arm. She took it and they walked home, not speaking much. When they reached Acorn House, they shared a small supper at the kitchen table, still saying little. Cormac couldn't help the despondent thoughts that flitted through his head: less than twenty-four hours remained for them to share together...this time tomorrow he would be on a ship surrounded by strangers...too soon he would not be able to put out his hand and simply hold hers...

He realised he had done exactly that when her fingers tightened on his. She stood. He half glanced at the table but she led him from the kitchen and up the stairs with Barnabas as their only witness.

In their bedroom, they undressed on either side of the bed before throwing off most of the bedcovers and slipping under the single sheet, the only covering they needed during the heat of June. They were naked except for the two rings on her left hand, one circle made of thread and the other of gold, and the band on his left wrist, which consisted of two braids of leather and a third of hair, her chestnut locks mingling with his own fair strands.

She lay on her left side facing him, both of her hands folded beneath her cheek. 'I'm not sure I'm entirely in the mood,' she admitted, her expression rueful.

'That's fine,' he said, tucking her hair behind her visible ear. 'We don't have to do anything.'

Lying back, he gathered her to him in a soothing embrace and she relaxed into his side, draping her limbs across his body. Her bare breasts pressed against his ribs and he savoured the intimate touch of her skin on his without any expectation. It was enough just to hold her.

'I'm scared,' she whispered, her breath grazing his collarbone. 'For Emily, and for you.'

He could have said 'don't worry' or 'there's nothing to be scared about' but she didn't deserve empty platitudes. Moreover, if he couldn't be honest with her, who could he be honest with?

'I am too,' he said. He feared the power that Garrett wielded and, worse, he was terrified that his daughter no longer wanted him to be her father. 'But I swear to you that I won't rest until Emily's safe.' He almost added 'no matter the cost' but gulped back the words before they escaped; while he valued truthfulness between them, he didn't think Bridget needed to hear that part.

She huddled into him, her thigh a comforting weight across his legs. 'This will be so hard,' she murmured. 'I can't fully articulate how much I'm going to miss you.'

'You don't need to,' he said softly. 'I already know because I feel the same way.'

It was a painfully familiar feeling. Too many times in their lives they had been parted against their will. When they were children, Bridget's mother had hauled her off to Dublin, breaking their innocent childhood friendship. Then, when Bridget returned to Oakleigh as a young woman, they had united as lovers and planned to marry until Lady Courcey had learned of their affair and banished Cormac from the estate. Seven and a half long years had passed before they had found each other again in London and summoned the courage to run away together. They had existed side by side from that day to this. And now, out of dire necessity, he was about to put an ocean between them.

'I'll be thinking of you every minute of every hour we're apart,' he promised.

'And I you.'

She looked up into his face and, without taking her gaze from his, she let her fingers trail all over his body. She traced the arc of his ear, the bulk of his shoulder, the jutting bone of his elbow.

'What are you doing?' he asked.

'Memorising every bit of you,' she replied. 'Raise your hip a little, will you?'

He obeyed and her hand snaked under him to caress the leaf-shaped blemish at the base of his spine.

'I love that no one else knows that's there,' she said, dropping a tender kiss on his chest.

Her fingers continued to roam over him and he copied her, his hand gliding along her waist and brushing the triangle of freckles on her right hip. He didn't need to glance down to find them; he already knew all of her by heart.

He couldn't say how long they remained like that, bodies entwined as they committed each other to memory, but he supposed they must have dozed off because he woke much later with the dawn. As the grey light filtered into the bedroom, he realised that Bridget had woken too and was touching him in a wholly different manner to the chaste way she had earlier in the night, her attentions concentrated on one region in particular. He exhaled in surprise.

She peeked up at him from beneath her eyelashes. 'Do you want to...?'

He didn't need to reply – his body had responded with alacrity to her stroking hand. He tumbled her back on the bed and joined his mouth with hers, determined to make this encounter a memorable one.

In the course of their endeavours, she was louder than he had ever heard her and it made him wonder whether these sounds were in fact her most natural reaction to pleasure. Had she always previously striven to restrain herself, even when they had managed to obtain the luxury of relative privacy? At present, in their completely empty house, they were enjoying a level of solitude hitherto seldom tasted and she could express her satisfaction as loudly as she liked – the nearest ears were Mr and Mrs Hill next door and neither Cormac nor, quite evidently, Bridget cared what their cantankerous neighbours thought of their wanton conduct. When they reached the culmination of their activities, he muted his own groans as much as he could, the better to hear her. Her joyous cry as she scaled that peak utterly demolished him.

They drifted off to sleep again without a word, only a breathy sigh and a gentle kiss. Despite the fact that they were both tangled up in the sheet, when Cormac awoke next it was to find that the sheet had somehow migrated to Bridget's side of the bed and his naked form was completely exposed. At least he could be thankful that it wasn't the heart of winter or certain parts would have retracted in protest. He chuckled and she stirred.

'Hmm?' she mumbled, cracking open one eyelid.

He tugged some of the sheet back over his body in answer.

'Oh,' she said. 'Sorry. I don't know how that always happens.' She yawned and sat up. 'How are your teeth this morning?'

'My teeth?' he repeated, baffled.

'You were grinding them so hard as you slept that I feared you would splinter them.'

He ran his tongue along his teeth but they seemed fine, if a little achy. 'I suppose I had a lot on my mind. To be honest, I'm surprised I was actually able to sleep.'

'Same here,' she said.

Her dark brown eyes connected with his and the reality of the coming day hit him all of a sudden, as brutal as a punch to the stomach. There were mere hours to go.

'Time to get up,' she said quietly and slid out of the bed.

When they left Acorn House, he was carrying his packed valise while she clutched a wide canvas bag with the white muslin gown folded carefully inside. His throat felt clogged with emotion throughout their walk to Broad Street and the sensation only intensified when they entered the Careys' rooms and Jack and Gus both came running to him for hugs.

Gus gave him a rough embrace around his middle before charging off again to wrestle with Brian Carey over the last slice of bread and butter left on the table for breakfast, but Jack clung to Cormac with a vehemence that conveyed his awareness of the day's significance. Cormac and Bridget had already told the boys that their sister and Rory had gone to visit a friend across the sea and that Cormac had to take a trip abroad too because he had some carpentry business dealings in England. He intended to meet up with Emily and Rory over there and the three of them would travel back together. While Gus's only reaction to this had been excited speculation about whether the captain would let Cormac sail the ship, Jack, who was the older and more sensitive of the two, had shown a better understanding that this would necessitate their father's absence for a very long time. Now, he hung onto Cormac's arm with a fierce possessiveness.

'Can I come with you, Da?' he pleaded.

Cormac placed an affectionate palm on his son's fair head. 'Not this time, *a mhac*. You need to stay here and look after your ma and your brother. Especially Gus. Who will mind him when he gets into scrapes, if not you?'

They both glanced over at the table, where Brian had won the tussle and was savouring his bread and butter with relish while Gus watched with a combination of seething envy and threatening tears. Jack peered up at Cormac with a resigned expression.

'It has to be me,' he said, nodding in acceptance of his duty.

'You are an exceptional big brother,' Cormac told him. 'As fine as your uncle Patrick was to me when he was alive.'

Jack puffed up with pride at this. He finally released Cormac's arm and ran to hug his mother, who was speaking in undertones with Derval by the window. Sorcha hovered nearby, feigning disinterest while clearly trying to eavesdrop, but there was no sign of Una who had presumably already headed off to work at the shirt factory. Setting his valise on the floor, Cormac called

Gus to him and the lad trudged across the room with a fleeting look of longing over his shoulder as Brian licked his fingers.

'I have to leave shortly, *a mhic ó*,' Cormac said. 'Will you do something for me?'

Gus narrowed his eyes, plainly expecting to be encumbered with chores. 'What?' he asked warily.

Cormac knelt and bent his head close to Gus so that only he could hear. 'As the youngest in the family, you have a grave responsibility when I'm not here. It will be your job to keep your ma smiling, and to help your brother while he's the man of the house. They will lean on you for cheer and support. Can you give them that?'

Gus's tubby body bobbed up and down with enthusiastic affirmation, although Cormac wasn't sure if the lad was just relieved that he hadn't received a concrete list of tasks. Tilting his head with an indulgent grin, he ruffled Gus's curls and stood, just as Orlaith came into the room.

'I thought I heard yous downstairs,' she said with a brave attempt at a smile, before her face crumpled. Letting out a sob, she fell into Cormac's arms and he held her tightly. She mumbled something incoherent, her words muffled against his chest.

'I didn't quite catch that,' he said, his tone gently teasing.

She drew back and he sobered at once when he perceived the deep distress in her features.

'We're the last two,' she said plaintively. 'Mary, Patrick and Margaret are dead, and Bronagh's nowhere to be found. I can't help thinking how sad Ma and Da would be to see all their children lost or scattered far apart. What if I'm gone west before you get back? What if this is the last time we ever see each other?'

He grasped her elbows firmly. 'It won't be. If you've already left Boston by the time I return, I'll come visit you in Chicago. Nothing will stop me.'

She sniffed. 'D'you promise?'

'I do,' he said and, despite the anguish of the occasion, his heart filled with gladness at such proof that his broken relationship with his sister had truly mended. Recollecting the fondness they had shared long ago at Oakleigh when she had been a little girl of five years old tending her hens in the McGoverns' cottage, he ventured to add, 'I promise, chicken.'

She beamed at him through watery eyes.

Derval approached him next and, to his astonishment, she embraced him with enough force to squeeze his ribs. 'Thank you for doing this,' she said, her voice hoarse in his ear. 'I'm counting on you to bring them home. Keep my boy safe.'

When she let go, he said with all his sincerity, 'I will.' The weight of expectation sat heavy upon him but he shouldered it without objection.

A subdued snuffle by the window drew his gaze to Bridget; she was valiantly pretending not to cry as a stalwart Jack stood by her side. Taking Gus by the hand, Cormac crossed the room to them.

'I'll go to the docks alone,' he murmured to Bridget. 'There's no sense in dragging you there too.'

She nodded in acquiescence. 'That's probably for the best,' she said thickly. 'Madame Roche is expecting me anyway.' A sudden thought struck her and she blurted, 'Did you remember to pack any food?'

'Yes,' he reassured her. 'I haven't forgotten anything.' He swallowed as the moment of parting arrived. 'All I need is a kiss to send me on my way.'

She flung her arms around his neck and pressed her lips to his, prompting quiet sniggers from Sorcha and Brian. Jack and Gus wrapped their arms around him too, one on either side of his waist, and the four of them huddled there like a cluster of animals trying to keep warm against a winter chill. He didn't want it to end but he knew it must and that he had to be the one to do it. He gently extricated himself from their knot of bodies and patted the two boys on their shoulders before cupping Bridget's cheek one last time.

'Love you,' he said, his words barely more than a breath.

'Love you too,' she whispered. She kissed his wrist where the braided leather band lay hidden beneath the sleeve of his coat. 'Be safe.'

He wasn't able to say anything more. He turned away, dug his flat cap out of his pocket and put it on. Chewing the inside of his cheek, he picked up his valise and walked to the door. His final glance encompassed them all, lingering longest on Bridget. Then he left, shutting the door behind him.

As he crossed the hallway to the front door of the building, he caught a movement out of the corner of his eye: a flash of red hair by the banisters at the top of the stairs. He pretended he hadn't seen it and strode out the door to the street.

CHAPTER 6

Bridget traipsed along Summer Street, carrying her canvas bag and stifling the urge to glower at the other pedestrians who had the audacity to smile on this black day. She had prevailed upon Derval to look after Jack and Gus for a little longer and was heading towards Madame Roche's establishment to present her progress on the white muslin gown, but fabric contours and embroidery stitches were the furthest thoughts from her mind.

Love was a wonderful, grievous thing. By building her life with Cormac, she had opened herself up to a tremendous happiness unsurpassed by any other but, in doing so, she had grown so intrinsically dependent upon him that it felt like his very absence had dulled the vitality of her senses. Colours seemed faded, surfaces rougher, sounds harsher. It was as though she and Cormac really had become one flesh after so many years together and that today's separation had sentenced each of them to exist as only a fraction of the whole as long as they were apart.

At least she still had her two boys. Cormac might be gone for now but she would continue to see glimmers of him in Jack's eyes or around Gus's mouth, and they themselves would bring light and energy and cheerfulness in their own special ways. They were just as much a part of her flesh as Cormac was, and Emily too. Three-fifths of her family were still together – she ought to be grateful for that and trust that they would be reunited with the other two-fifths in the fullness of time.

Resolving to remain optimistic, she pushed open the door to Madame Roche's shop and entered. The dressmaker was in the middle of serving a middle-aged customer who appeared to be grudgingly paying a number of outstanding bills, so Bridget waited discreetly in the background while the churlish woman concluded her business. Madame Roche did not even glance in Bridget's direction until the customer had stalked out of the shop, muttering about how outrageous it was that a good name did not seem to be worth anything these days.

Bridget perceived the deep frown lines on Madame Roche's forehead and gave her a sympathetic look. 'Difficult morning?' she said.

'Difficult week,' Madame Roche replied curtly in her strong French accent. She spun on her heel to march into the back room of the shop and Bridget followed. Madame Roche jerked her chin towards Bridget's canvas bag. 'Is that the muslin?'

'Yes.' Bridget carefully drew the gown out of the bag to display her work but Madame Roche didn't bother to examine it.

'Just leave it there,' she said, pointing at a table where several other half-finished garments lay spread out.

Puzzled, Bridget draped the gown over the table, taking care not to dislodge the pins she had left in it. When she turned back, Madame Roche was surveying her down the long slant of her nose.

'I have always held great confidence in your skills,' she said, 'and even greater faith in your integrity. I paid you more than fairly as an acknowledgement of your worth.'

Bridget blushed modestly. 'Thank you—' she started to say but Madame Roche interrupted her.

'Which is why your appalling deception wounds me all the more. How could you be so careless with the reputation of this establishment?'

Bridget's jaw dropped. 'Pardon me?'

Madame Roche sighed. 'And you choose to feign innocence. That is even worse. Ah, *c'est terrible.*'

Bridget was stunned. Had Madame Roche somehow learned of her adultery and her associated lies? But how could that be? Bridget and Cormac had only revealed the truth to Derval and Charlie, and both had promised to keep the secret.

Then it occurred to her with dawning horror. Could this be Garrett's doing? Had his insidious pen wreaked harm beyond the letter he had sent to Emily? Was he attempting to destroy their whole lives in Boston?

'Did you receive a letter?' she asked weakly.

'I received a visit,' Madame Roche snapped. 'From Mrs Halliwell.'

Now Bridget was completely baffled. 'Mrs Halliwell? What did she want?'

Madame Roche folded her arms. 'She came to return the blue silk gown.'

'Good gracious!' Bridget exclaimed. 'Why?'

'Because her daughter refuses to wear it.'

That was very upsetting to hear for Bridget had deemed it to be one of her finest pieces of work. 'Did she find some defect? Would she not seek to have it repaired rather than simply return it?'

'There was no defect.' Madame Roche's lips pressed together. 'Miss Halliwell has declared that she will never put the gown on because it has already been used by another.'

Bridget laughed. 'But that's preposterous! It was made *for* her. I took her measurements in this very shop.'

'She insists that she saw another girl wearing it.'

59

'When?' Bridget demanded. 'Where?'

'Less than two weeks ago, mere days before the Halliwells collected it from here. Miss Halliwell was attending a ball at Marlowe House on Beacon Hill and recognised her gown on another guest.'

Bridget's blood ran cold. God, no. Surely not.

'What did the guest look like?' she mumbled between frozen lips.

Madame Roche pursed her mouth. 'A slight girl with fair hair and blue eyes. Apparently, the young master of the house was quite taken with her. Miss Halliwell did not confront the girl on the night, but she grew convinced of her suspicion after she and her mother took the gown home from this shop. When her mother desired her to wear it to a soiree, she would not countenance it and divulged the reason why. Mrs Halliwell went to Mrs Marlowe, the hostess of the ball, but the girl in question did not match anyone on her guest list. Even her son was unable to put a name to her. In fact, she had vanished from the party before it ended. Highly irregular circumstances indeed.'

A wave of dizziness washed over Bridget and she stumbled back against the table, clutching it for support. She wanted desperately to reject the evidence before her but there could be no denying the blatant truth – Emily was the culprit of this offence. She had to be, for too many pieces of the puzzle could be connected to her: the description of the girl, the location of Marlowe House, the timing of the ball. For heaven's sake, Bridget remembered Emily admiring the blue silk gown laid out on her sewing desk and had even caught her holding it up against her body – to gauge the length of it, that was now obvious. But by what means had Emily managed to spirit the gown out of Acorn House and back in without Bridget knowing? And how on earth had she had the capacity for such abominable trickery? In a single instant, Bridget's daughter had become a stranger to her.

Madame Roche fixed her with a beady gaze. 'Do you know what is afoot here?'

Bridget gulped. 'I-I believe I do.' She wilted at the prospect of confessing to Emily's deceit and, inevitably, her own disgraceful secrets. 'I beg you not to ask me to explain but please let me plead for your forgiveness. While I was unaware of this dreadful incident until now, I apologise profusely that it happened.'

'So you assume responsibility for it?' said Madame Roche, looking dismayed that her accusation had been accepted without any contradiction. Perhaps she had hoped that Bridget would produce some credible proof to refute it.

'I must,' Bridget said bleakly.

Madame Roche shook her head. 'Such a waste. You were the most talented seamstress I ever had the fortune to employ.'

'You're going to dismiss me?' said Bridget, so nauseated that she feared she might be sick. She took a shaky step away from the garment-covered table just in case.

'With immediate effect,' said Madame Roche. 'It is regrettable, but it has to be done.'

Distressed, Bridget beseeched, 'May I be given the chance to make amends? I would be willing to compensate for the loss incurred by the returned gown, and to work on half pay thereafter.'

'*Ma chérie*, it is a great deal too late for that,' said Madame Roche, the edge in her tone belying the endearment. 'The ramifications of this deplorable state of affairs go far beyond the cost of reimbursing one gown. Have you considered Mrs Halliwell's reaction?'

'Was she very angry?' Bridget asked in a small voice, feeling like a disobedient child being castigated for the error of her ways.

'Livid. She informed me in no uncertain terms that she intends to take her custom elsewhere.'

'Oh no!' Bridget blurted. 'That's awful. I am so very sorry.'

'It is more disastrous than you imagine.' Unfolding her arms, Madame Roche reached up to pinch the bridge of her long nose before carrying on wearily, 'Mrs Halliwell has lost all trust in my establishment and feels obliged to warn her acquaintances of what has occurred. Soon, I shall be losing customers on all sides.'

Bridget covered her mouth with her hand, aghast. 'Do you really believe that will happen?'

With a wave towards the front of the shop, Madame Roche said, 'Why do you think I have insisted that the likes of Mrs Forbes-Cabot come in to settle their accounts? Once word of this gets out, even my most loyal patrons might see fit to disregard their debts to me. I will be branded unreliable and unworthy of their patronage. My reputation in the better circles will be ruined.'

And all because a silly girl wanted to dress up and go to a ball.

Bridget's temper rose, her guilt and embarrassment displaced by fury. That thoughtless child had wrecked so much with her rash behaviour. When she had stolen the gown, had she cared at all about the repercussions? Had it even occurred to her that she could devastate other people's livelihoods in the process? Shame flooded Bridget at her daughter's reprehensible selfishness.

Then the nature of her shame changed, turning inwards. This was the daughter she and Cormac had raised. Where could the blame for her conduct lie but in their hands? If Bridget was going to criticise Emily for not foreseeing the potential outcomes of her choices, then she must censure herself, and Cormac too, for the decisions they had made in the past which had detrimentally affected others. So many terrible things had happened to the McGovern family because Bridget and Cormac had been too wrapped up in their own selfish desires at Oakleigh to give a thought to what might happen afterwards. It would be hypocritical to condemn Emily for following the poor example set by her parents.

Particularly when their actions had had such a negative impact upon Emily herself. They had yet again placed their love higher than any other consideration when they had reunited in London and whisked Emily away in the full knowledge that they were forever cleaving her from the life of privilege and wealth that had been her birthright. Growing up in Boston in a situation of relative hardship was not something she had ever wanted or deserved. Was it any wonder that she had seized upon Garrett's offer to return to the aristocratic existence of her birth, paying no heed to the havoc she would wreak along the way? They should not be surprised in the slightest. In some ways, it appeared that Garrett understood Emily better than either Bridget or Cormac did.

With that dismal thought, Bridget's fury died, its heat supplanted by desolate cold. She raised her gaze to Madame Roche who was staring at her with palpable unease. What emotions had she read in Bridget's face?

'I cannot ask for your forgiveness,' Bridget murmured, 'but please know that my remorse is sincere. Thank you for the opportunity to work in your employ.'

She wouldn't dream of seeking payment for her labours on the white muslin. She left Madame Roche standing in the back room and exited through the front door of the shop with her empty canvas bag, her heart grieving for so many reasons.

CHAPTER 7

Emily shakily climbed the steerage stairs, taking care not to trip on her full-length skirts, and emerged onto the deck. Clouds scudded across the blue sky above the ship's sails and the invigorating wind buffeted her, revitalising her pallid skin. She inhaled as deeply as she could, relieved to be liberated from the confines below at last.

Another day had passed and so had the seasickness, at least for the most part. She still had no appetite but she had been able to keep down a cup of water and nibble on some dry biscuit that morning. However, she felt as weak as a kitten and resolved not to go anywhere near the edge of the ship, lest the wind blow her overboard.

Even as that vision occurred to her, a particularly strong gust rushed across the open deck and she wobbled, grabbing hold of her bonnet so it would not fly off her head.

'Watch out,' Rory said just behind her at the top of the stairs.

He stepped up to her side and awkwardly extended his arm to her. Although it galled her, she reached out and clung to him for support.

'Let's go this way,' he said, pointing further up the deck with his free arm. ''Tis usually a bit quieter in that area so you'll have more space to walk around.'

Of course, he had had plenty of time to explore the ship over the past four days while she had been stuck to her berth and her bucket.

'Good idea,' said another voice and Louise Shelby materialised next to them, one hand resting on her bump. 'What a welcome sight it is to see you back on your feet, Emily.'

Emily experienced a surge of gratitude towards the young woman, as well as a substantial measure of mortification. Louise had helped change her clothing, plied her with water, and even washed out Emily's vomit-stained valise. She exemplified the Good Samaritan from the Bible and Emily knew how lucky she had been that her arbitrary companion had turned out to have such a compassionate nature. She offered Louise a timid smile.

'Thank you for being such a treasure,' she said. She would have said more but her choice of words gave her pause. Her father had always addressed her as '*a stór*', which meant his 'treasure'. She had not spared much thought for her parents during the depths of her misery but now she felt a renewed stab of guilt behind her ribs at the surreptitious way she had deserted her family. She supposed that feeling would stay with her until such time as she reunited with them.

That was, if their door would even be open to her.

'I'm glad I could help,' said Louise. 'Excuse me, I must go...' She waved vaguely towards a queue of passengers on the far side of the deck and hurried off.

'What's over there?' Emily asked Rory.

He cleared his throat. 'The privy,' he replied.

She coloured and said nothing else. As she had not had enough energy to go above deck prior to this, her only option for relieving herself down in the steerage quarters had been a bucket screened by a roughly hung sheet of canvas. The smell in that corner had been so overpowering on the most recent occasion that, after Louise had assisted her back from it, Emily had resolved to overcome her accursed nausea so that she would never have to visit it again.

'Will we head that way so?' said Rory, pointing unnecessarily towards the same area as before.

She made a wordless sound of affirmation and let him lead her along the deck. His gaze darted all around them as they walked, seeming to scrutinise every person in sight, be they passengers taking the air or sailors climbing the rigging. She, too, stared about, absorbing the landscape of their new temporary home. Near the middle of the deck was a wooden structure with a mass of people crowded around it, smoke billowing from its entrance.

'What's that?' she asked.

'The kitchen shanty. You won't be going in there 'til you've your full strength back. 'Tis survival of the toughest in that sty.'

She watched as a pair of women came coughing out of the kitchen and two others immediately shouldered their way in past them, clutching cooking kettles and bundles of sticks. It was all too easy to picture her own small form getting trapped in that crush.

Grimacing with apprehension, she said, 'Is that the chief activity on board? Fighting for cooking space?'

Rory shrugged. 'We've had a bit of music too. A couple of the fellas from my part of the ship brought out a fiddle and a drum the first evening. And Captain Philips said there's to be Mass every Sunday.'

'For Catholics or Protestants?' she asked, reflecting upon the assorted nationalities of the ship's passengers and the numerous differences between their creeds.

''Tis a mishmash. The captain said we'll take what we're given and let there be no griping about it.'

They had reached the quieter part of the deck and Rory's green eyes, sharp as an eagle's, raked the masts above.

'Are you looking for someone?' she said, mystified.

His gaze snapped back to her. 'No. So are you going to tell me?'

'Tell you what?'

'What's so important in London that you were willing to throw up your guts for several days straight to get there?'

She clamped her mouth shut. His tone left her in no doubt that he thought she was daft.

'Well?' he prompted.

Feeling defensive, she said, 'I didn't know I would be so sick.'

'And if you'd known, would you still have got on the ship?'

'Yes,' she said mulishly.

He shook his head in disbelief. She withdrew her arm from his with an abrupt jerk.

'I can walk without help now, thank you,' she said, her back and her voice stiff.

She took a few steps away from him, her legs trembling, but to her surprise he stayed with her, matching her slow pace. What a peculiar, provoking creature he was; her snub had been the perfect opportunity for him to march off and relinquish his obligation to look after her. However, it seemed he was as stubborn as she was.

After letting an awkward beat pass, he said, 'D'you remember we agreed to a truce before we boarded the ship?'

'Mm-hmm,' she mumbled.

'That one only lasted about four seconds. Want to aim for ten this time?'

Against her will, the corners of her mouth turned up. He was being magnanimous and it would be terribly petty of her to throw his olive branch back in his face. 'Very well then.'

He offered her his arm again and had the grace not to look smug when she took it. He led her a little further along the deck before lightly pressing her elbow and she followed his cue to turn back the way they had come. She waited until they had rambled a full length down the deck and back before she spoke.

'My other life,' she said. 'That is what waits for me in London.'

His brow puckered in confusion. 'What d'you mean?'

She took a breath. 'What I'm about to tell you is a very great secret and it implicates my parents. You must promise not to tell another soul.'

'Your parents?' he said, his eyes widening. 'What about them?'

She said nothing, only gave him a meaningful look.

'I swear,' he said hastily. 'I won't say a word to anyone.'

'Thank you,' she said with a dignified dip of her head. 'I will hold you to that.' Before he could laugh at her pomposity, she went on, 'I was born in London, you already know that. What you don't know is that I was born in the grand townhouse on Berkeley Square which we are on our way to visit. It was my home for the first six years of my life. I had a governess and fine clothes, and there were servants who opened the door and drove the carriage and laid out a feast at every mealtime.'

She stole a glance at Rory. He wore a sceptical expression but he adjusted it to one of polite interest when he saw her looking. That annoyed her – what reason would she have to lie about this?

'I can assure you,' she said, raising her voice a tiny bit, 'that I'm telling the truth. Have you ever wondered why I speak the way I do? Why I don't say ''tis' or why I've always called my parents 'Mama and Papa' instead of 'Ma and Da'?'

'Yes,' he admitted. 'I've wondered that.'

'Well, it's because I had a genteel upbringing. I am a daughter of the aristocracy.' She paused. 'But I am also the daughter of a stable hand.'

Though she did not wish to sully her parents' characters when Rory held so much respect for them, her father especially, she could not relate the truth of her past without disclosing their indiscretions. It all spilled from her lips: the circumstances of her parents' affair at Oakleigh; their separation and her mother's coerced marriage to a man she did not love; the coldness that had pervaded Wyndham House while she and her mother had lived there with Garrett; the joy they had both experienced when her real father had re-entered their lives; her parents' decision to run away with her which had sparked a scandal in society circles; and the dangers and hardships they had suffered since that fateful day. Of course, much of it was second-hand information because she had not been alive to witness it or had been too young to remember it, but the hardships she certainly remembered. They were too recent and impactful to be forgotten.

Rory had stiffened when she had divulged her mother's – and thus, someday in the distant future, her own – claim to the title of Lady Courcey, but after that he had schooled his features so well that she could not tell whether belief or incredulity held sway over him. She carried on regardless.

'I understand that my mother and father acted out of the deepest love for each other,' she said earnestly, 'and that they have done their best to provide for me and my brothers by whatever means they could. But the fact is that they do not have the wealth or social standing to give me what I need, now that I'm no longer a child. Garrett, on the other hand, is both able and willing to improve my situation in the most marvellous manner.'

She relayed the contents of Garrett's letter, or at least what details she could recall, for she had only managed to read it three times before her father had burned it. As she spoke, the glittering promise of all that London had to offer practically shimmered before her eyes.

'Can you see now that I simply must do this?' she finished, almost pleading with Rory to take her side.

He bit his lip. 'No,' he said, drawing the word out slowly. 'I still don't see it.'

Exasperated, she clicked her tongue. 'Which part of it is not clear?' she ground out.

'Why d'you need so much money?'

'To pay for the fees at Brubaker Art Academy! It is the most direct path to becoming an accomplished artist.'

'And why have you got to be part of high society?'

'Because it's what I'm entitled to by my birth. And because—' She hesitated. Ought she to tell Rory about Samuel?

Before she could determine what to say, Rory twitched all of a sudden and pivoted to the side, compelling her to follow as he strode towards the gunwale of the ship. He stared out across the water as though some invisible force were pulling his gaze to the horizon. The wind battered them but she didn't protest their change of course, figuring that Rory would be tenacious enough to save her if a mighty gust endeavoured to blow her frail body overboard.

More importantly, the break in their discussion had given her sufficient time to make her mind up that Samuel Marlowe was none of Rory's concern.

'Because it's my entitlement,' she reiterated and left it at that.

He made a dubious sound in his throat. ''Tis a very fine life you're expecting to lead once you get to London, is it? When you're living in the house of a—what d'you call him again?'

'He's a viscount. Oh, yes, it will be quite splendid.'

'Then why was your ma so eager to run away from it all?'

Emily faltered. 'H-her situation was different. She was forced to marry someone against her will.'

'And the same won't happen to you?'

She opened her mouth and closed it again. Gathering her scattered wits, she said, 'No, of course not.'

'How can you be so sure?'

She raised her chin. 'For the simple reason that it's not Garrett's intention. All he wants is a child, an heir. He made no mention in his letter of marrying me off to anyone.'

Rory snorted. 'Of course he wouldn't. He'd wait 'til you got to London before he revealed a shocker like that.'

She felt as if the strands of their conversation were slipping out of her grasp, fluttering away on the wild wind. 'You're wrong about him,' she insisted.

'Am I? Seems to me he's done some nasty things to your folks in the past. What makes you think he's changed?'

'You didn't read his letter. The language he used was so contrite and sincere. I am persuaded that he is not the man he once was.'

Rory fell silent, gazing out at the rolling waves. When at length he spoke once more, his voice was calm and steady. 'I'm only going to say this once and if you choose not to agree then I won't mention it again.'

She narrowed her eyes at his profile. 'What is it?'

He hunched his shoulders. 'We got on the ship but that doesn't mean we have to see this plan all the way through. We could turn around in Liverpool, get the next ship back to Boston. There's no need to go as far as London if you decide that maybe Garrett isn't such a trustworthy fella after all.'

Doubt flickered in her belly. Could Rory be right? Her mother and father had been utterly convinced that Garrett had had an ulterior motive in contacting her.

But they were prejudiced against him. They hadn't been even the slightest bit open to the possibility that he might have reformed his character over the intervening years. Their opinion could not be deemed reliable. As for Rory, he had never even met Garrett, let alone read his letter.

Emily straightened her spine. 'We are going to London.'

Rory nodded glumly. 'Right so.'

CHAPTER 8

Emily cautiously twisted her body an inch to the right, trying to find a more comfortable position in the berth. She could sense her limbs wanting to loosen, to stretch out wide, but that was impossible with the supine form of the pregnant Louise lying close beside her. Louise had admitted that she had procured sleeping space in another berth while Emily was ill but she had come back to this one now that the worst of the seasickness was past. The disadvantage of this, aside from the tight confines of their accommodation, was that Emily was terrified she might accidentally knock against her companion's large bump in her sleep and cause harm to the unborn baby nestled within, so she could not relax and thus slumber continued to elude her.

She breathed shallowly through her mouth, although the smell wasn't quite as bad now that she had been back down in steerage for a few hours. Having said that, her initial return to the quarters below deck had been ghastly. The stink as she had descended the stairs had nearly knocked her backwards and she had needed to pause for a few moments to adjust to the noxious air rippling over her, the reek of filthy bodies and unwashed clothes interlacing with the pungent stench of vomit. It shamed her to comprehend that she, too, had contributed to this disgusting odour and it appalled her that she and the other passengers would have to endure it for the entirety of the voyage. No wonder everyone spent as much time as they could up on deck. Even the smoky, overcrowded kitchen shanty had to be better than this.

Sighing, she shifted again and nearly plunged off the edge of the bunk. She caught herself just in time and lay still, heart pounding. Louise didn't stir apart from a drowsy mumble but the fright left Emily wide awake and all hope of falling asleep vanished. It was the first time she had been so alert on the ship during the night and, to avoid noticing how bad the place smelled, she focused instead on the sounds she could hear. A human symphony permeated the darkness, the rhythmic breathing of slumbering passengers mingling with a muffled chorus of coughing, wheezing and breaking wind. A baby's fretful cry rang out but its mother hummed a soothing lullaby and the child quietened. There was the discordant splash of vomit being expelled into a bucket and Emily flinched, praying her own queasiness would not resurface.

Then she heard something else. A groan. Not one of sickly misery but what sounded like...pleasure. She held her breath and listened harder. It came from the middle section of steerage, where the husbands and wives slept. Except one pair were most definitely not sleeping. She blushed furiously and was suddenly very glad for the pitch black that had descended when the hatch at the top of the stairs had been closed for the night. It might have shut out the fresh air but it also prevented anyone from perceiving her bright red face.

The groan came again. By its deep timbre, she could tell that it belonged to a man. He appeared to be immensely enjoying whatever was taking place between him and his wife. The woman, on the other hand, was largely silent. Was she not getting as much satisfaction from their activities? Or perhaps she preferred not to express it aloud with so many

74

eavesdropping ears in the vicinity. Feeling guilty, Emily made a concentrated effort to stop listening but then the woman gasped and Emily's curiosity rose beyond her power to stifle it.

With a sinful thrill, she let herself imagine what was taking place in the couple's berth. Had they removed their clothes for the act? Were they touching each other in a very intimate way? Of course, she had no specific knowledge of the relations between a husband and wife but she knew *something* important happened when they married and that it must be of a physical nature. Why else were young unmarried men and women kept so stringently apart? She thought uneasily of the strict rules she and Rory had contravened by travelling together and acting as brother and sister. Well, at least nobody could accuse them of behaving improperly, in *that* sense at any rate.

Her thoughts strayed instead to Samuel. If her dream came true and he asked for her hand in marriage, what would their wedding night be like? Would he groan like that man? Would she gasp like that woman? With a jolt, she realised that her hand had crept across her body and was clutching her breast over her clothes. She snatched it away at once. Gracious, she was a wicked girl.

She needed to think about something else. Her other dream of becoming an artist, yes, that was much safer territory. How she missed—

Enthusiastic panting emanated from the middle section of the ship and she clamped her palms over her ears to block it out.

How she missed painting. She wished she could have brought some paper and the watercolour box her father had made for her but she had needed to prioritise space for clothing and food in her valise. Not to worry – Garrett would undoubtedly be able to equip her with a new set of brushes and watercolour cakes in London.

Throughout the upheaval of her life, art had always been her sanctuary. As she lay in the berth with Louise moving restlessly next to her, she found herself longing for the peace that accompanied the stroke of her brush and the swirl of the paint when she rendered the images from her head into tangible form. In her younger years, her preferred colour had been pink but she had since outgrown that inclination. Now she esteemed green above all others, for its spectrum of shades was unparalleled: the deep green of forest foliage, the blue-green of the sea, the emerald green of a gemstone, the yellow-green of parched grass in summer. The list was endless.

If she was being honest with herself, her favourite shade of all was the green of Auntie Derval's eyes which, she had to allow grudgingly, was also the colour of Rory's eyes. Separating the organs from their infuriating owner, she considered them to be quite striking, as vibrant as clover after rain. She thought she'd like to paint them sometime but suspected she might struggle to get the colour exactly right. She would probably need to spend more time looking directly into them, an idea which made her feel oddly self-conscious.

After she dozed off at last, she drifted into a dream where she lay confined in an open coffin in the middle of a forest surrounded by green-eyed boys who groaned in unison. She was unspeakably scandalised upon waking but the memory of it faded away as Miss Lovell came wandering past the women's berths, announcing in a slurred voice that it was time to rise.

When Emily reached the bottom of the stairs, Rory was nowhere to be seen and she had no intention of venturing into the men's section to find him, so she climbed up to the deck alone, Louise having gone ahead of her on an urgent mission to use the privy. It was just as windy as the previous day and this time raindrops spattered her bonnet as well. She didn't mind; it was a blessed relief to escape the prison below.

76

She eyed the kitchen shanty which was already thronged with people, mostly women but a number of men too. They must have scrambled up on deck as soon as the sailors opened the hatch. Unwilling to enter the melee, she passed the kitchen by and started ambling up and down the deck like yesterday, waiting for Rory to appear. A pair of deckhands were on their knees scrubbing the boards and she took care not to get in their way.

She had just pivoted on her heel for the fifth time when she spotted Rory emerging from the kitchen in the company of an old man, both of them gasping from the smoke. The stranger carried a cooking kettle in one hand; he clapped Rory on the shoulder with the other and made for the hatch leading down to steerage. Rory glanced around and caught sight of Emily. He visibly hesitated before stepping in her direction, a cup clutched in his fist. As he neared the two deckhands, he gave them a hard look but then seemed to dismiss them, sidestepping them without concern.

'Morning,' he said when he reached Emily, not quite meeting her eye.

'Good morning,' she replied. 'Who was that man you were with?'

'Henrik something-or-other, never caught his surname. Norwegian fella. Hasn't a word of English but he helped me make the porridge.' Rory held out the cup. 'Want some?'

To her astonishment, her stomach gurgled. 'I believe I do,' she said. 'What a marvel. I genuinely thought I'd never feel hungry again.'

She accepted the cup which was faintly warm to the touch. He dug a spoon out of his pocket and wiped it on his sleeve before handing it over with a self-conscious wince.

'Sorry,' he mumbled.

'No, this is perfect, thank you,' she said, even though she had to resist the urge to peer at the spoon before dipping it into the porridge. She took a mouthful; it was bland but she supposed that was just as well, given her delicate stomach. 'How satisfying it is. Are you going to have some too?'

He nodded and she passed the cup and spoon back to him. For an instant, she felt strangely embarrassed by the idea of the spoon going into his mouth after it had just been in hers, but then she cast the discomfort aside – there was no room for primness on board a ship. And heaven knew she had already lost all of her dignity when he had seen her throw up on herself.

They shared the porridge back and forth without talking until not even any dregs remained. It could have been a companionable silence only for the fact that Rory still wouldn't make eye contact with her and stood a few paces away as though she might have a contagious disease.

'Are you sharing a berth with Henrik?' she asked eventually, trying to break the tension.

'I am.'

'Is he travelling home to Norway?'

'No idea. No English, remember?'

She pursed her lips. 'What's the matter with you? Is our new truce over already?'

'No,' he muttered.

The rain fell a little harder but not a single passenger in sight made a move to seek shelter. Emily suspected that nothing less than a hurricane would force them below deck.

'I can tell there's something wrong,' she said relentlessly.

He clenched his jaw. She waited. At last, he blew out his breath in a gesture of surrender. She had assumed that it was just some trivial annoyance that had provoked him but, when he looked straight at her, she discerned with surprise that his expression was distinctly troubled.

'You're…' he began and stopped. He rubbed the back of his neck. 'You're…a lady.'

Startled, she said, 'No, I'm not.'

He scowled. 'You told me yesterday—'

'I'll be a lady someday,' she hurried to amend, 'but I have no existing title. Right now, I'm just a "miss".'

Would she be obliged to go by the appellation Miss Lambourne once she got to Berkeley Square? The notion unsettled her. Shedding the surname McGovern would feel like an outright rejection of her father, which she by no means wanted to do. She still cherished him, despite all that had happened.

'I don't understand,' Rory said bluntly.

She traced the rim of the cup, which had ended up in her hands after they had finished the porridge. 'If I were the daughter of an earl or a higher peerage, I would be addressed as Lady Emily from birth. But for lesser titles such as viscount or baron, daughters are known as Miss whatever-the-family-surname-is until they inherit a title or, much more commonly, marry a gentleman in possession of one.'

He chewed over that for a while. 'But you're still a member of the upper classes. You've got noble blood in you.'

'I do,' she allowed. 'However, like I said yesterday, I have lower class blood in me too.' She blinked. 'Are you worried that I'm going to put on airs and graces now that I've revealed my background?'

He swallowed. 'I'm worried that I'm going to be accused of kidnapping you.'

She laughed. While part of her wanted to make a dry remark about how he had form in that area, given that he had abducted Mabel when they were younger, she held her tongue on that score and said instead, 'What? Don't be absurd!'

The unease remained in his features. 'I mean it. You're not a carpenter's daughter needing an escort for protection anymore. You're a young lady' – he waved away her attempt to protest that term again – 'who has a claim to a future title and wealth. Jesus, there's a bloody lord in England planning to acknowledge you as his heir.' He flung his hands up in the air. 'And what am I? A lowly apprentice with nothing but pennies to my name. From the outside, it could easily look like I snatched you and mean to demand a ransom before handing you over.'

This time she didn't scoff but said calmly, 'And if anyone was stupid enough to accuse you of that, I'd set them straight in the most scathing language at my disposal.'

He stared at her, green eyes piercing. 'Would you though? It'd be a handy way to get rid of me, wouldn't it?'

Rather than feeling indignant, she found herself bitterly hurt by the insinuation. There was something very broken between them if he believed her capable of such spitefulness.

'Despite what you obviously think,' she said, her voice low, 'I am not a malicious person. I might not have desired your company on this voyage at the outset but I have been grateful more than once since then that you insisted upon coming. I wouldn't do or say anything to cause you harm.'

He flushed, his face turning pink all the way to the tips of his prominent ears which were visible whenever the wind tousled his shaggy hair.

'Right so,' he said with an awkward cough. 'Then we're sticking with the McCarey brother and sister story until we get to London?'

'If that's still acceptable to you,' she said formally. 'And please be assured of this: while I may be under your protection now, I guarantee that you will come under my protection then.'

Grasping the cup in her left hand, she held out her right. He looked down at it for a moment before shaking it with his own.

His big palm was warm despite the squally weather. When they let go, she thought – or at least hoped – that they had partly bridged the chasm between them.

The rest of that day passed similarly to the previous one and so did the next as they established both the reassurance and the tedium that came with daily routine. They walked the same expanse of deck over and over, and they listened to the fiddler and drummer play together in the evenings before the sun went down. They socialised with both Louise and Henrik, although conversation with the latter amounted to not much more than shrugs and hand gestures. Emily even braved the kitchen and learned how to start a fire beneath Henrik's cooking kettle – it wasn't a skill she would need once her new life began at the house in Berkeley Square but it was very useful to know in the interim.

Two days after she and Rory had shaken hands on their latest – and, with any luck, most abiding – truce, they were wandering along the stretch of deck that Emily had whimsically taken to calling the Promenade when she once again noticed Rory intently watching the sailors at work. His attention seemed focused on one man in particular who was hanging from some rigging above and laughing down at his fellows. She squinted at the man, thinking that there was something familiar about him. Then she gasped and clutched Rory's arm.

'Rory, is that your—'

He swiped at her other hand which was rising to point towards the man and pulled her away from the group of sailors, striding down the Promenade until they were almost back at the steerage hatch. She had to practically run to keep up. When he came to a halt, she tugged on his elbow to make him look at her.

'I'm right, aren't I?' she panted. 'That man back there is your father!'

Rory cast a fleeting glance over his shoulder before admitting, 'He is.'

Her mouth dropped open. 'Good gracious, how can that be? Did you know when we boarded the ship that he would be on it?'

'Yes,' Rory muttered. 'The *Integrity* was always his vessel. 'Tis been years since he sailed on any other.'

'Good gracious!' she said again, turning to peer back in the direction of the sailors. Rory's father had leapt down from the rigging and was tussling good-naturedly with one of the other men. What was his name again? Oh yes, he was known as Brian Mór so as not to confuse him with the youngest Carey child, little Brian. She hardly recognised him, but there were just enough similarities between him and his four children to make out the resemblance. Uneasiness stirred in her gut as it occurred to her that her lack of recognition equated to his very long absences from home – she couldn't recall him coming back to Broad Street on shore leave above three times in all the years her family had known the Careys.

'Stop staring or he'll notice us,' Rory barked and she hastily swivelled around to gaze out across the water.

'Is he the reason you came with me?' she asked, scarcely moving her lips even though Brian Mór was too far away to hear her.

Out of the corner of her eye, she saw Rory shaking his head. 'I'd already decided to come. But I guess he was a second reason.'

Shoulders slouched, he crossed to the edge of the deck and grasped the gunwale with both hands. Emily hesitated before joining him.

'You haven't spoken to him yet?' she said.

'No,' was his flat response.

'What do you intend to do?'

He sighed. 'I don't know. At first, I think I meant to find the sod and give him a piece of my mind. Maybe knock him to the boards.'

She was shocked. 'You wanted to hit him?'

'I still do.' He gritted his teeth. 'You've no idea how angry I am at him. Ma never told us what went on between them but he didn't treat her right, I know that much. And in the end he just stopped coming home. I wondered if maybe the *Integrity* had moved on to a new shipping route and that was why he never came back to Boston anymore. That would've suited him fine, and us too. We didn't want him anyway.' Rory's knuckles tightened on the gunwale until they went white. 'And then you said you were going to get a ticket on the *Integrity*. The bloody ship was in port and he couldn't even be bothered to get off it to go visit his wife.'

Emily wouldn't dare point out that Rory was contradicting himself by declaring in one breath that his family didn't want Brian Mór to come back and then vilifying him in the next for not doing so. He clearly harboured very complicated feelings towards his father.

If truth be told, she understood all too well what that was like.

'So,' she said tentatively, 'you still wish to confront him about that? Make him answer for his neglect of you all?'

Rory grimaced. He rubbed his jaw and she perceived the bristles growing there on his cheeks and chin. It was funny how she had so often regarded him as nothing more than an aggravating boy and yet he was actually a man now. In fact, thanks to his father's abandonment, he had become a man sooner than she had even realised. At eighteen, he was just three years older than her, but with this weight on his shoulders he seemed far older.

'I...' he said and trailed off. When he spoke again, she had to strain to hear his subdued voice over the crash of the waves

83

against the ship's hull below them. 'I always thought he was a boor, that he was unpleasant by nature and nothing could improve his humour, not even being with his wife and children.' Rory stole another furtive look up the deck but Emily didn't tear her gaze away from him as he went on broodingly, 'I was wrong though. I've been watching him for days here and he's different. He actually seems...happy.'

'In what way?' she asked quietly.

'He smiles,' said Rory, the incredulity evident in his tone. 'And laughs. He mucks about with the other deckhands and they appear to really like him. I just...it's hard to compare this version of him to the lout who griped all the time at Broad Street and couldn't wait to leave as soon as possible.'

Rory loosened his grip on the gunwale, flexing his fingers. Emily stood patiently beside him, not saying anything; she sensed that he was trying to unravel it all in his head before speaking it out loud.

'I think,' he said at last, 'that he must be a true seaman. That when he's on land he doesn't feel completely himself and he's only whole once he's back on the water again. That'd explain why he was never satisfied with us in Boston and why he's so content on this ship. Right?'

'Perhaps that is the case,' she said uncertainly.

Silence fell between them until he suddenly thumped his fist on the gunwale, causing her to jump.

'It shouldn't pardon him though,' he growled. 'Why am I trying to make excuses for him? He never should've married if he didn't want a family or a life on land. He *chose* to become a father, and a poor one at that.'

He whirled around and stalked towards the steerage hatch, even though there were still several hours until sundown.

84

Emily let him go. She was beginning to understand him well enough to recognise that there was nothing she could say in this moment to assuage his sense of betrayal.

CHAPTER 9

As Bridget roused from sleep, she enjoyed a split second of ignorant bliss, expecting to see Cormac lying next to her when she rolled onto her side.

Then she opened her eyes and reality took hold, as it had cruelly done every day since he had gone. Five mornings in a row the loneliness had hit her afresh upon waking, each one as raw as the first.

The bone-deep sense of loss echoed another dark time in her life, when she had moved to London with Garrett after their wedding. Her enforced separation from Cormac had left her numb and apathetic, not caring if she wasted away to nothing. She had stopped eating and her housemaid, Lizzie, had been obliged to spoon-feed her like a child. It wasn't until she had realised that Emily was growing inside her that she had motivated herself to try to live again.

There was no question of allowing herself to fall into that abyss this time, not when she already knew that she had two children relying upon her to be strong. Even as she thought of them, she heard Jack and Gus romping around in their bedroom and Gus's high-pitched giggle bursting out in response to something Jack had said in a softer tone. She smiled. Her boys needed her and, likewise, she needed them.

They would muddle through this together until Cormac and Emily returned.

She climbed out of bed, noting with a certain degree of smugness that the bedcovers were still spread across Cormac's side of the bed. She would take great pleasure at some future stage in informing him that this plainly meant he must play a contributory role in their persistent migration to her side of the bed when they slept together.

After dressing, she went downstairs, where she experienced a pang of anguish at the sight of her empty sewing desk. Shame still burned her skin at the memory of Madame Roche's disappointment in her. What a dreadful encounter that had been, receiving her disgraceful dismissal while at the same time comprehending with such terrible clarity the enormity of Emily's dissatisfaction with her life. How she and Cormac had failed their daughter.

The colossal risks Emily had taken to attend the ball at Marlowe House had felt like vital information which Cormac ought to know before he left Boston so, upon leaving Madame Roche's shop, Bridget had hurried to the docks in the hope of catching him ahead of his ship's departure. She had been too late. The ticket seller had pointed out the sails of the *Blue Onyx* leaving the harbour and she had watched it glide from view, fretful that Cormac had gone forth without knowing the full extent of Emily's discontent and the extreme measures she had resorted to in her quest to improve her circumstances. Convincing her to reject Garrett's dastardly proposition would likely be a more monumental task than he was even prepared for.

Bridget's gaze strayed to the floor in front of the fireplace, where a singed black spot was visible in the middle of the hearthrug. On the night of Emily's birthday last month, an ember had leapt from the grate and landed there, burning the rug until Bridget had stamped it out, while Cormac had sat frozen, powerless to move in the face of the danger. Fire was his vulnerability but there were few other challenges he could not conquer once he set his mind to them. He would be able to rescue Emily and sway her to the truth, Bridget was sure of it.

Turning away from the hearthrug, she summoned Jack and Gus downstairs and instructed them to feed Emily's hens. They ran to do her bidding, calling 'Delilah! Jemimah! Beulah!' as they scampered out to the back yard with a dish of water and a plate of vegetable scraps. Surveying them from the kitchen window, she decided that they would visit Broad Street today, in the hope that Orlaith would be home and not out tending patients. Jack's school term had finished and, since Bridget regrettably had no work commitments of her own, the coming day was uninhibited by any obligations. The stove did need a good scrub and blacking but that could wait. She imagined that Orlaith must be missing Charlie as much as she was missing Cormac and that they might provide consoling company for one another.

Waiting until a time when she could be certain that Tess had left to go to work at Tremont House, she set off with Jack and Gus and arrived at the building on Broad Street to find a cluster of people gathered on the street outside it. Some carried pots and armfuls of clothes, and all wore worried expressions.

'What's going on?' she asked a scraggy woman whom she recognised as being from another family who lived in the building, though not one with whom she had been on as friendly terms as the Careys.

''Tis the fever,' the woman breathed, her forehead creased with anxiety.

Before Bridget could press her for clarification, Orlaith came hurrying out of the building, clutching a stuffed sack. She spotted Bridget and came dashing up to her.

'God Almighty,' she moaned. 'What a misfortune this is.'

'What's happened?' Bridget asked, alarm rippling down her spine. She put a firm hand on both of her boys' shoulders, keeping them close to her.

'Scarlet fever,' said Orlaith and Bridget sucked in a breath of fear. It stuck in her throat when Orlaith added with another moan, 'The Careys.'

'Oh no,' Bridget gasped. 'How?'

'They think Una brought it home from the shirt factory. She got it first and Sorcha and Brian followed soon after. Derval's still well but she's blocked their door and refuses to allow anyone in. She won't even let me examine the young ones to see if there's anything I can do to treat them.'

That didn't surprise Bridget. Scarlet fever was highly contagious and, although it was most common in children, adults could catch it too. Derval wouldn't want to put Orlaith in jeopardy, no matter her valuable nursing skills.

'Derval called to me through the door and said I should warn the rest of the folk in the building,' Orlaith continued, 'so I've told them all and everyone's leaving with whatever they can carry until the danger's passed. They'll stay with other families along the street for now.' A shadow crossed her face. 'Except for Mr Lorenzo. He's already showing signs of it so he won't come out of his room either.'

Bridget recalled the evening she and Cormac had bumped into Una on the doorstep before the girl had headed up the stairs to visit Mr Lorenzo. For one horrific heartbeat, she wondered if Una could have passed the scarlet fever to Cormac too and that he was in peril of infecting all the passengers and crew on the *Blue Onyx*. Then her panic subsided as she figured that the odds of such a scenario occurring were so unlikely as to be almost nonexistent – after all, Bridget had also met Una that day and her own health was fine. The girl must have caught the fever at a later stage and gone up to Mr Lorenzo's room again since then. Bridget hoped the disease would not be too severe upon the elderly man, nor on the three Carey children whom she cherished as dearly as her own family.

'Will you come stay with us at Acorn House?' she said to Orlaith.

'Ah, thanks, I was hoping to do that, so long as I won't be a nuisance.'

'Not at all. Needless to say, Emily's room is currently unoccupied. We'd be very happy to have you. But—'

Bridget choked herself off as she recollected the fact that Tess would need a temporary place to reside as well. Orlaith's features contorted with discomfort.

'Don't worry,' she said. 'We found out about the fever just before Tess headed off to Tremont House so she said she'd ask for a bed in the servants' quarters there. She reckoned she wouldn't be welcome under your roof...' Her words faded away awkwardly.

Damn right, thought Bridget, but she just said, 'That's everyone sorted then.'

'Apart from the Careys and Mr Lorenzo,' Orlaith said, shooting an apprehensive glance back at the building. Most of the displaced occupants had begun drifting off towards the other dwellings along the street. Bridget espied old Mrs Kane standing on her doorstep beckoning to the scraggy woman she had spoken to before. At first, she speculated whether the tetchy old lady was just seeking gossip but she welcomed her neighbour across her threshold with a bracing pat on the back.

Orlaith dropped her sack on the ground, scurried up to the Careys' window and rapped on one of the panes. The original window had been damaged by hooligans during the riot between the Irish Catholics and Yankee Protestants but Charlie had organised its repair as a gesture of apology for the part his fire engine company had played in the violence, leaving it more pristine than any other in the building. Orlaith knocked on its glass persistently until Derval appeared and lifted the sash the tiniest crack. Her agitated voice floated through the gap.

'Don't come too near, for your own sakes.'

Orlaith stepped back, hovering an arm's length from the window. Bridget moved to her side, motioning at Jack and Gus to remain behind them. Weak coughs emanated from the room beyond Derval but Bridget couldn't see any of the children.

'Tell us what we can do to help,' she urged.

Derval wrung her hands. 'Just make sure everyone stays away. We can't let it spread any further.'

'The building's cleared out,' Orlaith assured her. 'It's only yourselves and Mr Lorenzo left so yous can bar the front door from the inside. I'm going to stay with Bridget but we'll come back with food, water, medicine, whatever yous all need. We can hand it in through the window or leave it on the doorstep.'

'Thank you,' Derval said fervently. She pressed her fingertips to her forehead. 'Lord bless us and save us—first Rory, and now this. What's going to be the third calamity?'

'The third?' said Bridget, puzzled.

Derval made the sign of the cross and bent closer to the glass, peering uneasily upwards to the sky as though she expected it to fall down. 'Bad things always come in threes.'

CHAPTER 10

Cormac leaned against the gunwale and whittled the block of wood with his pocket knife, nicking away at it without any clear idea of what it was to become. He figured that inspiration for its final shape would reveal itself to him in time. He blew at the shavings and they wafted over the side of the ship and into the churning water below.

Other passengers sauntered past him or laughed in groups nearby but he paid them no heed. He wasn't interested in making friends on this voyage. The bulk of his waking thoughts revolved around his two foremost concerns: the family he had left behind and the family he was heading towards. He felt suspended in limbo between them, unable to act while confined out here on the ocean. Longing and anxiety were his constant companions.

At least the weather had been fine thus far, and his sleeping accommodations were tolerable – he had purchased a ticket in steerage rather than a cabin in order to conserve as much of his money as possible, but the captain had been more preoccupied with taking on cargo than passengers prior to departure and so Cormac had managed to obtain a single berth for the journey. He kept to himself at mealtimes and remained on the edge of the jollity that took place in the evenings, quietly enjoying the music but never participating in the dancing. As he watched a knot of young Scottish folk skipping about to jigs and reels each evening, he wondered how Emily and Rory were spending their time aboard their own ship – he somehow couldn't picture them reconciling their differences and dancing harmoniously together.

A commotion further up the ship drew his attention away from his block of wood. He frowned as a pale-faced lad – he recognised him as the youngest seaman on board who was always consigned to swabbing the deck – came scrambling out of the hold and started shouting at his crewmates. Several sailors went dashing back down into the hold with him. Cormac glanced at the cluster of passengers nearest him; they all looked nonplussed.

'Probably a fuss about nuffin,' said one fellow with an English accent and a receding chin. He gave a dismissive shrug and returned to bantering with his companions. Cormac leaned on the gunwale again and resumed his whittling, peering out to the horizon every now and then as if that would make land appear sooner.

A short while later, they found out that it had in fact been a fuss about something very serious. In his peripheral vision, Cormac saw a passenger with a ginger beard clamber out of the steerage hatch and run up to the group near him. Wide-eyed, he panted to them, 'There was a fire!'

Christ, no.

Cormac's fingers went numb. The wood and knife slipped from his lifeless grip and he strove to recover his senses, grappling for the two items as they fell. He managed to catch the block of wood but the knife slithered out of his grasp, plummeting down the ship's hull and into the water with a splash. He cursed, then whirled to listen to what the ginger-bearded man was saying.

'—could hear them bellowing at each other in the hold. The fool of a boy was fed up of the ribbing he kept getting from the crew for not being able to smoke a pipe without heaving up his insides. So he hid down below among the cargo to *practise*, the idiot. Dropped the pipe on a ruddy bale of cotton. We're lucky the whole lot of us didn't go up in flames.'

The other men reacted with an assortment of exclamations and expletives but Cormac raised his voice above the rest. 'Is the fire under control now?' he asked urgently, stepping closer to the group.

The ginger man threw him a wary look; it was the first time Cormac had made an effort to converse with any of them. 'It is. They quenched it by emptying some of the water barrels over the bale.'

Cormac sagged, wordless with relief.

The ginger man turned back to his companions. 'It affected the supplies though. Our water will have to be rationed more tightly for the rest of the trip.'

'Better a dry throat than a scorched arse,' said the fellow with the receding chin, and the others all laughed.

Cormac swivelled away from them, resting his forearms on the gunwale as he waited for his heart rate to slow down. When would he overcome this damnable fear? He clutched the block of wood in his hands; it would remain a shapeless lump now that his pocket knife was sinking to the ocean floor. He clicked his tongue in exasperation and regret.

With a sigh, he spun on his heel and made for the hatch that led down to the steerage quarters. Below in the gloom, he located his valise in the storage bay between the empty berths. He opened it and tossed the useless piece of wood into it; his hands would have to be idle for the remainder of the voyage.

While he had the valise open, he felt about for the secret compartment Bridget had sewn into the lining and withdrew

94

the pouch he had hidden there. It jangled faintly. He had stowed most of his money on his person for safekeeping but had set this pouch aside so that all of his funds would not be in the same place. Now he envisioned a scenario where the ship became consumed by a blaze and he wouldn't have time to retrieve his luggage in the midst of trying not to burn or drown. Would it be wiser to keep this money on him too?

He heard a scuffle of steps and glanced up sharply. The English fellow with the receding chin was standing on the steerage stairs, staring at him. Cormac's fist tightened on the pouch. With a narrowed gaze, the other man pivoted and climbed back up to the deck.

Cormac swallowed. Then he tucked the pouch into his pocket and closed the valise.

He had been right to be cautious. The next day, he checked his valise and found that its contents had been disturbed. A ripple of unease skated over his skin.

***

Emily's day was going from bad to worse. She had volunteered to make the porridge for Rory, Henrik and Louise that morning and had ended up burning it to the point that it was almost inedible. The others hadn't complained but it had been an ordeal for them all to stomach it. Now she had a pain in her abdomen as she ambled along the Promenade and she hoped she had not made everyone ill with her dreadful cooking.

A seagull landed on the deck near her and she shooed it away irritably. It remained where it was, unperturbed, so she produced her handkerchief from inside her bodice and flailed it about until the seagull flapped lazily away. She tucked the handkerchief back into her bodice with a peevish sniff. While she usually had a fondness for birds, one of this creature's compatriots had defecated on her head the day before and a thoroughly unpleasant experience had ensued as she endeavoured to wash it out of her hair. It had left her thankful that Delilah, Jemimah and Beulah had never been able to fly to any great height.

Rory walked by her side, taciturn. He had made no further reference to the presence of his father on the ship and neither had she, although they both continued to keep a surreptitious eye out for him and she had learned to turn away inconspicuously whenever Brian Mór came within their vicinity. Perhaps Rory would resolve to confront his father, or perhaps he would reach land without ever approaching him. Either way, she would not push him on it.

Her stomach cramped again and, startled, she felt something wet seep between her legs. Had she lost control of her bladder? A flood of mortification swept over her from head to toe.

'Excuse me,' she muttered and scuttled away from Rory, ignoring his surprised expression.

She joined the queue for the privy which, mercifully, was not as long as it had been when the passengers had gone up to the deck first thing that morning. As she waited, she could feel the slickness at the top of her thighs and squeezed them together to stem the trickle, appalled beyond belief. If she really had urinated by accident, she thought she just might throw her treacherous body into the sea. She was too short, her breasts were too small, and now this!

She jiggled nervously on the spot as a hunchbacked woman entered the privy ahead of her. Only one to go. However, most vexingly, the woman spent an interminable length of time going about her business. When she finally exited the privy, it was with a shifty look which made Emily gulp a deep breath of air before she crossed its threshold herself.

The conditions inside the privy were only a marginal improvement on the bucket screened by the canvas sheet down in steerage. It was a ramshackle wooden structure with a hole in the floor and a messy pile of straw in one corner. The floor was always slippery and stained by the activities of previous careless users. Emily had established from the outset that it was prudent to make her visits as brief as possible and to only breathe through her mouth while she did the necessary.

Still, this occasion required rather more particular consideration. Fearful, she hiked her dress and petticoat up above her knees and put a timid hand through the gap in her drawers, touching the wetness between her legs. Then she pulled it back and examined her fingertips. They were red and slick with blood.

Realisation struck her like a ton of bricks. After yearning for so long to become a proper woman in every respect, it had happened at the most inconvenient moment imaginable. She was on a *ship*. How was she supposed to deal with her courses here?

She wished she wasn't alone for this. If only she were at home, her mother could have advised her what to do. Or, if it had occurred at Marlowe House, Matilda would have helped her. She felt quite forlorn and, as another painful cramp assailed her insides, increasingly sceptical as to why any girl would want to grow into a woman when this was the dubious reward.

Well, there was no use regretting the circumstances now. Her courses had arrived and this was where she must contend with them. To begin with, she needed to clean herself. She eyed the pile of straw but doubted its effectiveness in this scenario and pulled her handkerchief out of her bodice once more. She dabbed the affected region with it and then inspected the square of cloth, noting the bloody streaks with indecent fascination. Folding the handkerchief over on itself, she wiped again. This time, she observed only a faint crimson residue. There really wasn't so very much blood after all.

But how long might it continue to flow? What if it became heavier? How would she stop it from dripping down her legs onto the boards of the deck and revealing this most intimate information to all the other passengers, including Rory? That was a level of humiliation which could not be endured. She would have to stay away from everyone until the wretched affliction had passed.

She cringed as she remembered that it would likely return next month. And the month after that...

With a moan of despair, she let her skirts fall and regarded her soiled handkerchief. She wouldn't be able to wash it without someone else noticing the bloodstains. Sighing, she dropped it into the hole in the floor. On her next intake of breath, she forgot to only inhale through her mouth and the stink from the hole hit her nostrils. Good Lord, how could such a smell come from that stooped little woman? She hastened out of the privy to suck fresh, salty air into her lungs.

Returning to the Promenade was an impossibility so she instead slunk down to the steerage quarters. She crawled into the berth she shared with Louise, where she discovered that curling up into a tight ball alleviated the ache in her abdomen a little. Conscious that the blood would continue to leak out of her, she bunched her petticoat up between her legs to absorb what it could and tried not to feel sorry for herself. After all, this was a momentous event – although she did not know exactly how it correlated, she understood that her courses were a sign that she was now able to bear a child. She pictured Louise glowing with pregnancy and thought she would very much like to experience that joy herself someday. For now though, the whole affair brought only discomfort in her belly and a tenderness in her breasts and a childish craving for her mother's soothing embrace.

Louise sought her out a while later upon, she claimed, Rory's mulish insistence. 'He said you looked as pale as a sheet before you vanished.'

'Tell him I'm fine,' Emily reassured her in as robust a tone as she could muster, not wanting her companion to fear that she might become a burden again. 'I don't feel seasick, just fatigued. A spell of rest will put me to rights, I'm sure.'

She didn't rise for the rest of the day and slept fitfully that night, waking at intervals to find that the cramps had worsened whenever her limbs involuntarily stretched out, encroaching on Louise's side of the bunk. Each time, she folded herself back up like a hedgehog to ease the pain.

She dreaded that she would wake the next morning reeking and soaked in a pool of blood but, to her relief, no such awful incident occurred – in fact, she could no longer even feel any wetness between her thighs. Further inspection in the privy revealed that she had hardly bled much more and the meagre quantity that had seeped from her body had crusted in the creases of her petticoat. Perhaps the first time was always this swift. She was so glad at this rapid conclusion to her traumatic experience that for once she did not care about the stench of the privy.

She couldn't throw away her petticoat like she had her handkerchief so she changed into her spare one and, when washing day arrived, tried to scour the soiled article as inconspicuously as she could. However, Louise was kneeling ungainly at the tub of salt water next to her and she perceived the bloodstains despite Emily's best efforts to conceal them.

'Aha,' she said. 'Now I understand.'

Emily flushed and hung her head.

'Don't be embarrassed. It might be a bit unpleasant but it's natural for every woman.' When Emily glanced up, Louise offered her a sympathetic look. 'Was it your first time?'

She nodded mutely.

'And you weren't sure how to cope with it? Did your mother not forewarn you?'

'She did, but it wasn't until it happened that I realised I hadn't asked the right questions at all. I only wanted to know when I would get my courses, not what I ought to do when they actually arrived.'

Louise gave her a compassionate pat on her arm, leaving a wet handprint on her sleeve. 'Come to me the next time. I'll answer what I can.'

Emily thanked her most sincerely for her kindness. It cheered her to have a confidante in the matter although, needless to say, she intended for Rory to remain entirely ignorant of it. She would rather suffer a further ten days of bloody undergarments than explain to him the reason for her aloofness.

As she scrubbed hard at her petticoat, it struck her that, between her seasickness and her courses, she had spent an inordinate amount of time on the ship wishing she wasn't on it.

Chapter 11

Bridget entered the post office, trying not to feel self-conscious. While it wasn't an exclusively male domain, its current occupants were predominantly of that sex and their stares ricocheted towards her and away again like flies rebounding against a clear pane of glass.

At the counter, she enquired whether the post office held any correspondence addressed to the name McGovern and, upon confirming her spousal connection to Cormac, the clerk slid a single letter across the counter to her. She would have put it directly into her pocket but the postmark caught her eye: New York City. Her breath caught in her throat. It had to be related to Bronagh – Cormac had no acquaintances or business associates as far away as New York. Would it be yet another dead end, the third calamity Derval had predicted? Or, just perhaps, might it contain some good news at long last?

Too impatient to wait until she got home, she stepped over to the wall out of the way of the other queuing patrons and opened the letter. She had scarcely scanned the first lines when her gaze fell upon five marvellous words: *I have seen your sister.*

She let out a yelp of shock and joy. Disregarding the censorious glares this provoked in her direction, she read the letter eagerly all the way through.

It was from a Mrs Temple, who declared herself to be the manageress of Gallagher's Boarding House in the Bowery district of New York. She had been perusing a copy of *The Truth Teller* after the morning rush of departing patrons when she had turned to the missing persons section and, to her astonishment, caught sight of the portrait of a young woman she recognised. The woman in question had stayed at Gallagher's Boarding House only the previous week. Mrs Temple was certain that they were one and the same for the portrait was a very skilled likeness of her guest. It pleased her to be the bearer of such optimistic news for Mr McGovern and she urged him to come seek his sister in New York City at the earliest opportunity. If he called to the boarding house, she would be glad to assist him by whatever means she could.

Bridget's pulse thumped rapidly. *Only the previous week.* Allowing sufficient time for Mrs Temple to write her letter and for it to travel from New York to Boston, it could not be more than two weeks since she had seen Bronagh. It was the surest proof they had received to date that Cormac's sister was still alive, and very recently so.

Bridget sprinted from the post office, barely heeding the complaint of a man whose foot she trod on in her haste to leave. She tore home to Acorn House and burst through the door to find Orlaith seated on the sofa in the front room, a string of rosary beads entwined in her fingers. The doors to the kitchen and back yard were wide open, although no breeze blew through.

'Orlaith!' she exclaimed and then pulled up short. 'Oh, I'm very sorry. I didn't mean to interrupt your prayers.'

Orlaith stood. 'It's fine. I wasn't praying. I was just holding them.'

Bridget recognised the beads as Orlaith dropped them into her pocket – they were an old, plain set that had once belonged to Maggie McGovern, the only tangible object the McGovern siblings had left to remind them of their mother. They had once been such a large family, Maggie and Jack and their six children. Now just two of them remained.

But might there possibly be three?

'I have news!' Bridget blurted. 'Of Bronagh!'

She thrust Mrs Temple's letter into Orlaith's hands and watched her read it, easily identifying the point when she arrived at '*I have seen your sister*' by her loud gasp. Bridget curbed her excited impatience, clamping her mouth shut and listening to the faint sounds of Jack and Gus larking about in the back yard until Orlaith reached the bottom of the page. Finally, she looked up, her grey eyes shining like polished silver.

'God Almighty,' she rasped. 'After all this time. I can't believe it.'

'You can,' said Bridget, smiling. 'This family is well overdue some decent fortune, wouldn't you agree?'

Orlaith beamed back but her elation faded as her upper teeth worried at her bottom lip. 'We shouldn't get ahead of ourselves though. What can we actually do with this information? Cormac is away, and will be for months. By the time he gets back, the trail leading to Bronagh will have gone cold again.'

This dilemma had already occurred to Bridget during her mad dash home. 'Well,' she said, the exhilaration of good news encouraging her to speak her mind, 'not if we act upon it ourselves.'

Orlaith blinked. 'Ourselves?'

'You said it yourself—the trail will have gone cold long before Cormac returns. We may only be women but can we really forgo this chance to find Bronagh at last? Ought we not to pursue this knowledge now that we are in possession of it?'

In the ensuing silence, Bridget heard a distant shout as Mrs Hill next door scolded Jack and Gus over the fence for being too rowdy.

Orlaith raised her chin. 'You're right,' she said. 'It'd be excruciating to let this opportunity slip away just 'cause there isn't a man around. The pair of us are more than capable of doing this.'

'Furthermore,' added Bridget, 'we would be of far more use to our family investigating this promising clue about Bronagh rather than twiddling our thumbs waiting around to receive word from Cormac or Emily. I have no work commitments to detain me. Do you have any patients in grave health who are relying upon your aid?'

'As luck would have it, not at the moment,' said Orlaith. She peered at the letter still clutched in her hand. 'We could go to Gallagher's Boarding House and find out everything Mrs Temple knows, then try to trace Bronagh's steps wherever she went next. Imagine if we found her...' Orlaith's voice choked with emotion.

Bridget felt similarly moved but she strove to recollect the practicalities of the situation. 'If we are to truly undertake this, we shall have to be judicious in how we go about it. One thing we cannot deny is that there may very well be some danger involved—the last report we had of Bronagh was that she was keeping company with some men of a highly unsavoury sort.'

That report had come from Mr Todd, a stagecoach driver who operated the route from Boston to New York. Three months ago at The Bucking Deer Inn, he had informed Cormac that Bronagh had travelled on his coach seven years previously with another woman and two men who had been abusive towards both females on the journey. What if those brutes still occupied an unwelcome presence in Bronagh's life?

Orlaith squinted down at the page once more. 'Mrs Temple makes no mention of anyone else being with Bronagh. D'you reckon she might've managed to get away from those fellas since?'

'It's possible,' said Bridget. 'But I think we ought to still be on our guard just in case.'

Orlaith frowned. 'Might it be dangerous enough that we should wait for Charlie to return from Chicago before we go? He'll be back much sooner than Cormac and could come with us to New York.'

'That's an idea with potential. When do you anticipate his return?'

Orlaith thought about it before admitting, 'Not for another fortnight, in all likelihood.'

They glanced at the letter in unison and then their gazes met above it in silent agreement. It was too long to wait.

'We'll proceed with the greatest caution,' said Bridget. 'And we won't entertain any risk that could put us or the boys in the slightest jeopardy.'

'The boys?' Orlaith repeated, taken aback.

Bridget nodded, sombre but resolute. 'I considered the situation from all angles on my way home from the post office. If you and I go to New York, Jack and Gus will have to come with us for I cannot leave them on their own. Ordinarily, I would entrust them to Derval's care but that's not a viable option in the present circumstances.'

A week had passed but scarlet fever still reigned at the building on Broad Street, although thankfully none of the sufferers had significantly deteriorated in the interim.

'And is there nobody else who could mind them?' asked Orlaith, looking doubtful.

'I cannot encumber the Kanes or any of the other residents on Broad Street—they are already accommodating more than their fair share, thanks to the fever outbreak. Not to mention, we shall be obliged to appeal to them to assume the duty of bringing supplies to the Careys and Mr Lorenzo while we are gone.'

'What about your neighbours?' suggested Orlaith.

Bridget snorted. 'Mr and Mrs Hill view the boys as wicked devils hell-bent on disturbing their peace. They wouldn't tolerate them for an hour, let alone several days. I expect I'll have a hard enough challenge persuading them to look after the hens.'

Orlaith hesitated. 'There's Tess—'

'No,' said Bridget flatly. She downright refused to leave her sons in the care of a woman in whom she held absolutely no trust.

Orlaith didn't argue the point. 'I understand. In that case, there really isn't any choice other than to bring them with us, 'specially if we want to get going without delay. At least there'll be two of us to mind them.'

'Indeed,' said Bridget, impressed by how quickly she and Orlaith were formulating their plan while also heeding the pertinent complications.

In truth, she did harbour misgivings about taking Jack and Gus along on an enterprise fraught with so many unknowns, particularly when she hadn't even given a moment's consideration to the notion of them going with Cormac to England. However, a coach ride to New York would not be remotely as arduous or as lengthy a journey as crossing the Atlantic Ocean, and thus it was on the whole much more feasible to contemplate. Moreover, the exigency of the situation demanded that she and Orlaith take action swiftly.

She continued, 'I can envision us procuring a room at Gallagher's Boarding House while we are in New York. So perhaps we shall take turns staying with the boys in the room and going out to make enquiries. Who knows, there might even be time to explore the big city before we depart. With all the hullabaloo over Emily running away, it would be nice to make a fuss of the boys for a change.'

Jack and Gus had been entirely overshadowed by their sister's recent antics. They would deem this trip a magnificent treat – even travelling on the stagecoach would be an adventure they had not yet experienced in their young lives.

Nevertheless, searching for Bronagh would, of course, remain their primary objective. With the help of God, they might actually hope for success this time. Bridget imagined Cormac's stunned expression if he walked through the front door of Acorn House upon his return to Boston to find his long-lost sister standing before him. What a wonderful gift that would be. Bridget yearned to do everything in her power to achieve it.

CHAPTER 12

Emily and Rory were actually laughing together.

A fierce wind had whipped up around the ship in the afternoon, so strong that it had plucked the bonnet from Emily's head – evidently, she had not taken enough care in tying its ribbons. Rory chased after it but was obliged to fight off an audacious seagull which seemed to think that the bonnet might contain a tasty morsel. He drove the impudent bird away and returned to Emily, triumphantly carrying his hard-won prize. Placing it back on her head for her, he made a point of knotting the ribbons with fastidious precision beneath her chin. She giggled as he stepped back, his eyebrows arched and his arms folded in haughty appraisal before he, too, broke into laughter. It was a novel experience and she much preferred it to their frequent sniping.

'Thank you for rescuing my bonnet, noble sir,' she said with a curtsey.

That erased the grin from his face for some reason. He didn't remark upon it, only gestured for them to continue their walk along the Promenade, any trace of hilarity replaced by his more typical reticence.

What had she said to offend him? She had only thanked him, and surely he comprehended that her 'noble sir' comment had been in jest. Or could that in fact have been the cause of his abrupt change in humour? Had he thought she was mocking him from her own loftier position?

A stiff silence billowed between them as the wind also swelled, gusting harder than it yet had over the past three weeks they had spent meandering up and down the deck day in, day out. The ship pitched more deeply to one side and then the other. Unnerved, Emily peered out to sea and discerned a tall bank of black clouds roiling on the horizon. Below, the water heaved all around the ship in choppy waves.

'Um, Rory?' she said timidly. He gave her a sidelong glance and she pointed at the clouds. 'Is that...?'

He grimaced. There was no need for him to offer any additional response because now she could perceive the flurry of activity on the ship as the sailors scurried to and fro, furling sails and securing whatever loose articles could be tied down with rope. She quailed at the patent agitation in their movements.

'It'll be fine,' said Rory and she turned her anxious gaze back to him. 'When I was younger, my da told me stories about getting caught in storms at sea. The crew are experienced in these kinds of conditions—they know how to handle it.'

She tried to feel reassured but a shiver vibrated through her as the temperature dropped noticeably. She stared out at the cloudbank again – it was drawing nearer to the *Integrity* with frightening swiftness. The sailors started barking at the passengers on deck to make their way down to the steerage quarters. One man stuck his head into the kitchen shanty and ordered the occupants to douse their fires. There were a few grumbles from the passengers but most seemed to grasp the implication of the approaching peril and shuffled towards the hatch, casting fearful looks out to sea before ducking below.

A voice behind Emily and Rory said, 'Come on, folks, get moving,' and a hand shoved at Rory's shoulder. They turned as one and found themselves face to face with Brian Mór. Rory shook himself out of his father's grip at once.

'No,' he said defiantly.

Brian Mór scowled. ''Tis captain's orders, you pup—' He froze.

Rory clenched his jaw, holding his ground under the man's scrutiny.

'*Rory*?' Brian Mór said, dumbfounded. 'What the bloody hell are you doing here?'

When Rory didn't say anything, Emily said tentatively, 'Hello, Mr Carey.'

Brian Mór swung towards her, glaring. 'Who're you?'

'E-Emily McGovern,' she stammered. 'My family and I used to live in the rooms above yours at Broad Street.'

If possible, his gaze darkened even further at the mention of his family's home in Boston. He transferred his attention back to his son. 'Tell me,' he demanded. 'How in God's name did you end up on this ship?'

'I bought a ticket,' said Rory through gritted teeth. 'When it was in port. D'you remember where that was?'

Raindrops began to fall, leaving fat, wet splotches on the boards of the deck. Emily tugged her bonnet over her forehead but the two men acted like they hadn't even noticed the worsening weather. Their expressions mirrored each other, surly and mutinous.

'Get down below,' Brian Mór said gruffly.

He made to turn away but Rory seized his arm, jerking him back to face him again.

'Not until you answer me,' he snapped. 'You can't have forgotten where the ship was in port. Why didn't you go see your wife and children? How many times has the *Integrity* docked in Boston but you just stayed on board pretending we didn't exist?' Rory was yelling now, his face bright red. He grabbed the front of his father's shirt, his fists bunching in the folds of fabric. 'What made you abandon us, you bastard?'

Brian Mór flung Rory's arms away and cuffed him around the ear. Rory stumbled backwards.

'Don't you dare speak to me that way, whelp,' his father hissed at him. 'Shut your gob and get below before I throw you down there myself.'

Rory didn't budge. 'Tell me the truth. I want to know *why*.'

Equally obstinate, Brian Mór said, 'You'll get no answers from me.'

He whirled on his heel and stalked away, growling at another pair of passengers to hurry down to steerage before briskly scaling some rigging to help his crewmates finish furling the sails. The rain was now falling in earnest, soaking Rory's uncovered head as he glowered up at his father's agile form clambering among the ropes. Emily plucked at his sleeve.

'Come,' she said, wanting to speak gently but compelled to raise her voice to be heard over the roar of the waves and the wind. 'We need to get out of this weather.'

To her surprise, he didn't resist when she took hold of his arm and pulled him towards the steerage hatch. Even in the few seconds it took to reach it, the downpour rapidly became torrential and they dashed the final steps across the deck, gasping when they gained shelter but nearly tumbling down the stairs in the process.

As Emily caught her balance, she registered the strained atmosphere in the steerage area. Passengers were milling about aimlessly or huddling on their bunks, muttering to each other and eying the sides of the lurching hull as though they could see through it to the brewing storm outside. The tension was palpable, making the hair rise on Emily's neck and arms. Descending fretfully to the bottom of the stairs, she wheeled around to Rory, who was wiping rainwater from his eyes – at

111

least, she presumed it to be rainwater. She certainly wasn't going to question whether it was any other type of moisture.

But what could she say instead? *Are you hungry? Do you feel better or worse after confronting your father? Are you quite sure we're safe and not about to die?*

She was saved the trouble of deciding when another sailor – not Rory's father – appeared in the hatch opening above, shepherding a few straggling, drenched women ahead of him. Judging by the cooking kettles in their hands and the peeved expressions on their faces, he had shunted them out of the kitchen against their will. After prodding them to hurry down the steps, he stooped through the hatch himself and glanced around.

'Where's Lovell?' he hollered.

'No need to shout,' came the responding admonition. The matron appeared at the foot of the stairs, squinting in the light from the hatch and rubbing her temples. Having observed the woman's habits over the past three weeks, Emily had learned to recognise these as signs that Miss Lovell was recovering from her previous night's drinking and had not yet embarked upon her next bout.

The sailor gestured peremptorily from the matron to the confused mass of men, women and children. 'Make sure they tie up any loose baggage. It's going to be a rough night.'

Emily baulked at that. It was only late afternoon. How long did he expect this storm to last?

Miss Lovell flapped her hand at the sailor as though to say 'don't tell me what I already know' and with a shrug he vanished from the hatch opening. The matron turned and began issuing desultory instructions to the passengers regarding their belongings, while also making a reproachful remark to a nearby cluster of highly strung children about keeping the noise down. As the people scuttled about in response to Miss Lovell's orders, Emily shuffled out of their way, stepping back with Rory into the shadow of the stairs.

'What should we do now?' she asked him, her voice little more than an anxious squeak.

He exhaled a tired breath that she suspected had as much to do with the disastrous encounter with his father as it did with the advancing storm. 'Wait it out. 'Tis all we can do.'

'Ought we to go to our respective sections?' she said, wondering if the ship's rules tended to slacken during turbulent circumstances such as these.

'I guess so,' he said.

Neither of them made any move to part and, rather awkwardly, she started picking at the wet ribbons of her bonnet, which were still tied under her chin. To her exasperation, the knot was too tight and, after several unsuccessful attempts, Rory said, 'Here, let me.'

She could have refused out of silly pride but she dropped her hands and stood still, or at least as still as she could on the rolling ship. His knuckles grazed her chin as he teased out the knot. The ribbons fell apart and he removed her bonnet quite gently before handing it to her.

'Let me know if you need m—anything,' he said. He walked off into the men's section where she watched him join Henrik, who was hovering nervously in front of one of the berths. Was that where Rory and Henrik shared their bunk? It seemed like very intimate knowledge for her to have, but then she reasoned that Rory knew where she slept after all.

She made for the women's section where she found Louise pacing up and down the floorboards by their berth and rubbing her belly. When Emily approached her, she gave a hysterical laugh.

'How's this for timing?' she said and doubled over with a groan.

Emily gaped, nearly dropping her bonnet in shock. 'Your baby's coming? *Now?*'

Louise winced. 'Just my luck. Know any proverbs about babies who are born in storms?'

Emily shook her head, although she doubted any such sayings would contain optimistic prophecies about a child who entered the world while nature raged around it.

'What can I do to help you?' she asked, keen to reciprocate Louise's goodwill from when she had tended Emily during her seasickness.

'Not much for the time being, I think,' said Louise, panting. 'The pains have only just started.' She gasped and reached out to grab their bunk's bedpost, her fingers clenching it hard. An expression of fear shadowed her face. 'I wish Roger were here,' she choked.

He had to be her dead husband. She had never spoken of him before. Heart aching for the young widow, Emily tossed her bonnet on the bunk and clasped Louise's other hand with both of her own.

'I am no substitute for Roger,' she said, 'but I am here and I shall give you every ounce of support I can.'

Louise cast her a look of deepest gratitude. Then she uttered another groan of pain, just as the boom of an enormous wave crashing against the hull reverberated through the steerage quarters. A number of women emitted screams of fright and several children burst into tears. Emily swallowed her own terror as best she could but, between the hazardous weather and what little she knew of the perils of childbirth, she could not deny the profound fear that was settling into the very pores of her skin.

Her trepidation only intensified when she heard a further loud bang and the dim light below deck vanished altogether, plunging the steerage passengers into darkness. She recognised the sound as the shutting of the hatch at the top of the stairs but it was usually heard at ten o'clock each night when everyone was obliged to retire to their berths. Yet here they were in the late afternoon with the sailors expecting them to endure the entirety of the storm while surrounded by solid blackness. She was very glad that she was still clutching Louise's hand; she squeezed harder and Louise returned the pressure.

This only comforted her for an instant before realisation hit her – good gracious, Louise could not give birth in the pitch dark. It would be inconceivable.

'Louise!' she said frantically. 'We must tell Miss Lovell that you are in labour. She will have to permit us to light a lantern. Can you wait here by yourself for a few minutes while I go seek her out?'

'I can,' came Louise's reply, breathy and strained. 'Thank you, dear Emily.'

Emily patted her hand before letting go. 'I'll be back soon.'

Her eyesight was adjusting somewhat and the dense black had faded to a gloomy grey but, even so, she could not discern much more than the outline of Louise's pregnant figure. She stretched out an arm to locate the edge of the berth and ran her fingertips along it until she reached its foot. Then she proceeded cautiously to the neighbouring berth and the one after that, using her memory of the layout in steerage to guide her towards Miss Lovell's private compartment. She tripped over her own feet and bumped into other disorientated passengers, reeling when the ship heaved from side to side, but finally found her way back to the stairs below the closed hatch. It was latticed so some light still filtered down through the gaps, although its murky nature suggested that the thick bank of clouds she had seen on the horizon was now blocking out most of the sunlight above the ship. Rainwater also dripped through the wooden grid, creating wet patches on the stairs beneath.

'Miss Lovell?' she called out timidly and, when she received no answer, repeated herself in a more forceful tone.

The matron emerged from the shadows past the stairs. Emily could distinguish the shape of her head and body but the spidery veins on her face were imperceptible in the dimness. 'What is it?' Miss Lovell said, her tone curt.

'They closed the hatch,' Emily began, pointing upwards.

'Of course they did,' said Miss Lovell. 'The last thing we want is for the place to get flooded. They'll be covering it up shortly with canvas too.'

Emily swallowed. 'We need a light. Is there a lantern I could borrow to—'

'No lanterns,' the matron said dismissively. 'A lantern won't stay where it's put in these conditions. We don't want a fire down here either.' She turned away.

'But it's for my friend,' Emily said, her desperation and her voice both rising. 'She needs light to deliver her baby safely.'

Miss Lovell's head twisted sharply towards her. 'Baby? There's a woman in labour down here? Right now?'

'Yes, my friend, Louise Shelby—'

'Take me to her at once.'

Emily led the way back, fervently grateful that the matron was sober in this moment. When they reached the berth, they found Louise leaning her forehead against the side of the bunk above, moaning. A thicker mass in the darkness next to her indicated a small throng of concerned passengers. One woman's shadowy hand rubbed Louise's back and said reassuringly, 'You'll be grand, love,' but anything else she might have said was swallowed by an ear-splitting creak of the hull. The group uttered frightened gasps and Louise let out a sob.

'There, there,' said Miss Lovell, unperturbed by the noise. 'The *Integrity*'s a fine ship and we're all safe aboard her. Captain

Philips will steer her true, mark my words. Let's focus instead on delivering that little one without harm.'

'Is there a midwife on the ship?' Emily asked hopefully.

'Just me,' said the matron, her tone bracing. She grasped Louise's arm. 'Come with me now, Mrs Shelby. I'll take care of you.'

Emily was pleasantly surprised by Miss Lovell's kind manner – prior to this, she had not exhibited more than a passing interest in the welfare of the passengers under her supervision. Giving thanks that the woman had chosen this day of all days to show her compassionate side, Emily tailed her closely as she ushered Louise past the other berths back to the stairs. Louise was breathing heavily but she had ceased sobbing and it seemed Miss Lovell's confident presence had exerted a calming influence upon her.

They arrived at the stairs and Miss Lovell began leading Louise up the steps, holding her elbow to help her keep her balance.

'Miss Lovell?' said Emily behind them, confused. 'Where are we going? Your private quarters are over there.' She pointed past the stairs where the matron's compartment was hidden in the gloom.

Miss Lovell glanced over her shoulder with a scoff. 'You think she can give birth in that tiny hole? There isn't room to swing a cat in it.'

She climbed the stairs with Louise until they could go no further without knocking their heads against the closed hatch. Halting, she called up through it, 'Halloo! Simpson! You there?'

After a few seconds, the sailor from before appeared, his face peering down through the lattice.

'Oh, good,' said Miss Lovell. 'Open the hatch, will you? I've got a passenger here nearly ready to give birth. We need one of the crew cabins.'

Simpson didn't object so Emily supposed that this was not an uncommon occurrence. He retreated from the hatch and lifted it with a grunt. Rainwater sloshed down the steps and splashed across Emily's boots. She hurried to scramble up the stairs after the others but Miss Lovell shooed her away.

'You're not needed,' she barked over the howl of the wind and shepherded Louise up the final few steps onto the rain-lashed deck.

'I am!' protested Emily. 'I promised her I would help!'

When she tried to follow, Miss Lovell waved her back once more. 'Child,' she said with a laugh, 'how could you possibly help?'

She nodded at Simpson and the sailor moved to drop the hatch into place again, forcing Emily to take several steps back down the stairs. The wooden grid descended with a thud that resounded in her ears.

However, she was not so deafened that she missed what Miss Lovell said to Simpson next.

'Make sure the captain's informed about this. It's an extra task beyond my official duties. I'll expect a good bottle in recompense.'

'Miss Lovell!' Emily cried. 'Louise!'

They didn't hear her. Through the gaps in the lattice, she saw them bend forwards into the buffeting wind and vanish from view. She pushed on the hatch but it was much too heavy and wouldn't budge. In the next instant, Simpson strode across the grid dragging a sheet of canvas over it and all was sealed away from her: the rain, the light, and any hope of helping her friend.

Chapter 13

Emily stood motionless on the stairs in the dark, aghast. If the matron's only motivation was liquor, to what extent did she actually care about the lives of Louise and her baby? Would she be recompensed for her efforts regardless of whether the delivery was a success? It was less than encouraging that she was not skilled in midwifery like Auntie Derval, but if she was also indifferent to the outcome...

Emily whimpered in distress. She had been the one to alert Miss Lovell to Louise's urgent situation. She had placed her friend's life, and that of her unborn child, in the matron's questionable charge.

She would be responsible for whatever trauma befell them both.

After a long shudder of despair that seemed to tremble all the way from her scalp to the soles of her feet, she took a stumbling step down the stairs and then another. She picked her way through the gloom back to the women's section where she located her berth and crawled into it – there was nothing else to be done with the entire steerage shrouded in artificial night.

The bunk seemed far too large in the absence of her companion beside her. She stretched her limbs out wide in a starfish shape but felt vulnerable in that exposed position and instead curled herself up into a ball, as she had done when her courses came. She made herself as small as she could, glad for once that she had such a diminutive figure. All she wanted was to hide herself away from the world.

But the world would not let her hide, would not pretend that it had forgotten her existence, would not allow her to ignore the reality that she was here on this ship in the throes of an increasingly powerful storm. As she lay there with her knees huddled tight against her chest, the wind tossed the vessel about as wildly as if it were nothing but a bobbing twig in the water. Rain battered the hull like thousands of tiny spears and the wood groaned as it tried to resist the onslaught. Strangely, she did not feel seasick from the violent motion. However, a dreadful panic climbed up her throat, blocking it so that she could hardly breathe.

She might perish this very day. If the storm became much fiercer and the crew lost control of their vessel, it could very well capsize. Though she endeavoured to quash the image, her mind was able to picture it all too vividly: a gigantic wave crashing into the side of the ship with enough force to roll it over, the passengers within thrown from their berths, the seawater pouring in on all sides, the screaming silenced as the steerage quarters became a tomb. The *Integrity* and all who sailed upon her would sink to the ocean floor.

Her whole body quaked. She had brought this upon herself and, worse, upon Rory too. How fearful was he right now? How much more did he hate her because her foolish choices had brought them to the brink of death? Tears gushed from her eyes. She didn't want to be hated. She didn't want to die.

In the pitch black, her very worst thoughts swarmed their way to the surface of her mind, thrusting aside rationality and engulfing her with terrible feelings of doubt and shame and self-reproach. If these were the circumstances in which she was to depart from this life, how would she be remembered, should anyone care to remember her? She would never prove to her horrible schoolmaster, Mr Miller, that a woman could achieve more than an existence of mere mediocrity. Samuel would never know her as anything but the mysterious girl from the ball and she would slip from his memory, their love forever undeclared. And her parents... Without the chance to explain her actions or beg for their forgiveness, the abiding version of her that they would retain for the rest of their lives would be a selfish, irresponsible child who had abandoned them for the sake of her own self-serving ambitions. Heavens above, what if her papa went to his eventual grave believing that her decision to flee to England meant she had preferred Garrett to him as a father? What a cruel thing that would be. Oh, she was a wicked creature indeed.

The ship plunged to the side more deeply than it had yet done. Was this the fatal moment? She clung to her berth in petrified anticipation. Then it lurched back in the opposite direction and she expelled a quivering breath. A woman vomited in the adjacent berth and the reek of it drifted past her. Many of the passengers were shrieking or crying now but she imagined that she could hear a more distant scream of agony above the thrashing wind and lashing rain. Please, God, she prayed. Please spare Louise and her little baby.

Out of the blue, there was a series of heavy thuds across the floorboards and something struck her hard on the shoulder, eliciting a screech of fright and pain from her.

'Wh-who—?' she stuttered.

She put out a cautious, questing hand and her fingers touched leather and metal. Further exploration established that it was luggage of some sort – someone had evidently not tied down their possessions securely enough. Distraught from the scare it had given her, she shoved it off the berth onto the floor.

121

Her heart pounded, beating against her ribs like a trapped bird. Rubbing her aching shoulder, she tried to regain control of herself but her pulse continued to thump too fast and her breath came in short, rapid gasps so shallow that it seemed like scarcely any air was reaching her lungs. Could a person expire from fear itself? If so, she was lost. Trembling, she pressed her palms over her eyes and surrendered to her terror, the sobs ripping from her with raw ferocity. She wept and wished from the depths of her soul that she had never run away from home.

'Emily?'

She jolted at the voice that came murmuring out of the darkness, so shocked that the next sob lodged in her throat and ascended no further. Dropping her hands from her face, she squinted through the murk to glimpse a shaggy-edged silhouette kneeling by her berth. She struggled to speak.

'R-Rory?' she managed in a strangled whisper.

''Tis me,' he said and added awkwardly, 'I...just came to check that you're all right.'

A surge of gratefulness rose up in her, eclipsed instantly by her hysteria. 'Oh, I'm not,' she wailed. 'Louise and her baby might die tonight and it will be my fault! And you and I might die and that will be my fault too! And my parents must be so disappointed in me and I've set an appalling example for my brothers and I'm an absolute disgrace to them and I won't have the chance to say sorry to anybody and—'

He cut her off, not with placating words but by quite simply pulling her to him and pressing her face to his chest, physically stifling her outburst. The spectrum of her awareness narrowed to the rough texture of the cloth of his shirt and the pressure of his hands curving around her skull and the smell of his body that was an unexpectedly appealing combination of rain and musky perspiration. Her arms automatically wrapped around his torso and she latched onto him like a barnacle on a rock. She turned her head slightly so that her cheek rested against his chest and found that she was able to breathe a little easier. She couldn't tell whether his intention had been to silence her or to console her, but he had achieved both.

After a minute or two, she said without any trace of reproof, 'You shouldn't be here.'

Before he could respond, there was an audible exchange nearby between the two disembodied voices who had argued over Rory's presence in the women's section back when Emily had been sick.

'Too right,' retorted the tetchy one. 'It should be females only.'

'Ah, let the girl have some comfort,' the good-natured one countered tolerantly, with an underlying tremor in her speech that conveyed her own unease at being trapped in the thick of the storm.

Rory must have agreed with the second woman because he made no move to leave or even to disentangle Emily from their close embrace. He seemed to be waiting for her to act next.

Without any further clarity of thought other than that his knees must be growing sore from kneeling on the hard wooden boards, she tugged him forwards in a wordless invitation to climb into the berth. He rose and she shifted backwards to make room for him, releasing her grip around him so that he could manoeuvre his tall body into the narrow space. A few seconds of clumsiness ensued as each attempted to accommodate the other but at last he settled on his side next to her, his legs slightly bent. She was short enough that she could curve herself into the space in front of his torso, their heads and upper bodies not touching and only her shins grazing his knees. A vague consciousness of the impropriety of it crossed her mind but it promptly fled again – in the midst of her distress, she needed his warm, comforting presence more than she needed the approbation of a society who could not observe her current situation in any case.

The ship lurched once more and, whimpering, she scrabbled to seize the edge of the bunk.

Rory's steady voice emanated from the dark. 'You can hold onto me.'

She didn't think twice. Scooting closer, she buried herself in the circle of his arms and hung on tight. Logically speaking, she knew there was nothing he could do if the ship capsized but she nonetheless felt safer with his solid form surrounding her.

Time lost all meaning after that. The storm raged on, seemingly without end, pummelling at their vessel which felt about as substantial as a thimble as it floundered on the vast, seething ocean. Emily silently prayed several decades of the rosary, counting on her fingers because she had no beads. Rory lay there calmly, not speaking or moving much, just being quiet and as sturdy as an oak. There were further knocks and bangs as more baggage came loose from its ties but nothing else struck them or their berth. Other passengers prayed aloud, wept or retched. One man towards the front of the ship sang a strident, drunken rendition of 'Amazing Grace' numerous times before he subsided into a slurred burble.

She couldn't say for certain when day became night or how long it took for the storm to pass, but she gradually noticed that the hammering rain had ceased to a gentler patter and the teetering of the ship had eased back to a more regular motion.

'Thank the Lord!' the good-natured voice exclaimed nearby. 'We're saved.'

'Until the next one comes along,' her tetchy companion said ominously.

Emily couldn't bear to contemplate the idea of suffering another ordeal like this on their voyage so she firmly shut any such thoughts out of her mind. Instead, she allowed blessed relief to suffuse her as the tension began to drain from her taut limbs. She wriggled within Rory's embrace but when he didn't budge she realised he must have fallen asleep at some point and she fell still, not wishing to disturb him. She listened to his even breathing and tried to match him, but he was too slow and she was too fast – every time, she was obliged to draw her next breath before he did.

She didn't doze off herself so she was awake when the hatch opened an indeterminate time later and footsteps descended the stairs. Grey light – was it dawn? – seeped down into steerage, revealing the mess of scattered baggage and splashes of vomit on the floor around the berths. As the passengers climbed out of their bunks to survey the chaos and give thanks to God, a figure picked its way through the muddle and approached Emily's berth, cradling a small bundle.

'Louise!' Emily shrieked.

Rory startled awake and she immediately slithered out of his grasp, embarrassed by their unseemly proximity now that other eyes were upon them. However, Louise did not blink at the sight – after all, she believed that Emily and Rory were siblings and what kind-hearted brother would not seek to console his sister in the middle of such a traumatic event? In any case, Louise had far more important concerns. She beamed, displaying the bundle in her arms as Emily and Rory struggled to extricate themselves from the berth.

'A girl,' she said proudly. 'Strong and healthy with ten fingers and ten toes. I named her Philippa after Captain Philips—we all made it safely through the storm thanks to him.'

Emily peeked at the small face nestled inside the bundle and her heart overflowed with adoration. 'Oh, she is beautiful,' she breathed. 'And such a pretty, fitting name. We do indeed owe the captain our gratitude. What a terrifying night it was.'

She stole a self-conscious glance at Rory. He was rubbing his bristly jaw as he yawned, not appearing very interested in the new baby. His gaze flicked towards Emily and she looked away at once.

'Did Miss Lovell take good care of you?' she asked Louise. 'I was dreadfully worried when she wouldn't let me come with you above deck.'

'She did a fine job,' said Louise. 'Although she hadn't much to do, if truth be told—Philippa all but slid out by herself.'

Rory coloured at this and coughed. 'Did you meet any sailors on your way down?' he muttered. 'Are we allowed back up on deck?'

'We are indeed. The sun's just rising and it's wonderfully fresh, like the storm blew away all the cobwebs in the world.'

They weren't the only ones who craved to escape the confines of steerage. A crowd had gathered at the foot of the stairs and passengers were clambering up it and vanishing through the hatch with alacrity. Emily, Rory and Louise joined the throng, Louise cooing affectionately over the bundle containing her newborn daughter. What an enormous relief it was that Miss Lovell had, in whatever limited way, assisted mother and child safely through the birth. However, it did not restore Emily's faith in the matron – the events of the previous evening had been a hard lesson learned in comprehending both her own gullibility and the potential unreliability of others. She did not think she would trust any person so readily again.

Reaching the top of the stairs was like being birthed from the ship's womb – they emerged onto the deck gasping mouthfuls of air as if they were inhaling it into their lungs for the very first time. They navigated their way through the mob of passengers cheering and applauding the *Integrity*'s survival and found an empty stretch of gunwale to look out over the ocean. The sunrise was magnificent, the bright gold disc inching above the horizon and casting a spear of radiance across the tranquil water. Between Philippa and the sun, Emily felt quite overwhelmed by the sheer splendour that the world could contain.

She swivelled at the sound of clomping boots behind her; two sailors were striding towards the horde of passengers still streaming out of the hatch. With a gulp, she saw that one of them was Brian Mór. She wondered if she ought to alert Rory but, before she could decide, he had turned and spotted his father too. They stared at one another for a long, assessing moment as though they were each registering that the other had survived the storm and contemplating whether or not to resume their row from the previous day. Then Brian Mór glowered at his son and marched away, joining his crewmate to announce to the passengers that the captain had declared an extra Mass would be said later that morning to give thanks for their good fortune.

Rory's countenance hardened but he didn't pursue him. When he glanced at Emily, she once again hastened to focus her attention elsewhere. She wasn't sure if she would ever be able to meet his eye again.

She returned her gaze to the sea, absently massaging her shoulder that had been struck by the loose luggage. The waves lapped soothingly against the hull of the ship and she found it difficult to believe that mere hours ago the same body of water had nearly swallowed them whole. She recollected her consuming panic in the darkness, her awful conviction that extreme catastrophe was inevitable, her longing for reassurance that had driven her to embrace a young man more intimately than she had ever held her real brothers. It was astonishing how fear could distort reality to such an extent. She was very glad that she had her wits about her again.

But, having faced the wrath of nature in its humbling magnitude, she truly perceived her own insignificance in the world.

CHAPTER 14

Bridget grimaced when the stagecoach trundled into yet another hole in the road, jolting its occupants about and prompting a chorus of apologies as an elbow dug into a neighbouring rib or a hatbox fell upon an unsuspecting foot.

'That lunatic is going to get us all killed,' grumbled the owner of the hatbox, settling it firmly on her lap again.

Bridget, too, felt that the driver was operating the coach at a rather excessive speed, but it matched the pace of the previous couple of days which had flown by in a flurry of activity as she and Orlaith had made their plans for New York with impressive efficiency.

Standing at a safe distance from the Careys' window at Broad Street, they had informed Derval through the crack that they would be away for probably a week or so but that the Kanes had kindly agreed to take on the responsibility of leaving provisions on the doorstep in their absence. While acknowledging the risk, Derval had concurred that they were right to follow the encouraging clue about Bronagh and, after expressing her regret that she was not in a position to mind Jack and Gus, she had wished them the very best of luck.

'And please God the scarlet fever will be gone from here by the time ye return,' she had added and blessed herself, her hand flitting agitatedly from forehead to chest to shoulders.

Notifying Tess about their trip was a task which Orlaith had undertaken alone. Afterwards, she had come back from Tremont House to report that Tess had made an earnest offer to go with them but that Orlaith had gently declined her help. Neither of them had broached the subject of looking after the two boys – Orlaith hadn't wanted to throw another refusal at her friend, and it seemed that it had not occurred to Tess to wonder where Jack and Gus would be in the midst of all the commotion. Bridget was relieved to have avoided that confrontation entirely.

In the meantime, she had visited The Bucking Deer Inn to make enquiries about taking the stagecoach from Boston to New York. She would use a portion of the money Cormac had given her to pay for the four fares – it was not an expense either of them had considered when he had divided up his savings for Brubaker but it would be worth it if it led to them finding Bronagh.

Once she had ascertained from the innkeeper that the next coach bound for New York would be departing the following morning, she had gone back to Acorn House to pack for their journey. Cormac and Emily were currently in possession of the family's only two valises so she had resorted to using the canvas bag in which she had carried the white muslin to Madame Roche's shop, filling it with food for four and changes of clothes for herself and the boys, while tucking her money pouch and Mrs Temple's letter into her pocket for safekeeping. Orlaith still had the sack she had taken from Broad Street when the fever had broken out so, upon her return from Tremont House, she had sewn a strap onto it to make it easier to carry.

All that had remained after that was to meekly ask Mr and Mrs Hill to watch over the hens, which they consented to do with bad grace, and to tell Jack and Gus the news about their imminent expedition, which they greeted with roars of excitement.

The pair of them were right now bouncing in their seats on the stagecoach, enjoying the bumpy ride far more than the rest of the passengers. Gus, in particular, fizzed with exuberance and Bridget had to chide him on several occasions when he whooped too loudly at the coach's jerky movements or pointed enthusiastically at interesting sights beyond the stagecoach window, twice nearly knocking off the cap of the man in the adjacent seat.

'You need to calm down and behave, little miracle,' Bridget scolded when this happened a third time, 'or I shall get out the wooden spoon at our next stop.'

She didn't mean it because of course she had not packed the wooden spoon but Gus believed her and the threat was enough to persuade him to adopt a virtuous expression and perch obediently next to his meeker brother.

As the coach swung around another bend in the road, Bridget seized an arm strap and wished the driver would take a little more care. If he carried on in this fashion for the duration of the three-day journey, they would all have bruises by the time they arrived in New York. She had hoped that they would be fortunate enough to travel with Mr Todd who, according to Cormac, had seemed quite a decent sort even if he had been unable to assist Bronagh out of her troubling situation. However, it was a paunchy fellow called Mr Henson who sat up front and urged the team of horses onwards.

In between the towns and stagecoach stops, they traversed stretches of American countryside which, though striking in their own way, made her wistful for the hills and fields of home.

Eight years had passed since she had last stood on Irish soil and she felt the separation keenly. How saddening it was that both Emily and Cormac would sail within reach of Ireland but neither would actually set foot there.

Opposite her on the centre bench, Orlaith gazed out the window and Bridget wondered whether she, too, pined for Ireland...or did her daring thoughts possibly stray down a different path? Was the dreamy tilt of her head an indication that she was imagining the life that she, Charlie and Tess might soon lead in Chicago? A notion struck Bridget – if they indeed found Bronagh in New York, could that sway Orlaith from her desire to travel west? Perhaps the outcome of this venture would be the whole McGovern family remaining in Boston, more tight-knit than ever before. Buoyed by this marvellous image, she settled back in her seat, full of hope.

Unfortunately, her optimism took a severe blow as the day wore on and she had occasion to observe Mr Henson's behaviour when they halted at inns along the route to change the horses. While the passengers took these opportunities to stretch their legs and snatch a bite to eat, the coach driver spent the entirety of each stopover at a table inside the inn, drinking pint after pint of ale. This didn't appear to have a significant impact on his cognition or coordination, given that every time he climbed back up into the driver's box for the next stage of their journey and took the reins with a steady hand, seemingly unimpaired. But it was disconcerting all the same and Bridget found her cheerfulness gradually displaced by unease.

The first two days passed largely without mishap but the third day brought justification for her misgivings. Looking forward to reaching their destination that evening, the travellers rose from their beds in The Brigadier Inn, which boasted marginally cleaner accommodations than the inn they had stayed at the previous night, to realise that Mr Henson was nowhere to be found. Bridget and Orlaith gaped at the stagecoach in the inn's courtyard, where it stood without horses or driver, and exchanged mystified glances with the other milling passengers, while Jack and Gus weaved among the assortment of legs and skirts as they chased each other. An ostler crossed the yard leading a horse but he guided it past their coach and harnessed it to another waiting conveyance.

'Where on earth could Mr Henson be?' Bridget said, baffled.

Although some of their fellow travellers had come and gone over the past couple of days, embarking and disembarking at various stops along the route, the woman with the hatbox still remained part of the company and she now let out an indignant snort.

'Good Lord, there he is, the lout.'

Bridget swivelled in the direction the woman pointed and recoiled. Mr Henson had just stumbled into view around the corner of The Brigadier, scratching absent-mindedly at his stubbly cheek. To her dismay, the day-old beard was the least slovenly aspect of him. His hair stuck out at all angles, matted with dirt and straw. One sleeve of his stained shirt was rolled up to the elbow and the cuff of the other dangled at his wrist, while much of the shirt itself spilled out of his breeches. An indecent proportion of his unsightly paunch was visible due to the way a strip of the hem had rucked up at the waist, exposing a hairy mass of flesh. He looked like he had spent the night in the stables and, when he drew nearer, smelled like it too.

'Everyone ready to go?' he said to nobody in particular, his words so slurred that Bridget could hardly make them out.

'He's polluted with drink!' she exclaimed, appalled. He must have been imbibing something far stronger than ale and in vast quantities throughout the night to be still so inebriated this morning.

133

Orlaith's jaw dropped in incredulity as Mr Henson staggered sideways despite there being no obstacle of any kind near his feet. He barely managed to catch his balance but grinned proudly as though he had accomplished a remarkable feat of acrobatics.

'He's in no fit state to drive,' she said, disgusted.

'Indeed, he is not,' Bridget said flatly. 'And I have no intention of letting my children board that coach with an intoxicated man at the reins.'

'You'll be waiting a while so,' said the ostler as he strode back across the courtyard behind them. 'I've seen him like this before. He won't be lucid for hours yet.'

'But then how are we to get to New York today?' demanded the woman with the hatbox.

'You won't,' said the ostler in a matter-of-fact tone. Mr Henson obligingly supported this assertion by attempting to climb into the driver's box of the other coach in the yard, slipping off it and falling heavily on his backside. 'By the time he's sobered up, it'll be too late to get on the road.'

The woman gave a squawk of outrage. 'I'm supposed to reach my sister's house by tonight! Tomorrow is the Fourth of July—I have to be there for the celebrations!'

The ostler raised his palms as if to say 'That's your trouble, not mine' and disappeared around the corner of the inn.

'So we're expected to just tarry here for the day?' said the woman, staring in disbelief at Mr Henson, who had dragged himself into a sitting position against one of the other coach's wheels and, by his beatific expression, appeared to think he was resting on a bed of clouds. Jack and Gus paused in their chasing to gawk at him.

Bridget and Orlaith shared a grimace of frustration. Now that they were this close, even a day's delay seemed to put the success of their mission in jeopardy. But they were completely at the

134

mercy of a man who had neither regard for his personal dignity nor consideration for the service he was meant to be providing. Resigned, they towed Jack and Gus away from the disgraceful sight and spent much of their wasted morning and afternoon verbally composing angry letters of complaint to the company who operated the stagecoach route and allowed a reprobate such as Mr Henson to remain in its employ.

Just as the ostler had predicted, by the time the driver was lucid enough to take command of his coach again, it was far too late to set off. The travellers had gathered in The Brigadier's dining room that evening and were vilifying Mr Henson with one voice when he came through the door massaging his temple. The woman with the hatbox – whose name, Bridget had learned during the course of their denunciating, was Mrs Bergamot – laid into him at once, castigating him for his thoughtless conduct and blaming him for making her miss an important patriotic occasion with her family.

'Hold your tongue,' he barked at her. 'I'll get you there as fast as I can tomorrow. We'll leave at first light.'

Bridget wondered whether another night of drinking might controvert that promise but, no, they found Mr Henson sitting in his driver's box at dawn the next morning as sober as a judge and bellowing at them all to hurry up and get in. The ostler helped the passengers stow their baggage on the roof of the coach (apart from Mrs Bergamot's hatbox which she kept a firm grip on) and everyone piled inside, eager to finally depart The Brigadier Inn. However, minutes later Bridget sorely regretted putting her trust in Mr Henson when he took off at an alarming pace, whipping the horses so hard that they thundered out of the inn's courtyard as if a pack of hellhounds were snapping at their hooves.

'Hang on tight,' she said frantically to Jack and Gus and they grabbed the nearest strap, as did every other passenger who clung on for dear life as the coach careered down the road. With an ominous sinking sensation that seeped down into her bones, she had the sudden, definite sense that their whole journey was doomed to fail and that Mr Henson's dreadful behaviour was a portent of worse things to come.

'Please keep us safe,' she breathed and hoped God was listening.

They had already stopped once to change the horses when the inevitable happened. The coach was hurtling along at a renewed speed thanks to the fresh team up front when there came an almighty sound of cracking wood and it lurched to the side. Bridget lunged for Jack and Gus as the coach began to topple, clutching them to her breast amid a volley of shouts and screams and desperately hoping to shield them with her own body. She saw Orlaith grapple for an arm strap and miss it, while Mrs Bergamot's hatbox sailed across the space and collided with the far wall, smashing open and ejecting its precious cargo onto the floor. Its owner shrieked and scrambled after it even as the coach teetered further.

Then, impossibly, it righted itself, tilting back the other way and settling onto the road with a jarring thud. The passengers gaped around at each other, astonished to still be alive. Bridget ran her fingers over her sons' skulls and shoulders and arms, searching for blood or breakages and, thankfully, finding none. Her relief was quickly eclipsed by a blinding rage. She thrust the two boys towards Orlaith who was rubbing a red spot on her forehead – had she banged it? – and clambered over the seats to the door where an ashen-faced man was about to heave his shoulder against it.

'Let me pass,' she demanded. 'I want to give that animal a piece of my mind.'

'You and me both, missus,' the man said grimly.

He shoved the door open and leapt out to the ground. Bridget followed, almost tripping off the narrow step in her haste to get down. Once she was outside the coach, she had a clear view of what had occurred. The coach's front right wheel had splintered – fragments of it were scattered around the road while a few spokes dangled from the remains that still hung forlornly on the axle. A long, deep rut in the ground showed where the wheel had snagged and broken. Mr Henson had descended from the driver's box and was surveying the damage, hands on his hips and his face purple with apoplexy. Bridget huffed and stalked over to him, just as he kicked at a severed spoke and sent it flying across the road. She dodged out of the way as it shot past her and glared at the driver, her fists clenched and her blood boiling.

'Are you trying to murder us?' she shrieked at him. 'Two of my children are on this coach! If there had been so much as a scratch on either of them, I would tear your eyes out!'

Mr Henson's features darkened further to a deep violet. 'Calm down, woman. It's only a broken wheel. It happens all the time.'

'It shouldn't have happened at all,' she countered. 'If you weren't driving like a madman, you would have had enough time to see that rut and avoid it.'

Mr Henson tossed his head and grumbled something about 'female hysterics'.

'She's right, Mr Henson,' retorted the man who had opened the stagecoach door. Still very pale, he strode up beside Bridget and pointed an admonishing finger at the driver. 'You were driving recklessly. This accident is your fault.'

The other passengers were now surging out of the coach and gathering around, their expressions ranging from shock to resentment to fury. Mrs Bergamot was clutching her ill-fated hat, its contorted shape suggesting that it had been trampled in the mayhem. Her eyes glittered with condemnation. Mr Henson folded his arms defensively.

'I was just trying to get you there quickly like you wanted,' he muttered. 'We were making up for time lost yesterday.'

'Which *you* lost to begin with,' snapped Bridget. 'If you hadn't drowned yourself in drink the night before, we would not have been in such an excessive hurry today.'

Everyone made incensed exclamations of agreement and Mr Henson pinched his lips together sourly. Bridget spotted Orlaith emerging from the coach with Jack and Gus and, passing the role of accuser on to her fellow travellers, she scurried over to the three of them. A lump on Orlaith's forehead showed that she had indeed taken a knock but she seemed otherwise unharmed. Jack and Gus were practically jumping out of their skins with excitement.

'Ma, wasn't that just thrilling!' Gus gushed.

'On the contrary, it was very dangerous,' she said, performing another visual inspection on both boys. There wasn't a bruise or cut in sight. She turned her attention to Orlaith. 'Does your head hurt badly?'

Orlaith shook it experimentally. 'No, it's just a bump. I'll be grand. What did Mr Henson say?'

'That it's our fault for putting him under pressure to go so fast.' Bridget clicked her tongue. 'What a scoundrel he is.'

Twisting her mouth in contempt, Orlaith said, 'What happens now?'

'We certainly won't be getting back into the coach anyway, not with that blackguard at the reins.'

Regrettably, Bridget was obliged to eat her words. After Mr Henson had extricated himself from his small mob of dissatisfied customers, he set about retrieving a spare wheel and a box of tools from the rear of the coach, while at the same time informing the passengers that they were stuck with him until New York.

'You're stranded between stage stops with no means of getting to the next one,' he pointed out with a degree of relish.

'We'll wait for another stagecoach to pass by,' the pale man said obstinately.

'Suit yourselves,' said Mr Henson. 'But there's no telling how long you'll have to wait and no guarantee there'll be any space on it when it does come, definitely not for you all.' He heaved the wheel over his shoulder and added, 'So if you decide not to travel with me, you can either enjoy sleeping rough out here for a couple of nights or else attempt a very long walk to the nearest town. I wouldn't recommend either, especially not with youngsters in tow.'

He chuckled as he made his way to the front of the coach and Bridget fumed at his retreating back.

There followed much discussion among the passengers, which included a drastic proposal to wrest control of the coach from Mr Henson, but they ultimately rejected this in light of the fact that driving a team of horses required enormous skill that was beyond them all, even an accomplished horsewoman like Bridget. With a great deal of reluctance, they came to the galling conclusion that they would be compelled to rely upon Mr Henson to convey them to their destination. Together, Bridget and Mrs Bergamot, who was still cradling her crushed hat like a deceased pet, approached Mr Henson as he finished attaching the spare wheel to the coach. Kneeling on the ground, he glowered up at them as though anticipating another tongue lashing which, of course, he richly deserved. However, Bridget chose the path of civility – antagonising him further was not wise when they were dependent upon him to remove them from this predicament.

'The wheel is fixed, sir?' she enquired with admirable composure.

'It is,' he said shortly and got up from his knees, wiping his hands on the front of his breeches.

'Very good,' she said. 'Are you ready to depart then?'

'Suppose so. Are you lot coming with me?'

Mrs Bergamot bit out, 'We are. We've got no other choice.'

Mr Henson did not even try to hide his smugness. Bridget folded her arms.

'Having said that, we insist that you slow your pace,' she said tersely. 'No more careless driving or we shall have you arrested upon our arrival in New York.'

He shrugged. 'Fine by me. But it'll take longer to reach the city. Could be nightfall by the time we get there. You'll miss most of your Fourth of July celebrations,' he added, jutting his chin at Mrs Bergamot.

She looked pained but said, 'If it is a choice between the celebrations or survival, I choose survival.'

He snorted, plainly of the opinion that they were exaggerating the situation far beyond what it warranted. 'As you wish,' he said obsequiously and, picking up his box of tools, swaggered away from them, leaving the pieces of the broken wheel discarded at the side of the road.

A brief while later, Bridget ushered Jack and Gus back onto the coach with more than a little trepidation. As the travellers settled themselves, she ordered the boys to grasp the arm strap with both hands but, to her pleasant surprise, Mr Henson proved true to his word. The coach eased into motion and trundled off down the road at a pace barely faster than a walk. She let out a breath of relief.

However, as the rest of the day elapsed, her relief once again vanished, this time replaced by annoyance. Mr Henson seemed determined to provoke his passengers by any measure within his power for now he drove excruciatingly slow, far slower than necessary, until every form of transport was passing them out, even a wagon drawn by a mule that looked as ancient as the earth itself. Bridget ground her teeth but didn't complain – she would endure this temporary irritation if it meant that they would all arrive in possession of their lives and limbs.

The sky darkened beyond the stagecoach windows and Mr Henson stopped to hang a lantern above his driver's box which only lit a limited stretch of the road ahead. Bridget's worries surfaced again – now that visibility was so poor, were they at risk of another accident? Once more, she experienced the dreadful foreboding that this journey was destined to come to grief.

Miraculously, the coach did not break a second wheel nor veer into the ditch in the dark. It lumbered into the outskirts of New York City as night fell fully and a series of Independence Day illuminations flared in the distant sky. Jack and Gus pressed their faces to the stagecoach window, angling their heads to catch a better glimpse, but Bridget was too weary to look. She had been wound up so tight with anxiety for most of the day that it felt like a sheet of iron had been soldered to her back between her shoulder blades and she could not relax her muscles. She pressed her palm to her nape and tried to stretch her neck. Orlaith eyed her from the opposite bench.

'How're you doing?' she asked.

'I'll be better once we get off this godforsaken contraption,' Bridget replied tensely.

At long last, the coach rolled to a halt and Mr Henson hollered, 'New York City, final stop!'

The passengers emitted a collective sigh of thankfulness. Bridget didn't want Jack or Gus to get crushed in the commotion of disembarking, so they held back with Orlaith until everyone else had exited and eventually alighted last from the coach. Mr Henson was up on the roof, throwing the travellers' baggage haphazardly to the ground. The others had already seized their belongings and were dispersing into the night, hurrying away to whichever destinations they were a day late in reaching. Mrs Bergamot had placed her ruined hat upon her head, despite its sorry state, and walked off with as much dignity as she could muster.

Bridget scanned the street. A putrid smell drifted faintly on the air and there was no inn, only a series of dark, shuttered buildings on both sides. Was this even an official stop for the stagecoach or had Mr Henson simply discarded them as soon as it was expedient to do so?

As Orlaith gathered up Bridget's canvas bag and her own sack, Bridget marched to the front of the coach where Mr Henson was descending from the roof back to his driver's box.

'Excuse me, sir!' she said brusquely and he winced, clutching his temple like she had driven a blade into his skull.

'What do you want now?' he growled at her.

'Which street is this? And can you tell us where we are in relation to the Bowery district?'

He waved her away as if she were a troublesome gnat. 'My job was to get you to New York. Where you go next is none of my business.'

She refused to budge. 'But you must be familiar with the city if it's a regular stop on your route. We're looking for Gallagher's Boarding House. Do you know where it is?'

'Never heard of it,' he said, although she had the sneaking suspicion that he wouldn't tell her even if he did know. 'Off with you now. I need to tend to the horses.'

He needed his next drink, more like. Seething, she whirled on her heel, muttering, 'Unchivalrous cad,' along with several other choice descriptions that suited him very well. She stamped back over to Orlaith, Jack and Gus. The boys had expended the enthusiasm that had sustained them throughout the day

142

and were now sagging with exhaustion. The sooner they located Gallagher's Boarding House, the better.

'Come on,' she said. 'We'll manage without his help, seeing as he's not gracious enough to give it.'

She accepted her canvas bag from Orlaith and took hold of Gus's pudgy wrist, while Orlaith slung her sack over her shoulder and grasped Jack's hand. Bridget led the way to the end of the street and, acting on instinct, turned left onto the next one.

'Keep an eye out for any street signs,' she said. 'Or, better yet, we'll ask for directions from the next person we meet.'

Oddly though, the street was empty of any other people and lit poorly by a sparse scattering of lamps. She quickened their pace, keeping alert for voices or traffic indicating busier streets nearby. The night seemed to swallow all sound – the clearest thing she could hear was the distant bang of an illumination. That gave her hope; illuminations meant spectators so they couldn't be too far away from the celebrating crowds. Endeavouring to judge the direction of the bang, she guided them onto another street perpendicular to the one they were on.

Halfway up it, her skin prickled. There was nothing to distinguish it from the last one – it appeared equally deserted and gloomy and stank of rubbish. Nonetheless, a ripple of fear slithered down her spine. She sensed that they were not alone.

'I think we should go back—' she started to say.

Too late. Shadows detached themselves from the darkness a few yards ahead and three or four figures advanced towards them. Her breath snagged in her throat. She could only make out their hunching silhouettes but she knew beyond a doubt that they meant to do them harm.

'Run!' she croaked.

She hauled Gus around and saw Orlaith do the same with Jack and then all four of them were dashing back up the street the way they had come. Heavy footsteps thudded in their wake and Bridget's heart pounded just as loudly. Where could they run to? The buildings on these streets were all shuttered and, aside from the disbanded group of passengers who had all since disappeared, the only other person they'd seen in the vicinity had been Mr Henson. Would he still be there with his coach? Would he have the decency to help two women and two children in desperate need?

Those questions would remain unanswered for they never even made it to the end of the street. A hand snatched at her from behind, wrenching on a hank of her hair dangling below her bonnet. She cried out as several strands ripped from her scalp. The same hand tried to break her grip on Gus but she hung onto him as hard as she could, even though he yelped at the bruising force she exerted on his wrist.

'Let go of him,' said a male voice as rough as the hand. Was it an Irish accent?

No time to think about that. 'Over my dead body,' she snarled.

The man laughed harshly. 'That can be arranged.'

A fist came out of nowhere and struck her jaw. She had never been hit with such force in her life. Her nerves went numb and everything began to slip away from her: her sight, her balance, her bag, her child's wrist—

No. She fought to stay conscious and upright and tightened her grip once more on Gus.

'Ma!' he whimpered and the fright in his voice cut her to the bone.

'I've got you,' she rasped.

Only she didn't.

The fist struck her again and all of a sudden she was flat on her back and her hands were empty. Her little boy's screeching filled her ears and she struggled to rise, but her body wouldn't cooperate. She might as well have been severed from the neck down for all the response she got from her arms and legs. Her vision was blurry but her hearing compensated for the loss of her other senses and every horrifying sound became heightened.

'You bastards!' she heard Orlaith scream. 'Get away from us!'

There was the resounding smack of skin slapping flesh.

'Bitch!'

A thump like a sack of potatoes being thrown on the floor.

The wet noise of spitting. 'No, don't you dare touch him!'

A high-pitched gasp of pain. That was Jack, her precious lamb.

Please, she begged her limbs. Please move.

Her feet twitched and she raised her head an inch.

Calloused fingers pawed at her left hand.

Then another blow, this one to her temple.

No more sound. No more sensation.

Nothing.

CHAPTER 15

First came the pain. A throb in her jaw, a spike in her temple. Something hard was digging into her back.

Then came the confusion. Her eyelids cracked open and she saw a black, starless sky nestled between looming roofs. Disorientated, she realised that she was lying on the ground. Had she fallen?

Then came the memory of what had happened. With a strangled cry, she shot up, ignoring the pinch of stones as she braced herself on her hands and knees. She could perceive nothing but shadows in the dark street.

'Gus!' she cried. 'Jack! Orlaith!'

A muffled groan answered her. Frantic, she crawled in the direction of it and found Orlaith prostrate on the ground nearby, her bonnet missing and her hair a bedraggled mess. Bridget grasped her shoulder and rolled her over, squinting through the gloom at Orlaith's face. Her eyes were closed and a trickle of blood trailed from the corner of her mouth.

'Oh, God!' Bridget exclaimed, shaking her. 'Orlaith! Speak to me!'

Orlaith's eyelashes fluttered. 'Bridget?' she mumbled. 'What happened?' In the next instant, her eyes widened. 'God Almighty, I remember. Those damn thugs! Did they hurt you?'

Bridget didn't care about that right now. 'Help me find the boys,' she said urgently. 'It's dark and I can't see where they are.'

She stood, ignoring the dizziness that washed over her. Orlaith struggled to her feet too, wiping her mouth with the back of her hand, while Bridget turned in a circle, peering about her.

'Jack!' she called. 'Gus!'

'Maybe they're hiding,' said Orlaith. 'In case the rats come back. Yous can come out now, lads!' she added in a raised voice. 'The men are gone.'

There was no response from the ostensibly deserted street. Bridget realised that she couldn't hear the bang of the illuminations anymore. How long had they been unconscious?

She gulped down her mounting panic. 'They could have been knocked out like us,' she said, wanting to wring the necks of the beasts who had done this. 'Let's search around for them.'

They were in a pool of darkness right here, the nearest lit lamp at least half a dozen yards further up the street beyond the point where the men had materialised. Gritting her teeth, she took slow, methodical steps in one direction and then another, praying that her foot would nudge a knee or an elbow and simultaneously dreading that she might discover an inert body.

Orlaith's voice erupted from the other side of the street. 'I found—!' She cut herself off almost immediately. 'Never mind,' she moaned. 'It's just my bonnet.'

By the time Bridget's steps took her within the ring of the lamplight, she could scarcely breathe – a vice of terror had encircled her, squeezing all the air out of her lungs. There wasn't a trace of her boys to be found. Where on earth were they?

Orlaith scurried up behind her. 'Anything?' she asked hopefully.

'N-nothing,' Bridget managed to force out. Her teeth had started to chatter, the snapping sound amplified in the silent

147

street. Distraught, she spun around to Orlaith. 'There's no s-sign of them at all!'

In the glow of the lamplight, Orlaith could not conceal the alarm that filled her features. She valiantly tried to cover it up by saying in a bracing tone, 'They have to be here somewhere. Let's look again.'

Together, they combed the street from one end to the other, calling out Jack and Gus's names over and over. They stumbled upon several piles of refuse heaped against the walls of the buildings and disturbed a large rat which scampered away from them, its long tail whipping out of sight as it ran under the gap at the bottom of a boarded-up door, but found not a shred of evidence of either boy. Bridget quietly began to sob but she kept staggering on until they reached the top of the street for a second time, at which point her legs gave out and she collapsed to the ground.

'They're gone!' she wailed. 'Dear God above, my boys are gone!'

Orlaith dropped to her knees beside her and wrapped her arms around her, wordless. What could she say after all? There was nothing in heaven or on earth that could console Bridget as the awful reality crashed over her. Jack and Gus were lost, snatched away from her by strangers in an unfamiliar city.

'Why would those men take them?' she sobbed. 'What could they possibly want with two little boys?'

'Maybe they didn't take them,' said Orlaith, rubbing Bridget's back. 'Maybe the boys ran away when we were attacked and then couldn't find their way back to this street. They might be wandering around somewhere close by.'

Optimism soared in Bridget before evaporating. 'Surely they would have heard us shouting,' she said bleakly.

'Not if they went very far,' said Orlaith, her conviction strengthening as she warmed to her theory. 'They could've easily gone astray in this maze of streets.' She pulled back and squeezed both of Bridget's hands with her own. 'Have faith. We'll find them.'

Bridget swallowed her next sob and latched onto Orlaith's sliver of hope, even though her intuition whispered that they were clutching desperately at straws. 'You're right,' she said, sniffing. 'We need to search further. And perhaps we'll have the good fortune to meet someone who came across them.'

Even as she said that, she wondered why they had not encountered any other people up to this point. It might be night-time but this was a city, for God's sake – how could a street remain empty for so long?

Orlaith rose and encouraged Bridget to stand as well. As she clasped Orlaith's left hand with her right one and climbed to her feet, Bridget had recovered her senses enough to notice that something else was missing.

'Orlaith!' she gasped. 'Your wedding ring!'

Her fingers flew to her own left hand. The rough circle of thread was still there but her beautiful gold ring was gone. She let out an incoherent cry of anguish. Cormac had given it to her in Cove after they had suffered Agnes McLoughlin's censure for sharing a bed in her boarding house while unmarried. How Bridget had admired the striking metalwork depicting a love heart topped with a crown and cradled by a pair of hands. She had worn it continuously for eight years and now, in its absence, she felt as if those vile creatures had ripped away yet another piece of her body.

'*Go ndéana an diabhal dréimire dá gcnámh droma ag piocadh úlla i ngairdín ifrinn*,' she spat in the Irish tongue, because no curses in the English language seemed strong enough to express her hatred of them. It was a phrase Cormac had once taught her in jest: *may the devil make a ladder of their backbones picking apples in the garden of hell*. That was what she wished for them and, by God, she meant it.

Orlaith, too, was clutching her bare left hand, tears escaping from her eyes. 'Oh, Charlie,' she lamented. 'I'm so sorry.'

As the shocking theft of their rings sank in, it occurred to Bridget that they had not happened upon her canvas bag or Orlaith's sack when they had scoured the street for any sign of the boys. Swiftly, she delved into her pocket for the money pouch containing the remainder of her portion of the Brubaker savings but found nothing other than Mrs Temple's letter. The men had stolen everything of value bar the clothes they wore. What a barbaric state of affairs. While she supposed she ought to be grateful that they had not defiled her and Orlaith on top of their other crimes, she knew she would have borne that horror in exchange for having Jack and Gus by her side right now.

She could have let her distress overcome her again but instead she felt defiance fire through her veins. Silently sentencing the criminals to even more torment in hell, she said earnestly to Orlaith, 'The boys are our most imperative concern. We must keep searching.'

With renewed determination, they left that street and ventured into the surrounding neighbourhood, careful not to lose their bearings as they called out to Jack and Gus at regular intervals and hunted for them in shadowed doorsteps or behind abandoned crates or other detritus. Hope leapt inside Bridget every time she discerned a movement in the murk but it was only ever a rodent or a cat, never her beloved boys. In desperation, they even went back to the first street where they had disembarked in an attempt to seek aid from Mr Henson. Unsurprisingly though, he and his coach had disappeared. Have faith, she reminded herself, chanting Orlaith's advice in her head repeatedly until the two syllables became gibberish.

'Once the sun rises, we should go back to the street where it happened,' she said out loud, unable to control the wavering pitch of her voice. 'We might detect some clue that we missed in the darkness.'

Before Orlaith could respond, a faint racket drifted to them on the night air: clopping hooves and creaking wheels. Orlaith's expression lit up and together they took off, dashing towards the noise. They rounded the corner onto the adjoining street and stopped dead when the stench nearly knocked them over.

'Good gracious, what is that?' said Bridget, gagging.

Orlaith pressed her sleeve to her nose, looking around for the source of the revolting smell. 'Night soil cart,' she choked out.

It came trundling through the gloom, its bed piled so high with excrement that some of it dripped onto the ground in its wake. A man sat up front clutching the reins and wearing a cloth tied across the lower half of his face. In the midst of her nausea, Bridget felt a surge of relief at seeing another human being at last. She ran towards the cart, waving her arms.

'Please stop, sir!'

With a startled expletive, the man jerked the horse and cart to a halt. 'What do you want?' he barked. 'If you're gonna cause mischief, you'd better know I'm armed.'

She faltered. 'We mean you no harm, sir, I swear. We are just desperate for help.'

He peered down at her and Orlaith suspiciously. 'What sort of help?'

'We're trying to find my two sons who went missing tonight in this area.' The situation was so horribly familiar that her mind flashed back eight years ago to Cormac's agonising search for his family at Oakleigh and in Dublin. Were the McGoverns destined to always be cruelly pulled asunder? 'They're aged seven and five and the older is fair while the younger has curls the same colour as mine. Please, have you seen them anywhere in this locality?'

The man shook his head, not in answer but in disbelief. 'What possessed you to go wandering around here at night? And with children besides? Do you wanna bring trouble on yourselves?'

'Of course not! Our stagecoach was delayed by a broken wheel so we didn't reach the city until after nightfall, at which point we were set upon by thugs. They robbed everything we had a-and possibly kidnapped my children too. If they didn't, then it's likely that the boys ran away and hid someplace in fright. I just want to know if you've seen them? I'm begging you, please tell me if you have.'

The man's eyes had narrowed above the cloth around his face and now he glanced uneasily over his shoulder. 'Thugs?' he said. 'They still about?'

'We're not sure,' said Orlaith, lowering her sleeve from her nose to speak. 'We were knocked unconscious and don't know how much time passed before we woke up.'

The man tightened his grasp on the reins. 'I'm gonna get out of here now. You should both do the same, if you know what's good for you.' He flicked the reins and the horse started to move off.

'Wait!' Bridget exclaimed. 'Have you seen my children?'

'No,' he called without looking back. 'And if they were snatched by who I think, you'll never see them again either.'

She felt like he had punched her brutally in the gut. Tears of despair stung her eyelids. Gathering up her skirts, she darted after him, sidestepping the filth that fell from the cart.

'Don't leave, sir!' she blurted, almost screaming at him in her fear. 'Those men—who are they?'

He stared straight ahead as if he hadn't heard her. The horse was nearing the end of the street and picking up pace; she would not be able to keep up much longer.

'I implore you!' she cried. 'We are utterly lost. At least tell us the name of this neighbourhood!'

He still didn't glance down at her scuttling by the side of the cart, but he replied, 'Five Points. You don't wanna stay here a second longer than you have to.'

Wishing he would offer to carry them away from the place, she entreated, 'Then how do we get to the Bowery district?'

The cart began to turn the corner and she was obliged to stop running after it. As she gasped for breath, he cast a fleeting look back at her.

'Head east,' he called and, pointing, added, 'That way.'

With that, man, horse, cart and excrement vanished from view, although the reek remained. Bridget cared not one iota about the foul odour. She covered her face with her hands and broke down, bawling into her cold palms. Orlaith caught up to her and stroked her arm but Bridget hardly registered her touch. The man had confirmed her very worst nightmare and her heart was shattering into a thousand pieces.

'Bridget,' Orlaith said after some time, her throat sounding strangled with emotion. 'Dawn's coming. Will we go back?'

Bridget let her hands fall. The sky above the city roofs had brightened a little and she could distinguish Orlaith's features more clearly now. Her cheeks were wet and her tears had mixed with the residue of blood at her mouth, leaving a red streak down the side of her chin. Still crying herself, Bridget reached out and dabbed the smear away with her thumb.

'Do you remember how that happened?' she asked thickly, showing Orlaith the smear.

Orlaith grimaced. 'One of the fellas hit me. I think I bit my tongue when I landed on the ground.' She poked the inside of her cheek experimentally with her tongue. 'It doesn't hurt too bad.'

'That's good,' Bridget said in barely more than a whisper.

Orlaith pointed at Bridget's face, her expression sympathetic. 'You've got an awful bruise on your jaw. And the side of your head is swollen as well.'

'Oh,' she said, too numb to dredge up a more substantial response.

Mutely, they retraced their steps to the site of the attack. In the grey light, they could make out scuff marks on the dirty ground. Was that where Orlaith had fallen? Was this where Bridget had crawled to her? Could those grooves be a sign of someone digging in their heels trying to resist being dragged away? It was impossible to know for sure.

The only certainty was that Jack and Gus were not there. They had fled or been carried off into the recesses of this treacherous city and Bridget had no means by which to find them.

How in the world could she tell Cormac that she had lost his sons?

Her knees trembled and she thought she might crumple again. Orlaith, bless her, kept her upright with a solid grip on both of her elbows.

'We need to think straight,' she said robustly, even though her round eyes still glistened with sorrow. 'It's a hideous situation but we can't give up. We have to seek help.'

'From whom?' said Bridget, doing her best not to sound despairing. 'We don't know a single person in New York.'

'That's not true,' said Orlaith. 'We were on our way to visit Mrs Temple before all this happened, weren't we? Maybe we're not on personal terms with her but there's still a connection on account of Bronagh. Let's go to her as we'd planned. She's already proven to be a charitable soul just by writing to Boston in the first place—if she wasn't the type of person who's willing to help others in need, she wouldn't have bothered getting in touch with Cormac at all. Am I right?'

'Yes,' said Bridget in a tiny voice.

'At the very least, she should be able to tell us where we can find a constable who'll have the resources to expand our search. The authorities will know where the New York crooks hide out, wouldn't that be fair to assume?'

Bridget swallowed, a minuscule flame of hope flickering to life in her belly. 'Yes,' she said, stronger this time.

'Then let's find her,' Orlaith said and added softly, 'And may God watch over the boys until we find them too.'

With a final, anguished glance behind her, Bridget followed Orlaith away from the loathsome street. She knew it would occupy her nightmares for the rest of her life, whether or not she ultimately reunited with Jack and Gus. Please, please, *please*, God, guide us to them.

They headed east like the night soil man had advised and as the sun began to emerge, so too did the local inhabitants. Bridget deduced that Five Points must be a dangerous area indeed if its denizens kept out of sight during the night-time hours. Of all the places Mr Henson could have deposited his passengers, why had he picked there? His negligence had brought about the most unfathomable trauma.

She eyed the people but didn't approach any of them to ask about her missing children – they would not have seen anything while holed up in their houses behind their shuttered windows. Orlaith, however, went up to a pair of women to solicit clearer directions to the Bowery district. They were belligerent to such a degree that Bridget suspected they would have tried to rob them if it was not patently obvious that two battered women with no baggage had nothing left to steal. Still, they eventually divulged the details of how to get to the Bowery and, in a stroke of luck, could even describe where Gallagher's Boarding House was located.

Mercifully, their directions proved sound and at length Bridget and Orlaith found themselves standing at the foot of a flight of steps leading up to a narrow building which had polished windows framed by pretty shutters and a red front door with a gleaming knocker. Bolstered by the wholesome impression it gave, they dragged their exhausted legs up the steps.

Bridget pushed open the red door and they entered. The lobby was bright and welcoming with a vase of roses perched on a counter. Behind the counter stood a woman of middling years who gave them a friendly smile as they limped across the room towards her.

'You're up and about early,' she said. 'I've only just unlocked the door.' Her smile faltered when she took in their dishevelled appearance. 'Oh, you poor dears, what happened to you?'

Bridget made a heroic effort not to weep at the woman's kindly tone. 'Are you Mrs Temple?' she asked.

The woman's smile vanished. 'No,' she said tightly. 'You have the wrong establishment.'

Perplexed, Bridget said, 'This is Gallagher's Boarding House, is it not?'

'It is. I am Mrs Gallagher.'

'I do beg your pardon. Could you direct us to Mrs Temple?'

'There is no Mrs Temple under this roof.' Mrs Gallagher folded her arms. 'Please leave.'

Bridget looked at Orlaith, completely thrown by this unexpected development. Orlaith murmured, 'Show her the letter.'

Bridget fished Mrs Temple's letter out of her pocket with a shaking hand and laid it on the counter. When Mrs Gallagher made no move to touch it, she explained, 'We received this a week ago from a Mrs Temple with news of a missing relative of ours. She instructed us to visit her at this address.'

Mrs Gallagher's mouth compressed, her initially warm demeanour now as chilly as a Boston winter. 'She told me to expect someone to call for her here,' she muttered. 'Only she believed it would be a man.'

Bridget nodded, her spirits lifting a fraction. 'Yes, she wrote to my husband but he was unable to come so my sister-in-law and I responded to her invitation instead. Where might—'

'I want to make something abundantly clear,' Mrs Gallagher interjected. 'I have no connection with that woman and no desire to accommodate anyone who does. I must ask you once again to leave.'

Bridget stared at her, her spirits plummeting back to their previous depths. 'How have we offended you, pray tell?'

Mrs Gallagher's lip curled. 'Your acquaintance with that woman is offence enough. For a third time, I insist that you—'

'Where can we find her?' It was Orlaith's turn to interrupt, her grey eyes as hard as flint. 'The sooner you tell us, the sooner we can stop soiling your establishment with our presence.'

Mrs Gallagher seemed to recognise the wisdom in this for she said swiftly, 'Orange Street. That is where her premises is.'

'And where's Orange Street?' asked Orlaith. 'We've never been to New York before.'

To Bridget's dismay, Mrs Gallagher replied, 'The Five Points district.'

'Five Points?' Bridget uttered, aghast. 'But we've just come from there. It's a wicked place.'

'Quite,' said Mrs Gallagher.

Horror crept up Bridget's spine. Mrs Temple resided in Five Points? How could that be? Whether through grief or fatigue, she no longer understood what was going on. All she could grasp was that she and Orlaith were not welcome at Gallagher's Boarding House and that the woman in whom they'd put their trust apparently dwelled in the very neighbourhood where they had been assaulted. It was too much. She began to cry again. As she did so, her gaze fell upon the vase of roses. It seemed incongruous to her that such beauty could exist when such evil had transpired and it made her weep all the harder.

Orlaith draped a supportive arm around her shoulder. 'Tell us the way to Orange Street,' she said, 'and we'll be gone.'

Mrs Gallagher, who looked highly uncomfortable at Bridget's emotional state, hurriedly imparted succinct directions to get from the Bowery to the intersection in the Five Points district where five different streets met, one of which was Orange Street. Bridget hoped that Orlaith was absorbing the information for not a word of it had sunk into her own addled brain.

'Thanks,' Orlaith said curtly when Mrs Gallagher had finished speaking. 'And goodbye.'

She snatched the letter off the counter and guided Bridget back to the front door. Just as they were about to cross the threshold, Mrs Gallagher called after them in a disapproving voice, 'By the by, Hester Temple is a Madam, not a Mrs.'

With that dreadful parting comment ringing in their ears, they emerged onto the sunny top step and Orlaith shut the red door behind them. Bridget endeavoured to staunch the flow of her tears.

'What will we do?' she croaked.

'The only thing we can do,' said Orlaith.

Full of foreboding, they descended the flight of steps and went back the way they had come, their feet as heavy as their hearts. When they reached Five Points again, Orlaith led the way and found the place where the five streets converged as Mrs Gallagher had described. It was quite possible that they had strayed through this particular area the previous night but, if they had, it had been too dark then to perceive its distinctive layout. The five streets extended out from the intersection and were now full of people making a din as they bustled to and fro. Bridget and Orlaith located the junction between Cross Street and Orange Street and proceeded along the latter, their gazes raking the facades of the buildings while they kept a wary eye on the locals hurrying by. Even in the midst of their exhaustion, neither of them would let their guard down again, not here.

Mrs Gallagher had told them to search for an establishment with a pink lantern. Several of the buildings on Orange Street had lanterns hanging above their doors and some of these had red ribbons tied around them, rippling in a gentle July breeze. More than halfway along the street, they came to a door whose lantern bore pink ribbons – or rather, they looked like they might have once been red but had faded, whether through repeated washing or sun exposure. As they were paler than all the other ribbons on the street, Bridget and Orlaith had to assume that this was their destination. Lamentably, both the ribbons and Mrs Temple's true title left them in no uncertainty as to what lay beyond the door.

They exchanged a miserable glance. Orlaith sighed.

'We've come this far,' she said. 'And things really can't get any worse.'

She knocked on the door.

It took a long time for someone to answer it and the girl who peered out was yawning and bleary-eyed. Of course, by this time of the morning the employees within must have finished their night's labours and were doubtless gone to their beds, to rest rather than to work.

'What do you want?' she asked, blinking. Bridget supposed that the girl was more accustomed to seeing men on the doorstep.

'We wish to speak to Madam Temple,' she said, feigning a brisk manner.

The girl shook her head. 'She isn't taking on anyone new at present. We've got a full house.'

'We're not seeking employment,' Orlaith hastened to assure her.

The girl's countenance grew wary. 'We don't cater for females here. If you're looking—'

'We're not seeking the services of the establishment either,' Bridget said just as swiftly. 'This is a personal matter. We're here in response to a letter we received from Madam Temple.'

'Oh, is she expecting you?'

'Yes,' said Bridget.

'Well then, come on in,' said the girl, her face clearing. 'You can sit in the parlour while I go fetch her.'

The 'parlour' turned out to be a cluttered room containing several cushioned chairs and a few low tables with half-empty glasses abandoned on their surfaces. A faint odour of sweat lingered in the air. Bridget could all too easily envisage the men who frequented this room, growing steadily drunker while they waited for their turn to slake a different kind of thirst.

Reluctant to take a seat, she and Orlaith remained standing awkwardly in the centre of the room until they heard heels clacking in the hallway outside and a woman entered the parlour. She had brown skin and coffee-coloured hair shot through with streaks of grey but Bridget had no time to register more than that for the woman's expression transformed from curiosity to outrage when she perceived her visitors and she let out a shriek.

'You!' she cried and launched herself at Orlaith, fingers primed to gouge out her eyes.

'What the—' Orlaith exclaimed, ducking aside. She darted around the back of a tatty armchair and Madam Temple pursued her, bumping against a table and knocking over a glass in the process.

'I'll kill you if you don't tell me where he is,' she snarled.

Bridget leapt after her and seized her arm. 'Stop it, you've made a mistake!'

Madam Temple tried to shake her off but Bridget maintained a steadfast grip, allowing Orlaith enough time to retreat to the furthest corner of the room. The madam glared after her until by degrees her fury gave way to confusion.

'Holy hell, you're not—' she said, her eyes widening in astonishment. 'You look just like her.'

Orlaith nodded, panting from the fright. 'So I've been told.'

Bridget released Madam Temple's arm once she felt the tension leak out of it. As the woman recovered from her shock, Bridget took the opportunity to observe her appearance in greater detail – she had quite an attractive face marred only by a slight gap between her front teeth. However, a careworn look had emerged more prominently upon her features as her anger receded, the dark circles under her eyes and the pinched skin around her mouth telling of sleepless nights and persistent worry.

'Who are you?' she asked them wearily.

'We came in response to the letter you sent to Boston,' said Bridget, 'after you recognised Bronagh McGovern in the missing persons section of *The Truth Teller*.'

Madam Temple frowned. 'But I wrote to a Mr Cormac McGovern.'

'You did. I am his wife, Bridget, and that young woman is his sister, Orlaith Adams. They are both siblings of Bronagh.'

'Why didn't Mr McGovern come himself?' Madam Temple demanded.

'He is gone to Europe on an urgent family matter.' Bridget gulped – how could it have come to pass that not just one but all three of their children were now in the gravest of danger? Heart aching, she strove to go on, 'G-given the pressing nature of your correspondence, we thought it best to take action without delay.'

An air of palpable disappointment exuded from Madam Temple. She dropped into the tatty armchair Orlaith had skirted earlier, her whole body sagging. 'I needed a man,' she muttered. 'Two more women are no good to me.'

'What d'you mean by that?' said Orlaith, edging out from the corner. 'Why d'you need a man?'

Madam Temple grimaced. 'Because I have an urgent family matter too.'

All sorts of wild ideas stampeded through Bridget's head. Was the madam a mother or did she consider the prostitutes her family? Did she need a man for protection? To impregnate her? To perform some sort of depraved role in the brothel? But New York was full of men – why attempt to lure one all the way from Boston? Furthermore, what could any of this have to do with Bronagh?

Bridget felt hollow as she said, 'You haven't even seen Bronagh, have you?'

'On the contrary, I have,' said Madam Temple, her gaze glittering with unmistakable loathing.

'Does she work for you?' asked Orlaith.

'I would never employ that bitch.'

Bridget and Orlaith goggled at each other across the room.

'Please tell us what your connection is with her,' said Bridget, fearing what they would hear.

Madam Temple shrugged. 'No point. You can't help me. You might as well leave.'

At that, something splintered inside Bridget, leaving a raw, ragged wound as it fractured her very being. She had brought her sons to this city where they had been cruelly separated from her, and it had been on account of the letter this woman had written. Mr Henson had mistreated them, thugs had attacked them, Mrs Gallagher had turned them away, and now Madam Temple wanted to cast them out too without offering the smallest clue as to Bronagh's whereabouts. Had everything they'd suffered and lost truly been for *nothing*?

She felt light-headed and her vision went white and the next thing she knew she was sprawled on the tatty armchair, the concerned faces of Orlaith and Madam Temple hovering above her.

'Wh...?' she mumbled.

'You fainted,' said Orlaith, touching Bridget's forehead with the backs of her fingers. 'Just for a minute. How do you feel?'

'Wretched.' Her stomach churned but she didn't get sick. She stared up at Orlaith in desolation. 'Oh God, if only we could wake up from this nightmare.'

Madam Temple glanced between the two of them. 'What nightmare?'

Bridget squeezed her eyes shut, expecting more tears to seep from them but none came. Dazedly, she said, 'My two little boys. They're gone.'

'Were they abducted from you?' Madam Temple gasped, her tone aghast.

Bridget's eyelids flew open. 'How did you know that?'

The woman's attractive features flooded with dismay. 'Because the same thing happened to me. My darling Willie was snatched away right from this very house.' She paused. 'By that bitch Bronagh.'

CHAPTER 16

Madam Temple didn't tell them to leave again. Instead, she ushered them to a comfortable sitting room at the back of the brothel which she said belonged to her private quarters. She made tea and they sat on three mismatched chairs, clutching their cups. Bridget willed the warmth of the liquid to leach into her fingers but they remained stubbornly cold and trembling.

'W-will you tell us what happened to your son, Madam Temple?' she said, her voice shaking as much as her hands.

'You can call me Hester,' said Madam Temple. 'There shouldn't be any formalities between childless mothers, right?'

A tiny exhalation of anguish escaped Bridget's lips.

'Sorry,' said Hester, dropping her gaze. 'I've had a few months to get used to my loss. Yours is still fresh.'

Bridget couldn't imagine ever getting used to this excruciating pain.

'Months?' Orlaith echoed. 'You said in your letter that you saw Bronagh much more recently than that.'

'I also said I was the manageress of Gallagher's Boarding House,' said Hester wryly. 'I wrote whatever lies I could think of to persuade Mr McGovern to come to New York.'

'What did you expect him to do when he got here?' asked Orlaith.

'Find his sister and, with any luck, my son with her.'

Orlaith chewed her lip. 'I can't understand why she would kidnap him from you. It beggars belief.'

'I may have told a few fibs in my letter but I'm not lying about this,' Hester said sharply. 'So if you're gonna accuse—'

'No, I do believe you,' Orlaith hastened to assure her, although Bridget detected a hint of lingering doubt in her grey eyes. 'It's just hard to accept that my sister could be capable of doing something so wicked.'

'Well, accept it. She robbed me of the greatest joy in my life.'

'How old is Willie?' Bridget asked, careful to use the present tense. The child might have been missing long enough at this stage for all hope to be lost but she refused to consign him to the past – after all, she would inflict critical injury upon anyone who dared do the same to her own boys.

'Nine,' said Hester. 'I had him when I was near forty and beyond any expectation of getting with child, given that it hadn't happened up to that point.' She lifted one shoulder. 'I don't know who his father was and I don't care. My Willie has been a gift from the moment he was born and all I've desired since that day is to give him a decent life. So I learned my letters and worked hard to become the madam here, doing my best to make sure he never wanted for anything. When he was old enough, he started to help around the place, fetching things and running errands. He was always such a good boy—the girls doted upon him. There was nothing grand about our lives but we were happy.' She glared down at her teacup. 'And then I made the mistake of inviting that woman into our home.'

Bridget perceived Hester's extreme remorse and wondered miserably whether she would someday find herself relating a tragic tale that included her own confession: 'And then I made the mistake of bringing my boys to New York'.

Suppressing her overwhelming guilt, she said, 'How did Bronagh's path cross with yours?'

Hester pointed towards the back wall of the sitting room where a door was partly visible behind a half-drawn curtain. 'When I went out into the alley for a breath of air one night. I'd just had to eject a customer for getting nasty with one of my girls and needed a moment to recover from the unpleasantness.' Her shoulders curved in as though she were hunching away from the bad memory. 'It was late January. There was snow on the ground and I remember thinking that Willie would want to play in it the next morning.' She shook her head sadly. 'I had no sooner gone outside than I heard awful sobbing and saw her crouching there in the alley, crying her heart out.'

Orlaith shuddered involuntarily at this. Wicked or no, Bronagh was still her family. It had to be very difficult for her to hear of her sister's suffering.

Hester glanced at Orlaith with a shrug. 'Sorry for mistaking you for her back in the parlour. You do share similarities but I can see now that your eyes are quite different. Not to mention, you've got a full set of teeth.'

Startled by this, Orlaith didn't respond.

Hester continued, 'I took pity on her, of course, and wanted to help. She was like a frightened animal when I came near, almost feral, but eventually I calmed her down and coaxed the truth out of her. Turned out she was pregnant. I told her there were ways of getting rid of it but she said she desperately wanted to keep it and that she was crying because she was terrified the baby's father would cause this child's death just like the last one.'

Bridget could offer nothing but stunned silence in reaction to these words. Orlaith, too, stared at Hester in shock but she managed to get out, 'She...lost a child?'

Hester nodded grimly. 'She didn't say how and I didn't pry. I just urged her to come inside out of the cold. To my eternal regret, she did.'

Hester went on to say that she had brought the weeping woman into her sitting room and sent Willie to fetch something to eat and drink. After further cajoling, she had learned that the stranger's name was Bronagh and her compassion had increased for, although she had an Angolan father, her mother had been Irish and she knew the people of Ireland looked out for their own, especially when they were far from their homeland. She had sympathised with Bronagh's plight and offered practical assistance in the form of employment – Bronagh might not have been in the first bloom of youth but she was still an acceptable age and would meet the tastes of the brothel's patrons, bad teeth and delicate condition notwithstanding. Crucially, such an arrangement would give her the liberty to free herself from the control of the baby's vile father.

'She said she couldn't though and mumbled something about not going the same way as her sister.' Hester eyed Orlaith. 'Did she mean you?'

Orlaith swallowed. 'No. Years ago, our older sister Margaret was forced to sell her body on the streets of Dublin. She died, and then so did our ma, and after that Bronagh disappeared.'

A ripple of pity crossed Hester's face. 'I see. Anyway, Willie came back with some bread and ale and while Bronagh wolfed it down I told her she could stay for a few days at least without having to earn her way. I think she appreciated the offer but she said that if she disappeared for too long then her man would hunt her down and beat her for running away. So I told her to run far enough away that he wouldn't find her. Honestly, she looked so broken when she admitted that she wasn't strong enough to do that and that she still loved him despite his faults.

She felt she had no choice but to go back to him, even though it would mean putting her child's life at risk.'

Bridget took a mouthful of tea, her sympathy for Bronagh's predicament warring with her personal agony. She understood the importance of uncovering what had happened to Cormac's lost sister but she longed to head back out into the city and keep searching for Jack and Gus. She wanted to walk every street, knock on every door, trawl through every gutter, and never stop until she found her beloved boys.

Except what if her single-minded determination simply wouldn't be enough?

The warm tea slid down her throat but she tasted nothing.

Hester carried on with a morose sigh. 'That was when one of my girls came dashing into the room in a panic. The nasty customer from earlier had returned and was causing a rumpus in the parlour. I told Bronagh to rest for a few minutes while I dealt with the crisis and to send Willie to the kitchen if she needed anything more to eat.' Her hands clenched around her cup. 'I was gone for maybe a quarter of an hour. Once I'd kicked the drunken sod out again, I came back to the sitting room. Bronagh wasn't there, and neither was Willie. At first, I thought she'd just buggered off without a word of thanks and that maybe Willie had gone upstairs to empty the pots, but I searched high and low for him in vain. None of the girls had seen him and he didn't reappear, not that night nor the next morning nor any day after that. It was so unlike him—he's always been a soft-hearted boy sticking close to me most of the time. So I knew he couldn't have run off. I knew she must have snatched him.' Her voice cracked. 'I just had no notion why.'

Angry tears glistened on her eyelashes but she brushed them away without letting them fall.

'God Almighty,' murmured Orlaith. 'You must've been insane with worry. Did you notify a constable? That's what we're hoping to do with—'

Hester shot Orlaith a derisive look that cut her off mid-sentence. 'Really?' she said. 'You think someone like me can just walk up to a constable and get help? What do you suppose will make him eager to provide his services—my profession or the colour of my skin?'

Regrettably, she was not wrong. In a flash of desperation, Bridget reflected that a constable might be more willing to aid her if she revealed her true status as a viscountess. It had been a very long time since she had entertained the idea of making such a claim in a public context but she would go to any lengths for the sake of her sons.

To her consternation, however, Hester added, 'Besides, no constable would be interested in finding a kidnapped boy in this city. Children go missing on a daily basis. They couldn't care less about it.'

Bridget whimpered. 'Is that truly the case? We thought they would assist us in searching for my two boys.'

'Not if they disappeared in Five Points,' said Hester bluntly. 'The authorities stay well away from here and the gangs have all the power.'

'There are gangs?' said Orlaith, her brow puckering.

Hester's lip curled in disdain. 'Plenty of them. The Forty Thieves, the Dead Rabbits, the Kerryonians, to name but a few. Men fighting for turf and respect and killing or dying in the process. It's rare for a night to go by without a murder. The locals have learned to keep off certain streets after dark.'

With no warning at all, Bridget's bile rose and, leaning forwards past her knees, she threw up onto the floor.

'Oh, I'm so sorry,' she moaned in humiliation, wiping the corner of her mouth with her palm.

Hester waved a dismissive hand. 'Don't worry about it.'

Putting down her teacup, she got to her feet, rooted through some clutter on a nearby table for a cloth, and bent to mop up the small puddle of vomit. Bridget shuffled her skirts out of the way.

'Please forgive me. I just cannot fathom how our stagecoach driver could have set us down in a district known for its monstrous criminal activity. And I unwittingly led my sons right into its very centre! How I fear for their safety!'

Hester rolled up the soiled cloth and dropped it into a corner of the room where some other items of clothing lay discarded. 'Believe me, I get it. I've cast up my accounts plenty of times these past few months over the same fear.'

Bridget winced, tasting acid on her tongue. 'You didn't stop seeking Willie, did you? Even though you lacked the support of the authorities?'

'Of course I didn't,' Hester replied as she sat again. 'I've spent every day since he vanished looking for him. My girls have tried to help too but, to be frank, there's not much a madam and a bunch of whores can accomplish on their own, even with our very persuasive set of skills.' A strand of hair had fallen across her face and she blew it off, her despair audible in the exhalation of air. 'We asked about him throughout the neighbourhood, every tenement and brothel, every tannery and slaughterhouse, even the slum of the Old Brewery which is about as dangerous as it gets. What made it so disheartening wasn't that the people we spoke to hadn't seen Willie—it was that they *refused* to say whether they'd seen him or not. As far as we could gather, one of the gangs has gained a reputation around the place for pinching children off the streets and they're such a foul lot that nobody wants to get on their wrong side. I used all my powers of persuasion but I couldn't find any man lustful enough to tell me anything useful beyond the name of the gang. They're known as the Kelly Greens and supposedly their leader's a real son of a bitch. I've no idea where they hide out or what in holy hell they do with the children they take. The trouble is I'm only a woman and as such I'm not allowed inside the worst taverns, which is probably where the best information is to be had. So, after all my searching, I'm no better off than I was the day Willie disappeared and he's gone over five months now.'

Again, she looked like she might cry but she held her emotion back.

'And you think he's fallen into the hands of this gang?' said Bridget, appalled. 'Do you believe Bronagh is somehow connected to them?'

Hester set her jaw. 'I can't say for sure. But there's no evidence to say she's not.'

An uncomfortable silence swelled. Hester had made several leaps to convince herself that Bronagh and these Kelly Greens were responsible for her son's prolonged absence but, while many aspects of the situation did point in that direction, she was sitting in the company of two individuals with kinship to Bronagh who badly wished it to be otherwise. If any one of them put tinder to that spark of conflict, their tentative amity could go up in flames.

But then, by some unspoken agreement among the three of them, they chose not to address it. Bridget got the impression that they all sensed they were better off together than divided. Their children needed them and there was no time to clash over unsubstantiated accusations. Hester would make her assumptions and Bridget and Orlaith would let her.

After several tense seconds, Hester broke the silence, acting like the pregnant pause hadn't happened. 'I haven't lost hope but it's dwindled over the months with still no sign of Willie or Bronagh anywhere around Five Points. I started to wonder if she'd taken him to another part of New York, or maybe out of the city altogether, or if the gang has some sort of underground lair where they're able to hide out of sight. I've been saving pennies wherever possible so I can eventually go looking further afield or offer bribes for information. Life has to carry on in the meantime though and the house continues to be as busy as ever. And here I am in the middle of it, feeling like a clockwork toy, just moving mindlessly from one task to the next.'

As she listened, Bridget lifted her cup to her lips and, instantly conscious of the automatic action, understood what Hester meant. The tea had gone cold and she swallowed it uneasily.

'Then I happened to be tidying up the parlour one morning a couple of weeks ago when I discovered that a customer had left his newspaper behind, a Catholic one called *The Truth Teller*, although I bet the fellow wouldn't be mentioning where he'd been at his next confession. I flicked through it idly and swear I nearly had an apoplexy when I reached the missing persons section. There she was staring up at me. The print was a bit clumsy but I recognised her face at once because I'd imagined scratching her eyes out so many times.'

To cut off another discomfiting silence, Bridget said, 'My daughter, Emily, drew the original version. She's never met Bronagh so she created it from Orlaith's likeness.'

'Talented girl,' said Hester.

'She is,' said Bridget, her chest tightening with sadness. Emily seemed very, very far away from her right now, not just in space but in affinity. All three of her living children were at this torturous moment in time as elusive to her as shadows on a cloudy day.

'It was enough to give me more optimism than I'd had in months,' said Hester. 'I saw that the author of the notice, Mr McGovern, was based in Boston and figured that if he had sufficient funds to get a notice printed in a paper in a different state from where he lived then surely he'd have the resources to ferret Bronagh out and, with the help of God, my son along with her. Most important of all, he was a man. He would command more respect from the cowardly locals, he'd be able to enter the taverns women couldn't go into and, unless he was an invalid or a dwarf, he'd have the strength to use brute force if necessary to unearth the answers I needed. I was prepared to do anything to get him to New York as soon as possible.'

Orlaith nodded. 'Which meant you had to invent a story,' she said, her tone pensive rather than accusatory as the pieces of this puzzle began to fall into place.

Hester let out a mirthless laugh. 'Exactly. My address was not a respectable one to write from after all. So I sent my letter to Mr McGovern, telling him that I ran Gallagher's Boarding House in the Bowery district and that a woman matching Bronagh's description had stayed at my boarding house only the week before. Needless to say, I lied about the time frame to add urgency and hope. Then I paid a visit to Mrs Gallagher and told her to expect a letter or, more likely, a man in the near future looking for Hester Temple and, if either came, where she should send them. When she realised I was a madam, she ordered me to get out and stop staining her establishment with my disreputability but I refused to move until she promised to direct any correspondence or caller for me to the house with the pink lantern on Orange Street. She agreed just to get me to leave.'

'She passed your message on just to get rid of us too,' said Orlaith. 'At least she told us the truth about where to find you.'

'And here we all are,' said Hester bleakly. 'Three powerless women.'

Bridget wanted to get so angry. She wanted to be shocked by Bronagh's unspeakable behaviour and outraged by Hester's deceit. She wanted to slap Mr Henson for his negligence and to burn down the post office for delivering the letter that had precipitated this disastrous trip. She wanted to rant and rave at God for allowing all of it to happen.

But she couldn't muster the heat for any of it. A terrible chill had seeped right down to her marrow and taken an icy hold.

Orlaith spoke up, her voice clear and steady. 'D'yous suppose this is just a coincidence? Or d'yous think maybe God actually meant for us to meet?'

Scepticism filled Hester's expression. 'To what end? Why would he bother putting us all together in a brothel in Five Points? I can't see him making sinners of you two or a saint of me.'

'Think about it for a moment,' urged Orlaith. 'Bridget's sons are missing and so's yours. We're searching for Bronagh and so are you. Our troubles and our goals are the same. It's got to be more than chance that our paths crossed. And now we're here, we should band together to find all three boys, and Bronagh as well.'

Hester folded her arms. 'While I reckon it's probably just a coincidence that an oaf forgot his newspaper in my parlour, I agree that working in tandem is a good idea. The problem is we're still only women. What do you imagine you can do that I haven't already tried?' Her features brightened. 'I don't suppose you left any other menfolk back in Boston who can come to our aid? You've got a different surname to your siblings so does that mean you're married?'

'Yes,' said Orlaith, 'but I'm afraid my husband's away in Chicago.' She paused, chewing on her lip. 'Wait, what date is it?'

'The fifth,' said Bridget dully. It was the day after the Fourth of July, and the bang of those celebratory illuminations would now forever be synonymous with horror and pain for her.

'I wonder has Charlie finished his business in Chicago by now?' Orlaith said with a palpable surge of hopefulness. 'He's gone almost three weeks. If he's already on his way back, it might not be very long before he returns to Boston. A week maybe?'

Bridget quailed at the thought of being parted from her boys for another hour, let alone a whole week, but the pragmatic part of her brain reminded her that Hester had so far been without Willie for over five months. There might very well be no swift resolution to this hellish ordeal, and she would have to latch onto the slimmest of hopes wherever she could find them.

'We should send a letter to Boston immediately,' she said, her voice barely audible, 'so it will be there for Charlie whenever he arrives.'

Orlaith straightened her shoulders with purpose. 'I'll do it right away. Poor fella, he'll be so alarmed when he gets back to find I'm not there—we never intended to be gone longer than him. He won't have any warning about the scarlet fever either, but he'll see the barred door and Derval will be able to talk to him through the window.' She hesitated. 'I should write to Tess too. If she already knows what's happened, then she can tell Charlie as soon as he turns up, just in case he doesn't think to check for letters at the post office.'

Bridget didn't argue because Orlaith was right.

'Who's Tess?' asked Hester.

Orlaith coughed. 'A friend of mine,' she said delicately.

Hester didn't pry further. 'The two of you can stay here for the time being,' she said instead. 'I haven't got any spare beds but we can gather some blankets on the floor in this room.'

'Are you sure?' said Orlaith. 'We're basically strangers to you.'

Hester shrugged. 'I don't trust anyone anymore but that doesn't matter. I've nothing left worth stealing.'

Orlaith looked both sorry for Hester and mightily relieved for herself and Bridget. 'Thank you very much. Could I trouble you for some paper and a pen as well?'

As Hester rummaged through the items on her cluttered table once again, she said, 'After you've written your letters, I'll go post them for you while you both eat something and get some sleep. You must be dead on your feet.'

Bridget watched Hester's fingers dart among the odds and ends, her mind in a daze. Although she and Orlaith had been awake for more than twenty-four hours apart from their brief spell of unconsciousness, the concept of sleep was incomprehensible to her. She didn't think she would ever rest again if her boys were not found.

CHAPTER 17

Emily breathed in deeply as she stepped from the gangway onto the wharf, her valise swinging at her side. The Liverpool air was pungent with the reek of rotten fish and stagnant water but she didn't care; she had never been gladder to set foot on dry land. The month-long ordeal at sea had finally ended. While of course necessary, it had also been so dreadful that in this present moment she couldn't even contemplate the return crossing to America, whenever that might be.

Admittedly, there had been some bright aspects to the remainder of the voyage after the occurrence of the storm. No weather so violent had assailed the *Integrity* again and the passengers had enjoyed pleasant if unvaried days on deck. To Emily's monumental relief, her blood had not made a reappearance so she hadn't needed to endure the embarrassment of seeking Louise's advice on that distasteful matter. In the evenings, she had delighted in learning the steps to a traditional Norwegian dance from Henrik, despite the lack of a common language between them. Louise had joined in sometimes, although Rory, predictably, had not. Above all, while Emily's heart still belonged to Samuel, she had fallen in love anew – little Philippa was a cherub to be utterly adored.

However, the final week of the journey had not been without its tribulations. A sickness of the bowels had spread through steerage and several small children had succumbed to it, as well as a few of the older men and women. It was horrendous that they had died mere days away from their destination. The ship's carpenter had built coffins to bury the bodies at sea and the passengers had listened to Captain Philips read from the Bible as their deceased family members and friends had sunk into the ocean out of sight. Among them, on the second to last day, had been dear old Henrik. Philippa, too, had fallen ill but she had thankfully survived, leading Louise to declare in tearful joy that babies born during storms must be blessed with an exceptional form of resilience.

Emily glanced over her shoulder at Louise who was stepping off the gangway behind her, her thriving daughter cradled in her arms. This would be the cruellest part of leaving the *Integrity*, that she would have to bid farewell to the kind-hearted friend she had made. The regrettable deaths on board had meant that the passengers could spread out a little more among the berths so Louise and her baby had been able to occupy a bunk by themselves, but that had not led to any lessening of the friendship that had blossomed between her and Emily. They had bonded to such a degree that they had promised to correspond with each other in the future, and Louise had already given Emily the address in Yorkshire which she was travelling on towards; she intended to return to the family she had left behind when she and her husband had emigrated to America. Emily sincerely hoped that they would take good care of her in the absence of her beloved Roger.

Beyond Louise, Rory trudged down the gangway, his canvas bag dangling from his hand. He had grown very quiet on the ship, especially since Henrik had passed away, and there had been no more instances of laughing like the day Emily's bonnet had blown away along the Promenade. She supposed she ought to be glad that London loomed ever nearer and she would not have to put up with his taciturnity on a full-time basis for much longer, but part of her wished she could draw that laughter out of him again.

'Do you want one last cuddle before we go our separate ways?' Louise asked Emily, holding Philippa out to her.

'Oh, yes, please!' Emily set her valise down on the wooden planks of the wharf and eagerly accepted the swaddled child. At nine days old, Philippa did little more than sleep, feed and soil herself, but Emily was fascinated with every bit of her, from her minuscule fingers and toes to the way her mouth opened in a tiny 'oh' when she yawned. She embraced the little girl gently and kissed her sweet-smelling forehead.

'I hope you have a beautiful life,' she whispered. 'Look after your mother, won't you?'

They took their leave at the end of the wharf, Emily and Louise exchanging emotional hugs while Rory mumbled an uncomfortable 'G'luck'. Emily waved after Louise and Philippa until they vanished from view among the crowds thronging the docks. Then she wiped away a tear and said to Rory, 'I suppose we'd better seek a stagecoach bound for London.' It was already mid-afternoon but, if they could find a coach with two available seats, there would be enough time to complete at least one stage of the journey before dark.

'Not yet,' he said. 'We need to wait.'

'Wait for what?'

He didn't reply, only strode away towards a low stone wall and sat on it, dropping his bag at his feet. She followed with her valise and stood glaring at him; she wished she had the height to look down upon him but his torso was so long that they were at eye level with each other.

'What are you doing?' she demanded. 'We have to go.'

'Not yet,' he repeated.

When he refused to relent to further prodding, she huffed in defeat, deposited her valise next to his bag and perched on the wall too. In truth, her legs were feeling somewhat shaky after getting off the ship – perhaps it would be wise to rest for a few minutes until she had adjusted to the sensation of being back on land again.

She tapped her fingertips on her knees and lifted her face to the overcast sky, thankful that at least it wasn't raining while they dallied. Rory didn't move beside her. He just sat there, his green eyes narrowed and fixed upon the docked *Integrity*, and gradually it dawned on her what – or rather, who – he was waiting for.

She chewed on her lip. 'Rory?'

'What?'

'Are you planning on making a scene?'

His gaze cut sideways to her. 'No,' he answered in a noncommittal tone that didn't reassure her at all.

A few minutes turned into an hour and she grew more and more anxious that they would miss all of that day's departing coaches. She twisted to face Rory, about to launch into a renewed plea to leave, when he stiffened. Shifting her attention back to the *Integrity*, she discerned Brian Mór striding down the gangway with two of his crewmates, all three of them grinning and shoving at each other. Emily expected Rory to march up to the group to confront his father but he swivelled away so that his back was to them. When they reached the end of the wharf, they headed along the docks in the direction that Louise and Philippa had gone so they didn't pass by the wall where Emily and Rory sat.

Baffled, she said, 'After waiting so long, why didn't you—'

He peered around at the men's retreating backs, then grabbed his bag and stood up. 'Let's go,' he said, his eyes still locked upon the men.

Her mouth fell open. 'Surely you don't mean to follow him?' she squeaked. 'I don't think that's a good—'

'You coming or not?'

Not pausing for her response, he set off and she was obliged to seize her valise and scurry after him, or risk becoming separated from him in this unfamiliar town. He stalked ahead of her, weaving in and out through the stream of passengers, sailors and dockworkers hurrying about their business on the docks, careful to maintain a sufficient distance between himself and the three sailors so that he was able to keep them in view while never getting too close to become conspicuous. Emily scuttled on his heels, wishing she could conjure up the right words to convince him to abandon this scheme. She was certain it could not end well.

The trio of men left the docks and entered a warren of streets nearby, striding along companionably until they reached a corner where they parted, Brian Mór heading left and the other two branching off to the right. Rory followed his father and Emily kept pace with him even though she almost had to run to keep up, her valise banging clumsily against her thigh.

'Rory,' she panted, 'maybe you should reconsider this. You remember what he was like on the ship. If he catches sight of you, he could get very angry.'

Rory tossed his head as if her warning were an irritable fly buzzing in his ear. 'I won't let him spot me. I just want to see where he goes.'

They shadowed Brian Mór down the next street and then onto another where Rory held back at the corner as it proved to be a narrow alley leading to a dead end. Terraced houses lined both sides of the alley and in the space between a handful of young boys were rolling hoops with sticks. Two of these detached themselves from the group as Brian Mór approached and ran up to him, yelling in excitement.

'Da!'

'You're back!'

Brian Mór swung the smaller of the two boys up into his arms and affectionately ruffled his hair while the bigger boy scampered towards an open doorway in one of the terraced houses and dashed through it, shouting, 'Ma! Ma, he's home!' Chuckling, Brian Mór disappeared into the house after him, still carrying the younger boy.

Flabbergasted, Emily swivelled towards Rory. He stood immobile beside her, unblinking and white-faced. In the next instant, a wave of red flooded his cheeks and he spat out a swear word so foul that she gasped in shock. He didn't notice; he was already marching in the direction of the house with the open door.

'Oh, no, you mustn't!' she cried, hastening after him.

He reached the house swiftly with his long-legged stride but he paused on the threshold in an attitude of disbelief which gave her the chance to catch up. She peered past him to witness the scene within.

In the centre of the small room, Brian Mór had put down the child and was shrugging out of his coat. A plain, frizzy-haired woman took it from him, planting a kiss on his cheek as she did so. She started to step away but he said, 'Not so fast, my queen,' and pulled her back, pressing his lips ardently upon hers. She giggled and yielded to him, folding herself into his embrace. The two boys didn't bat an eyelid at this demonstrative behaviour as they announced at the top of their lungs that they'd found an injured fox in the alley while Da was away and nursed it back to health and named it Ginger until it got better and ran off. In the meantime, a third child – a little girl with a frizzy mane of her own – had latched herself onto Brian Mór's leg and was peeping up at him with a worshipful expression.

Emily clapped her free hand to her mouth to curb another shocked gasp. Rory had no such self-control. A growl of fury rumbled from his throat and he stamped across the doorstep and into the house. The family – for a family they clearly were – turned in surprise at his entrance. The woman looked puzzled and the children curious, but Brian Mór's countenance went from stunned to enraged in one second flat.

'What the bloody hell!' he spluttered. 'Get out of my house!'

Rory dropped his bag on the floor and crossed his arms purposefully in an action that was eloquent to all.

'Who are you?' the woman asked suspiciously in a nasal English accent, her initial polite puzzlement quickly souring into hostility.

Rory's chest heaved with a furious intake of breath but before he could reply Emily rushed into the room and grabbed hold of his arm.

'Don't,' she implored him. 'Not with the little ones here.'

He hesitated, glancing from her to the three children. The eldest was probably no more than eight years old and the girl had to be scarcely three. He jerked his chin at his father.

'Send them out,' he said, his tone gruff and uncompromising.

Brian Mór looked incensed but he must have seen the wisdom in Rory's command for he touched the older of the two boys on the shoulder and muttered, 'Take your brother and sister outside to play and don't come back in until I say so.'

'Maybe I should stay, Da,' the boy said, glowering at Rory.

'No, lad, go on now.'

Brian Mór shoved harder on the boy's shoulder and, reluctantly, he took the hands of his younger siblings and led them back out to the alley, throwing an ugly scowl at both Rory and Emily as he passed them. When the three children had left, Emily closed the door behind them; the room became dim but that was preferable to the possibility of innocent ears overhearing the coming altercation.

The woman pushed a hank of her frizzy hair back from her face and repeated, 'Who are you?' with a noticeable quiver in her voice this time.

Rory pointed at Brian Mór. 'I'm his son,' he snarled. 'But I wish I wasn't.'

The woman sagged. Still clutching Brian Mór's coat, she turned to him and said, 'He's a grown man so this obviously happened a long time ago. Is it too much to hope that you've lost contact with his mother or is she still your mistress now?'

'What're you on about?' Rory spluttered. '*You're* the mistress!'

'Shut your bloody trap,' Brian Mór snapped as the woman drew herself up and said haughtily, 'I'm his *wife*, I'll have you know.'

That knocked all the wind out of Emily like she'd been kicked in the chest by a horse, so she could only imagine how brutally it hit Rory. He gaped, speechless, for several seconds, his features contorting with stupefaction and dawning horror.

'You're trespassing on my property,' Brian Mór barked with a distinct tinge of panic in his tone. 'I want the pair of ye gone right this very—'

'You lousy bastard,' Rory broke in, his hands curling into fists at his sides. 'My God, you rotten, foul, lousy bastard.' His gaze swung back to the woman but Emily was glad to see it contained pity rather than blame. 'Did he give you his name?'

Her mouth opened and closed like a fish. At last, she stammered, 'M-my name is Maud C-Carey.'

Emily couldn't help the tiny moan that slipped from her. This was utterly inconceivable. The poor woman.

And poor Auntie Derval.

Rory's mother was evidently at the forefront of his thoughts too for he said to Brian Mór with complete incomprehension, 'How could you do this to her? For all these years? *How*?'

Brian Mór's jaw worked but no explanations or excuses issued forth. Emily surveyed him with revulsion. Did he feel any sense of disgrace or was he just annoyed that his deceitfulness had been uncovered?

'Brian?' Maud said tremulously. 'Can you please tell me what's going on?'

Instead of answering, he shifted his weight from one foot to the other and avoided her eye.

'Come on, you coward, own up,' said Rory. He added threateningly, 'If you don't tell her, I will.'

That spurred his father into retorting, 'The only thing you'll do is clear off and never darken my doorstep again.'

Rory snorted with disgust and turned to Maud who was now clasping her apparent husband's coat tightly to her bosom as though it might save her from drowning.

'I'm sorry to hurt you this way,' he said, 'but back in Boston—'

Brian Mór lunged at Rory and struck him across his mouth. He staggered but managed to stay upright.

'Be quiet or I'll break every bone in your body,' his father growled.

Maud looked shocked. 'Brian!'

He flinched, the closest he had yet come to showing shame for his despicable behaviour. 'Don't believe a word he says, love,' he muttered. ''Tis all lies.'

Rory laughed without a trace of amusement. 'Coming from the master liar himself.' He spat a globule of blood into his palm and wiped it away on the thigh of his trousers. 'And a criminal too.'

'Criminal?' said Maud, wide-eyed with alarm.

'Being married to two women at the same time is a crime, right?' Rory flung at his father. 'Or have you never heard of that law?'

Maud emitted a weak gasp. Emily approached her and put out a faltering hand, not quite touching her arm. She wanted to offer consolation even though it wasn't her place and there was none to be had. Still, they were the only females in the room and the unfortunate woman deserved some clarification about this atrocious situation, despite the fact that there could be no solace to accompany it.

'It's true,' she said. 'There is another Mrs Carey living in Boston and Mr Carey has four children by her. I'm so very sorry.'

Maud blinked and her chin trembled. She could have fallen to her knees weeping or lashed out at Brian Mór with her fists but she only cast a look of desolation at the closed front door and whimpered, 'O-our children.'

What was the legal status of offspring born into a bigamous marriage? With a start, Emily realised that the two boys and girl outside were Rory's half siblings. His own attention, however, was still entirely focused upon his reprobate father.

'I could go to the authorities,' he said. 'They'd cart you off to jail for sure.'

Brian Mór grimaced. 'You'd have a lot of lives on your conscience then, lad. Who'd provide for this family if I'm locked up? Not to mention, I support your mother too. I've never stopped sending her money all through the years.'

This time it was Rory who threw the unanticipated punch. His curled fist connected with his father's chin and suddenly Brian Mór was sprawled on the floor. He stared up at his son, slack-jawed.

'D'you expect gratitude or something?' asked Rory, breathing heavily. 'Stop sending Ma money. *I'll* support our family. We don't bloody need you.'

And, whirling on his heel, he thrust open the front door and stormed out of the house, leaving a resounding silence in his wake.

Emily glanced between the trembling Maud and the spread-eagled Brian Mór and gulped. 'I'd better...' she said awkwardly, then snatched up Rory's canvas bag from the floor and ran from the house and the devastation they had caused.

There was no sign of Rory outside but the three children were hovering in the alley. The eldest gave her another nasty scowl as she passed and her guilt intensified for she and Rory had just destroyed what had plainly been a happy home. And yet, the foundation of that happiness had been built upon a grave falsehood and an unlawful marriage contract. Granted, Emily herself had been raised in a home with no marriage contract whatsoever, but at least her parents had both knowingly entered into those circumstances. Maud had been totally deceived – wasn't she entitled to learn the truth?

Reverting rapidly to her own concerns, Emily emerged onto the street at the top of the alley in a panic, afraid that she might have lost Rory in his haste to put distance between himself and the man who had failed him as a father. Luckily, she glimpsed his tall, shaggy-haired form pounding away up the street and she hurried to follow, hampered somewhat by the two pieces of baggage she now carried.

Whether by intention or instinct, Rory somehow found the route back to the waterfront. Still trailing behind him, Emily caught herself sighing with relief when she espied the masts of the ships docked in the estuary. Good gracious, she couldn't be feeling nostalgic for the *Integrity*, could she? She pushed the absurd notion out of her head and continued after Rory. He finally came to a pier that seemed less busy than the others and, walking its full length to the end, he lowered himself to sit on the edge and dangled his feet over the water.

She wondered whether she should join him until she saw the violent shake of his shoulders and decided emphatically against the idea. No, he would not appreciate her presence at this juncture. Instead, she put their baggage down on the ground at the near end of the pier and sat on her valise to wait.

She kept her gaze upon him and, after a time, the shaking stopped. He stayed there a little longer, head bent and shoulders slumped, until all of a sudden his head jerked up and he lurched to his feet, looking around wildly like he had misplaced something. Emily got up from her valise and waved timidly down the pier at him. His demeanour calmed and, pausing briefly to press the heels of his palms hard into his eyes, he jogged towards her. When he reached her, he halted with a mortified expression on his face.

'Sorry for forgetting about you,' he mumbled.

She flapped his apology away. 'You had other things on your mind.' Her eyes flicked from the cut at the corner of his mouth to his bruised and swollen knuckles.

He winced but didn't comment on either the injuries or the encounter with his father. Reaching for his bag with his undamaged hand, he said, 'Thanks for grabbing this. Will we go find a stagecoach to London so?'

She bit her lip. 'We can make enquiries but I believe it's grown too late for today.'

He glanced up at the sky. Although it was too overcast to accurately tell the time, both of them knew that too much of it had passed since they got off the ship. 'Sorry,' he said again.

'Perhaps it's for the best,' she said, affecting a cheery manner. 'Let's seek out an inn for tonight. After so long at sea, we deserve a decent meal and comfortable lodgings before we travel any further.'

CHAPTER 18

It wasn't until they were sitting at a table in the dining room of The Knight's Arms with two bowls of steaming stew in front of them that it occurred to Emily that there was a significant snag in this plan.

'Rory,' she hissed at him across the table, keeping her voice down so the other patrons nearby would not overhear.

'Hmm?' He was already delving into his stew and no wonder for it smelled divine.

'Stop eating, for heaven's sake. We don't have the money to pay for it!'

He paused with the spoon halfway to his mouth. 'I thought you still had some left in that coin purse from Tess?'

'I do but it's dollars,' she said, growing frantic. 'They use *pounds* in England. Gracious, this is theft. We're criminals!'

His countenance darkened at her choice of word. 'We're not. 'Tis an honest mistake. We'll find a place to exchange the dollars for pounds in the morning. There's got to be somewhere near the docks—sure we aren't the only folk who just arrived from America.'

She calmed a little. 'Yes, good thinking. But what if we don't have enough for the inn as well as the stagecoach fares? It's very likely we're going to be short the full amount.'

He shrugged. 'Then we'll have to stay in Liverpool until we do. I can probably find a few days' labour hereabouts, maybe as a dockworker like your da used to do in Boston.'

It vexed her that their arrival in London might be delayed even longer but she said, 'Perhaps I could seek a temporary maid's position in one of the inns or boarding houses too.' She swallowed uneasily. 'Are you sure you want to work at the docks? What if you bump into...'

Rory glowered. 'I'll knock his block off again.'

Discomfited, she busied herself with taking a spoonful of the hot stew. It tasted strongly of onions and contained an unidentifiable stringy meat. She made use of her time spent chewing to formulate her next question and, after she had gulped the mouthful down, said quietly, 'What were you expecting to find today?'

He stared down into his bowl, pushing the meaty lumps around with his spoon. 'Honestly? I was expecting him to go straight to a brothel. I figured he must have gotten tired of my mother over the years and that whenever he was in port he just wanted younger, prettier things with no inconvenient brats to bother him.' He dropped his spoon into the stew and sat back, looking sick. 'I didn't expect *that*.'

'I don't think anyone could have,' she said sympathetically. 'It was truly shocking.'

A glimmer of embarrassment flickered across his expression. 'It was, but I think I could've handled it better.' He ran a hand down his face in a dispirited gesture. 'Jesus, how do I tell my ma?'

She was saved from responding by the rotund innkeeper who toddled over to their table and said, 'Everything satisfactory here?'

Emily froze but Rory collected himself enough to say, ''Tis grand, thanks. Can we take lodgings here tonight and pay for the meal and accommodation in the morning?'

The innkeeper squinted down at them both, his gaze lingering especially upon Rory's bruises. 'So long as you actually mean to pay and don't plan to run off first thing without settling what you owe.'

Rory motioned towards Emily. 'My sister has our coin purse. Take it out and show him, Emily.'

The innkeeper waved a pudgy hand. 'That's fine—I'll take your word for it. We're almost full up but I reckon we can accommodate two more. What's the name?'

'McCarey,' said Rory.

'Righto, let me know when you're finished here and I'll show you upstairs.'

As he started to move away, Emily thawed enough to ask, 'Excuse me, sir, can you tell us where we can catch a stagecoach tomorrow that will take us as far as London?'

He frowned back at her, puzzled. 'Stagecoach? Why not go by rail? It's much quicker.'

With the air of a seasoned urban dweller speaking to a pair of country bumpkins, he advised them as to where they could locate the railway station on Lime Street and even the approximate departure times and fares. When he left their table to approach another patron entering through the dining room door, Rory threw Emily a glum look.

'It sounds like the better option but we don't have enough money, do we?'

'No,' she said dismally. Taking into account their bed and board at The Knight's Arms, she was certain that they would not have sufficient funds to travel to London by coach or rail. This extra day had proved a costly delay. Still, she could not blame Rory for what he had done – he had been entitled to learn the truth about his father, even if it had brought fresh misery rather than a sense of closure.

They finished their stew in low spirits and afterwards followed the innkeeper's waddling form up a staircase so narrow that Emily was positive the man would become wedged between the walls. He attained the landing at the top without mishap, however, and led them into a tiny room with a slanted ceiling where Rory couldn't stand fully upright and three bodies along with two pieces of baggage was an exceedingly tight squeeze. Most pertinent of all, there was only one bed.

'Oh!' Emily squeaked. 'We actually require two rooms. Or, at the very least, two beds.'

The innkeeper raised an eyebrow. 'What's wrong with this? You're brother and sister, ain't you?'

'Yes, but—'

'Like I said earlier, we're almost full up. It'll be this or the front door.'

She considered the front door option for half a second but if they left to seek another inn that could provide two beds, then they would be obliged to immediately pay for their meal here with English currency that they did not have. She deflated. 'Well, then...um...thank you.'

Rory didn't say anything and she couldn't bring herself to look at him.

'It's quite roomy for two,' said the innkeeper, sounding a touch defensive. 'Four slept here last night without complaint.'

'I'm sure it will be more than adequate,' Emily replied with an attempt at a gracious smile. 'Thank you again.'

Appeased, he said, 'Righto, see you in the morning.'

He had to reverse out of the room and rotate his large bulk on the landing before he could make his way back down the narrow stairs. At least the room did not feel quite so cramped after his

193

exit but, when Emily peered at Rory, he was still stooping to avoid smacking his head against the ceiling.

'You ought to sit down so you don't get a crick in your neck,' she said, striving to sound pragmatic and not at all horrified by the situation.

He lowered himself onto the bed because it was the only furniture – the room contained nothing else apart from a ledge upon which stood a candlestick and a basin of water. Emily bustled about, shutting the door and pushing her valise into the corner and peeking out the small window at the now-dusky sky, but eventually she had to confront the glaring issue. She turned to face Rory and found him watching her.

'Which side do you want?' he said without preamble.

He didn't offer to sleep on the floor and she didn't ask him to – the space wasn't large enough for her to stretch out, let alone him. She eyed the bed. It was not much wider than a berth on the *Integrity*. On the other hand, it was definitely longer; Rory would be able to lie back without bending his legs which meant that their bodies would not have to touch. This was doable.

'The left, please,' she said.

'The left when you're looking at it or the left when you're lying down in it?'

'Oh,' she said, flustered. 'Um...the left when I'm looking at it. I suppose it's the right when I'm...lying down...' God above, was she really about to share a bed with Rory Carey?

This was so very different to the day of the storm. Everything about that incident had felt unreal – her fear had wrapped itself around her like a shroud, obscuring any sense of reality to the point that she could almost pretend afterwards that it had all been a feverish dream. But there was no near-death scenario taking place tonight at The Knight's Arms and they were both in full control of their faculties. This was tremendously inappropriate.

And yet, it was happening. He had slid to the right side of the bed and was shucking off his boots. She removed her own boots too but not another stitch came off. By wordless agreement, they would brazen this out fully clothed.

She edged along the tight gap between the wall and the left side of the bed, pulled back the covers and scooted beneath them. Staring fixedly up at the slanted ceiling, she watched out of the corner of her eye as Rory climbed in on his side. The mattress compressed with his weight mere inches away from her and she shifted to put as much distance between them as she could without falling out of the bed. Neither of them spoke.

They hadn't lit the candle so it didn't need to be blown out. Dusk turned into night beyond the window and she continued to lie there motionless and alert, wondering whether Rory was finding their proximity as excruciating as she was, given that they were not stranded on a ship in danger of sinking. What on earth would her parents say if they could see her right now in this scandalous position? Even worse, what would Samuel think of her?

Another ghastly thought struck her – supposing her courses returned in the middle of the night? She would die of humiliation if she woke up smelling of blood or, God forbid, had stained the sheets with it.

After a while, a slow, steady breathing emanated from the other side of the bed and she inclined her head to listen more intently. The wretch, he had managed to fall asleep. Clearly, he wasn't as perturbed by their situation as she was. Then again, his reputation was not at risk, whereas she had her standing in society to think of. She was about to join the ranks of those who dictated the acceptable standards of propriety and who would judge her accordingly – she had to ensure that she would be worthy of their esteem.

But what could she do to resolve this predicament? She and Rory would be stuck in Liverpool, and thus this inn and this bed, until they accumulated enough funds to travel onwards. They could seek alternative lodgings where they would not be obliged to share a bed, but paying for two beds would postpone their departure for even longer since they would need to earn more money to cover the additional cost. Would the protracted delay be preferable to the risk of bringing her character into disrepute?

Before a solution presented itself to her, she felt her eyelids droop and at last she drifted off to sleep.

She was jerked awake some time later by an insistent hand shoving at her arm.

'Would you ever stick to your own side of the bed, for God's sake?' came Rory's complaining voice from the darkness.

'Wh-what?' she said, startled.

'Budge over,' he demanded.

As she regained her wits, she realised that she was spread out under the bedcovers like a starfish, arms and legs stretching in four directions. Mortified, she curled her limbs up tight.

'Thanks,' he said and added in a grumble, 'I can't understand how you managed it. You're such a small person.'

'Sorry,' she bleated and tucked herself as close to the edge of the bed as she could.

When she woke the next time, she found herself enveloped in a snug, musky warmth which was quite pleasant until she became conscious of the arm draped heavily across her waist. She uttered a muffled shriek and batted at it.

'Now who's hogging all the space?' she exclaimed.

Rory stirred beside her. 'That was on purpose,' he said drowsily, not lifting his arm. 'You sprawled out again when you went back to sleep so I figured the only way to keep you on your own side was to pin you in place.'

'There is absolutely no need to do that,' she said in a high-pitched tone. 'I'll stay put without your assistance, thank you.'

He made a sceptical noise but rolled away from her and dropped off again almost at once.

She pinched the skin on the back of her hand repeatedly to stop herself from falling asleep after that – she knew she had no control over her limbs when she was unconscious so she would have to remain awake until morning. This whole fiasco really was downright untenable.

Just as her hand began to sting, a promising idea popped into her head. With a hiccup of apprehension, she analysed it from every angle – yes, it would address all of their difficulties in one go. Indeed, if it worked out then they ought to be able to leave Liverpool the next day after all. There was a significant flaw, however.

Rory wouldn't like it one bit.

CHAPTER 19

Emily waited for the dawn to break beyond the room's small window before gently extricating herself from the bed and pulling on her boots. Rory was lying on his stomach fast asleep and didn't rouse at her quiet movements. Checking that Auntie Tess's coin purse was in her pocket, she slipped from the room, crept down the narrow staircase on tiptoe and scurried out of the inn, hoping that the innkeeper would not spot her. She made it outside without being assailed by accusations of dodging payment and, relieved, she hurried away through the Liverpool streets.

To her surprise, she only made one wrong turn before she found her way back to the alley with the dead end. There were no children playing in it this early in the morning although she spotted a hoop and stick abandoned in the shadows near one doorstep. The door to the Carey house was closed and she tried not to envision the distressing scenes that must have taken place there after she and Rory had fled the previous day.

Drawing in a deep breath to fortify her nerves, she approached the door and knocked. She had expected that it would take a few minutes for anyone within to stir from bed and come downstairs, but her knock was answered almost immediately and Brian Mór stood there with dark circles under his eyes and a bruise on his chin. Indignation and anger flushed his features and, she thought, not a little trepidation. His gaze darted past her to the alley.

'Rory isn't with me,' she assured him. 'I came alone. Please may I speak with you, sir?'

'I've got nothing to say to you,' he said snidely.

'Let her in,' admonished a voice from the room beyond him and Maud appeared at his side. She, too, looked exhausted, her cheeks pale and her frizzy hair in disarray around her shoulders.

Brian Mór instantly obeyed her command and pulled the door wide to allow Emily to enter. She crossed the threshold tentatively and Maud gestured towards a stool. She sat, absorbing the details of the room which she had not had the opportunity to take in yesterday. Her stool was one of five standing in the vicinity of a table that appeared to function both as a kitchen workbench and a sewing desk, judging by the cooking utensils and fabrics strewn across it. There was a fireplace on one wall, its bricks blackened from use and a blanket spread across the floor in front of it. Was that evidence that Maud had not let Brian Mór share her bed last night? Emily did not know whether to feel vindictive triumph on Auntie Derval's behalf or sadness at being witness to a ruined marriage, fraudulent though that union had been.

She cleared her throat. 'Rory doesn't know I'm here. He'd be furious if he found out.'

'Sounds like the typical Carey temper to me,' said Maud and Emily was astonished to see a rueful smile curve the woman's tired mouth. She caught Emily's astounded look and shrugged. 'If I don't laugh about it, I'll cry.'

Emily nodded despondently. 'Mr Carey told you everything?'

'He did.' Maud paused. 'And I've decided to forgive him.'

Emily goggled at her in sheer bewilderment.

Maud moved closer to Brian Mór and linked her arm through his, gazing up into his face with an expression verging on reverence. 'After the children went to bed, we sat in front of the fire and talked for the whole night. He told me how he married his first wife too young and that they weren't a good match for each other and that he didn't understand what love truly meant until he met me.'

Emily thought that even she wasn't so gullible as to swallow such claptrap from a man well established as a liar. And yet, he returned Maud's gaze with an adoring one of his own, tucking a wayward wisp of her hair tenderly behind her ear. Could it be true? Had he been overcome by an emotion so strong that it had compelled him to abandon his wife and four children? But he had made a solemn vow to Auntie Derval – would he not have felt duty-bound to keep it, even if his heart had yearned for another?

Emily gulped. Her own mother had broken her wedding vows for the sake of love. Goodness, how complicated this all was.

'Does that mean...you don't intend to ever go back to Broad Street?' she asked Brian Mór timidly.

'The lad made it clear I'm not welcome there anymore,' he replied. 'So 'tis probably best for all concerned to leave things be.' A surge of sudden alarm crossed his face. 'Unless he's going to follow through on his threat and send the authorities after me?'

'I don't think he'll do that,' she said without real conviction.

The tension in the room heightened. Maud shifted her body forwards in front of Brian Mór as though to shield him from attack.

'Why are you here?' she asked, her tone hardening.

Emily wrung her hands in her lap. This had seemed like a sound idea beforehand, but now she wasn't so confident. 'I was w-wondering,' she said falteringly, 'if you might be able to...help us.'

'Help you?' said Maud, her brow furrowing. 'How?'

Emily squeezed her knees together. 'Rory and I need to get to London but we don't have enough funds to cover our travel there and we're stuck in Liverpool until we do. I thought perhaps you could assist us in departing as swiftly as we can.'

'The cheek of you!' spluttered Brian Mór over Maud's shoulder. 'After causing havoc yesterday, you now come begging us for money?'

'I know it's terribly impudent of me,' she hurried on. 'But Rory's talking about getting temporary work at the docks to earn the rest of the money we need. Can you imagine what will happen if you and he run into each other again? Wouldn't it be better for us to be gone rather than risk another dreadful encounter?' Her feet felt sweaty inside her boots. 'I'm not asking for the whole amount. We have some funds at our disposal so we would only require enough to make up the difference. Nor am I suggesting that it would be a gift for I will be in a position to repay it to you in full, or with interest if you prefer, once we get to London.'

Brian Mór looked ready to refuse her outright, but Maud screwed up her mouth as she contemplated Emily.

'We'll give it to you,' she said at last.

'What the—' Brian Mór started to object.

'On one condition,' she went on in a loud, firm tone. 'And you must swear to it or else there's no deal.'

Emily's heartbeat hammered with nervousness. 'What is your condition?'

'If we give you the money today, then the boy can't report Brian to the authorities. Not now, not ever.'

That was hardly surprising, she supposed. What was less certain was whether she possessed the ability to persuade Rory to consent to it. Still, she had come this far and could not back down now.

'I swear it,' she said, swallowing her misgivings.

She left the house a short time later with English coins in Auntie Tess's coin purse and directions to an establishment back at the waterfront where she could exchange her American dollars. Unfortunately, she had to wait for the money changer to arrive and open his shutters and, as the minutes dragged by, she grew anxious that she had been gone from The Knight's Arms for too long. By the time she had conducted her business, the sun was well up and the docks were teeming with people. She hastened back to the inn as fast as she could, hoping that Rory might have been tired enough to sleep late.

No such luck. When she entered their room at the top of the narrow stairs, a cranky voice snapped, 'About bloody time,' and she cringed. He was sitting on the end of the bed, his expression stormy and his knees bouncing in agitation. He looked like he would have been pacing the room if there had been space to do so.

'Oh, you're up!' she said with false cheeriness. 'Are you awake long?'

He levelled a reproachful gaze at her. 'Where've you been?'

'I went to the docks to exchange our money,' she said, which was the truth, if not all of it.

'Why didn't you tell me you were going?'

'You were still asleep and I didn't want to wake you. I would have left you a note except I wasn't sure if you could—' She broke off awkwardly.

His green eyes flashed. 'I can read,' he retorted. 'I didn't manage to learn much from your ma years back because you hated when I went anywhere near you at Broad Street, but Orlaith taught me a bit after your family moved out. And I've improved a lot since taking on my apprenticeship with your da.'

'I-I'm very pleased to hear it,' she stammered, mortified. 'I do apologise if I insulted you. I truly didn't mean to.' In an effort to detract from her blunder, she rushed on, 'I have some good news! It turns out we misjudged how much money we had left and we do in fact have enough to pay for the inn *and* purchase railway tickets.'

His knees stopped bouncing. 'Really?' he said suspiciously.

'Yes, so neither of us will have to look for work and we'll be able to leave Liverpool today after all.' She beamed at him.

He stared back. 'I don't see how that's possible. You were positive yesterday that we were short.'

'I was mistaken,' she said lightly.

He frowned. 'Are you lying?'

'N—' she began but the word wedged in her throat. She couldn't say it. She supposed she must have betrayed her guilt on her face for he sat up very straight.

'Where'd you get the extra money?' he asked, his voice measured.

She just stood there, mute and flustered.

'Jesus Christ. Tell me you didn't.' He rose abruptly, keeping his head bent so that it would not hit the ceiling. His tall, hunched form seemed to loom over her. 'Tell me you didn't do what I think you did.'

She wavered. 'I did,' she said, compressing her lips together and bracing herself for the onslaught.

An infuriated swear burst out of him. Though it wasn't as foul as the previous day's awful expletive, he did appear to be remarkably comfortable with uttering profanities around females – but then perhaps such salty language was only to be expected from the son of a sailor. He ran his hands through his hair, glaring down at her.

'You're unbelievable,' he muttered through gritted teeth. 'D'you ever think of anyone but yourself?'

That stung her, probably because there was too much truth in his accusation to deny it. Nonetheless, she protested, 'I was thinking of you too! This way you won't have to seek labour at the docks and run the risk of walking into your father at any moment. Wouldn't you prefer to avoid that?'

'Not if it means I'm in the bastard's debt!'

'You won't be,' she said, eager to mollify him. 'I promised Mr Carey and Maud that I would reimburse them once we got to London. They said I didn't need to but if it would put your mind at ease—'

'What else?' he interrupted.

'Pardon?'

'What *else* did you promise them?'

'Oh.' She peered down at the toes of her boots and took a quick breath. 'That we wouldn't report Mr Carey to the authorities.'

She heard a thump and another curse. When she glanced back up, Rory was rubbing the crown of his head, a mixture of pain and rage colouring his features.

'Are you hurt?' she asked, moving towards him with her hand outstretched.

He reared away from her and knocked his head against the ceiling again; the candlestick and basin both quivered on their ledge. 'Damn it!' he exclaimed.

She might have giggled under less upsetting circumstances. Instead, she took a timorous step back and said, 'I'm sorry. When we talked on the pier yesterday, you suggested going to find a stagecoach there and then, so I assumed you didn't intend to follow through on the threat you'd made to your father. I thought you would welcome any chance to get away from the place where his sins had come to light.'

'I'd rather work a hundred days in the worst pits of this town than owe that louse a single penny,' he growled.

'Does your pride really mean that much to you?' she said, growing exasperated at his pig-headedness.

'It does!' he practically yelled.

Into the ensuing, echoing silence, she said in a small voice, 'Do you want me to bring the money back?'

He clenched his jaw. ''Tis too late now. We might as well leave. That's what *you* want, isn't it?' He swiped his bag up off the floor and strode to the door. 'Let's head for Lime Street. And don't bother speaking one word to me between here and London.'

CHAPTER 20

Once again, Cormac found himself leaning on the same section of gunwale that he had frequented daily for the past three and a half weeks. Today, however, was different as he scanned the horizon hungrily for any sign of land. The *Blue Onyx* was still a few days away from reaching Liverpool but, according to the deckhands, somewhere out there just beyond his sight lay the coast of Ireland.

His heart ached to be so near to his homeland and yet unable to reach it. Although Boston had become a special place for him and his family, it could never quite evoke that profound sense of 'home' that Ireland did, entangled as his beloved country was in emotions of nostalgia and sorrow and joy.

'Thinking of swimming the rest of the way?' asked an English voice close at hand.

He turned to see the ginger-bearded man who had come running to tell the other passengers about the fire when it had started down in the hold – he had propped himself on the gunwale a little way down from Cormac and was regarding him with a grin. He jerked his head towards the sea. 'You're leaning so far out that you look nearly ready to jump overboard.'

Cormac grimaced self-consciously. 'Just trying to catch a glimpse of home.'

The man gave him an appraising glance. 'You Irish? Wouldn't have been able to tell from your accent.'

Cormac lifted one shoulder in a shrug. 'I guess I lost it over the years,' he said vaguely.

'Must be a while since you've been home then.'

He didn't offer any response to that. He had continued to remain largely anonymous during the voyage, even after the man with the receding chin had observed him taking his money pouch out of his valise down in steerage. Following that incident, he had been on his guard for any trouble from that fellow or the rest of the group of English passengers he fraternised with, but nothing had happened thus far. Still, he had sensed their attention aimed in his direction on more than one occasion and hadn't slept easily since. At least there were only a handful of days to go – soon he would be back on land and able to shed their watchful gazes, though of course then he would have to be vigilant for a much more official kind of attention.

The ginger man was part of that group too, but he gave no impression of antagonism towards Cormac as he said blithely, 'I'm heading homewards myself. Ronnie Tucker's the name, a Manchester man born and bred. Me and my mates are all navvies down on our luck. We thought America was the best place to get plenty of work, only that weren't the case. But the railways are booming at home so that's why we're going back. Not to mention, we're all in agreement that we prefer wholesome English roses to those American bints,' he added with a husky chuckle.

Cormac thought it odd that they had encountered difficulty in finding employment, considering O'Mali's report that the country's economy seemed to be improving again after the financial crisis a number of years ago, but he chose not to comment.

'What's your own name?' Tucker asked suddenly.

'O'Malley,' Cormac replied without missing a beat. He had no intention of giving his real name to this stranger, nor using it at all once he reached England.

'Nice to meet you, O'Malley.'

He returned the greeting with civility but not sincerity.

'You're quite the loner, ain't you?' Tucker said with a wink. 'I haven't seen you join in with those Scottish dancers even once.'

'I'm content just to watch and enjoy the music.'

Tucker laughed and went on casually, 'What're your plans when we get to Liverpool? You sticking around or travelling on?'

Cormac stiffened. Endeavouring to adopt the same offhand manner as his companion, he said, 'Oh, travelling on,' and divulged no more than that.

After a further couple of desultory attempts at conversation, Tucker left him alone on the deck. Cormac blew out a breath, uneasy at the man's obvious interest. He wished the one defensive object he'd brought on this journey hadn't sunk to the bottom of the ocean to rust. He supposed the block of wood might do in a pinch if he needed to whack an assailant over the head but it was no match for a sharp blade.

Casting thoughts of his shifty fellow passengers aside, he returned his gaze to the horizon and pretended that an infinitesimal speck far out to sea was the green coast of Ireland. Would he and his family ever return home? With a start, he realised that, even though he regarded all three of his children as Irish, none of them had actually been born there. In fact, Emily – who, he had to allow, had quite a bit of English in her too – was the only one who had even set foot on Irish soil, and that had been for a scant few months eight years ago.

How he looked forward to the day he would bring his two sons home for the first time.

***

Nine days. Nine whole days had passed since Bridget had last seen Jack and Gus, and so much time had gone by that at this desolate point she very much feared they were—

No, she refused to think that word. They were alive. To believe otherwise was to give up hope, and hope was the only force that was keeping her going when despair threatened to engulf her.

Every day had become the same as the next. She rose from her blanket at the brothel each morning when dawn broke, splashed water on her face, and returned with Orlaith to the street where her boys had disappeared, desperate to find some clue they might have overlooked before. Then they spent the entirety of each day trawling through the streets of Five Points, making enquiries about Jack, Gus and Willie to anyone who would listen and generally being ignored or scorned for trying to find missing children in such a cesspit. They were gone, everyone told them without exception. Move on. No point pining over what was lost for good. Sometimes their heartlessness was too much to take and Bridget would stumble out of the dwelling or premises and throw up into the filthy gutter.

She and Orlaith called daily at the post office but no correspondence arrived from Charlie or Tess and they had no way of knowing if their messages had even been received, let alone whether Charlie might be on his way to New York. What if Orlaith's letters had gone astray and never reached Boston? Hester advised her to write fresh ones and again posted them on her behalf. Bridget promised her weakly that they would pay her back but Hester just said, 'Finding my Willie will be thanks enough.'

And so they searched and they waited, praying with all their might that Charlie would come to their rescue soon or that some other good fortune would befall them. Even a scrap of information about where the Kelly Greens were known to hide out would have felt like progress, if only the locals weren't so afraid to cross that gang's leader. Bridget did try to march into an exclusively male tavern once because it was rumoured to be a favourite haunt of more than one gang in Five Points, only to be unceremoniously ousted from it with nothing but a bruised arm to show for her efforts.

The injuries she and Orlaith had sustained on the night of the attack had mostly faded but she didn't have space in her mind to care about that. She would have neglected her own needs entirely had Orlaith and Hester not forced her to eat and rest, although food tasted like chalk in her mouth and slumber amounted to nothing more than short bursts of hellish dreams. She lay down for barely three or four hours a night, insisting upon combing the streets even after darkness fell.

'That's when it's most dangerous,' Hester had warned her.

'Then that's when we're most likely to happen upon the thugs we seek,' she had replied grimly.

She was fully prepared to flaunt herself as prey if it would bring her into contact with her sons' captors. For she harboured little doubt now that Jack and Gus had been kidnapped from her. If they had managed to run away from their assailants that night, she would have found them since, she was sure of it. The fact that there was a gang in this neighbourhood notorious for snatching children, and that so much of what Hester had told her corroborated the insidious nature of the ambush, meant she was certain that Jack and Gus had tragically become the latest two to fall foul of that band of villains.

If only the thugs weren't so adept at their despicable line of work. They spirited children away as though they had never existed and left virtually no trace of themselves or their quarry behind. The day after the attack, Bridget and Orlaith had gone back to the street again after Orlaith had finished writing her letters and scoured it once more for clues. They had noticed nothing new apart from a streak of deep black dirt on the ground that looked and smelled like soot. Whether it had been smeared there prior to their arrival with the boys, or during the violent confrontation, or in the intervening period before they returned, they could not tell. And now so many days later, thanks to trampling feet and a brief spell of summer rain, there was nothing to distinguish this street from the others in its vicinity apart from the spectre of grief that hung over it.

As twilight deepened on the evening of this ninth day of agony, Bridget and Orlaith trudged along the outskirts of the Five Points neighbourhood where it merged with the Bowery district. They had broadened their search every day in expanding circles throughout the area and were beginning to give credence to Hester's theory that the Kelly Greens either concealed their kidnapped victims in some sort of underground lair or else removed them to another part of the city altogether. Bridget was endeavouring to suppress an anguished crack in her voice as she suggested to Orlaith that they venture beyond Five Points the next day when she perceived two bulky figures ahead of them, carrying lanterns and staffs. Her heart lifted.

'Night watchmen!' she exclaimed, pointing them out to Orlaith. 'Oh, please God they can help us.'

She picked up her skirts and dashed towards the two men, Orlaith on her heels. As soon as they drew near enough, she cried out, 'Please, we need your help!'

The men whirled around at her call. Both stout with clean-shaven jowls, there was little to differentiate between them except for a prominent scar underneath the left man's eye. He straightened and said promptly, 'What's happened, ma'am?'

211

She skidded to a halt. 'My two boys have been abducted. Help us find them, I beseech you!'

As Orlaith scuttled to her side, the second man held his lantern higher to peer at them in the waning evening light. 'We'll do what we can, ma'am. What ages are they?'

'Oh, thank you!' she said, almost bursting with relief. 'They're seven and five years old.'

'And where were they taken?'

She gestured behind her. 'On a street back there. We can show you the precise spot.'

The unscarred man's eyes narrowed. 'You mean they were taken in Five Points?'

She barrelled on, 'And we can tell you the places where we've made enquiries and where we've been aggressively prevented from doing so. Those uncooperative persons will surely be obliged to submit to questions from you as agents of the night watch.'

The man with the scar winced as he leaned on his staff. 'Not a chance. The folk in that dunghill of a community have no respect for the law.'

She drew herself up. 'And will that hinder you from assuming your duty, sirs?'

'Yes, when it's futile to even try,' said the second man firmly. 'We'd be driven out or murdered in the attempt.'

'And what about her boys?' Orlaith said shrilly. 'Are those two precious children to be abandoned because neither of yous have the spines to do your jobs?'

The man with the scar glanced aside in embarrassment, while his companion's cheeks suffused with anger. 'We're not sticking around to listen to your sass.'

As he started to turn away, Orlaith blurted, 'No, please don't go! It's been more than a week since we've seen them and the longer time goes on, the less hope we have. We're begging you.'

He swivelled back. 'A week? You mean it didn't even happen just now?' He snorted. 'Ditch your hope. There's no point holding onto it at this stage.'

Distraught, Bridget gasped, 'How can you say such a thing? Have you no pity?'

Perhaps the scarred man did, for he hung his head in shame, but the other was unmoved. 'I have sense,' he countered.

She bridled and, in her desperation, made an instantaneous decision. 'Then tell me, have you pockets? And a desire to fill them with money?' Though hating herself for resorting to this, she carried on in an assertive tone, 'I am married to the Viscount Wyndham who is a member of the House of Lords in London. As a wealthy and influential peer, he is in a position to pay you handsomely for your efforts in locating his missing sons.'

The second man tittered.

'Did you not hear me?' she said. 'I am a viscountess!'

'And I'm the King of England,' he said and swaggered away, holding his staff and lantern aloft as though he bore the royal orb and sceptre.

The man with the scar grimaced in apology at Bridget and Orlaith and hurried in pursuit of his companion. His voice drifted back, 'You know, I think they've got a queen over there now...'

Orlaith stared after them. 'Thanks for nothing,' she muttered caustically.

Bridget watched in despair as the light of the two bobbing lanterns became swallowed by the growing darkness. Her disloyal declaration coated her tongue like sawdust and she felt the urge to spit. She would have to add it to her list of reasons why she would never be able to face Cormac again. Dear God, their family was in ruins and he did not even know it yet. She only prayed that, where she was conspicuously failing, at least he might succeed in saving one of their children.

CHAPTER 21

They had arrived in London at last.

Emily gazed across Berkeley Square at the grand facade of Wyndham House. Night had fallen and warm lamplight glowed in its windows. The very extravagance of so many lights illuminating a single residence was gobsmacking. What conceivable need could there be for such lavishness? Garrett lived alone, did he not? She felt uneasy – what if he was hosting a gathering for his acquaintants? She had no desire to intrude upon such a situation while wearing her drab, travel-stained attire.

Glancing sideways, she saw Rory surveying the townhouse with crossed arms, his face impassive. As per his instruction in Liverpool, she had not attempted to speak to him since they had left The Knight's Arms apart from the basic communication necessary to purchase their tickets and board the railway carriage. The journey south-east to London had been unbearable, both of them too angry and miserable to be awed by the speed at which they crossed the country. Upon reaching London in the late evening, they had spent their final shillings on a hackney from Euston Station to Berkeley Square, maintaining their silence the whole way.

She broke it now. 'Shall we...?' she said and gestured across the road.

His jaw twitched which she interpreted as acquiescence. She waited for two fine carriages to pass by and then stepped out onto the street. She didn't take her gaze from the house as she approached it, her feet feeling both heavy and light on account of the apprehension and excitement wrestling for dominance inside her. Rory plodded in her wake without a word but, when they got to the front steps, he surprised her by reaching for her valise.

'Don't think you should knock on that door with baggage in your hand,' he said gruffly.

Astonished, she let him take it. He motioned for her to go on and she climbed the flight of steps, her blood thrumming in her ears. She rapped on the knocker and waited.

The door was answered by a handsome footman whose face was vaguely familiar. She combed through her memory for his name.

'Peter?' she tried.

He looked surprised and puzzled. 'Can I help you, miss?'

He didn't recognise her but that was to be expected; she had been a little girl of only six years old when they had last met.

'I'm very sorry to arrive unannounced,' she said. 'I...I used to live here a long time ago.'

His mouth dropped open and his gaze landed upon the golden curls escaping from her bonnet. 'M-Miss Emily?' he said, utterly astounded.

'Oh, I'm so pleased you remember me,' she said with a smile. 'I seem to recall that you used to slip me biscuits from the kitchens when my mother wasn't looking, didn't you?'

He blinked. 'Yes, I did.' His gaze flitted to Rory standing on the step just below Emily.

'This is Mr Rory Carey,' she announced formally, indicating him with a tentative wave of her hand. 'He's my—' She had been about to say 'friend' but she didn't think Rory would appreciate the appellation, given the frosty nature of their current relations. 'He escorted me on my journey here.'

Eyes as round as saucers, Peter said, 'Very good, miss. Do you wish to come in?'

'Yes, please, if...' – how on earth should she refer to Garrett? – '...your master is in a position to receive visitors?'

'I'll check at once,' he said, opening the door wider to admit them. As they crossed the threshold, he seemed to recover some of his equanimity and said warmly, 'You're very welcome home, Miss Emily.'

'Th-thank you,' she stuttered. Was this her home? A fleeting image of Acorn House with its brown front door and grey shutters entered her mind and she pushed it away. 'How kind of you to say so.'

The sound of brisk footsteps heralded the arrival of another man into the hallway; his dark clothing marked him as the butler but Emily could not for the life of her recollect his name.

'Mr Thrussell, sir,' said Peter, saving her. 'Look who's here. It's little Miss Emily, though she ain't so little anymore.'

Apart from a slight widening of his eyes and a barely perceptible crease between his brows, the butler betrayed no shock at Emily's unexpected presence.

'It's an honour to have you under this roof again, miss,' he said, bowing to her.

Peter, a little flustered, belatedly did the same. She coloured at their deference and studiously avoided Rory's eye.

'His lordship will be very pleased to see you,' Thrussell continued.

'He's here, then?' she said nervously.

'Indeed, he is enjoying a glass of brandy in the drawing room as we speak, miss. Shall I announce your presence?'

She peered down at her plain, grubby clothing and surmised that there was nothing she could do about it. 'Please do, if it is convenient.'

Thrussell's attention slid to Rory. 'And your...companion?'

She flushed. 'Um...'

Rory's countenance was inscrutable as he said, 'I'm sure you'd rather meet him in private, would you?'

Even though she felt that having Rory by her side would be a reassurance despite their latest rancour, she knew she had already asked enough of him. 'It is probably for the best. But where will you go?'

'Peter can bring him below stairs,' said Thrussell.

'Rory isn't a servant,' she said, vexed by the insinuation. She had promised him on the ship that he would come under her protection once they reached London and she intended to stand by that promise.

'Of course not, miss,' Thrussell said smoothly. 'I only meant to imply that the kitchen staff haven't yet finished cleaning up after dinner so the young man might obtain a meal downstairs if he is hungry. One of Monsieur Lévêque's underlings would no doubt be happy to oblige.'

'Oh,' she said, embarrassed. 'That is very considerate of you.' She glanced at Rory for his reaction.

'Sounds good, thanks,' he said and, still carrying both his canvas bag and her valise, he followed Peter through a door out of the hall without looking back at her.

'This way, miss,' Thrussell said and ushered her towards the staircase. As she climbed the steps, she recollected having done so more than once as a little girl in the company of her governess, Miss Davison, returning from a walk in the gardens across the street bearing a bunch of daffodils or some other flower in

217

bloom. Her memory was so hazy that she might very well have dreamed it or read about it in a book. How extraordinarily real and unreal all of this felt.

They stopped outside a closed door on the next floor.

'Please wait here,' Thrussell said and slipped inside. She hovered anxiously until he reappeared a minute or two later. 'You may come in now, miss.'

He conducted her into the sumptuous drawing room and promptly departed with another bow. She lingered near the door in uncertainty as a tall figure rose from an armchair by the fireplace and came towards her.

What struck her first was the colour of his hair which, though it retained a small number of black strands, had turned predominantly silver on his crown and at his temples. Rather than aging him in an unfavourable way, it in fact lent him an aura of debonair magnetism. This, coupled with his attractive hazel eyes, left her somewhat dazzled by the spectacle and she swallowed, striving to find some semblance of self-possession.

'My darling Emily,' said Garrett.

He approached and grasped both of her hands in his. As he looked down at her, a slow, satisfied smile spread over his face.

And an inexplicable thrill of fear ran the length of her spine.

'I am so very glad you came,' he murmured. 'You must be tired after your long journey. Come sit down.'

Drawing her over to the fireplace, he encouraged her to take the armchair opposite the one he had been occupying. He let go of her hands and sat too, that disconcerting smile still lingering at the corners of his mouth.

'Did you travel alone?' he asked.

She shook her head. 'An acquaintance accompanied me. He is getting something to eat in the kitchens now.'

Garrett's lip curled as she spoke, although he fixed an amiable expression back onto his face almost at once. 'That is quite a mixed accent,' he remarked. 'Your years abroad have left their mark on you.'

She squirmed with shame. 'Will it have an impact on my suitability for joining society?' she asked, developing an instantaneous aversion to her subtle American twang.

He cocked his head to the side. 'Let us hope that it does not.' That didn't make her feel any better and neither did his next revelation. 'On that matter, I regret to inform you that you are too late to make your debut in this year's season—it came to an end in June. We shall have to postpone your official coming out until the next season begins after Christmas.'

Her gut clenched with disappointment and apprehension. Such a delay would be substantial enough to thwart the wish she had expressed in her letter to her parents that she would see them and her brothers again within the year.

'I-I see,' she said. 'And in the meantime?'

'We can take advantage of the marvellous opportunity to become reacquainted with each other,' he said, 'and rejoice that father and daughter have been reunited at last.' Had his lips twitched as he said that or had she just imagined it?

She squirmed again. 'Ought I to call you...um...'

All traces of amusement vanished from his features. 'I suppose *he's* "Papa" now,' he said coolly.

She withered, both at his tone and at the fact that she had stopped calling her father 'Papa' some time ago. She had believed it had made her more mature to address him as 'Father' but now it struck her as quite unfeeling. Could he have interpreted it as a demotion in her affections for him?

Garrett compounded her guilt by carrying on, 'You can call me "Father" if that makes it easier to differentiate between us.' He shrugged. 'Or "sir" if you prefer.'

She relaxed a little. 'Thank you,' she said and added delicately, 'Sir.'

He sniffed as though to convey that her choice made no odds to him. 'Are he and your mother aware that you have come here?'

How had this man such an extraordinary talent for provoking her guilty conscience? 'I left them a note,' she admitted.

His mood seemed to lift again at that. 'Tell me, how do they fare?' he asked in apparent geniality. 'Are they content in Boston?'

A sense of alarm skittered across her skin. 'They are well,' she said cautiously. 'My father runs a successful carpentry business and my mother is a seamstress. I have two younger brothers as well, Jack and Angus.'

Garrett didn't so much as blink at any of this information so she supposed he must have already been apprised of it. 'They have been blessed with great happiness,' he said, still maintaining a pleasant manner. 'How very fortunate for them that so much luck has fallen into their laps, when others lamentably come by so little of it.'

She had no response to this disquieting statement. Mercifully, a timely knock on the door announced Thrussell's return and he entered the drawing room accompanied by—

'Lizzie!' Emily cried with joy, leaping to her feet.

The housemaid beamed at her. 'Good evening to you, miss.'

Her forehead and cheeks were no longer covered with the red pimples she had suffered in her youth, although a scattering of pitted scars showed where those blemishes had once been.

'Lizzie will see to your personal needs for the time being,' said Thrussell with a slight bow at Emily, 'as we have no lady's maid in residence at present.'

'Alas, I was obliged to dismiss Audley after your mother's departure,' said Garrett regretfully. 'I do hope she managed to find employment elsewhere and wasn't left impoverished by the incident.'

Before Emily could do anything more than register the snide undertone of this, he carried on, 'We shall install you in your mother's old bedchamber, if that is agreeable to you? It will be a little cold from lack of occupancy but the staff will ensure its cosiness as swiftly as possible.'

'There's really no need to go to any trouble,' she said, feeling self-conscious at the idea of servants preparing a bedchamber for her, even though it was an expected aspect of this life she had come to claim.

'It's no trouble at all, Miss Emily,' said Thrussell. 'I offered a guest bedchamber to Mr Carey but he declined, preferring to accept accommodation in the servants' quarters instead. He has already retired for the night but he gave your valise to Peter and it is now in your chamber.'

She nodded mutely. Although the notion of Rory sleeping in a servant's room made her very uncomfortable, she supposed she could not protest if he had not objected to it himself.

Thrussell and Lizzie exited the drawing room and Emily sat back down, eyeing Garrett who reclined in a relaxed fashion in his armchair even while he regarded her with the faintest impression of...dislike? A grain of doubt lodged inside her as she struggled to recall the words of the letter he had sent to her in Boston. She couldn't remember the precise language he had used but his sentiment had been very clear – he had been repentant of his past failings and desirous of rekindling a relationship with her as his daughter. And yet, right now he exuded a curious combination of smugness and resentment.

Endeavouring to set her qualms aside, she said politely, 'May I enquire after your own wellbeing, sir? How have these past years treated you?'

He propped his elbows on the arms of his chair and steepled his fingers. After a long moment of scrutiny aimed at the ceiling, he said in a clipped tone, 'Unfavourably.'

She shivered. And she began to suspect that her parents had shown a great deal more perception than she had when they burned Garrett's letter.

CHAPTER 22

Despite her mother's luxurious four-poster being the largest, cosiest bed she had slept in for years, Emily dozed fitfully throughout the night. When dawn broke and light leaked into the bedchamber, she found herself staring at the underside of the bed's canopy, wide awake. How often had her mother lain in the same position and shrank from the thought of encountering Garrett that coming day?

A long time passed before Lizzie bustled in with a scullery maid who prepared a hip bath of fragrant warm water for Emily in front of the hearth. After a rather indulgent spell of bathing that left her feeling tremendously refreshed, she donned a robe and went over to the bed where Lizzie had spread out a dress on top of the covers.

'This used to belong to your mother,' said Lizzie, fingering its cuff fondly. 'The master kept all her clothes, even after—' She reddened and coughed, before continuing, 'I can tell you ain't quite the same size as her so I stayed up late last night to take it in a bit and shorten the hem. It might not fit perfect but it'll do until we can get you to a seamstress for proper fittings. You'll want new things anyway 'cause the fashions will have changed since—' She cut off mid-sentence again and busied herself with straightening a nonexistent crease in the skirt.

'You oughtn't to have worked so late on my account,' said Emily, 'but thank you very much for your kindness.'

Lizzie looked up. 'It's nuffin. I'm happy to do it.' She offered Emily a small smile. 'You're very like her, if you don't mind my saying so.'

'Am I? Most people say that I take after my—' It was Emily's turn to choke off her speech. How could she be so indiscreet? She was thankful that at least the scullery maid had left the bedchamber. But how much had Lizzie known about her parents' affair?

Lizzie kept her gaze steady as she said quietly, 'Mr Davenport?'

Emily gulped. 'You knew?'

'No, but I guessed.' Lizzie toyed with the dress's cuff again. 'It was almost as if the air hummed whenever the two of them were in a room together. The way they looked at each other... I walked in on them in the hallway once and I reckon they'd been just about to kiss. So I wasn't all that surprised when, you know...'

'When they ran away together, and took me with them,' Emily said.

Lizzie nodded. 'Your hair and eyes were so similar to his that I couldn't help making the connection. I didn't know for sure until now though.' She bit her lip. 'I hope you don't think it's too bold of me to talk about it.'

'I don't,' Emily assured her. On the contrary, she was grateful to have a confidante, especially now that she and Rory were barely on speaking terms.

'That's what I meant when I said you're very like your mother. The way you greeted me last night and then how you said just now that I shouldn't have worked so late on the dress. She was like that too. She treated us servants like human beings.' Lizzie paused. 'Is she happy with Mr Davenport?'

'Very much so.'

'I'm glad. She deserves to be with a good man.'

Emily flinched. 'Are you implying that your master isn't?'

Lizzie glanced away. 'That ain't for me to say.'

The bottom dropped out of Emily's stomach. 'Have I made a terrible mistake in coming here?' she asked miserably.

Lizzie picked up the dress and draped it over her arm. 'I think it's time to check whether this fits you,' she said, even though Emily would have to put on several other layers before she would be ready for that outermost garment.

Emily dipped her head in resignation. 'I understand that you can't speak against him,' she said. 'This is your employment. I wouldn't want to jeopardise your position in any way. But could I perhaps rely on you to be my ally in other matters?'

Lizzie's expression lifted. 'I'll do whatever I can for you, miss.'

'Thank you. To begin with, I need to ask your advice on something awfully private.'

Lizzie's eyebrows shot up but settled again once Emily revealed the nature of her concern. Although she was undeniably loath to bring it up, she had been so fretful that her courses might come during her bath and leave a stain on the tub that she had to acknowledge the wisdom in being fully prepared for their next onslaught. Lizzie went a little pink at the introduction of this taboo topic but didn't shy away from it. As she helped Emily to dress, she described the bodily signs that indicated when the monthly blood might be approaching and also where Emily could find cloths in the chest of drawers to contend with their arrival. Thus armed with knowledge, Emily resolved not to be so fearful of them next time.

After she had finished dressing, she descended the stairs for breakfast, feeling rather regal. Her mother's clothing was still a touch too big, even with Lizzie's hasty alterations, but it was of a finer quality than anything Emily had worn since she had last resided in this house. She was also wearing a dash of her mother's lilac perfume, a true indicator of luxury.

When she entered the breakfast room, the splendid feeling vanished. Garrett was seated at the table reading a newspaper and some obscure part of her memory nudged forwards and reminded her that he didn't like to be disturbed when thus occupied, so she slid silently into a chair. He glanced over the top of the paper, gave her a brief nod and returned to his perusal of the news.

Peter stood unobtrusively next to a sideboard laid out with breakfast platters. When he came forwards to place a toast rack on the table, she asked him, 'Where is Rory? Does he know that it's breakfast time?'

Peter darted an apprehensive look in Garrett's direction. 'I did tell him, miss, but he said he'd prefer to eat downstairs in the kitchens.'

Would Rory choose to avoid her entirely now that his self-imposed duty of bringing her to London had been discharged? Perhaps he would seek a sum of money from Garrett to arrange his immediate passage back to America. Such a prospect ought to have engendered a sense of relief in her and yet she couldn't bear the idea of them parting in acrimony. She owed him a great deal of gratitude for accompanying her safely all this way and especially for calming her at the height of her hysteria during the storm.

Murmuring her thanks to Peter, she rose and filled her breakfast plate at the sideboard with ham and eggs. Returning to the table, she polished off every morsel with relish – she had forgotten how delicious food could taste when it was cooked to perfection. Peter served her cocoa and she was in the process of devouring a hot buttered scone when Garrett at last set down his newspaper.

'You may leave, Peter,' he said and the footman bowed and departed from the room.

Garrett took a sip of his coffee as Emily raised a wedge of the scone to her mouth.

'Have you compromised yourself with this Rory boy?' he asked bluntly.

She gaped. 'Pardon me?' she said in a shrill pitch.

'You've been travelling for weeks in close quarters with him. Were you tempted into impropriety?'

She recalled the ship's berth and the bed in The Knight's Arms with a degree of uneasiness. However, both of those occasions had been out of necessity, and nothing unseemly had occurred. Nobody needed to ever find out about them. 'No,' she said, making sure she looked offended by the insinuation. 'It was all perfectly proper.'

'You cannot reproach me for asking,' he said. 'After all, you could have inherited such promiscuity from your mother.'

Hot butter dripped from her neglected scone as she stared at him, open-mouthed and appalled. 'How d-dare you—!' she spluttered, outraged on her mother's behalf.

'Please do enlighten me if I have made a fallacious allegation against her,' he said, and the sneering curve of his mouth told her he knew she could not contradict him.

Feeling sick, she put the wedge of scone down on her plate.

'I have offended you,' he observed. 'Do forgive me for asking that impertinent question. I merely wanted to ascertain whether you remained unsullied for your coming out next season.'

She studied him with gritted teeth. His language was courteous but his mocking tone was anything but. He made no pretence this morning; last night's conviviality had evaporated. It was as though he had shed his skin and she could perceive the snake hidden beneath.

227

'I won't be having a coming out next season, will I?' she said, quite calmly.

He took another very deliberate drink of his coffee and placed the cup back on its saucer in an unhurried motion. 'No,' he said with equal serenity.

Her heart plummeted as she comprehended the enormity of that one syllable. What an utter fool she had been. She needed to proceed with extreme vigilance from this point onwards for she understood now that she was the mouse into which the snake intended to sink its fangs.

She swallowed a mouthful of her cocoa and sat back in her chair. 'Shall we speak plainly then?' she said. 'Your letter was a ruse?'

'Naturally.'

She kept an iron grip on her composure. 'Was there even a single word of sincerity in it?'

'Hmm, let me try to recall. I wrote it quite some time ago.' He made a show of tapping his finger on his cheek before he abruptly sobered. 'What I said about your brother James was entirely true. His birth and death were the zenith and nadir of my life. But my sentiments and promises in relation to you?' He shrugged. 'All lies.'

'So you do not wish to leave me your inheritance,' she said bleakly, 'nor introduce me into society as your daughter.'

'Of course not, though I must confess my pride in having penned such convincing fiction. I wondered whether the letter would be enough to lure you to England, especially as I'm certain your parents would have done all they could to persuade you against its contents, but clearly you yearned to believe in the fantasy.' He smirked. 'How it must have stung *him* when you proved yourself willing to reject his claim to fatherhood in favour of mine.'

'That's not what I did,' she retorted, aghast at the suggestion. 'He's still my father and I cherish him with all my heart.'

'That may be what you say but your actions speak otherwise.'

Those sharp fangs pierced her and their venom spread through her veins. Oh, her poor papa. How cruelly she had treated him in her vain pursuit of social advancement.

'Why did you construct this deception?' she asked, baffled. 'What possible motive could you have for luring me here?' She gasped. 'Am I a ransom? Do you mean to coerce my mother into returning to you?'

He arched an eyebrow. 'What makes you think I would care to have her back?'

She floundered at his obvious disdain. 'If not that, then what? What do you want?'

'Your assistance,' he said unexpectedly.

She goggled, so taken aback that she couldn't find her tongue.

He gave a dry chuckle. 'I'll explain all in good time, my darling daughter. For now, suffice to say that you are in a unique position to help me with a particular objective I am trying to achieve.'

'Pray, what would induce me to help you?' she asked with excessive civility.

He smiled and she was almost surprised not to see actual fangs behind his lips. 'I said that I had no desire to leave you my inheritance. But that's not to say that I'm averse to giving you some of my fortune. In fact, I am prepared to part with a very handsome sum in exchange for your willing participation in this venture. It will be more than ample to enable you to travel back to America in luxury...and to cover the costs of attending Brubaker Art Academy.'

She started. 'How do you know about Brubaker?'

He just sat there, a glint of arrogance in his beguiling hazel eyes.

229

'How do you know about Brubaker?' she repeated loudly, masking her alarm with a burst of temper.

He spread his palms above the tabletop in a nonchalant gesture. 'How did I learn of your address? How am I already cognisant of your parents' occupations and the existence of your two brothers? How was I able to identify the dream you coveted most? Did none of those questions ever occur to you?'

Her breath snagged in her throat as the magnitude of her own folly became horrifyingly clear to her.

He sniggered and his air of self-satisfaction swelled into crowing triumph. 'I have had eyes upon you, and your family, for years.' He shook his head. 'How your mother ever believed she could abscond from England without eventual detection is beyond me. She took steps to thwart me, insisting that our correspondence go through the intermediary of Oakleigh, but I knew she had gone to America and that was enough to work with, given the substantial wealth and resources at my disposal.'

Emily couldn't look at his smug countenance any longer. She focused instead upon her plate, where the butter had cooled and congealed into lumps.

'I hired an agent and sent him to America with the sole purpose of tracking your mother down. She could have been anywhere on the continent, but the eastern seaboard was most likely—New York, Boston, Philadelphia, all the cities known for letting in the Irish rabble. I assumed *he* would want to be with his own kind.' Garrett's voice dripped with contempt. 'My agent was meticulous and ultimately discovered you all living in inferior circumstances in Boston. When he reported that a second child had been added to the family, and a son at that, I instructed him to determine the boy's parentage by any and all means. What if your mother had been with child before she fled London? If there was the remotest possibility that her son was mine, I would have taken possession of him without

230

compunction. My agent tailed your mother along the streets of Boston until he finally got close enough to discern that the boy with her was in fact fair-haired.' Garrett snorted. 'That's one thing I'll say for the stable hand—he certainly stamps his get.'

Emily sent up a quick prayer of thankfulness that Jack had so blatantly taken after their father in looks, leaving no question mark over his paternity. Even an ounce of uncertainty would have spelled disaster for their family – she couldn't begin to imagine the grief they would have suffered had her brother been abducted from them.

But in the end disaster had still come; it had only been delayed for a number of years until Emily had fallen into Garrett's trap.

'Why interfere again now?' she asked, looking up at him. 'Why me?'

'It wasn't just "now". This plan has been in motion for a long time and I have had to exercise great patience in waiting for it to come to fruition. My agent continued to monitor your family, at first purely for my own information but then with more specific intent when I identified a new purpose for his surveillance. An...event, shall we say, occurred in my own life that had the potential to accomplish a personal aspiration of mine, but an obstacle stood in the way. I deemed you to be the ideal candidate to nullify that obstacle so I gave my agent orders to concentrate his attentions upon you in particular and deduce how you might be persuaded to assist me. It helped immeasurably that you proved to be the vulnerable link in your tight-knit family's chain.'

'I'm not a vulnerable link!' she said, highly affronted.

He waved a lazy hand in her direction. 'Given your current situation, I would respectfully disagree.'

She drooped with shame.

'My agent observed the various facets of your existence in Boston and over a period of time was able to establish that you nurtured an earnest passion for art and an ambition to study it at Brubaker.'

'How could he possibly have learned that?' she demanded, bewildered and not a little frightened that a stranger had burrowed so deeply into her life without her knowledge.

'He generally only apprised me of his conclusions, not his methods,' said Garrett, 'but I gathered that he inveigled some of the pertinent details from one of your friends at Hawes School. She said you announced in front of the schoolmaster and your classmates that you intended to become a great artist and you were subsequently strapped for your insolence.'

Emily felt crushed by both the distressing memory and the school friend's betrayal. She could easily surmise who the friend had been for she had made only one throughout her time at Hawes. 'Emmeline told him that?' she said. 'Why would she reveal such things to a man she didn't know?'

Garrett angled his head. 'Who's to say she didn't know him? One of my agent's supreme talents is insinuating himself into the confidences of people who are privy to the information he needs, no matter how long it may take him to acquire it.'

'I never said anything to Emmeline about Brubaker though,' said Emily, perplexed.

'But you discussed it with your teacher, did you not?'

With wretched realisation, Emily said, 'Yes, with Miss Green—that is to say, Mrs Kendrick since she married. She was the one who suggested I apply to the academy in the first place.'

'And no doubt a proud teacher will enthuse about her favourite student to anyone who will listen.'

Emily pressed her fingertips to her cheek in dismay. 'I can't fathom how this man discovered so much about me and I've never even met him.'

'On the contrary,' said Garrett cheerfully, 'you have indeed met him. I received a letter from him mere days ago which reported your commencement of service at Marlowe House and in it he mentioned that he had accidentally bumped into you. However, he believed he had managed to evade your suspicion on that occasion.'

'What!' she exclaimed. 'I don't remember that. What does he look like?'

'Another of his fine attributes is possessing quite a forgettable face. Big lips are perhaps his only distinguishing characteristic. Although I suppose in America his English accent might stand out as well.'

She gasped. 'I do remember him! We walked into each other on Boston Common on my first day of service.' She gasped again, louder and more horrified than before. 'Oh, good gracious, and I've seen him since then too!'

'Have you indeed?' Garrett said with the polite curiosity of one enquiring about the weather. 'Under what circumstances?'

Given that she was already caught in his snare, she could see no reason not to divulge the details. It had been the night of the ball at Marlowe House and, following her wonderful encounter with Samuel Marlowe and the uncomfortably close call with the girl who owned the blue silk gown, she had returned to the servants' quarters by way of the servants' door on the upper floor. When she had darted through it, she had stumbled upon two figures flirting in the stairwell: her fellow housemaid Matilda and a liveried coachman who had purportedly conveyed some of the guests to the ball. It had seemed like a chance incident at the time, but Emily recollected his big lips...and afterwards Matilda had admired his English accent. Somehow in the course of his spying, he must have learned that Matilda was Emily's friend and had targeted her as a potential source of information. How far would he have been willing to go in the flirtation to obtain any useful knowledge? Thank goodness Emily had intruded upon them.

She hiccupped with shock as another revelation struck her. Before Matilda had sent her coachman back down to the kitchens, his gaze had seared into Emily on that stairwell and now she understood why. He hadn't perceived her as a guest who had become lost on her way to the commode – he had seen a girl whom he knew full well to be a servant dressed in a beautiful gown that she had no business wearing. Why would she have risked such a reckless exploit if she had not deeply desired to move in upper class circles? She had unwittingly laid her dreams, and her weaknesses, wide open to him for manipulation.

And Garrett's letter had arrived on the doorstep of Acorn House the very next day.

Garrett slapped his knee. 'I must say, I do admire him for immersing himself into the role with such commitment. He has more than earned his stipend for that day's work alone.' He chuckled with appreciation. 'I had given him leave to deliver my letter when he deemed it would be most effective. I heartily concur that the day after this ball was excellent timing. My, how you must have thought I had answered your prayers. You would have been forgiven for suspecting me of clairvoyance.'

Emily yearned to scream at her past self for her immense stupidity. She had fallen for his deception like the helpless mouse she was. Did a mouse have any power at all to resist its predator? 'What if I refuse to help you?'

He took another unconcerned sip of his coffee, though it must have grown cold by now. 'You are free to depart from this house whenever you wish,' he said. Her heart leapt and her feet would have too if he hadn't carried on, 'I assume you have enough funds to take you back to Boston?'

His clairvoyance appeared to extend to Auntie Tess's empty coin purse discarded upstairs in her mother's bedchamber. 'I don't,' she bit out.

'What a shame.' He adjusted the position of his coffee cup; its porcelain bottom scraped against the saucer. 'I'm afraid I cannot facilitate you in that regard if you are unwilling to assist me with my own request. So, for both our sakes, I do hope that a profusion of money is incentive enough for you to cooperate.'

She glared at him. 'If I do what you ask, you will allow me and Rory to leave?'

'Certainly.'

'How soon can I do it?'

'Soon. I shall need to make some arrangements first. Once the deed is accomplished, I will recompense you accordingly.'

'Then we have an agreement.' She stood up from the table. 'You lousy sod,' she threw at him and fled from the breakfast room. She hated the genuine laughter that followed on her heels.

Dashing angry tears from her cheeks, she located the nearest door that the servants used to enter and exit the family section of the house and hastened through it. Her mother had never taught her to shun the servants' quarters so she had explored those spaces as a child while trotting after Lizzie or sometimes Peter, and she could just about remember her way around them now. She scurried down the servants' stairs and rushed along the flagstone corridor to the kitchens.

The chef, Monsieur Lévêque, was making an almighty noise as he banged two pots together and barked instructions at an underling who cringed and hurried off to do his bidding. He turned at Emily's entrance and his bushy moustache quivered.

'Little Miss Emily!' he bellowed so stridently that she would have anticipated a scolding, save for the shining delight on his face. '*Je suis enchanté* to see you again.'

She halted and groped for her good manners. 'And I you, Monsieur Lévêque,' she said with a brief curtsey. 'Thank you for a delicious breakfast this morning.'

'That was nothing!' he hollered proudly as he dropped the pots onto a nearby bench with a pair of thuds. 'Wait until this evening's feast. It will be *magnifique*.'

'I look forward to it with eagerness,' she said, hoping her smile wouldn't fracture as she envisioned sharing another meal with the fiend upstairs who called himself a gentleman. 'Please, Monsieur, have you seen a young Irishman down here?'

'*Oui*, you mean Ror-ee. He is a good worker—he sliced *le jambon* for me with a fine steady hand. He is partaking of a second *petit-déjeuner* in the dining hall.'

With a swift murmur of thanks, she scuttled away to the adjoining hall where the servants took their meals and found Rory seated at one end of the long table; the room was otherwise empty since the servants were engaged in their morning chores. Rory was shovelling a forkful of ham into his mouth and nearly choked on it when Emily appeared. He swallowed hastily.

'I wasn't expecting to see you down here,' he said. Then he squinted at her. 'Have you been crying?'

She was almost overcome by an absurd urge to fling herself into his arms but she restrained herself. 'I—oh, R-Rory,' she stammered. 'I've been so foolish. I can't tell you how sorry I am.'

His expression hardened. 'I don't want to talk about my da.'

'It's n-not about him.' She covered her face with her hands. 'You were right,' she said, her words muffled. 'I ought to have listened to my parents. They were able to see through his lies.'

She heard Rory's sharp inhalation. 'You mean Garrett?'

'Yes,' she said wretchedly, gulping back a sob.

'Jesus.'

He said nothing else and she couldn't bear to drop her hands and perceive the condemnation in his eyes. After a long moment, however, she heard the scrape of wood on the flagstone floor and felt a touch at her elbow.

'Come on,' he said. 'Sit down.'

She allowed him to tow her over to the chair next to his and they sat on either side of the table's corner, their knees close beneath the table but not touching.

'Tell me all of it,' he said, and she did, from the English agent who had tracked her family's movements in Boston to the bargain she had been compelled to make with Garrett. She kept her voice low to avoid being overheard even though Monsieur Lévêque continued to roar away in the neighbouring kitchen.

When she had finished, Rory blew out his cheeks. 'Can you make any guess as to what he wants you to do for him?'

She shook her head in misery. 'He said he wasn't trying to force my mother into resuming her marriage with him.'

'What about you?' said Rory. 'Could he be planning to marry you off?'

She recalled dismissing that theory when Rory had made it back on the ship but didn't think she could be so blasé about it now. 'To what end though?' she wondered aloud. 'He's rich. He doesn't need to form a strategic alliance with another wealthy family.'

'Maybe his money's run out?'

'Maybe...' she said doubtfully. The affluent lifestyle she had witnessed and experienced in Wyndham House so far spoke to the contrary. 'I suppose I shall have to wait until it suits him to tell me. He said he had some "arrangements" to make, whatever they may be. We are at his mercy until then.'

Rory didn't reply to that, only glanced away and poked at the few fragments of ham remaining on his breakfast plate.

She grimaced. 'I meant to say, *I* am at his mercy. There is no obligation for you to stay, of course. He has only demanded assistance from me so perhaps he will agree to give you the money to travel back to America if we ask for it.'

Rory looked back at her. 'I'll stay.'

'But you have already done so much and it's my fault that you're caught up in this mess. You really don't need—'

'I'll stay.'

She didn't argue any further. Secretly, she was relieved. Lizzie might be her ally to a degree but Rory was the only person under this roof whom she could wholly trust.

'What will you do?' she asked, surreptitiously wiping away a grateful tear. 'I don't know what kind of demands Garrett will put on me to accomplish this mysterious task of his. If it's time-consuming or takes me away from the house, how will you occupy yourself?'

He prodded at the ham again. 'Work in the kitchens?'

'You can't do that,' she said, aghast. 'Monsieur Lévêque said you sliced ham for this morning's breakfast fare. Rory, you aren't a servant here!'

He frowned. 'I'm not a guest though either, am I? I don't belong above or below stairs. If I have to pick one, I'll choose below.'

She fell silent. At last, she said, 'I'm very sorry for putting you in this position.'

'No more of that,' he said firmly. 'You're sorry and I accept it. Now you've got to stop saying it.' Before she could apologise for apologising, he added, 'Maybe I'll walk around the city a bit. I've never been to London before.'

She brightened. 'You could go to Westminster Abbey. Mama and I visited it when I was younger. It's a beautiful building and many distinguished people are buried there.'

'There you go. That's something for me to do. We'll both be grand.' His knee knocked against hers under the table but she couldn't tell whether it had been a friendly nudge or a mere accident.

'We'll both be grand,' she repeated.

238

Would they? It all depended upon Garrett who very much had the upper hand. The snake had coiled itself tightly around its prey.

CHAPTER 23

The tenth day had slipped past and still nothing. Bridget and Orlaith returned to the brothel very late that night, dead on their feet after another long day of fruitless searching. As they entered the brothel, two generously bosomed girls passed by them in the hall; one of them whispered something to the other and both cast looks of pity towards Bridget and Orlaith before climbing the stairs to go about their own business.

Exhausted, they dragged themselves in the direction of Hester's private quarters at the back of the brothel. When they approached the sitting room, they found the door ajar. Two or three voices came floating through the gap, and one of them was male.

Orlaith's brow furrowed. 'That sounds like—'

She gasped and dashed for the door. Together, she and Bridget rushed headlong into the room to find two figures seated with Hester.

'Charlie!' Orlaith cried with passionate relief.

He stood up and she fell into his arms, clutching him around his neck like she would never let him go. Bridget's heart lifted with unfathomable gratitude until her gaze fell upon the other figure who had risen from her seat next to Hester.

Tess.

Before she could say anything, Charlie mumbled, 'I can't breathe, sweetheart.'

Orlaith reluctantly loosened her iron grip on her husband and, with an affectionate pluck of her chin, he turned to Bridget. A quiet sob escaped her as she, too, embraced him with all her might.

'Thank you,' she whispered. 'God bless you for coming.'

When she released him, Orlaith and Tess were sharing a hug as well. Bridget had no intention of doing the same. Why in God's name was Tess here? They needed a man, not another ineffective woman, and heaven knew there were already enough harlots under this roof.

'Are you here to gloat?' she said, her voice full of frost. 'Do you believe he will go running to you for consolation after he learns that I've lost his sons?'

Orlaith and Tess separated, enabling Bridget to read the genuine hurt in Tess's eyes.

'No,' she said quietly. 'I'm devastated and I'm here to help however I can. I love those two boys and can't stand the thought of anyone harming a single hair on their heads.'

Bridget accepted that she was speaking the truth. She also realised that she could place the blame for this calamity nowhere except upon herself and her own stupid pride. If she had not objected to Tess looking after Jack and Gus while she and Orlaith went to New York, then the boys would be safe in Boston right now.

'I'm sorry,' she muttered. 'That was unfair of me. I'm just so tired.'

'You were out very late,' Hester put in, looking discomfited by the tension that stretched between Bridget and Tess like a taut, invisible wire. 'Where did you go today?'

'North beyond Five Points,' said Orlaith. 'All along Canal Street. The folk there weren't quite as unfriendly as they are around here but they still had no information worth telling. Same dead end as everywhere else.'

'Our luck might be about to change,' said Hester with a gleam in her eye. 'We have Mr Adams now. He'll be able to ferret about in places we couldn't.'

'Please call me Charlie,' he said.

'Well, that's the first problem we'll have to fix,' she replied. 'There's no such thing as polite manners among the rats you're gonna be mixing with.'

His forehead creased with uneasiness, and guilt suffused Bridget; they were laying an enormous burden upon his shoulders.

'Has Hester told you everything?' she asked.

'I have,' Hester said before Charlie could respond. 'And I've already got suggestions for the places we should send him first. There are a couple of taverns near the Old Brewery, The Coney Stew and The Gorget, where we might have a decent chance of finding out what we need to know.'

Bridget winced. 'I tried to enter The Gorget before, but they threw me out.'

'They'll have no reason to throw out a man looking to drown himself in drink,' said Hester. 'That'll probably be the best approach—if he's three sheets to the wind, they won't pay him much attention or guard their tongues too closely.' She eyed Charlie. 'I hope you're a good actor. You'll need to convince them you're a drunkard while staying sober enough to glean some useful information.'

He squared his shoulders. 'I can do it. What about my accent though? Won't I be too conspicuous among the Irish?'

'There should be a mix of all sorts in the taverns, Irish and blacks and Americans too. Although to get in with the Kelly Greens, you'd better say your folks were Irish. Make sure you know the name of some tiny village in Ireland where they came from and be able to list off a few of your kin too. If you can invent a distant connection with someone else's third cousin without getting caught in the lie, then you're golden.'

'But what if he does get caught?' Orlaith said anxiously.

'I won't,' Charlie reassured her, even though he had never displayed any kind of discernible flair for artifice in the past – Bridget couldn't recall him telling so much as a harmless white lie. Even now, he seemed so guileless as he said earnestly, 'I'll do whatever it takes to infiltrate this gang and I'll be very careful how I go about it, I promise. If there's any knowledge to be gained about their diabolical activities, I'll get a hold of it.'

There were further hugs and sobs of gratitude in response to this valiant speech, following which Orlaith remained clinging to Charlie, peeking up at him with adoration.

'I missed you,' she murmured.

'Missed you too,' he said, his eyes fixed upon hers with equal devotion. 'I have plenty to tell you about Chicago.' He hesitated. 'But we have news from Boston too.'

Bridget drew in a sharp breath. 'The fever?' she said, full of dread.

'It's gone,' said Tess. 'And the Careys all recovered fine.' She lowered her gaze. 'But it took Mr Lorenzo, the poor fella.'

'Oh no, how awful,' moaned Bridget.

'May God rest his soul,' said Orlaith sadly.

As they mourned the loss of that dear old man, Hester poorly concealed her impatience, shifting her weight from one foot to the other and glancing towards the door.

'You know,' she said, 'it's late but the taverns will be hopping until dawn. There's still time to head out tonight.'

Orlaith glanced up fearfully at Charlie but his expression grew resolute. 'Then I'll go right now,' he said. 'Where will I find them?'

After Hester had described how to get there, he detached himself gently from Orlaith. She trembled as she let him step out of her embrace.

'Stay safe,' she begged him and then added desolately, 'They stole my wedding band. I'm so sorry.'

He bowed his head in what Bridget took to be an expression of regret until he lifted Orlaith's left hand and pressed a kiss to her bare ring finger. 'Don't give it another thought,' he said. 'We know what really matters.'

Then he marched out of the sitting room, his back straight and his step purposeful.

***

Cormac trudged along the Liverpool docks carrying his valise, torn between gladness and vexation. The *Blue Onyx* had arrived safely and the first thing he had done upon disembarking was to enquire from the nearest port official whether the *Integrity* had also reached its destination. Happily, he had determined that it had but, to his dismay, he had also learned that it had docked four days ago, meaning he had lost yet another day in his pursuit of Emily and Rory.

'Aye, the *Integrity*'s a good 'un,' the port official had said sagely when Cormac had expressed his frustration about this. 'She keeps up a good speed, even when she's hit by a storm.'

Although relieved that Emily had chosen a solid vessel upon which to flee across the ocean, Cormac was exasperated that it had been one with such a reputation for swiftness. A passage of four days since coming ashore meant that she and Rory must surely have got to London by now, and consequently his mission to make contact with them would be that much harder.

Then again, could there be any chance that they were still in Liverpool? What if they had become stranded here without enough funds to accomplish the final leg of their journey? How could he travel onwards himself before ascertaining whether they had done the same? A protracted search for them around the town would cost time and might be in vain if they had indeed already left, but he would have to make sure.

After thanking the port official, he had traipsed away along the docks and was now seeking a money changer's establishment to exchange his dollars for pounds. He found one further along the waterfront and went inside. As he waited for the man to deal with another customer ahead of him, it occurred to him that Emily and Rory would have needed to pay a visit here too, if they'd had any dollars left to exchange. Hence, when his turn came, he prefaced the transaction with a query.

'Did a tall young man with green eyes come in to do business with you in the past few days? He would have been Irish although he would have had American currency.' He assumed that Rory would be the one to handle such matters but, to be thorough, he added, 'A petite, fair-haired girl might have been with him.'

The money changer regarded him with narrow eyes – Cormac couldn't tell whether he was giving him a distrustful look or whether he had a permanent squint from peering at coins day in and day out. 'I remember the girl but not the young man.'

That surprised and worried Cormac. What if Emily and Rory had somehow become separated? It had provided him with a great deal of comfort these past weeks to know that Emily had not travelled alone, but now that consolation leaked away. 'Can you recall anything about your dealings with her?'

'She was a stunner,' the man said and Cormac bristled at his undisguised lechery. 'She didn't seem to even realise how pretty she was, which made her all the more appetising if I'm telling the truth. Very tasty on the tongue, I'd wager.' He uttered a guttural laugh.

'I'm her father,' said Cormac.

The man's laughter abruptly stopped. 'Right,' he croaked. 'Uh, what is it you want to know?'

'Every detail you can remember of your encounter with her. Leave nothing out.' Cormac gave him a hard stare, hoping it communicated eloquently just what he would do to the money changer's tongue if he had touched his daughter.

'It was all above board,' the man said hastily. 'She was my first customer that day—she'd been waiting outside before I'd even opened the shutters. She seemed to be in a hurry and kept saying she needed to return to the inn. I took her dollars and gave her pounds in return and she went on her way. That's all that happened, I swear!'

'Did she mention the name of the inn?' Cormac asked coolly.

'No. All I could tell was that she was anxious to get back there. She must've had a debt to pay because she counted her money very carefully before she left and I heard her mutter something about having enough for the innkeeper and the station master too.'

'Station master?' Cormac repeated, alert. 'As in the railway station?'

The money changer shrugged. 'Probably.' In a patent effort to get rid of Cormac, he said, 'The station's on Lime Street—might be worth checking out?'

Cormac didn't disagree and obtained the necessary directions forthwith.

'I'd also like to avail of your services before I go,' he said. He produced his money pouch and, after haggling to counter an extortionate exchange rate, he took his leave to the money changer's obvious relief.

Tugging his flat cap low over his eyes, he departed from the docks and made his way through the Liverpool streets in the direction of Lime Street. If he could confirm that Emily and Rory – please God he was still with her – had boarded a railway carriage and thus avoid trawling through every inn in town looking for any trace of them, that would be ideal. He tried to evade attention by matching his pace to the others around him and focusing his gaze in the middle distance so as not to make eye contact with anyone. However, the inevitable still happened.

'O'Malley!'

He halted and slowly turned – unsurprisingly, he spotted Ronnie Tucker a few yards behind him. Tucker broke into a jog to cover the gap between them.

'I thought that was you, mate,' he said. 'Fancy coming for a sup and a bite? Reckon we deserve to wet our throats properly after the water rations these past few weeks. I know a good place nearby.'

When he jerked his thumb towards an alley on the other side of the street, Cormac knew that he definitely had to head in the opposite direction.

'No, thanks,' he said civilly. 'I'm afraid I've got to be going.' Keeping a tight grip on his valise, he whirled around and strode away.

'Wait—'

Cormac sped up and entered an alley a little further along on the near side of the street, hoping he could cut through it and lose Tucker at the far end.

What he didn't expect was to find the group of English passengers he had wanted to elude waiting for him halfway down it. The man with the receding chin stood at the head of them, his mouth twisted into a smug sneer. Cormac came to a standstill.

'Sorry, mate,' came Tucker's voice from the mouth of the alley. 'I was trying to lead you away from them.'

He didn't dare take his gaze away from the men clustered in front of him, so he waited until he sensed Tucker's presence at his back before saying, 'Why would you do that?'

Tucker made a noise that sounded like the equivalent of a lethargic shrug. 'You seem like a decent enough sort. Maybe you don't deserve to be beaten up and robbed.'

'Don't go getting any high-and-mighty ideas, Tuck,' growled the leader of the group. 'You're as crooked as the rest of us.'

'I'm well aware, Shaw,' said Tucker wearily. 'No need to remind me of the mess we left behind in America.'

So it wasn't the lure of English roses that had impelled them back across the Atlantic. The knowledge brought clarity but not ease – if they were capable of perpetrating criminal activity to the extent that they had been obliged to flee the country where they had committed it, then that did not bode well for Cormac's chances here in this Liverpool alley, particularly when he was outnumbered and unarmed. He lamented once again the loss of his pocket knife which would have felt most reassuring in his palm right now.

The last time he had found himself ambushed in an alleyway, he had departed from it with a severely battered body and a pistol wound in his arm – Cunningham, Munroe and the other men had very nearly finished him off that night and his injuries had taken a significant time to heal. He would be of no use to his daughter if he allowed anything of the sort to happen again today.

He held out his valise. 'Take it,' he said to Shaw. 'I'm not going to fight you for it.'

Shaw regarded him with suspicion. Cormac tossed the valise to him and he caught it, astonished. After a split second of indecision, he shoved it into the hands of one of the men beside him and pointed at Cormac.

'I'm betting there's nothing worthwhile in it. Empty your pockets.'

Cormac clenched his jaw and pulled out his money pouch.

'I knew it,' said Shaw. 'Give it here.'

Cormac tightened his grip on the pouch and the coins within clinked together. Then he drew back his arm and lobbed the pouch as far as he could over the heads of the men. They swivelled as one to see where it landed and, while their backs were turned, he spun around towards the mouth of the alley. Tucker grinned and stepped back, letting him sprint for the street beyond.

He dashed down the street, dodging shocked pedestrians as he put distance between himself and the men. With any luck, by the time they checked the contents of the pouch and commenced their pursuit of him, they wouldn't know which way to go. He followed a haphazard course through the maze of streets until he eventually came upon a church. It wasn't a Catholic place of worship but he slipped inside and found a stairs to the upper gallery. Crouching inside a box pew, he prayed his hiding place would be good enough to escape detection from thug, clergyman or parishioner.

They had probably been tailing him since he had disembarked from the ship. He couldn't have prevented that but he hoped he had now done enough to throw them off his scent. He was prepared to linger here until nightfall if that's what it took.

He twitched his feet and felt the simultaneously uncomfortable and comforting dig of the money he had wedged inside his boots before leaving the *Blue Onyx*. He had known for days that a confrontation with those Englishmen would be unavoidable – when they hadn't accosted him aboard the ship, he had been prepared for it to happen on land instead. Consequently, he had consigned a small portion of his funds to be set aside for the anticipated theft and requested that the money changer substitute the meagre sum of American currency he had given him for the smallest denomination of English coins possible. The money pouch had contained only pennies and halfpennies which, until inspection, would pass for the shillings and pounds the crooks had no doubt counted upon finding.

While not a catastrophic loss, it had nevertheless depleted his hoard enough to leave him apprehensive. He still had a sufficient amount to pay for at least two ship tickets back to America, but not three. No matter – he would prioritise passage for Emily and Rory and worry about securing his own later. As for the valise, he resigned himself to the loss of both it and its contents which, to be fair, had not held great monetary or sentimental value in any case.

He heard movement below in the nave of the church and held his breath. Whispers drifted up to him but he couldn't hear what they were saying. After several tense minutes, the low voices faded away again and he relaxed. Perhaps they had merely been members of the congregation seeking a quiet moment with God. Fortunately, it wasn't a Sunday so he didn't have to fear an influx of worshippers for a formal service.

Given the likelihood of other pious individuals coming along, however, he decided that his best course of action would definitely be to wait and leave the church later under cover of darkness or even at first light the next morning if the doors were locked overnight. It would be a challenge to contend with the resulting thirst and hunger but he could cope with it – after all, he had survived both for longer in the past.

Once he emerged from his refuge and made certain that he was not being followed, he would return to the money changer to exchange the remainder of his dollars currently secreted in his boots. Then he would go to Lime Street and find out if Emily and Rory had indeed purchased tickets at the railway station there. Thank goodness Emily's features were striking enough that she was memorable even to strangers. It ought to be a straightforward matter to determine whether she and Rory had left Liverpool on a locomotive bound for London.

If they had, he would follow. And, God willing, he would find them safe and sound.

CHAPTER 24

Garrett had made his secretive arrangements with alacrity. Only three days had passed since Emily and Rory had arrived at Berkeley Square and yet here she stood in the entrance hall of Wyndham House, full of trepidation as she prepared to leave for some unknown destination. She wore one of her mother's pretty bonnets and a reasonably warm shawl (the English weather being nowhere near as pleasant as the conditions she had left behind in Boston), but Lizzie had not been instructed to furnish her with a packed valise so that meant Garrett's task must lie within the bounds of London. She would surely return to the house by that night and it gave her solace that she would have the opportunity to confide in Rory before the day was through.

He was nowhere to be seen at present but she did not expect him to appear – he still hadn't made Garrett's acquaintance and had expressed no desire to do so unless, he said, Emily saw a need for it. She didn't want to place him in an uncomfortable position so she had not pressured him to change his mind, even though she did feel that having him at her side at the breakfast table or in the drawing room would have been akin to facing Garrett from the battlements of a castle rather than meekly lowering the drawbridge for him. Nonetheless, given that Rory shunned the family section of the house and Garrett never strayed into the servants' quarters, it was feasible that the two might never meet.

'Are you ready, my daughter?' Garrett's voice preceded him as he came into the entrance hall. He was accompanied by his valet, Brewer, who carried his gloves and hat.

Emily flinched at the address. 'I am.'

'Then let us be on our way,' he said with an air of eager anticipation, accepting his gloves and hat from Brewer and putting them on.

Peter opened the front door for them and Emily stepped outside first. She was surprised to discover that the carriage was not waiting below in the street – were they close enough to walk to their destination?

Garrett joined her on the top step and, when the door shut behind them, he offered her his arm. 'Shall we, my daughter?'

She sensed that he was gaining an enormous amount of enjoyment from her reaction every time he called her that. She took his arm without a word and they descended the flight of steps to the footpath. To her puzzlement, he led her straight across the street to the private gardens in the centre of Berkeley Square. Producing a key, he opened the gate and they went through it, leaving it unlocked behind them.

The weather was dry and the leaves of the plane trees rustled in a cool summer breeze. Emily and Garrett strolled along the path beneath them without comment. They completed a full circuit of the gardens before she lost her patience and said, 'Sir? What exactly are we doing here?'

'You'll see,' he replied, refusing to say any more than that.

They had made their way around the gardens one and a half more times before a male figure walked through the distant gate and glanced about. Garrett at once steered Emily in the newcomer's direction. As they approached, she could see that the stranger was well dressed but young, his rangy body not yet filled out to full manhood. He caught sight of her and Garrett and sauntered forwards, his demeanour relaxed. When he reached them, he spoke first.

'So she exists,' he said with faint amusement.

'I told you she did,' Garrett answered in a remarkably similar tone.

Emily stared at the boy – she could hardly call him a man, could she? He scarcely looked a year or two older than herself and, much as she regretted to admit it, her recent actions had been those of a silly girl, not a sensible woman. She studied his features; he was strikingly handsome with black hair and hazel eyes and he carried himself with an easy confidence. Why did he look so familiar? She had never met him before, had she?

Eerily reading her mind, Garrett said, 'The two of you are already acquainted but you might not remember the meeting. You were only six and seven years old when it occurred. For the sake of thoroughness, allow me to reintroduce you. Miss Emily Lambourne, this is your cousin and half brother, Master Patrick Lambourne.'

Before she could even begin to absorb the implications of this announcement, the boy rolled his eyes and stuck out his hand. 'Edward Whitmore,' he said with the long-suffering air of one who has made the correction many times before.

'Emily McGovern,' she declared and, disengaging her arm from Garrett's, she shook the boy's hand firmly.

Garrett grunted at the exchange but didn't gainsay either of them. 'What a joyful occasion,' he said sardonically. 'Two siblings reunited after so long apart.'

Emily frowned at him. 'Why do you say that? He's not my brother.'

'On the contrary,' said Garrett. 'He is my natural son, and legally you are my daughter. My blood might not make you brother and sister but the law does. Furthermore, you share a genuine kinship as cousins through the connection between his mother and your father.'

Emily goggled at him. 'Who is his mother?'

'Your aunt Mary.'

That left her speechless. She had been vaguely aware of the existence of other aunts on her father's side of the family but she knew they had died many years ago and that it pained him to talk about them. There had been an Auntie Margaret and, yes, an Auntie Mary too. Was this boy truly a son of hers...and Garrett's? How could that be possible?

'I see she has been erased from your family history,' said Garrett tersely. 'Permit me to reinstate her where she belongs.'

He clasped his hands behind his back and faced Emily straight on. Edward – for she would think of him the way he wished and not by how Garrett had addressed him – observed them with an attitude of indifference, as though none of this was a surprise nor even of mild interest to him.

'Few people appreciated Mary for the astonishing woman she was during her all-too-brief life,' Garrett continued in a much softer voice. 'I met her on my father's property in Ireland by providential chance and felt like I had only taken my very first breath at the age of three-and-twenty. Though a union between a gentleman and a peasant girl ought never to have existed, we entertained the possibility because both of us were young and naive and smitten.'

His face seemed to shine with an extra intensity and Emily's heart pounded to witness it. She knew she must not trust him and yet she could not be unmoved by such an ardent disclosure. Much as she didn't want to admit it, it reminded her strongly of her own parents' devotion to each other.

'We wed in secret in Dublin with the intention of revealing the marriage to our families afterwards, at which point any

255

objections from mine would come too late. However, whereas I remained intoxicated by my passionate feelings, she, alas, regained her senses. She became convinced that my family would never accept her and that it would be best for me if we parted. So she ran away, leaving me with no hint as to where she had gone.'

He swallowed. Emily eyed him warily. Was that real remorse in his countenance or merely a fine display of acting?

'Some time later, I discovered her whereabouts on the Oakleigh Estate but she—' His words caught in his throat and he drew in a shaky breath. 'She took her own life before I could make contact with her. I never knew that she had carried my son and given birth to him before she died. I believed myself to be a childless widower and that I must now do my duty and marry a lady from my own class to satisfy my family's wishes. I married your mother and, needless to say, you know what happened after that.'

His mouth twisted with resentment. Emily cast a quick look at Edward – she was learning about his origins but how much knowledge did he have of her own? He returned her gaze with a raised eyebrow and a knowing smirk. An ample portion of it, then.

Garrett ignored this silent communication. 'Do you remember the Earl of Bewley?' he asked Emily and, startled, she nodded, for she could dimly recall the jovial gentleman and his plump wife who had been so kind to her. 'He pursued your miscreant parents when they fled to Ireland, wanting retribution for your father's impersonation of his nephew, Oliver Davenport. Upon his return to England, Lord Bewley informed me of the events that had taken place, including the fact that your father had alluded to a nephew of his living with an upper class family on St Stephen's Green in Dublin. Perhaps it was wishful thinking on my part to believe that a fragment of Mary had lived on. Still, I had to find out for certain.'

Just then, an elderly couple entered the gardens and came ambling along the path towards Emily, Garrett and Edward. When they neared, the gentleman offered a civil greeting of 'Wyndham' to Garrett while the lady batted her eyelashes at him in quite a coquettish manner for her advanced years. Bowing, Garrett returned charming salutations to them both and Emily curtseyed as they passed but Edward scarcely inclined his head, apparently unstirred to behave with proper courtesy. He caught Emily staring at him and his lip curled in an uncannily familiar expression.

'Something to say?' he enquired lazily once the elderly couple were out of earshot.

'No,' she said quietly.

Garrett chuckled. 'Patrick has little appreciation for social niceties. Too intent on indulging in life's pleasures, isn't that right?'

'It's Edward,' was the boy's only response to this.

A muscle twitched in Garrett's jaw. 'Would you care to take a stroll around the gardens while I finish acquainting your sister with the particulars? You are, after all, already cognisant of them yourself.'

'You've told me the yarn enough times before,' Edward muttered, 'but I'll hang around anyway. I want to see her reaction.'

Garrett didn't object and Emily got the impression that it pleased him to command Edward's attention. But what could be his actual objective here? She was at a total loss to understand what was going on and couldn't even begin to fathom how to parse the lies from the truth.

Glancing over his shoulder to make sure that the elderly couple had definitely meandered on, Garrett resumed his tale.

'As you can imagine, it was no small challenge to discover the whereabouts of this nephew Lord Bewley had mentioned. All I had to go on was the name of a square in Dublin and an estimation of the boy's age based on how old he must be if he was genuinely a product of my marriage with Mary. However, you are already aware that I have both the means and the patience to authorise such a thorough, lengthy search.'

The gleeful glint in his eye made Emily shiver and she tightened her shawl around herself.

'After much painstaking investigation, my agent—a different one to the fellow you met, naturally—detected the presence of a boy living in the residence of Anner House on St Stephen's Green who matched the child I sought. I travelled to Ireland to see for myself and observed the boy from a distance when he left the house in the company of Lady Anner. Good Lord, how my heart soared to look upon him. I knew unquestionably that he was mine for who could view us side by side and doubt it?'

Emily appraised their identical pairs of hazel eyes, their equally thick and silky hair beneath their hats (albeit one head black and the other silver), even the similar nonchalance in their postures, and could not deny it. Admittedly, there was something different around the boy's mouth but perhaps that had come from his mother.

Her aunt. Her dear father's long-dead sister. Could this actually be true?

A shadow of regret fell across Garrett's features. 'He was ten years old by that stage and I grieved to have missed out on a whole decade of his life. I was determined to do all I could not to miss any more of it. But my agent had learned that Patrick had been raised under a fabricated identity without a whisper of his humble beginnings. It would not be an easy feat to convince him of the truth of his past, especially when it was tainted by a lower class connection. Though it agonised me to bide my time,

I returned to London and merely kept eyes upon him in Dublin while he remained there cosseted by his adoptive mother.'

Emily expected Edward to get riled up at that, either in indignation on his own behalf or in defence of Lady Anner, but he maintained his languid disposition. Gracious, did he bestir himself for anything apart from insisting that he be addressed by his correct name?

'My patience was eventually rewarded,' said Garrett, 'because my agent discovered that Patrick was due to come to England at the age of thirteen for his formal education at Eton College. At last, he would be removed from Lady Anner's suffocating influence and, I hoped, in a position to broaden his mind. As an Old Etonian myself, I easily gained access to the school by joining its ranks of affluent benefactors. The headmaster welcomed my generous contribution and sanctioned my request for a private meeting with one of the pupils without question.' Garrett lifted a pointed finger as though he were delivering a lecture and had arrived at the crux of his hypothesis. 'And here was the greatest challenge thus far. How could I make my son receptive to the revelations I intended to impart, several of which would be unpalatable to one raised in the bosom of nobility? I led with what I could count on as being the best temptation for a young man of the upper classes: my title and my wealth. I introduced myself as a viscount with a vast estate and emphasised just how fortunate my heir would be to inherit it all. When I saw his eyes light up with envy, I knew I had a chance. Then I revealed that he was that heir.'

Despite herself, Emily was intrigued. She would have dearly liked to witness that encounter. 'And how was that news received?'

Garrett let out a humourless laugh. 'With derision and mistrust. But I persisted. I visited Eton College on numerous further occasions, bestowing donations and seeking an

259

audience with my son each time. I repeated the facts of his parentage over and over, insisting that he listen to me and accept the reality.'

Emily cocked her head at Edward. 'Did you think he was a madman? Or a liar?'

'Both,' Edward said dispassionately. 'But if truth be told, it wasn't the first time an alternative account of my family history had been presented to me. I'm old enough to remember the day that a man—your father, I suppose?—came to the front steps of Anner House and professed to be my uncle. His story and Lord Wyndham's corresponded to a certain degree so I began to harbour doubts. When I went home to Dublin at the end of that school term, I asked Lady Anner about both men's claims.' He rolled his eyes. 'Her outraged denial was enough to verify it.'

'But yet you still haven't accepted it?' she said cautiously.

He emitted a scornful snort. 'Of course not. Why would I wish to acknowledge the existence of a dead peasant mother? If her connection to me were made widely known, it would only diminish my status in society. I see no advantage to that, not when I am currently regarded as the respected nephew of the Lord and Lady Anner who took me into their home when my father's health was ailing. My father, George Whitmore,' he added with emphasis. 'As he is now deceased, I am next in line to inherit the Anner title.'

Garrett nodded indulgently. 'Such a pity that the barony of Anner is of lower standing in the peerage than the viscountcy of Wyndham, and comes with less wealth. I am tremendously well-heeled, you know.'

Edward's handsome hazel eyes narrowed with greed and resentment. 'An unblemished pedigree is more important.'

'Is it?' said Garrett. 'Dear me, I would have thought an immense fortune would hold greater sway. You could lead a dissolute lifestyle for all your days and never run out of funds.'

He clicked his tongue in mock disappointment before adding rather wistfully, 'Of course, I would much rather you accepted my claim from a heartfelt desire to acknowledge me as your true father. Nevertheless, I am prepared to use material enticements to achieve my ambitions if I must.'

Emily stared from the unrelenting man to the obdurate boy and wondered how she had ended up caught between them.

'Why am I here?' she asked, mystified.

Garrett bared his teeth, reminding her that the wistful father was still a snake underneath. 'That is quite the excellent question, my daughter.' He turned to Edward. 'Well, Patrick? Can you offer any speculation?'

The boy just shrugged, seemingly unwilling to respond verbally to the name.

'Come now,' said Garrett, his tone light. 'I warned you that this moment would arrive sooner or later. You doubted her existence but here she is. And now a decision is upon you, Patrick.'

Edward crossed his arms, still mulishly refusing to speak.

'A decision?' said Emily.

Garrett sent a look of exasperation towards Edward before returning his attention to Emily. 'I am tired of waiting,' he said. 'My son is sixteen years old and has known for three years that I am his father, yet still he declines to admit it publicly. I want him to live under my roof, I wish to fund his education, I yearn to announce to the world that this fine young man is my progeny. Yes, we can expect an adverse reaction from society because of his mother's lower class background but I am past the age where that is of any great consequence to me.' He gesticulated like he was brushing society's critical opinions under a rug. 'However, Patrick will not permit any of this. He sees no reason to act because he believes that he will inherit my title and wealth upon my death without needing to make the slightest effort to earn them while I live. But I take a dim view of this cavalier attitude. So I am going to force his hand.' Garrett paused. 'Unless he agrees to openly acknowledge his filial relationship to me, I will settle my entire estate irrevocably upon my only other legitimate child. You.'

Emily gazed at him with utter incredulity. This had to be another deception.

Edward sniggered. 'I don't think she believes you, sir.'

'Do *you* believe him?' she demanded.

'I didn't up to now.' His lips twisted. 'Not until you actually showed up.'

Rage simmered within her. Had Garrett really dragged her all the way across that awful ocean just to have her stand in front of this boy and prove that she was not fictitious? In her anger, she forgot that her return to Boston was contingent upon successfully assisting Garrett in his no-longer-mysterious task.

'Don't trust a word he says,' she asserted. 'He has already informed me that he does not intend to leave me his inheritance or even arrange my coming out in society. This is an empty threat.'

'On that I must contradict you,' Garrett said smoothly. 'I told you I had no desire to grant you those boons but that does not mean I shall not bestow them if I am left with no other recourse. Should Patrick choose not to recognise me as his father, then I vow to take his birthright away out of spite. I do not covet a shadow of a son waiting in the wings for my exit. I shall have the entire paternal experience with him or nothing at all.'

Edward's apathy had at last been eclipsed by actual emotion – a dull red flushed his features and the corners of his mouth turned down as though he were a petulant child whose favourite toy had been snatched away from him. Emily half expected him to stamp his foot and whine, 'But I don't *want* you to take away my birthright!'

262

To avert any such embarrassing spectacle, she said to Garrett, 'May Edward and I speak in private for a moment?'

'For what purpose?' he asked, more with curiosity than suspicion.

'So that we can complain about you freely,' she replied in a matter-of-fact voice.

He laughed, bowed and sauntered away along the path. She turned back to Edward and scrutinised his sullen face.

'We are in a bind,' she said. 'Much as I should like to thwart his wishes, he has me completely in his power. The only thing I want is to leave London with my friend and go back to Boston but we don't have the means to do so. We are reliant upon Garrett to pay for our passage and he won't provide the necessary money unless or until he achieves his goal with you. I may have to accept what he's offering with no other alternative to escape his influence.'

'It's a nuisance,' Edward grumbled. 'If only I had the funds, I'd help you escape myself. Unfortunately, my allowance has been cut off—my adoptive parents deemed me too wasteful with it.'

'What a disappointment,' she said, vexed. 'It would have been a marvellous solution to this dreadful predicament.'

His brows knitted together. 'Why do you speak as though it would be a burden to receive Lord Wyndham's bounty? He's talking about bequeathing everything he possesses to you.'

She grimaced. 'I don't crave that kind of wealth. Not in this manner and certainly not from him, now that I perceive the kind of man he really is. He is a snake.'

Some of Edward's sulkiness dissipated as he grinned. 'His underhandedness bothers you? I quite admire it about him. I think he deserves a measure of approbation for constructing this scheme so neatly, don't you?'

She pursed her lips. 'I do not. Have you any inclination to consent to his proposal?'

He shrugged and looked away.

'Or do you wish to remain loyal to Lord and Lady Anner on account of their past benevolence to you?'

He peered down at his boots and remained mute.

'Why did you come here today?' she asked, struggling to make sense of this boy.

'Boredom.'

She regarded him with a degree of dislike but not a little sympathy as well. 'How do you feel about what he has told you? About your lower class background and your real mother?' She, too, had been the recipient of such a revelation but her father still lived and she had adored him ever before she knew the truth. Edward's experience was not the same.

His eyes rose to hers. Jaw set, he said, 'What's America like? I have it in mind to visit there someday.'

She bore the rebuff without protest; no doubt his feelings were difficult to process and she was, after all, a stranger to him despite the blood they shared. 'It's...fine. The weather's hotter there than here in the summer. Um...' She cast about, trying to imagine what aspects of the country might interest him. 'The railway system isn't as advanced as it is in England.'

His attention shifted past her shoulder. 'He's coming back.'

She didn't glance around but listened to the jaunty beat of Garrett's approaching footsteps with a ripple of loathing. He joined them wearing a broad smile.

'Well, my darling daughter? Have you managed to convince him to welcome me with open arms?'

'Alas, she has not,' Edward said with mock sorrow. 'I'll need some time to think upon your ultimatum so you won't have an answer from me today. I bid you both good day.'

With that abrupt farewell, he spun on his heel and walked away. Garrett's longing gaze lingered on the boy until he had disappeared through the gate.

'What did you think of him?' he asked, returning his scrutiny to Emily.

She hesitated. 'He...looks very like you.'

This seemed to please him. 'I think so too. There really can be no uncertainty about his parentage.'

She chewed on her lower lip. 'Did you truly marry my Auntie Mary?'

'I did,' he replied, his tone clipped. 'At the time, we told no one but the minister and the two witnesses who attended the ceremony. They were the baker for whom Mary had worked in Dublin and his wife. Sadly, no written record of the union survives—when I contacted the minister after discovering Patrick's existence, he informed me that several of the church registers had been lost in a fire.'

That was remarkably convenient, Emily thought.

'However,' Garrett continued, 'all three of them have signed declarations swearing that the wedding took place.'

'You've gone to some lengths to prove the validity of your first marriage,' she said.

'Of course I have. It was vital to ensure Patrick's legitimacy before I could present him to society as my son and heir.'

She nodded wryly. If there had been no legal union, then the boy was a bastard and not entitled to an iota of Garrett's estate.

'I see,' she said. 'And you believe you will realise that ambition? And that an ultimatum is the best way to achieve your son's affection and allegiance?'

He scowled. 'I perceive no other way.'

All of a sudden, Emily felt very sad for the man standing in front of her. He didn't know how to attain anything in his life other than by employing some form of threat or deceit or

265

bribery. Furthermore, he had spent a vast portion of the past number of years tracking the movements of the woman who had deserted him and the boy who refused to acknowledge him, and not really living himself.

'Are you very lonely?' she asked. 'Did you try to seek another wife after Mama and I left? You could have divorced her and created a new family.'

'Females are a scourge,' he muttered. 'Why would I invite further grief upon me? No woman could ever compare to Mary. No child could ever compare to her child.' He swallowed, perhaps aware of how tender he sounded and how vulnerable that made him. He straightened his shoulders. 'A wife's chief duty is to provide a son and I already have one of those. That is all I desire: a worthy heir for my estate when I die.'

She wrinkled her nose. 'In that case, you cannot mean to follow through on your vow to name me as your heir, should Edward choose not to assume that honour. You surely do not deem me worthy, even if I am the daughter of a baroness.' She sucked in a breath. 'Oakleigh! What will happen to my entitlement to it if Edward does indeed become your heir?'

One corner of his mouth lifted in a smirk. 'Your mother is still my lawful wife which means that both she and her estate are my property. Oakleigh is mine to do with as I wish—I have every right to bequeath it to Patrick along with everything else I possess. Of course, the Courcey title itself would have to remain within your mother's legitimate bloodline but you would be penniless without the land and wealth attached to it.' He angled his head to the side, giving her an assessing look. 'Having said that, I also have the power to specify you in my will as the beneficiary of all of Oakleigh's assets. Perhaps you would consider that to be an extra incentive in serving as my ally in the matter of Patrick's acceptance of my proposal?'

Emily crossed her arms, tucking the folds of her shawl into her elbows. 'What guarantee would I have that you would not renege on that promise as soon as you got what you wanted? Why would you bother to keep your word?'

He barked a laugh. 'Because I could not care less about that Irish scrap of earth. It has been somewhat revived after Lady Courcey's ill-management of it but, apart from its income, it means nothing to me. On the other hand, I know that it bears a great deal of sentimental value for your mother. By controlling its fate, I retain a hold over her—and, by association, you. Nevertheless, I am prepared to place that card on the table and lose the hand in order to win the game.'

Emily wavered as she imagined returning to Boston and telling her mother that she had rescued Oakleigh from Garrett's clutches – would it help to soften the pain she had caused her parents? But how could she rely upon any pledge that came from Garrett's deceitful mouth?

His expression turned rueful. 'I am conscious of the fact that you deem me an untrustworthy creature,' he said, 'and you are justified in your opinion, I'll grant you that. Still, I have already demonstrated that I do not intend any harm to the Oakleigh Estate. I could have wreaked havoc had I overturned the forged signature that your charlatan of a father made at Webb & Brereton Solicitors, but I let the matter be. Once I learned about the existence of my son, Patrick became the only focus in my life. He is all that is important to me now.'

He spoke with the same earnestness as his pestilential letter. Where did his honesty end and his falsehoods begin? She couldn't let herself be duped as she had before, and yet she would have to at least pretend to cooperate for now.

'I can try to speak to Edward again if you'd like,' she said. 'But what extraordinary powers of persuasion do you think I have? He appears to have full dominion over his own mind.'

'You don't give yourself enough credit,' Garrett said, wagging his finger at her. 'If you want to go home desperately enough, I'm confident you'll find a way to encourage him in the right direction.'

She abhorred the fact that he had given her multiple reasons to exert herself in his favour. And all to what end? 'Why are you striving so hard to win him over when he continually resists your efforts?'

Garrett sighed and stared off across the gardens. 'Whenever he smiles or frowns, he looks just like her.'

CHAPTER 25

A new routine had been established at Hester Temple's brothel. Charlie left each night as soon as darkness fell and Bridget, Orlaith, Tess and Hester remained wakeful until the dawn waiting for his return, the hours endless and torturous as they prayed for good fortune.

The third night brought progress at last, but at a cost. Charlie stumbled into Hester's sitting room just before daybreak, weariness outlining every contour of his body and a haunted look in his eyes. A powerful stench of drink rolled off him and yet he seemed stone-cold sober. He sank into the chair Tess offered him and dropped his head into his hands. They all stood staring at him.

'Charlie?' Bridget said tentatively.

'Just...give me a minute,' he mumbled to his knees.

Orlaith knelt by his legs and leaned against them, gazing at her husband's bowed head with concern. Slowly, he lifted it and offered her a grimace that no one in the room could interpret as a smile.

'I'm fine,' he said.

'You're not,' she replied.

He sighed. 'I'm not.' He glanced around at them all. 'I have news and I do think it's promising. But it won't be easy to hear.'

Bridget felt like her insides had been doused with ice water. 'Tell us.'

'I went to The Gorget again,' he said. 'Lord, it's a rough crowd in there. When I think back to the day of the riot on Broad Street, those vandals ran wild but that's because their bloodlust was up. The brutes in that tavern...they're wicked every minute of every day just because it's in their nature.' He looked queasy and gulped a mouthful of air.

'You witnessed some nastiness behind those doors tonight?' said Hester.

He shifted his gaze to the floor. 'More than witnessed.'

When he didn't elaborate, the worry deepened on Orlaith's countenance. 'What happened?'

He flinched. 'Please don't ask me to tell you. I did what was needed to gain their trust. Will you simply believe me when I say that I hate myself for what I did but that it was worth it for the information I gained?'

She squeezed his knee. 'I believe you,' she said, her voice barely louder than a whisper.

Bridget perceived the gratitude and guilt in his face and experienced similar emotions within her own breast. How she appreciated Charlie's selflessness and how she mourned the loss of his innocence. He might be a married man in his mid-twenties but he had always been a wholesome soul, and his good-heartedness had borne an endearing, childlike sort of quality. Evidently, an incident had occurred tonight that had sullied him in some irrevocable way. By the misery in his demeanour, he had suffered a wound deeper and far more consequential than his maimed ear.

'You will receive no condemnation from anyone in this room, Charlie,' she said earnestly. 'You are a champion in our eyes.'

Even Tess sounded sincere as she said, 'You can just tell us what you found out. You don't have to say how you came by the information.'

His troubled expression diminished just a fraction. 'All right then. First of all,' he said, turning his attention to Hester, 'I reckon your hunch is right about the Kelly Greens. Their reputation for snatching children seems undisputed, so if Jack and Gus are anywhere, they're almost definitely wherever the Kelly Greens are.'

Bridget's stomach churned at his use of the word 'if' but she couldn't reproach him for it. Too much time had passed since this nightmare had begun on the Fourth of July – at this stage, there could be no guarantee that her sons still lived.

Swallowing the bile that seared the back of her throat, she croaked, 'Were you able to determine why they kidnap children? What is their motive for such heinous villainy?'

'Greed,' Charlie said, sounding sickened. 'The Kelly Greens are known for thieving children—boys, mainly—except they actually thieve plenty more than that but make the lads do the rest of it for them. Once they identify a target, they sit back and let the poor creatures carry out all the dirty work. And they abandon them to suffer the consequences if they get caught.'

'That's monstrous!' Orlaith exclaimed.

'What kind of targets?' Hester asked, her gaze intent upon Charlie.

'Wealthy homes,' he answered. 'I'm disgusted to admit this but their scheme is fiendishly clever. On the surface of it, the men in the gang act as chimney sweeps. They enter a house to clean its chimneys and bring a climbing boy with them. While they're working, both man and boy surreptitiously scout around for any valuables worth stealing. If they spot something with potential, the boy is tasked with either pilfering it right away or contriving the means to sneak back in at a later stage—maybe pocketing a key or leaving the latch open on an inconspicuous window that a small form could squeeze through.'

As Bridget tried to absorb the horror of this awful news, Hester's mind had jumped straight to the practicalities of it. 'How can they get away with it though? If valuables go missing from a home right after a chimney sweep's been in it, wouldn't the owners know who to blame and take steps to hunt them down?'

'They go into hiding so they can't be traced,' said Charlie. 'We already know how good they are at that. What's more, no man works the same house twice to avoid being recognised and connected to a previous theft. They rotate, each claiming they'll be more trustworthy than any that came before.'

Orlaith let out a gasp. 'Chimney sweeps!' she exclaimed. 'Soot! We found a streak of it on the ground where the boys were taken. God Almighty, this makes sense.'

Did it? None of it made sense to Bridget. How could such evil exist in the world, where callous men exploited small boys like they were disposable chattel? How could God allow this?

It tore at her heart to picture Jack and Gus being coerced into such criminal endeavours. Even worse was imagining those thugs forcing her precious sons to climb chimneys, an occupation notorious for its terrible dangers. She could not prevent herself from envisioning their dreadful plight: soot becoming wedged in their lungs and throats and eyes, their elbows and knees bent into unnatural positions, the chimney sweep lighting a fire in the grate below to compel them to climb faster. Most horrendous of all was the risk of getting stuck in the narrow flues – she had heard tell of climbing boys losing their lives that way.

She must have made some sort of despairing sound for everyone's heads turned in her direction and Orlaith leapt up to grasp her hands.

'We can take courage from this,' she said fiercely. 'We know now that those men had a purpose in kidnapping the boys. Wicked though that purpose was, it means they had a reason to keep them alive. They're still alive—we *must* believe it.'

Bridget nodded numbly.

'And I have more to tell,' said Charlie, the haunted look in his eyes giving way to something resembling optimism. 'I pieced together a couple of indiscreet remarks from two different men during...the course of the night. One mentioned having to guard the boys in a stinking warehouse and the other hinted at a personal grievance with a butcher from a neighbouring slaughterhouse. Between the pair of them, I think we might be able to figure out where the Kelly Greens keep themselves and their captives holed up.'

Orlaith's expression lifted. ''Specially if we combine those details with any signs of soot!'

An ember of hope flickered to life inside Bridget, melting away some of the numbness.

'There you go,' said Tess in a cheery voice. 'We're another step closer to getting Jack and Gus back.'

'And Willie too,' Hester added with a warning tone that dared them to forget that they also had a third boy to find. Like a dog with a bone, she still refused to view the Kelly Greens and Bronagh as separate entities and continued to assume that some kind of connection existed between them.

'Jack, Gus and Willie are all in our thoughts,' Orlaith reassured her without denying or endorsing the possibility of Bronagh's involvement. 'Now, let's make a plan to go search for this warehouse.'

Though Bridget would have preferred to set out immediately, the others agreed that they should all take time to rest after the long, sleepless night they had just endured. Charlie, in particular, was so exhausted that he only needed to sit back in his chair before he dropped off at once. Bridget gazed down at his slack face and was glad to see some of the grimness fading out of it as he slumbered. She hoped the wholesome soul within could come to the fore again without having suffered too much damage.

After a few hours' sleep – or, in Bridget's case, a poor approximation of it that consisted of a nightmare in which she stumbled upon the burnt and disfigured bodies of her children – they decided on what to do next. They would divide into two groups and begin combing the Five Points district for a location that matched the clues Charlie had uncovered. Searching the area in daylight brought a modicum of safety but neither group was to act upon their findings until they all returned to the brothel that evening. Given Bridget and Orlaith's intimate acquaintance with Five Points and Charlie and Tess's relative lack of familiarity, it made sense to distribute their expertise accordingly and, with little discussion, Orlaith paired up with Tess and Bridget with Charlie. Hester then added herself to Orlaith and Tess's group to bolster their numbers in the absence of a male asset.

'May God bless us with good luck,' Orlaith said bracingly as they parted at the front door of the brothel. She, Tess and Hester went in one direction while Bridget and Charlie headed the opposite way. The day was muggy and overcast but Bridget fervently hoped that it would not rain – now that they had learned about the link to chimney sweeps, she would be looking everywhere for sooty footprints.

'I have a suggestion for where we ought to start,' she told Charlie as they walked briskly. 'There is a cluster of slaughterhouses at the southern edge of Five Points. It's possible that the warehouse we seek is nestled inconspicuously among them.'

'You know this place better than I do,' he said. 'By all means, lead the way.'

She strode onwards with a greater sense of purpose than she'd had for days. Her skin itched with a deep yearning to finally make tangible progress. To her dismay, however, their initial search yielded nothing of note – the slaughterhouses hunched side by side with shabby tenements and other rundown premises but no structure large enough that it could be deemed a warehouse. Disappointed, she and Charlie proceeded from street to street with less certainty, keeping a vigilant eye on the buildings that lined both sides and peering down the alleyways in between them.

Her hopefulness had long since ebbed and she was beginning to pray that Orlaith, Tess and Hester had encountered better luck when Charlie stiffened beside her.

'Don't look up ahead,' he hissed urgently.

Of course, her instinctive reaction was to do precisely what she had been forbidden to do and her gaze started to shift from the adjacent building to the path before them. In desperation, he grabbed her wrist and swung her towards him. Wrapping his arms around her, he pressed her into his chest and burrowed his face against her neck.

'Just pretend,' he breathed in her ear.

This time, she managed to obey. Pulse pounding, she leaned into his intimate embrace and let him stroke her back and her hips. He pushed her against the wall of the building next to them and tilted his head in a convincingly amorous fashion over her throat – only she could have known that his lips were not actually caressing her skin. All she felt was the graze of his anxious breath.

After a moment, he murmured, 'Look over my shoulder as casually as you can and tell me if you see a bald man in a long coat.'

Raising her head dreamily like she was relishing his attentions, she peeped past his misshapen ear and nonchalantly scanned the street to the left and right. She spotted a haggard woman nearby who muttered 'Hussy!' as she limped past and, beyond her, a man without a hair on his head, the ends of his coat flapping around his knees. He stumped by but didn't spare a glance for Bridget and Charlie's demonstrative behaviour.

'I see him,' she mumbled.

'Let me know when he reaches the corner.'

She rubbed her cheek flirtatiously against his and angled her head to follow the man's progress along the street. 'He just turned the corner now.'

Charlie pulled away from her, grasped her arm and urged her to hurry with him in the wake of the bald man. 'I couldn't risk him seeing me and getting suspicious. He's the fellow who said he had a grievance with a butcher.'

A frisson of fear and anticipation shuddered through her. 'You mean he's a member of the Kelly Greens?'

'Yes. Here's hoping he leads us right to them.'

Heart in her mouth, she hastened to keep up with Charlie and together they reached the corner where the man had disappeared. Rounding it with caution, they espied him marching further along the street so they followed as swiftly and as discreetly as they could. Charlie's grip felt tighter than a coiled spring and Bridget sensed that if the bald man so much as turned a fraction of an inch back towards them then Charlie would embrace her as ardently as he had before to avoid detection. But the fellow seemed quite intent on getting to his destination and he pounded forwards without even a fleeting look over his shoulder.

They tailed him through various streets and alleyways until he came to a stop in an alley that looked and smelled no different from the others, its buildings just as ramshackle as the rest of Five Points. However, he rubbed a nervous hand over his bald pate before stepping up to a door, thrusting it open and striding through it.

Bridget and Charlie edged closer to the building until they came upon a window set high in its wall, its square panes of glass murky with grime. She wasn't tall enough to look through it but he managed to peek over the sill by stretching up on the balls of his feet.

'I can see carcasses hanging in a line,' he muttered. 'It's a slaughterhouse.'

In the next instant, they heard a bellow from within the building. 'You'll fork out what you owe me or I swear to God I'll string you up next to your pigs!'

Bridget spun around to take in the rest of the alley. The opposite side was occupied by a long brick structure at least three storeys in height. She discerned a pair of double doors further along it with a smaller door set into the left-hand one. All of the windows were boarded up and the whole place appeared deserted...and yet, scuff marks in the dirt in front of the small door indicated that it was not entirely unused. Moreover, that dirt was as black as soot.

She seized Charlie's arm as tightly as he had clutched hers. 'This is it,' she rasped.

He dropped back to the flats of his feet, whirled about and assessed the warehouse across the alleyway. 'I think you might be right,' he said, his face flushed with relief. 'Come on, let's find a place to hide.'

They retreated from the window, sidling back to the corner of the slaughterhouse where a narrow passageway separated it from a storage shed of some kind. Creeping into the passage, they huddled against the wall of the slaughterhouse. A short ramp beside them led up to a side entrance and through its closed door they could hear muffled shouting. Ignoring the altercation, they peered out from their hiding spot, relatively concealed from view but still able to observe the warehouse across the way. Its filthy brick facade spoke of utter abandonment but an enormous pile of refuse shoved up against its wall said otherwise for it stank of rotting food and human waste, too freshly pungent to be long discarded. And when Bridget perceived the sparse bristles of a crooked chimney brush sticking out of the mound, she cast aside any further doubt. Her boys were in that building, she knew it.

As if Charlie could sense her blazing desire to barge straight in there, he said calmly, 'We need to wait and watch. We don't know how many are inside or how well it's guarded. I know it's difficult but we've got to be canny about this.'

She swallowed. 'I understand,' she said, even though every fibre of her being screamed to take action after having been impotent for so long.

They refocused their attention on the warehouse just in time to hear the screech of a rusty bolt, audible despite the ruckus taking place inside the slaughterhouse. The small doorway set into the double doors opened and a female figure stepped clumsily through it carrying a bucket. Charlie jerked with surprise and Bridget gasped in disbelief.

'Dear God in heaven,' she said hoarsely.

The dark-haired woman was noticeably pregnant which made it more awkward for her to hold the bucket. She lurched over to the rubbish pile and tossed its contents onto it; a foul smell of slops wafted through the alley. Instead of returning immediately inside, she put down the bucket and rubbed the small of her back. Her lips drew back in a grimace and Bridget glimpsed the cracked, blackened lumps of her teeth as well as the gaps between them. Then she picked up the bucket again and went back into the warehouse, shutting the small door behind her.

'God Almighty,' Charlie croaked in an echo of his wife's oft-uttered exclamation. 'For a second, I honestly thought she was...'

'You'd be forgiven for the mistake,' Bridget managed to reply. 'They're as alike as two sisters can be.'

She could hardly believe it. They had found Bronagh, right here in the den of the Kelly Greens. Hester's suspicions had been correct.

'We have to go after her,' Bridget said, her anger rising. 'We must find out what's going on and whether she's seen my boys.' Of course, if Bronagh had met Jack and Gus it would not have been in the knowledge that they were her nephews, but how could she look upon Jack and not recognise her older brother in his distinctive features?

Before Charlie could once again advocate caution, the yelling in the slaughterhouse grew even more strident and, all of a sudden, something large and heavy thumped against the side door next to Bridget and Charlie. They both jumped with fright. Was the bald man about to burst through it, or perhaps the butcher?

'We'd better leave,' Charlie muttered. 'We don't want to be discovered lurking here.'

He started to move out of the passageway but Bridget yanked him back. 'Wait! Listen!'

There were pounding footsteps out in the alley and then a man rushed past. Bridget only caught the swiftest glimpse but it was enough to distinguish the fellow's bald head and his panicked face as he tucked a bloody cleaver inside his long coat.

'Oh no,' she moaned after the bald man had vanished from view. 'Did he just kill that butcher?'

'Now we definitely have to go,' said Charlie, his hand at her elbow. 'The last thing we need is to be implicated in a murder. Come on.'

Casting a longing glance at the warehouse, she yielded to his insistent tug with reluctance. They emerged warily from the passage and darted from the alley, leaving so many unanswered questions behind them.

When they got back to the brothel, they discovered that Orlaith, Tess and Hester had not yet returned. Bridget paced the sitting room restlessly while Charlie leaned against the table and watched her with a morose expression.

'I must apologise to you,' he said at last. 'What I did was uncouth and invasive.'

She halted in her pacing. 'It wasn't. It was quick-witted and necessary.'

He shook his head. 'I feel like a cad. And after what happened last night...'

'Do you wish to talk about that?' she asked tentatively.

'No,' he said in a flat tone. He sighed. 'I'm just not being a very good husband at the moment.'

'You mustn't think that way. You have done these things for a selfless purpose. I for one will be forever grateful to you for all that you have sacrificed.'

He looked unconvinced. 'But Orlaith—'

'Orlaith would say the same,' she said firmly. 'I'm certain she'd understand that what occurred between us was not untoward. She is sure of you, Charlie, and that speaks volumes because for a long time she wouldn't let her guard down with anybody.'

Some of the worry lines cleared from his forehead. 'You really think so?'

'I do. And if you would feel uncomfortable disclosing it, I'd be willing to tell Orlaith on your behalf.'

'Tell me what?' came Orlaith's voice from the sitting room door as she, Tess and Hester plodded into the room.

Charlie's eyes widened with alarm but Bridget said blithely, 'Charlie had to pretend to kiss me on the street in order to avoid being recognised by a man he met at The Gorget last night. The subterfuge proved fruitful for it led to us gaining some vital information about the Kelly Greens.'

'I'm sorry,' Charlie began but Orlaith cut him off with a flap of her hand.

'Don't be sorry—this is welcome news! We came back here with nothing to report from our own efforts so I'm very glad yous had better success than us.'

'What information did yous find out?' Tess asked as she flopped into a chair.

'Did you locate the warehouse?' Hester demanded. 'Did you figure out where they're hiding the boys?'

'We believe so,' said Bridget. 'But there's more than that.' She bit the tip of her tongue. 'We found Bronagh.'

'God Almighty!' Orlaith exclaimed, dumbstruck. 'She's alive? Where is she?'

Bridget hesitated. 'We saw her at the warehouse.'

Hester's eyes almost bulged out of their sockets. 'I knew it! She's in league with the Kelly Greens!'

'It does appear that way,' Bridget said heavily.

'Hold on a second,' Orlaith retorted. 'We don't know that for sure. Didn't we learn from Bronagh Mac and Mr Todd back in Boston that she'd been keeping company with some very violent men? There's no way she's voluntarily involved in kidnapping children. They're obviously forcing her to take part in their crimes.'

'No one forced her to snatch my Willie,' snapped Hester. 'She did that all by herself.'

'What if she was under orders to do it?' Orlaith said, desperation shimmering in her grey eyes. She turned a pleading gaze to Charlie. 'Mightn't that be possible?'

'It might be,' he said and Bridget could tell that he was torn between pragmatism and an impulse to support the wife he felt he had betrayed. 'We only saw her emptying slops outside the warehouse. Maybe those men make her act as a servant for them?'

'That has to be it. They must bully her into doing whatever they want.' Orlaith looked around at them all. 'Please. She's my sister. I can't believe the worst of her without proper proof.'

Hester opened her mouth but Bridget cut in. 'It's entirely natural that you should feel that way. And she deserves the benefit of the doubt. We won't level any further accusations at her unless we can acquire said proof.'

'So what d'you suggest?' asked Tess. 'Knock on the warehouse door and demand a confession from her?'

'Nothing so blunt as that,' said Bridget. 'But we do need to find some way to speak to her. That will have to be our next step. And if we can determine that those men are her captors, then we must do everything in our power to rescue both her and the children.'

CHAPTER 26

Cormac pulled his cap down further over his forehead and scrutinised Wyndham House from beneath its brim. Hovering a little way down the street on Berkeley Square, he was strongly reminded of when he had done this before – eight years ago, he had stood in this very spot waiting for Bridget to emerge alone from that house and, minutes after he had approached her on the front steps, they had fallen into bed together, reigniting the passionate love affair they had begun so many years before at Oakleigh.

The precious result of the first chapter of that affair was currently ensnared within those walls. Now that he had finally reached London, what should his next move be? Needless to say, he couldn't announce himself at the front door. Ought he to wait until Emily emerged, as he had done with her mother? But how likely was it that she would be in Garrett's company? He could not risk being discovered by Garrett – secrecy in this city was key.

As he dithered, a tall form came around the corner onto the square, walking along the opposite side of the street. He discerned the figure's shaggy brown hair and exhaled a deep sigh of relief. The sight of Rory Carey here on Berkeley Square confirmed that he and Emily had not become separated on their travels and must surely be indicative that Emily was, at the very least, physically safe. And, thank God, here was an opportunity for Cormac to reach her.

Hurrying across the street, he neared Wyndham House just as Rory was placing his hand on the iron railing of the gate leading down to the servants' cellar access. He passed Rory without breaking his stride, only turning his head slightly to mutter, 'Don't let on that you recognise me. Just follow casually.'

He didn't pause to witness Rory's shock but kept going to the end of the square and on to the next street. Halfway along it, he glanced back to make sure that Rory had indeed followed – the young man was trailing a few yards behind with an expression of fervent hope on his face.

On the street after that, Cormac slowed his pace to allow Rory to catch up with him. Rory drew level and mumbled, 'I'm beyond glad to see you, sir.'

Cormac motioned forwards to indicate that they should keep moving. 'Do you have a few minutes to talk? Or are you expected back at the house?'

'I'm free, sir. There are no demands on my time.'

Cormac led the way past a pair of men conversing on the street, careful not to make eye contact with them. 'Tell me first: is Emily safe?'

His heart seized when Rory hesitated. Then he said, 'On the whole, yes.'

Throat tight, Cormac said, 'But she's in trouble? Did Garrett prove false?'

Rory nodded glumly. In faltering words, he relayed the subterfuge behind Garrett's letter and the challenging duty the gentleman had placed on Emily's shoulders.

'*Patrick*?' Cormac said, astounded. 'Garrett wants to acknowledge his by-blow?'

'He says that the boy's birth is legitimate, that he married your sister.'

Cormac clenched his teeth. 'That's a lie. He never did anything so honourable.'

Rory grimaced. 'From what Emily's told me, he can make any lie as convincing as the truth.'

As they navigated their way through the city streets, he admitted that Garrett had Emily caught in a trap – she was obliged to go along with his scheme for she didn't have the means to leave London without his financial aid.

'Well, that's where I can assist,' said Cormac, his heart lifting to know that he could be of use to his daughter at last. 'If she wants to leave, she can do so this very afternoon.'

He urged Rory towards the wall of the nearest building to step out of the way of the other pedestrians. They were on a shopping street and the majority of the passersby were ladies meandering in and out of jewellers and other fashionable establishments. Digging into his pocket, he covertly passed his supply of money to Rory, who pocketed it at once to conceal it from view.

'That will be sufficient to cover passage back to America for both you and Emily,' Cormac told him in a low voice beneath the rattle of passing carriages.

'Thank you, sir,' Rory said earnestly. 'Have you enough left for yourself?'

'I do,' Cormac lied. 'You may need to concoct a story about how you came by this money if it would upset Emily to know that I followed her.'

'I don't think so,' said Rory. 'Honestly, I reckon she'd be overjoyed to see you. Will we all journey back together?'

Evading the direct question, Cormac said, 'I'll head to the docks next and check if there are any ships departing on a suitable route. If not, another option might be to travel by rail back to Liverpool and board a ship there.' So as not to look straight into Rory's eyes as he skirted the truth, he let his gaze stray to a trio of ladies who had just emerged from a nearby jeweller's – their backs were to him as two of them bade a cheery farewell to the third.

'We could meet you at the docks,' said Rory. 'Emily's not at Wyndham House right now but when she returns I'll tell her I've seen you. What if we arrange to—'

He cut himself off as a shriek tore the air. Cormac's feet were already moving for he had witnessed what was happening. The third woman had stepped off the footpath onto the street but halfway across she had stumbled and, unable to catch herself, she had fallen to the ground. The shriek had erupted from her when she had looked up to see a carriage flying recklessly along the street, bearing down upon her with frightening speed. Even in the course of his headlong dash, Cormac could identify the precise moment when the coachman comprehended both the calamity lying in his path and the reality that his horses were going too fast to stop in time. Letting out a roar of alarm, he pulled vainly on the reins.

As Cormac dashed towards the woman, her only reaction to the impending disaster was to cover her head with her arms. With her two companions' screams echoing in his ears, Cormac dove to the ground, grabbed her bodily and rolled her back towards the footpath out of harm's way. The carriage missed them by mere inches and clattered to a jerky stop several yards further down the street.

Shaking like a leaf, the woman emitted a sob as she lowered her hands from her face. 'Oh, thank—' she began to say before she stuttered to a halt. Any words of solicitude also died on his own lips. He recognised the woman enveloped in his embrace.

Miss Alice Caulfield.

He reared back from her. Her eyes sprang wide in sheer shock and then narrowed with unmistakable resentment. A delicate patter of footsteps coupled with anxious bleats of concern heralded the arrival of her companions. Still on his knees, he looked up and his stomach dropped to see two more familiar faces: Lady Newby and Lady Radcliffe. Alice, Lucy and Cassandra had been Bridget's closest friends during the years she had lived in London and they had only ever been acquainted with him as Mr Oliver Davenport, the admired nephew of Lord and Lady Bewley – that was, until he and Bridget had absconded with Emily in a cloud of scandal. He wasn't sure how much of the truth about his fraud had circulated around London after their disappearance but one thing was certain: they knew he was definitely not the man he had claimed to be.

Lucy and Cassandra's mouths fell open in identical expressions of bewilderment as other inquisitive onlookers gathered around, drawn by the heroic spectacle. Well-dressed ladies mingled with errand boys and liveried servants, all agog, while the coachman descended from his carriage and also hastened to join the growing cluster of people. Cormac found himself penned in on all sides and unfortunately Alice was the first to recover her wits.

'Seize him!' she cried shrilly to the surrounding bystanders even as she lay sprawled on the ground. 'He is a criminal!'

Their admiration for his heroism vanished at once to be replaced with suspicion.

'A criminal?' repeated the coachman. 'What's he done?'

'He's an impostor!' she declared in even more strident tones than before. 'He professed himself to be an earl's nephew when in reality he is nothing but a—a knave of the most egregious kind!' Her mousy features appeared almost rat-like as she gesticulated towards Lucy and Cassandra. 'These ladies have also been exposed to his duplicity.'

When everyone's attention swung in their direction, Lucy faltered but Cassandra wasted no time in adding her voice to Alice's accusations. 'Indeed, it is true,' she exclaimed. 'He is a blackguard and must be apprehended this very instant.'

Of course, the ladies couldn't supply any evidence to support their allegations but the coachman seemed very eager to believe them regardless – perhaps he was of the opinion that if the crowd's hostility was trained upon the so-called criminal, they would forget to call him to account for his own reckless driving. He strode forwards and, hauling Cormac to his feet, he motioned for a liveried servant and an errand boy to grab each of his arms. Both sprang to obey.

'Someone run for a constable!' he commanded and another errand boy took off at a sprint amid a hum of animated chatter.

As the men's fingers gripped him with pinching force, Cormac spotted Rory squeezing through the excited onlookers, clearly about to come to his aid. Very subtly, he shook his head at him. At first, Rory frowned in confusion but then understanding dawned. If he revealed his association with Cormac, he would probably be decried as an accomplice and seized as well, and it would do no good for Emily to have them both detained. Face contorted with anguish, Rory held back and did nothing as the crowd threw insults at Cormac.

'You'll get your comeuppance, you scoundrel,' one woman cried while the coachman offered his hand to Alice to help her to rise. Standing shakily, she kept her livid gaze fixed upon Cormac, her countenance a blotchy combination of flushed and ashen skin.

Lucy, too, continued to stare at him, although her expression was harder to read. She took a step or two closer to him.

'Did she go with you willingly?' she asked, her words almost lost beneath the abuse from the bystanders. 'That's what she claimed in her letter but...'

Despite his desperate situation, he managed to give her a reassuring nod. 'She did. We have led a very happy life together.'

Lucy eyed him doubtfully but didn't say anything further because the errand boy returned at that moment in the company of a giant of a constable – the man had to be nearly seven feet tall. Towering over everyone, he glowered at the sight of Cormac restrained between his two captors.

'Right, what's going on here then?' he demanded.

'We wish to report a crime,' Alice announced. Where had this forthright woman come from? She had always been so timid before. 'It happened some years ago but this man has evaded capture until now. You must take him into your custody at once and ensure that the might of the law is exacted upon him without mercy.'

She glared at Cormac and he felt her loathing as hotly as the blaze from a fire.

'Do you have anything to say for yourself?' the constable asked him brusquely. 'Do you deny the lady's charge?'

Cormac surveyed the scene bleakly. He had no means of escape. 'No,' he said.

His past had caught up to him at last.

***

In the course of her second meeting with Edward, Emily came to the definite conclusion that the boy's kinship to Garrett could not be refuted – quite apart from their physical resemblance, they were both as insufferably arrogant as each other.

On this occasion, Edward had consented to join her and Garrett at the National Gallery on Trafalgar Square. She had looked forward to viewing the masterpieces but, between the pair of them, they quite ruined the experience. Instead of taking the opportunity to study and savour the great artworks on display, they spent the entire visit trading jibes back and forth, each trying to gain the upper hand in their battle of wills. Garrett persisted in putting pressure on Edward to yield to his desire to publicly acknowledge their father-son relationship, while Edward continued to resist, even with the threat of Emily's claim dangling over him.

However, before they departed from the gallery, Garrett accelerated the timeline of his ultimatum. He summoned Emily away from her veneration of Sebastiano's *The Raising of Lazarus* to insist that she heed his conversation with Edward.

'I want the two of you to pay close attention,' he said, 'for we are approaching the point of no return.'

Edward folded his arms. 'Is that so?' he said indifferently.

Though he exuded an apathetic attitude, Emily noticed a glow in his cheeks which suggested that he had been rather enjoying the repartee with his father.

'Tomorrow evening,' Garrett said, 'there is a small soiree taking place at the Swaneset residence. As both of you are aware, the official season has ended and many of the ton have retreated to their country estates for the summer. However, Lord Swaneset's youngest sister, Lady Emma, had her debut this past year and made quite a failure of it—the poor girl was tongue-tied beyond belief. So her family has decided to host a number of minor gatherings during this quieter period to help her acclimatise to the rigours of the social scene by gentler degrees.'

Edward rolled his eyes, plainly bored by the woes of Lady Emma. 'What has that got to do with us?'

'I have secured an invitation to the Swanesets' soiree.' Garrett smiled. 'An invitation that has been extended to include my heir.'

That hooked Edward's attention. 'Who do you intend to bring?'

'That depends entirely upon you, Patrick,' Garrett said, still smiling in a most predatory way. 'As I said, we are approaching the point of no return. In the event that I escort Emily to this soiree, that shall settle the matter irrevocably. It may not be a court presentation in front of the queen but it will still be regarded as an entry into public society. She shall be formally recognised as my daughter and your claim as my son will be silenced forever. Of course, to soften that blow you will remain the heir of the Anner barony. If that is adequate for you, then you need not act at all.' He paused. 'If, on the other hand, you deem my superior title and fortune worthy of your consideration, you must present yourself at Wyndham House tomorrow evening before the soiree begins. Any time after that will be too late.'

Edward gave Garrett a long, assessing stare before turning to Emily. 'Do you mean to attend?' he asked her evenly.

She threw him a helpless look. 'I don't see how I can refuse,' she said, even though the idea of openly acknowledging Garrett as her father made her sick to her stomach. I'm so very sorry, Papa, she thought miserably.

After a contemplative moment, Edward unfolded his arms and let them hang lazily by his sides. 'Sebastiano beckons,' he said, jerking his chin towards the nearby painting. 'Let's go admire his work.'

Emily registered the profound disappointment on Garrett's face as she passed him but he did not voice it. In fact, he barely spoke another word until they had parted from Edward at the entrance to the gallery and climbed into the carriage to return to Berkeley Square.

'Perhaps I was too premature in trying to force his hand,' he murmured almost to himself.

'There's still time to decline the Swanesets' invitation,' she said hopefully as the carriage jolted into motion.

He shook his head. 'I cannot back down now. The die has been cast.'

What stupid obstinacy. She yearned to roll her eyes in the same manner as Edward. Instead, she flopped back in her seat and stared out the window. She hoped Rory would be at Wyndham House when they got back. He had planned to head to Westminster Abbey today while she was gone to the National Gallery and she wanted to ask him which monarchs' and poets' graves he had visited before she imparted her less palatable tidings regarding Garrett's latest stipulation.

She was envisioning the reaction she might read in his green eyes – which were often more eloquent than any words he could offer – when Garrett broke into her reverie. 'Has Lizzie altered any of your mother's more fashionable gowns for you to wear? If not, she will have her work cut out to make one ready for tomorrow evening.'

Emily gulped at the insinuation that she would definitely be his companion to the Swanesets' soiree. Did he truly mean to present her there?

He confirmed the ghastly reality of his intentions by continuing, 'You will actually know two of the other guests at the gathering.'

'I will?' she said, baffled.

'Yes. Do you remember your mother's acquaintance Lady Newby? I believe you once fraternised with her two daughters, Angela and Valerie. If you recollect, they are not much older than you. Valerie came out this past season while Angela entered society a year ago. The Newbys did not remove to the country for the summer so both of them will be in attendance.'

She pondered this during the rest of the short journey back to Berkeley Square. She, Angela and Valerie had once trod the same path until her own had diverged quite severely from theirs. An encounter with them would likely be the truest way to ascertain how her life might have turned out had her parents not whisked her away from her privileged circumstances.

Not that such knowledge was enough incentive to submit to Garrett's scheme. Perhaps she could feign illness to avoid the event altogether – that would give her a reprieve and also allow Edward more time to decide whether he wished to have this wealthy, charismatic bully permanently in his life.

The carriage stopped and they alighted in front of Wyndham House. Emily could hardly wait to escape Garrett's company – his presence seemed to leave an intangible, oily layer on her skin. However, they had scarcely crossed the threshold into the entrance hall when Thrussell greeted her with a grave countenance.

'Mr Carey desires to speak with you, miss,' he said. 'He entreated me to convey the urgency of his message as soon as you returned.'

Startled, she wondered whether something had happened during his visit to Westminster Abbey. 'Please tell him I'll meet him downstairs in the dining hall at once.'

'No,' said Garrett. 'Tell him to present himself in the drawing room.' At her protestation, he went on smoothly, 'If you are going to be a viscount's daughter, which now appears to be the case, then there will be no more loitering around the servants' quarters.'

Reluctantly, she capitulated. Divesting herself of her bonnet and shawl, she handed them to Peter and made her way to the drawing room. To her annoyance, Garrett followed in her wake.

'I would prefer to speak to Rory alone,' she said, her tone clipped.

'I'm sure you would,' he replied but did not deviate from his course. Did he suspect that an impropriety might occur if he was not there to protect his newly established asset from contamination? Or perhaps he feared that Rory would conceive of some way to help her evade his machinations. But surely Garrett comprehended that she was wholly within his power and had no capacity to resist him.

In the drawing room, they occupied the same armchairs they had on the night she had arrived and waited for Rory to appear. A minute later he was ushered in by Thrussell, who looked unperturbed to be conducting a lower class young man into the room as though he were a gentleman. At Garrett's dismissive wave, the butler then withdrew.

'Rory?' Emily said anxiously as he approached their two chairs. He did not seem to be harmed in any way but he was as pale as a sheet. 'What is the matter?'

He glanced from her to Garrett, making no effort to hide his hostility. 'I don't want to talk in front of him,' he said bluntly.

'It's a pleasure to make your acquaintance too, Mr Carey,' Garrett said with sardonic amiability. 'You may converse freely. I shall not impede you.'

Rory snorted and turned back to Emily. 'Can we go somewhere else?'

'Yes, let's,' she said, starting to rise.

'I think not,' said Garrett, his attitude relaxed but uncompromising. 'The more you try to conceal whatever this is, the more determined I am to hear it. You shall have to divulge it here or not at all.'

She sank back down. Rory grimaced, his shoulders sagging.

'Your da,' he said, barely moving his lips. 'He's here. In London.'

A burst of pure joy exploded inside her. Oh, God bless her marvellous papa. Although she did not deserve it, he had come to her rescue.

'That's wonderful!' she exclaimed, throwing an exultant look in Garrett's direction as she felt his oppressive influence falling away from her like shackles from an emancipated prisoner. She would have leapt to her feet and run from the house with Rory that very instant, only for the morose expression on Rory's face which stayed her movement. 'I-isn't it wonderful?' she said falteringly. Perhaps her father was terribly angry with her and didn't mean to rescue her after all.

Rory shook his head unhappily. 'He's been arrested.'

She gasped and clapped her hands over her mouth, utterly aghast. 'What on earth happened?' she blurted through her fingers.

'He was recognised by some ladies who called him a criminal,' Rory mumbled. 'I think they knew him from long ago when he'd pretended to be someone else.'

'Mr Davenport,' she breathed. Of course, that past deception would have made it exceedingly dangerous for him to set foot in London again, yet he had still risked it for her. After all the hurt she had caused him and her mother, she had no entitlement to such selfless love. And now her foolish actions were to blame for his capture by the English authorities. She moaned with self-loathing.

Opposite her, Garrett sat back in his chair looking enormously satisfied. 'My, how this is music to my ears,' he said. 'Finer than any aria I have ever heard at the opera.'

Too cowardly to bear the brunt of her loathing alone, Emily directed its force towards him. 'Did *you* orchestrate this?' she cried.

'I did not,' he said. 'However, when I set my plan for you in motion, I calculated that the likelihood of him coming after you was a realistic possibility. How delighted I am to hear that my speculation proved accurate and that he has ended up in this predicament. Moreover, I know someone else who will relish the news almost as much as I. I must write to the Earl of Bewley forthwith. No doubt he will wish to attend the trial in person.'

'Trial?' Emily repeated, horrified.

Garrett nodded buoyantly. 'Now that the miscreant has been arrested, he will have to be tried to determine his guilt. In the meantime, he will be incarcerated. Do you know where they have taken him?' he asked, aiming this question at Rory.

Rory's responding nod was as glum as Garrett's had been cheerful. 'Newgate Prison, the constable said.'

A cold shiver ran down Emily's back. Her father had been put in prison because of her, and worse than that was yet to come. What might be the potential outcome of the trial? She knew nothing of the English judicial system – was fraud a hanging offence?

Without any kind of conscious decision, she shot out of her seat, rushed across to Garrett's armchair and swung out her arm. He saw the blow coming and easily cuffed her hand away.

'Now, now,' he chided. 'That is no way for a future viscountess to behave.'

She gave a hysterical laugh. 'After all this, you think I shall willingly go along with your scheme? If you wish to announce me as your heir at the Swanesets' soiree, you will have to bind my hands and feet and drag me there for I will not go of my own volition.'

'But what of your own incentive in that regard?' he enquired lazily.

'I don't want a penny from you,' she retorted and even in the heat of the moment she began to understand why Rory had been so against the notion of accepting money from Brian Mór. 'Rory and I will find some other means of returning to America. I'll whore myself if I have to.'

Rory made some kind of movement in her peripheral vision but she didn't tear her defiant gaze away from Garrett. She was relieved that her voice hadn't trembled when she had made that desperate declaration.

Garrett sighed. 'Let us not consider such a vulgar option. Allow me to sweeten my bargain. If you attend the soiree, I will use my influence to free your father from Newgate.'

She gaped at him. 'You have the power to do that?'

He spread his palms in a munificent gesture. 'I do.'

She narrowed her eyes. 'Even if you can do it, I don't believe that you would.'

'That doubt is for you to overcome,' he said with a shrug. 'I have given you my word. Only you can decide whether or not to trust it.'

Trust the lying, manipulative snake? Ludicrous. But how could she ever face her mother again if she turned away from an opportunity – dubious though it might be – to liberate her father from imprisonment? Of course she must do it, even if the public announcement at the Swanesets' soiree would be the dreadful price she had to pay.

She glanced at Rory. His expression was as dour as she had ever seen it as he glared at Garrett. Then, when his gaze shifted to hers, she read the bleak truth in his eyes.

'I have no choice, do I?' she said and he pressed his lips together in grim agreement. Somehow, that gave her strength. She looked back at Garrett. 'I will go with you to the soiree if you can guarantee my father's release.'

'We have a deal,' he replied without enthusiasm and she reflected that little happiness would arise from their arrangement – he would have his heir but not the one he wanted, while her father would attain his freedom but lose his daughter in the process.

Still, though she would hate doing it, she would betray him in order to save him.

CHAPTER 27

Bridget, Orlaith and Tess huddled in the passageway beside the slaughterhouse while Charlie crept up to its side entrance and pressed his good ear to the door. After a minute, he cautiously pushed on it and it opened. Gesturing to them to wait, he sidled through the gap and disappeared. Orlaith tapped her fingertips repeatedly against each other and stared unblinkingly at the door until Charlie re-emerged.

'It's empty,' he said in an undertone.

Without a word, they followed him inside. Bridget stepped over a patch of crusted blood just beyond the threshold and wondered if it had seeped from a carcass or whether it indicated the site of the butcher's violent demise. When Hester had learned of the murder, she had said it would not be long before another lout took over his business, but right now the slaughterhouse lay vacant apart from discarded chunks of meat rotting on the butcher's block, buzzing flies swarming around them, and hooks hanging from the ceiling caked with blood. The thick, cloying smells of iron and decay clogged Bridget's throat and she struggled not to gag.

Tess pressed the back of her hand to her nose and mouth. 'Is it too late to swap places with Hester?' she choked out.

Hester had reluctantly remained behind at the brothel because five was too great a number to be skulking about when they needed to be inconspicuous. Bridget and Charlie had been the natural choices to go, given that they knew the location of the warehouse, and, in making allowances for two more, they had reckoned that Bronagh would respond better to Orlaith and Tess's familiar faces. That was the ostensible reason anyway – in reality, Bridget had encouraged Hester's absence as there was no guarantee that she would not lunge forwards to scratch out Bronagh's eyes as soon as she appeared.

If she even appeared. They had arranged their return to the alley to coincide with the approximate time that she had emerged from the warehouse the previous day, but what if that had been an anomaly? Perhaps the men in the gang kept her confined inside on an almost continuous basis and only let her out on rare occasions. In that case, they could watch the building for hours or even days without success. Should she not materialise within a reasonable time frame, Bridget resolved to devise some other means of infiltrating the Kelly Greens, no matter how desperate those means might be. However, for now she would remain optimistic. After all, slops needed to be emptied regularly – if that was Bronagh's dedicated chore, then she would have to come outside sooner or later.

Charlie sidled over to the high window and rose up on his tiptoes.

'I've got a partial view of the double doors from here,' he said. 'All we can do now is wait to see if she comes out.'

'There won't be much time to act,' said Bridget, anxiety coiling in her stomach. 'Yesterday, she lingered for less than a minute.'

'We'll have to be quick then,' said Tess, her muffled tone suggesting that she was breathing only through her mouth. 'I'll stand by that side door to be ready.'

This could have been construed as a selfish endeavour to return to fresher air, but the truth was that Tess had a specific role to play. Whether it would work or not depended on whether Bronagh was a mother or a monster.

Tess stepped back to the side entrance, positioning herself at the gap in the doorway, while Orlaith joined Charlie by the window, even though she was too short to look out through its murky panes of glass. Bridget hovered in the space between, undecided, before moving over to Tess's side. What was happening here was much bigger than their personal grievances.

'Let us know as soon as you catch sight of her,' Bridget called softly across to Charlie and he nodded without taking his gaze from the alley outside.

After that, the tedium of waiting gradually set in. All four of them remained standing but Bridget could discern the painful stiffness developing in the lines of Charlie's body as he continued to balance on the balls of his feet. The odour of the slaughterhouse diminished only slightly the longer they wallowed in it and she wondered if it might seep into the very fabric of their clothes, never to be fully washed away, even with the strongest lye soap.

She shook her head in disgust. How incongruous to be thinking about laundry at such a critical juncture. The everyday concerns that had occupied her mind in the past were inappropriate in this nightmarish present. Nothing mattered except—

'The door's opening!' Charlie's urgent whisper broke the silence.

Bridget's nerve endings flared with apprehension. 'Is it her?'

'I can't tell. No one's coming out. Hold on, here's someone now...yes, it's her!'

Tess wasted no time. Slipping through the side door out into the passageway between the slaughterhouse and the storage shed, she heaved a deep breath and began to wail.

Bridget was prepared for it and yet she still couldn't curb the chill of unease that skittered across her scalp, because Tess sounded exactly like a child in grievous distress. Ragged sobs erupted from her throat and she howled with the anguish of a little girl who had been abandoned by her mother and left all alone in the world. She had practised at the brothel before they left and had been so convincing that two of Hester's girls had come running to their madam's sitting room in panic, looking for the distraught infant.

That was what they were counting on with Bronagh. She had borne a baby once before and lost it, and was carrying another now. What mother would be able to resist the cry of a sobbing, helpless child? If she could close her ears to such a sound, then she truly was a monster.

As Tess continued to bawl with remarkable authenticity, Orlaith darted across the stained floor to Bridget.

'Charlie says Bronagh's put down her bucket and is looking all around with worry. This might actually work.'

The words were hardly out of her mouth when Charlie uttered a low exclamation. 'She's coming your way!'

Bridget scurried out through the side door to tug on Tess's arm. 'Pull back,' she muttered. 'We need to draw her inside.'

Tess didn't even break for breath as she retreated over the threshold; her bloodcurdling cries ripped from her, loud and unnerving, and Bridget didn't doubt that Bronagh could still hear them out in the alley. Charlie hurried over.

'She's gone from my line of sight,' he said. 'But I could see her heading for the corner of the slaughterhouse.'

Bridget pictured Bronagh peering into the passageway, seeking the source of the wailing. Would she pursue it? And, if so, which part of her character would compel her to do so – a maternal instinct to soothe a suffering child, or the shrewd recognition of a potential recruit for the Kelly Greens?

Tess had left the door ajar behind her. She carried on with her hysterics but backed away, hiding behind the door so that Bronagh would not catch a glimpse of her before she entered. Bridget, Orlaith and Charlie slunk up to the adjacent wall and pressed themselves against it, craning their necks to train their gazes upon the doorway. Charlie stood nearest to the jamb, his body poised in readiness.

A shadow fell across the threshold and a hand pushed the door open wider. Bronagh stepped through, one arm curved protectively over her pregnant bump and palpable consternation in her expression. She glanced around, her eyes slanted downwards as she sought the small, forlorn creature making those agonising sounds.

Before she even had time to register that four adults were waiting there instead, Tess ceased her screeching and swung the door shut, while Charlie leapt towards Bronagh to grab her. Her head shot up like a wild animal sniffing danger and her eyes widened in fright and confusion. When her lips parted to scream, he clamped his hand over her mouth to muffle the noise. She fought in his grip as Bridget rushed forwards.

'We don't mean any harm to you or your baby,' she said in earnest. 'But we urgently need to speak with you, Bronagh.'

Bronagh stopped struggling at the mention of her name, shock written all over her face. Her grey eyes – their shade familiar but their shape not as round as Orlaith's – focused more closely upon Bridget but she didn't seem to recognise her. It wasn't until Orlaith and Tess also stepped into her eyeline that her countenance filled with dawning recognition. She emitted a horrified gasp behind Charlie's fingers.

'Charlie will let go of you now,' Bridget said as calmly as she could, even though she ached to demand answers about her boys at once. 'Please don't flee. We won't hurt you.'

Cautiously, Charlie loosened his grasp on Bronagh but he remained hovering beside her, ready to seize her again if needed – after all, he had sacrificed a portion of his own honour to obtain the information that had led them to this point. Bronagh didn't try to run but her gaze flitted all around the slaughterhouse as though trying to spot its exits. She wrapped both of her arms around her swollen belly and stared at her captors with blatant unease.

This close to her, Bridget was appalled by her haggard appearance. Bronagh was seven years younger than her but she looked a decade older. Premature wrinkles lined her forehead as well as the corners of her mouth and eyes. Veins stood out on the backs of her hands and every one of her grimy fingernails was either broken or bitten down to the quick. Even her delicate condition could not lend her the plump glow of an expectant mother; her joints looked bony and her skin pasty.

Judging by the jubilation in Orlaith's features, she perceived none of this. All she saw was the dear sister she had lost so long ago. The final McGovern sibling had been found after so many years of fruitless searching.

'Bronagh,' she breathed, overjoyed.

She reached out to hug her but Bronagh recoiled from her like a feral cat. Hanks of her straggly hair, far greyer than the dark colour she had once shared with her sisters and their mother, fell across her face. She peered through the strands.

'What're ye doing here?' she mumbled, revealing the blackened, chipped teeth Bridget had glimpsed yesterday. She had retained her Carlow accent but her voice was hoarse, as though she rarely had cause to use it. Before anyone replied, she

303

raised her left hand to push back her hair and Bridget caught the glint of gold on her ring finger.

'That's my ring!' she burst out.

Startled, Bronagh hid her hand behind her back but Bridget knew she was right. She would have recognised that distinctive gold metalwork anywhere for she had lovingly traced the shapes of the crown, heart and hands countless times since the day Cormac had placed it on her finger. Relief suffused her that it had not vanished for good, but it was quickly surpassed by anger that another woman had claimed it as her own.

'Give it back,' she commanded, her palm outstretched.

Bronagh shook her head mutely and Bridget's ire rose further.

'I want what's been taken from me!' she snapped. 'My ring, and my sons!'

Bronagh gaped. 'Your sons?'

Bridget jabbed a finger in the general direction of the warehouse without taking her eyes off Bronagh. 'The Kelly Greens have them and I want them back! They'd better be unharmed or I swear to God I'll kill whoever hurt them.'

A series of emotions flashed across Bronagh's expression so swiftly that they were almost too fast to identify – there might have been astonishment, doubt, sympathy perhaps? However, they culminated in one very clear sentiment: fear. She drew in on herself and her gaze darted around once again, alighting on the side entrance she had come through.

Orlaith put out a pleading hand, although she didn't attempt to touch her sister this time. 'Please don't run away from us,' she entreated. 'We need your help. They're your nephews. They're Cormac's two boys.'

Bronagh's eyebrows sprang up. 'Cormac?' she said in wonderment, like she was speaking the name of some mythical being. Then, to herself, she murmured, 'He warned me. Said I'd be ruined. He saw the reality long before I did.'

'The reality of what?' Bridget demanded, bewildered. The last contact Cormac had had with Bronagh had been back on the Oakleigh Estate sixteen long years ago. What could he have warned her about then?

Bronagh didn't respond. She wearily passed her hand over her forehead, realised it was the one bearing the gold ring, and concealed it behind her back again. Bridget pursed her mouth at the childish action but decided to put the ring out of her mind – Jack and Gus were more important than a pretty piece of metal, and she knew Cormac would agree with her.

'That warehouse,' she said, striving for composure so that she could wrest at least some scrap of useful information from Bronagh. 'That's where the Kelly Greens hide the kidnapped children, isn't it?'

Bronagh bit down on her cracked lower lip as if to stop the words from leaking out but Bridget got the confirmation she needed from the flicker of guilt in her eyes.

'You don't help them to do it though, right?' said Orlaith, her tone beseeching. 'They're forcing you to be here against your will?'

The guilty flicker remained in the grey irises. Orlaith shrank back, utterly dismayed. Charlie looked like he desperately wanted to comfort her but he didn't abandon his wary position near Bronagh's side.

Bridget clenched her fists. 'You have to tell us,' she said and tried to soften the order with a fervent, '*Please.*'

Bronagh clamped her lips together. Bridget couldn't tell whether it was defiance or shame that kept her silent. Despairing, she wondered what to do.

That was when Tess spoke up. 'I'm a whore,' she said, her voice quiet and clear. Everyone looked at her in surprise, including Bronagh. 'I don't make a living that way anymore, but I did in the past so it'll always be a part of who I am. There's

305

no getting away from that.' She took a breath. 'I also kissed a man who belonged to another woman. I should apologise to her but I don't want to because I'm so jealous of what she has. I'm a resentful bitch, to be honest.' She gesticulated to the rest of them. 'Anyone else want to have a go?'

Orlaith cottoned on the quickest. Squaring her shoulders to face them all but addressing her words mainly to Bronagh, she said, 'I bartered my three-year-old nephew for a roof over my head and food in my belly. Now he no longer remembers that we were once his family.' She winced. 'And I accused my brother of being the reason our mother died, when I knew full well that what happened to her was out of his control. It was spiteful and I did say sorry afterwards but I'll always feel ashamed about it.'

Bridget squeezed her fists even tighter as she offered her own confession. 'I'm an adulteress and I have never repented that sin, even though my actions have had dreadful consequences for many others.' She gulped as the most disgraceful moments of her life all vied for prominence in her mind. 'I begged the man I loved to walk into a burning building to save my despicable mother, despite the fact that no other creature on this earth had wronged him more than she had. And I have failed all of my children in more ways than I can count.' She could have gone on but she left it at that, her heart throbbing with sorrow.

Bronagh's wide-eyed gaze shifted around the group to Charlie. He baulked and Bridget realised that his own shameful declaration would include whatever awful deed he had committed two nights ago. Surely that was too raw yet for him to admit.

Tess must have thought the same because, as Charlie opened his mouth, she hastened to interject, 'Charlie's an angel. It'd be no use comparing yourself to him.' She shrugged. 'But us normal folk have all done things we're not proud of.' She held eye contact with Bronagh, steady and calm. 'The point is, there isn't anyone here who thinks you're the worst person in the room. You can tell us what you've done and we won't judge.'

Bronagh swallowed. Her whole body trembled as she glanced between each one of them. Was she weighing up their transgressions against her own?

'I fell in love,' she croaked. 'With a wicked man.'

Bridget certainly couldn't impart any criticism for that. She knew better than most that the recipient of one's affections didn't always show their true colours until it was too late – she had once believed herself to be in love with Garrett, after all.

'The fault is not with you but with him,' she said compassionately. 'Did he hurt you?'

'Me and others.' Bronagh bowed her head. 'I didn't know a man could be that cruel. Growing up, I saw Da be so gentle and kind with Ma, and Patrick and Cormac always looked out for us girls. But Malachy isn't like them at all.'

Bridget felt winded, as though something large and heavy had just struck her square in the chest. 'Malachy?' she echoed disbelievingly. 'You don't mean...Malachy *Kelly*?'

Still looking downwards, Bronagh nodded miserably.

'My God,' said Bridget, stunned. Even as all sorts of questions erupted in her brain, one answer slotted itself neatly into place: the *Kelly* Greens.

'Who's Malachy Kelly?' Orlaith asked, frowning. 'And how do you know him, Bridget?'

Bridget bypassed all explanations and hurtled straight to the most pertinent detail. 'He's meant to be incarcerated in an Irish prison!' she exclaimed. 'What on earth is he doing in America?'

Bronagh's hair fell across her face again. Hiding behind it like a mask, she mumbled, 'I helped him escape.'

Bridget clapped her hand over her mouth to muffle the sound that slipped from her because, despite Tess's promise that they would not judge Bronagh, she could not prevent her tone from filling with condemnation at such a revelation.

Tess knitted her brows. 'Any chance yous can enlighten the rest of us?'

Bridget shot a wary look at Bronagh. 'May I tell them?'

Bronagh only grimaced but Bridget interpreted that as permission. She glanced from Orlaith to Tess and over to Charlie whose expression was equally perplexed. 'Malachy Kelly was a young under gardener at Oakleigh and grandson of the head gardener. In the summer of '28, he and two of his companions were caught stealing silver from the manor in the middle of the night. By my mother's orders, they were imprisoned for the crime.' She bit the tip of her tongue. 'Cormac and Bronagh were also implicated but were subsequently absolved of any culpability. In Cormac's case, he was innocent. In Bronagh's...' She trailed off. Bronagh had in fact aided Malachy and his cronies in entering the house but Bridget had vouched for her and ensured her exoneration. She cleared her throat. 'She harboured an attachment for Malachy which spurred her to act the way she did. However, all contact between them came to an abrupt end after the events of that night.'

Or at least it ought to have.

'I never forgot him,' Bronagh whispered. 'Before the constables took him away, he whispered in my ear, "Remember that the silver was for our future. Come find me. I'll wait for you." It was my fault he ended up in prison. He only wanted to save up enough money to marry me and take me to America. So I had to save *him* if I could.'

Bridget blinked in incredulity. 'How did you even find him? You and your family left Carlow that autumn when my mother evicted you from your cottage and you all ended up in Dublin. Orlaith and Tess told us what happened in the city.'

'And when you disappeared from there,' Tess put in, 'I assumed you went to America. You'd always talked about it.'

Behind her curtain of dishevelled hair, Bronagh said softly, 'I wanted to, but I wouldn't go without him. After I ran away from Dublin, I headed south and begged for rides from farmers passing in their carts until I found my way back to Carlow.'

Bridget's jaw dropped. 'You returned to Oakleigh?'

'No, I didn't need to go that far. I made for Carlow Town because one of the farmers told me that criminals are usually taken to the county gaol if they're sentenced to imprisonment instead of transportation. So when I got there I asked around and a local greengrocer gave me directions to Carlow Gaol.'

'And Malachy was there?' Orlaith said, dumbfounded.

'Yes.' Bronagh's lips twisted as she shoved back her untidy hair again. 'Along with the two fellas who'd got caught stealing with him, Seamus Sheedy and Billy Maher. I would've been happy to leave them behind but Malachy said they had to get out too.'

'But,' said Bridget, perplexed, 'how did you manage to speak to him in the first place? And then facilitate the flight of three men from a place secured by locks and guards?'

A spot of colour appeared high in each of Bronagh's pale cheeks. 'I found a gaoler with a weakness. He confirmed Malachy was in there and let me visit him in exchange for a groping.' Next to her, Charlie's own cheeks reddened. 'For the escape, I had to pleasure him with my mouth and steal his keys.'

Tess cringed in sympathy. 'Sometimes that's worse than the other way.'

'I know,' said Bronagh as though they were having a matter-of-fact discussion about the weather. 'But I wanted to save myself for Malachy.'

In that moment, Bridget experienced a great rush of pity for Bronagh and, yes, for Tess too. She understood what they meant and she endeavoured to hide her own blushes for she had also engaged in that very private deed, never with Garrett but on several occasions with Cormac. While it felt tremendously debauched, it was always an expression of passion that she could not contain and it so thoroughly undid Cormac every single time that it gave her an overwhelming sense of euphoria. But to perform such an intimate act as a means of negotiation or exploitation...that was a sign of profound desperation.

'You must have truly loved him,' she said to Bronagh without a trace of censure.

She glanced away. 'More fool me,' she said.

Indeed, for she had liberated a delinquent who ultimately graduated from thieving silver at Oakleigh Manor to thieving children on the streets of New York.

Had Bridget's mother or her land agent, Mr Enright, been informed of the breakout from Carlow Gaol after it happened? If they had, Bridget wouldn't have heard of it because she and Lady Courcey had not been on speaking terms at that stage, not since Bridget had expelled her from Wyndham House on the night of Emily's birth some years before. Would Lady Courcey have feared that the three criminals might attempt to burgle the manor again? How many sleepless nights had that brought her?

'Did you go back to Oakleigh after that?' Bridget wondered aloud.

'No. Malachy didn't want to risk getting caught again. Our goal became America so we stole whatever we could 'til we had enough money to purchase passage on a ship.'

'And you went from Cove to Boston,' said Orlaith.

Startled, Bronagh said, 'How do you know that?'

'We've been trying to track you down for years. It's why we came to this country in the first place. And now we've found you at last.' Orlaith offered a tremulous smile.

Bronagh did not return it. 'I wasn't worth finding.'

A discomfiting silence followed. Charlie broke it with an awkward cough. 'What made you choose Boston?'

It was the first time he had spoken since Bronagh had entered the warehouse. She jerked away from him. 'He's a Yankee?' she said to the others in revulsion.

'He's my husband,' Orlaith said unflinchingly, her assertion laced with defiant pride.

Bronagh looked taken aback. 'You're married,' she said. Bridget couldn't tell if it was amazement or envy in her tone.

'To an angel,' Tess said. 'Tell us why yous picked Boston.'

Bronagh hesitated. Was she having second thoughts about revealing her past? Then she shrugged. 'It was Malachy's decision. Seamus wanted to go to New York 'cause he had an uncle there but Malachy wasn't keen on being under someone else's heel so he chose Boston. We thought Seamus and Billy might go their separate ways from us until they joined us on our ship at the last minute. They didn't have the spines to go against Malachy in anything.' She wrinkled her nose. 'He was different when they were around, always acting tough and making crude jokes. I hated being the only girl among them so I was glad when Seamus got friendly with a fellow passenger called Cáit. She'd a great sense of humour and she fancied Seamus enough to stay with us after we got to America.' Bronagh sighed. 'Only trouble was that eventually he started treating her like dirt, pushing her about and telling her what she could and couldn't do. And Malachy didn't want to be outdone so he copied Seamus and treated me the same way. It got so bad that we needed their say-so just to get past the front door of the house where we were staying.'

That house, according to the information that Cormac and Orlaith had garnered, had been on Charter Street in Boston's North End. Where a murder had taken place.

Tentatively, Bridget said, 'By the time we traced you there, you'd disappeared. We heard about Bully Billy and what happened to him.'

To her surprise, Bronagh snorted. 'He was a bit of a fool to be honest, never had the grit of Malachy or Seamus. He gave himself that nickname to make him sound like a menacing fella but we used to laugh about it behind his back, and sometimes to his face.'

'Who killed him?' Charlie asked bluntly. 'And why?'

Bronagh's scorn fled. 'Seamus,' she said. 'In a jealous temper. You see, Cáit's plain enough in looks apart from her, ah, chest area. Honestly, her pair are the biggest I've ever seen, even bigger than Mrs Kavanagh's.' It was odd to hear Bronagh speak so naturally of the cook at Oakleigh while relating the details of the sordid life she had led since she had left there. 'Seamus came back to the house drunk one evening to find Billy pawing Cáit and he didn't wait for an explanation or an apology before laying into him. The first blow knocked him out cold but Seamus didn't stop at that and Billy never woke up afterwards.'

Bridget felt a little sick at this cool delivery of Billy's violent demise but supposed that Bronagh's attitude might stem from a sympathetic outrage on her friend's behalf at his detestable behaviour. 'Had he been taking advantage of Cáit?'

'No,' Bronagh admitted. 'She told me in confidence later that she'd encouraged him. She'd just wanted to fool around with someone who didn't get aroused by hitting her.'

Bridget's nausea worsened. 'And this...incident is what prompted you to leave Boston?'

'Sort of. Malachy had already been toying with the idea of moving on—the city hadn't lived up to his expectations of an easy life so he'd sent me out to ask about stagecoach routes to other places. But when it became necessary to get away fast, he made the obvious choice. Seamus's uncle was still living in New

York and he'd surely be willing to hide four people on the run from a crime if one of them was his own blood.'

From Cormac's past enquiries, Bridget knew what had transpired next: Bronagh, Cáit, Malachy and Seamus had boarded Mr Todd's stagecoach to New York and somewhere along the route the two women had tried to flee from their abusive men, possibly impelled by the hideous realisation that at least one of them was capable of killing. However, the men had caught them and dragged them back to the coach, and Mr Todd had later confirmed that all four of them had arrived in New York together.

'So that's how you ended up in Five Points?' said Orlaith.

Bronagh nodded. 'Seamus's uncle, Blackie Sheedy, had been working here long enough to become the owner of the warehouse across the way, but he'd given up on using it for honest employment and had started running a gang named the Sheedy Greens. They posed as chimney sweeps and thieved valuables from the homes where they worked.' She swallowed. 'It was Malachy who first hit upon the notion of getting the small climbing boys to do all the scouting and filching. He called them "expendable". If they were seized by the law, the gang could always find more.' Her palms crept defensively over her round stomach again. 'Blackie wouldn't agree to it. Him and Malachy constantly butted heads over how the gang should operate. And then Malachy killed him.'

They all stared at her in shock. She blinked back at them.

'It was an accident,' she said. 'They were having an argument about a damaged wall in the warehouse—the place has been in a shambles for years. Malachy rushed towards Blackie who stepped backwards, tripped and fell hard on a pile of bricks. Cracked his skull. The wall's never been fixed—no one will go near it now. They say 'tis haunted by Blackie's ghost.' Her fingers flexed on her bump. 'Malachy only told the truth about the accident to me. Everyone else believed he'd murdered Blackie to become the head of the gang, 'specially when he renamed them the Kelly Greens. They grew afraid of him, and Seamus thought he didn't have one up on him anymore now that they had a kill each. When Malachy ordered the men to start using the climbing boys for their burglaries, nobody refused. They snatched urchins off the streets or set upon unwary travellers who had children with them. They even made an arrangement with a few crooked stagecoach drivers to drop their passengers off in dodgy areas around the neighbourhood if they had young boys on board.'

Bridget sizzled with fury; it surged up through her like molten lava and seared her insides.

'That's what happened to us!' she burst out. 'Our driver abandoned us in the heart of Five Points and we were ambushed almost immediately.'

She wanted to slaughter the diabolical Mr Henson and she didn't care if it looked like an accident or not. Off the back of this revelation, another dreadful thought occurred to her – had he engineered the breaking of the wheel to ensure their arrival into the city late at night? The possibility that the catastrophe in that dark street had been premeditated hours or even days in advance was stomach-churning.

She went on urgently, 'My two sons were abducted and I desperately need to know if they're in that warehouse. Jack is the image of Cormac at seven years old and Gus is two years younger with a head of curls the same shade as my own. It's been fourteen days since I've seen them alive. I'm begging you, Bronagh, tell me they're alive. Please tell me they're safe.'

Bronagh gulped. She backed up a step, eyeing the closed side door only a few feet away from her. Charlie shifted a subtle pace or two as well.

'We did get two new boys recently enough,' she said, her voice husky and cautious. 'I suppose a couple of weeks ago sounds about right.' She added haltingly, 'I-I didn't look at them too closely though. I never do. I just bring them their meals and leave again.'

The lava gushed up inside Bridget but before she could erupt, Tess said, 'I know we promised not to judge but, Jaysus, that's pretty heartless.' Though her manner was composed, the tautness in her jaw betrayed her anger. 'Jack and Gus are sweet lads. They sure as hell don't deserve to be ignored or shoved up chimneys or any of the rest of it, and neither do the other children locked away in that godforsaken building. Surely you can't stand being mixed up in all this? We heard that you ran off a few months ago. Why didn't you keep on running when you had the chance?'

Bronagh's eyes bulged. 'H-how do ye—?'

'Hester Temple,' said Orlaith.

Bronagh sucked in her breath and her countenance filled with dismay.

'She's looking for you,' Orlaith pushed on, the harsh edge to her tone conveying that her sisterly compassion had reached its limits after all that Bronagh had disclosed. 'She wants her son back too.'

Bronagh's skin turned ashen and she appeared to be on the brink of throwing up. 'God, that poor woman,' she rasped.

'Poor woman?' Bridget spluttered in return, comprehending that Hester had been right all along in her conviction that Bronagh had taken Willie. 'Your sympathy strikes me as peculiar, given that you were the cause of her suffering and that you have the means to bring it to an end if you so wish.' She was growing more and more infuriated with Bronagh by the second. 'Can we presume then from your reaction that Willie is being held captive in the warehouse as well? Unless he has been apprehended by the authorities in the course of a failed burglary?'

'He's in there,' Bronagh said through frozen lips.

Bridget experienced a ripple of relief on Hester's behalf – Jack and Gus's two-week disappearance was discouraging enough but Willie's absence of five months had been verging on hopeless.

'At least you are able to remember one of the boys in your charge,' she said tartly.

'He's not easy to forget,' said Bronagh. 'Not after what I did to him.' Her inflection of self-reproach was unmistakable. 'Did Hester tell ye how I came to be at her brothel that night?'

Orlaith's voice softened. 'She said you were very upset.'

'I'd just found out I was expecting this little one,' Bronagh said, waving towards her belly. 'And I was damn terrified, 'cause of what happened to my first child.'

She shuffled closer to the door, making Charlie twitch in readiness, but she only turned and leaned her back against it for support.

'I fell pregnant not long after we got to New York,' she said quietly. 'I thought we'd get married at that point but Malachy didn't want to. Said there was no need for it—he already considered us to be husband and wife. Sometimes he could be real romantic.' The corner of her mouth curved upwards, the closest she had yet come to a smile. 'Then I had my baby and nothing else mattered in the world. He was the most beautiful thing I'd ever seen. All I wanted was for him to be safe and happy.'

There it was: a glimmer of the caring mother who had been irresistibly drawn into their trap by the apparent wailing of a distraught child.

'We named him after his da but called him Mal for short.' Her features hardened. 'He was all of four years old when his da decided it was time to join the family business.'

'Oh no,' breathed Orlaith.

Bronagh's chin quivered. 'He got stuck in a chimney and didn't know how to get back down. By the time an older boy climbed up and managed to pull him out, he'd suffocated on the soot, the craythur.'

Bridget listened in horror. The poor child – the last moments of his short life must have been petrifying. She would do absolutely anything to prevent the same from happening to Jack and Gus.

Grief darkened Bronagh's grey eyes to deep slate. 'I was devastated beyond words but Malachy shrugged it off. All children were "expendable" to him, even his own. I couldn't fathom how he could be that way. Cormac had warned me long ago of the sort of person Malachy was, but at last I saw the reality for myself. I only wish I hadn't had to lose my little Mal to see it.'

Orlaith stepped closer to Bronagh and, when her sister didn't shrink away, touched one of her hands which was cupping her bulging stomach again. 'It's just heartbreaking,' she said thickly.

The cloying air within the slaughterhouse became heavy with sorrow, pressing down on them from all sides. After a beat, Bronagh let her fingers link with Orlaith's. They both seemed far removed from the two innocent McGovern girls whose greatest worries had once been trying not to burn the servants' porridge at the manor or struggling to catch wayward hens at their family's cottage.

Bronagh's throat bobbed as she choked back her emotion. 'When I realised earlier this year that I was with child again, I panicked. I was so afraid for my baby's life, 'specially if it was a boy, that I just bolted without any notion where to go. I found myself crouching in a snowy alley sobbing for all I was worth when I heard Hester's voice.' She shook her head, her lashes lowered with guilt. 'She treated me kinder than I deserved. She brought me inside her brothel, gave me food, suggested ways to help. I thought about accepting her offer to work for her but the brothel was too near the warehouse—Malachy would find me and force me to return to him. I actually considered running away back to Ireland but figured there was no point without any family to go home to.' She squeezed Orlaith's fingers. 'I assumed you and Patrick had to be dead by then. I didn't think there was any chance ye could have survived in that awful city.'

Bridget allowed herself a fleeting moment to imagine what might have happened had Bronagh indeed boarded a ship back to Ireland. If she had found her way home to Carlow, the denizens on the Oakleigh Estate would have been able to tell her that some of her family members were still alive and, ultimately, they would have all reunited. Meanwhile, Willie Temple would have remained safe with his mother and Hester would have had no personal motivation to respond to the missing persons notice she came across in *The Truth Teller*.

Bronagh sighed a slow exhalation of shame. 'In the end, it made no odds 'cause I knew I couldn't bring myself to leave Malachy. I'd depended upon him for too long. Sure, I'd never be able to stand on my own two feet without him. Except going back meant my baby would be in danger once he grew old enough to climb chimneys, and the very thought of that damn near crushed me.'

'Ah, Bronagh,' Orlaith murmured. 'I can't describe how sorry I am for you.'

Very deliberately, Bronagh extracted her fingers from Orlaith's grasp. 'You won't feel the same after you hear what I did next.'

'You mean Willie?' said Tess. She crossed her arms as she surveyed Bronagh. 'We know what you did. And I think now I can guess why.'

Bronagh gave a dispirited nod. 'When he brought me something to eat, the most awful idea came to my mind. Hester went off to deal with an unruly customer and while she was gone I convinced Willie to leave through the back door with me. I reminded him that his ma had said to help me if I needed anything—he was a soft lad so he went willingly enough. I took him to the warehouse and offered Malachy a bargain: he could have Willie as a climbing boy so long as he swore that he wouldn't recruit our own child in the future. To my utter relief, he agreed.'

The silence was deafening. Orlaith took an unsubtle step backwards.

'I know,' said Bronagh dully. 'I'm a hideous human being. But I couldn't think of any other way to protect my baby. I told Willie that his ma had sent him to us for his apprenticeship and made sure all the men knew never to let him anywhere near the vicinity of the brothel when they took him out on a job. Needless to say, I stayed well away from there myself. To be honest, I hardly ever leave the warehouse anymore, apart from emptying the slops. Cáit's the one who goes out now to get food or other supplies.'

Because she didn't feel capable of addressing any other part of this heinous speech, Bridget said, 'Is Cáit still involved with Seamus?'

'Occasionally. She and I share a den on the upper floor and we don't come out much, but she has to be available when the mood takes him. Same with me and Malachy.'

What an atrocious state of affairs. Bronagh claimed that she could perceive the reality of her situation but Bridget doubted it very much. If she truly comprehended it, she would

319

recognise that Malachy's disinclination to marry her had been a blessing. No legal contract bound her to that fiend, unlike the all-encompassing power Garrett wielded over Bridget. She could flee, had even had the opportunity and justification to do so, and yet she continued to stay. Of course, fear played a significant role in keeping her confined in these circumstances, but so did her own delusion of love, as evidenced by her wearing the purloined gold ring on her wedding finger.

Bridget eyed the ring, her naked left hand twitching with longing. It was so close and yet frustratingly out of her reach. Then she remembered that she was not the only one who had suffered such a loss.

'Were there any other rings in the spoils from our attack?' she demanded, gesticulating towards Bronagh's hand. 'Orlaith's wedding band was stolen as well. Could Seamus have taken it for Cáit?'

Bronagh flinched. 'I'm not sure. Malachy always gets first pick of whatever comes into the warehouse so he gave this to me. I don't know if there was any other jewellery.'

'Can you find out from Cáit for us?' Orlaith asked, her tone hopeful.

Bronagh shot her a dubious glance. 'I'm not going to become some kind of messenger for ye. Malachy would go into a rage if he found out and I won't do anything that'll put my baby at risk.'

'But Jack and Gus!' Orlaith protested. 'You'll help us free them, won't you?'

Bronagh shook her head, her expression regretful but unmoved. 'I'm sorry. I can't.'

'So you're just going to walk away?' said Tess in disbelief. 'After all this, you're fine with acting like you never saw us and pretending that it isn't your own nephews locked up in there?'

Bronagh's face contorted into an anguished grimace. 'After everything I've told you, how can you even be surprised? Like I said before, I wasn't worth finding.'

She pushed off from the door and turned as though to open it. Charlie stepped closer and pressed his forearm against it to keep it shut.

'Listen,' she said wearily. 'There's nothing you can say or do to change my mind. I fell for a wicked man but I've become as bad as him.' She stroked her bump. 'The only thing that matters to me now is keeping this craythur safe.'

Bridget appraised the gaunt woman before her. She had sacrificed all of her integrity for the sake of her unborn child.

Would Bridget do any differently?

'We'll let you go,' she said, resigned to the fact that they could not rely upon Bronagh's assistance and already concocting an alternative plan. 'Will this prolonged absence get you into trouble when you go back inside?'

'I'm hoping no one will notice how long I've been gone,' Bronagh replied. 'The double doors aren't guarded, only the room where the boys are held.'

She held Bridget's gaze intently for a moment and Bridget understood that that was as much as Bronagh could give her.

'Good luck to you,' she said before nodding at Charlie. He stood back to let Bronagh open the door and, with a swift look of remorse over her shoulder at Orlaith, she darted out through it. A waft of slightly fresher air floated in as they heard her rapid footsteps fleeing up the passageway.

'Jaysus,' said Tess, releasing a breath through her teeth.

Charlie tried to wrap his arms around Orlaith but she stood rigid within his grasp. 'I hate Malachy Kelly!' she cried. 'I wish he was anywhere else on this earth but here!'

Bridget didn't have the courage to tell her that it had once been in her power to grant that wish. Though she presently stood in a stinking slaughterhouse, her mind drifted back to the candlelit study at Oakleigh Manor in the dead of night when Lady Courcey had delivered her judgement upon the silver thieves. She had intended to punish them with transportation to Australia but Bridget had persuaded her to reduce their sentence to imprisonment instead. After the criminals had been escorted from the study, Lady Courcey had said to her, 'I hope you will not learn the hard way the consequences of such leniency.' The lesson had been harder than Lady Courcey could ever have imagined.

Only for Bridget's intervention, Malachy Kelly would be languishing right now in a colony on the other side of the world.

CHAPTER 28

The guard unlocked the iron door and shoved Cormac roughly through it. Head down, he stumbled inside the cell to find that it was already occupied; several figures shrank back into the shadowed corners like rodents retreating from a bird of prey. The sound of tiny paws skittering over stone indicated that actual rodents inhabited the cell as well. A smell of urine filled the air.

'Sit there,' the guard barked and pointed to a stretch of wall, bare apart from the shackles hanging off it. Cormac lowered himself to the flagstones, propped his back against the damp wall and let the guard clap the shackles into place around his ankles and wrists. He had spent the previous night manacled in a holding area in some other part of the prison and his joints already showed signs of abrasion.

'Here, Roper,' came a gruff murmur from the opposite side of the cell. A shaft of murky light fell in through a high grate across the middle of the floor but the speaker remained beyond its reach in the gloom.

The guard's head turned towards the voice. 'What?'

'Got something for you.' Cormac discerned the Dublin accent and wondered if it was a policy at Newgate Prison to detain all the Irishmen together.

Roper made certain that Cormac's shackles were secure before he crossed over to the other prisoner. Cormac heard the metallic clink of coins and then the voice muttered, 'Bring the decent bottle, there's a good fella.'

'I'll see what I can do,' said Roper, 'but I ain't making any promises.'

As the guard exited the cell, Cormac reflected that he possessed no such leverage himself – he had given all of his money to Rory just before he was arrested. No matter. Enabling Emily and Rory to escape from London was a far more vital use of those funds than bribing the prison guards.

The door clanged shut and its heavy key turned in the lock. A gentle rustle of irons suggested that the other prisoners had relaxed again now that the guard was gone. A new voice spoke, this one in a broad Ulster accent, strengthening Cormac's theory that this was a cell designated for Irish inmates.

'What're you in for then?'

He didn't answer. He hugged the shadows that blanketed his section of the wall, yearning so badly to reverse the events of the past twenty-four hours. If only he and Rory had taken a different turn, if only they had walked along a different street. But then Alice Caulfield would have been crushed under the wheels of the carriage and, try as he might, he couldn't muster that level of vindictiveness towards her. She had been instrumental in his arrest yesterday but, judging from her actions, it appeared that her heart had been a grave casualty in his and Bridget's love affair eight years ago.

'You waiting for a trial at the Old Bailey?' persisted the Ulster voice.

Cormac eased the shackle along his left wrist so that it would not chafe on the braided leather band Bridget had given him.

'Och, not really the talkative sort, are you?' This was accompanied by a rasping chuckle.

'Not really,' he replied. 'But thanks for trying.'

There was a loud clanking as one of the other prisoners stirred suddenly. A low ejaculation of 'What the hell?' confirmed that the noise had issued from the Dublin man. 'Show your face, you!' he demanded.

Cormac hesitated, apprehension rising in him. He considered refusing until he realised that that would be pointless in these close quarters. He couldn't hide indefinitely, but at least neither could the other man get close enough to assault him. Pulling on his shackles, he shifted forwards into the shaft of daylight slanting across the middle of the cell.

'Well, if it isn't my old pal, McGovern.'

The other man leaned forwards too and the dim light illuminated a thickset fellow with a neck like a bull and an expression full of loathing. A chill rippled over Cormac's skin – he must have truly been preoccupied by his tribulations not to have recognised that voice sooner.

'Munroe,' he said coolly, trying not to betray the fact that the thug's appearance had just made his abysmal mood ten times worse.

Henry Munroe, on the other hand, said, 'This is the best news I've had all day—nah, all *year*. Sodding McGovern, in chains at last.' Though he sounded gleeful, his countenance did not lose its look of ugly dislike. 'I hope you're headed for the noose. I'll help them knot the rope myself.'

The Ulsterman cleared his throat. 'You two have some history, I take it.'

He was the only other occupant of the cell who showed any interest in Cormac and Munroe's not-so-touching reunion. The rest of the prisoners – from the movements in the shadows, Cormac estimated that there must be half a dozen in the cell altogether – either grunted with apathy or started to snore.

Munroe emitted a laugh that mutated into a snarl. 'History? You can say that again.' He lifted his hand to point a threatening finger at Cormac, the shackles clinking around his wrist as he did so. 'I had a good thing going until that bastard smashed it all to smithereens.'

Still shrouded in darkness in the corner, the Ulsterman said mildly, 'Is that so?'

Before Munroe could launch into a tirade of his past transgressions, Cormac asked succinctly, 'What happened to Cunningham?'

Munroe glared. 'He's dead. You killed him.'

'Is *that* so?' The voice in the corner sounded much more curious now, as though Cormac's capacity for murder had made him considerably worthier of attention.

'Dead,' Cormac repeated as he endeavoured to absorb the information. In his mind's eye, he once again saw the dagger sail from his own hand across the Dublin alleyway to lodge in the money lender's gut.

'And a nasty death it was too,' said Munroe. 'The man lingered in agony for two days while his insides turned foul. Called down every curse he could think of on you until he didn't have enough breath to speak anymore, and then he went blue and kicked the bucket. Stank to the high heavens, let me tell you.'

So Cormac had slain the son of a bitch. He had always suspected it but now he knew it for certain. The knowledge brought a fresh measure of guilt tempered with grim satisfaction – he had taken a man's life but countless people were better off without that blackguard ruling the streets. Apart from his lackeys, apparently.

Cormac tilted his head. 'Did no one take over his business?'

Munroe snorted. 'We made a dog's dinner out of that. It obviously should've been me to take charge but Lawlor thought he could do a better job so, instead of the pair of us putting up a united front, we divided the loyalties of the others. Ended up splintering the gang into bickering factions and the whole thing fell apart.'

Cormac could easily envisage how greed had got in the way of intelligence among those thugs. 'So you left seeking your fortune elsewhere?'

'I did. Decided to come across the Irish sea and chance my luck in this country. Fell in with a band of smugglers which proved fairly lucrative until the excise men caught us.' Munroe raised his palms as expansively as his chains would allow to indicate where that had got him. 'I'm waiting on my own trial too.' He eyed Cormac. 'So who managed to get your sorry arse behind bars? I owe the fella a drink.'

Cormac didn't reply. He imagined that Alice would faint if she came face to face with Munroe, a seasoned criminal of a much more brutal kind than himself.

'Och, you have to tell us,' the Ulsterman said encouragingly. 'I'm dying to know what a well-spoken blighter like yourself is doing in here with us.'

Cormac was saved from answering by the scrape of iron across flagstones as the cell door opened once more and Roper strode through it. He carried a bottle which he dropped into Munroe's lap.

'Take it easy with this one, right? I don't want to hear you singing Irish ballads in the middle of the night again. Believe me, you ain't no nightingale.'

Munroe chuckled huskily. 'Right you are. Cheers.' Before the guard turned to leave, he added, 'Question for you, Roper. Say a fella had some information about another fella that could contribute to the case being made in court against the second fella, would the first fella be able to negotiate a more lenient

327

sentence for his own crimes if he were to share that information like a decent citizen?'

Roper frowned as he tried to decipher this. 'I reckon so,' he said at last.

Munroe grinned. 'Then I need you to tell your higher-ups that I've got some information.'

Cormac's stomach sank.

CHAPTER 29

Emily sat at her mother's dressing table, fingering the red velvet of the gown she wore while Lizzie stood behind her stool and arranged her hair in a flattering style. She stared at her reflection with a heavy heart; less than an hour remained until she and Garrett had to depart for the soiree at the Swaneset residence and Edward had not shown up at Wyndham House. Her introduction into society was about to happen and she had never desired it less.

'Thank you for altering the gown so quickly,' she said faintly, shifting her focus to meet Lizzie's gaze in the mirror. 'You've done a marvellous job.'

'You're welcome, miss,' said Lizzie, her voice equally subdued. She slotted the final pin into place. 'All done.'

Emily took a deep breath before rising from the stool. She was about to step away when Lizzie caught her arm, arresting her in place.

'You're as strong as your mother,' she said, her tone now low and fierce. 'I know you can bear whatever he throws at you, just like she did.'

Emily felt her chin tremble and she bit down hard on her lower lip to stop it. 'I'll try,' she whispered.

She descended to the entrance hall where she found Peter hovering in readiness for their departure.

'Could you please ask Rory to come to me before I leave?' she said to the footman. She didn't dare incur Garrett's displeasure by entering the servants' quarters herself, not while her father's liberty hung in the balance, but she yearned for Rory's reassurance that she was doing the right thing.

Peter looked uncomfortable. 'I'm afraid I can't, miss. Mr Carey left the house a couple of hours ago and hasn't returned yet.'

'Oh,' she said, surprised to feel her spirits drop even lower. Gracious, she was a delicate creature at the moment. 'Thank you for telling me. I shall go wait for your master in the drawing room then.'

'No need. I am here.'

Her skin crawled. She didn't turn to greet Garrett but he walked right in front of her to appraise her appearance.

'Lovely,' he said with what seemed to be genuine appreciation. 'You are truly captivating in red, my daughter.'

Her stomach pitched with nausea. How appalling that her actions tonight would bind her irrevocably to this odious man.

Garrett grinned. 'At least you ought to be easy to marry off—no man in possession of his bodily functions could resist such a charming bauble. Indeed, I wager you shall marry up. Should we seek the interest of an earl or do we dare attempt to hook a marquess?'

Now her spirits plummeted through the floor. Samuel Marlowe was neither an earl nor a marquess. Worse still – in Garrett's eyes, at any rate – he was an American. Was she going to end up losing the love of her life by the very means with which she had been striving to make herself worthy of him?

There was a sharp rap on the front door. Emily and Garrett both looked at it with astonishment.

'Is it Patrick, do you think?' Garrett said to Emily, his feigned air of nonchalance not quite concealing the note of hope in his voice. 'Or Sawyer coming to tell us the carriage is ready?'

Or Rory, she added silently with her fingers crossed, even though there was no rational reason why he would want to enter the house by its main entrance.

Peter pulled the door open wide.

'Edward!' Emily exclaimed, astounded and utterly relieved.

He stood on the top step wearing a scowl but clad in finery appropriate for a social evening with the ton.

'I suppose you'd better call me Patrick,' he said to Emily before his gaze slid to his father.

Garrett's face was incandescent with stunned delight. 'T-truly?' he said. Emily wondered if he had ever stammered before in his life.

'You played a good game,' the boy replied. 'I tip my hat to you.' He shrugged but Emily thought he actually seemed impressed beneath his casual manner. Like father, like son in so many ways.

'I am overjoyed,' said Garrett, beaming. 'And I hope that in due course your esteem for me will extend beyond my guile and my fortune.'

'Who knows?' said Edward – or rather, Patrick. 'It's an adequate start though.'

They shared a smirk. Emily could only imagine the deviant relationship that would develop between them from here. It could all go horribly wrong...or it was possible that they just might be perfect for each other.

Urgent, clacking heels heralded the arrival of another visitor. A tall lady with flaxen hair came into view behind Patrick, her skirts bunched in her hands so that she could climb the steps unimpeded. Her nostrils flared as she let go of her skirts and looked around at them all, before focusing her attention upon Patrick.

'Edward,' she said in a soft voice that didn't match the simmering anger in her expression. 'Come away from here at once.'

She put her hand on his shoulder but he shook himself out of her grip.

'No, Mother—that is to say, Lady Anner. I have already explained my reasoning to you. You have suffocated me with your lies for long enough.'

'But you cannot mean to do this,' she said, waving in Garrett's direction with palpable dislike. 'It is too drastic, too public.' Her jaw tightened. 'Too permanent.'

Edward raised his eyebrows. 'I understand that the choice I'm making hurts you but you in turn must acknowledge that our familial tie was built upon a gross deception which *you* chose to perpetuate.' He twisted his mouth. 'Besides, my real mother was a peasant. Why would you and Lord Anner wish to be associated with someone polluted by lower class blood?'

'Because you're all we've got,' she hissed between clenched teeth. 'We have spent a great deal of time moulding you into a desirable form despite your objectionable origins. Without you, the barony will pass to a distant relative who is entirely unworthy of the honour. After all our efforts, that would be unconscionable.'

'I do apologise for having wasted your time,' he said with exaggerated politeness and took a deliberate step across the threshold into the house.

Emily goggled. How unfeeling of him to discard her just like that, but then the lady's own attitude was just as cold. She offered no protestations of adoring love for her 'son', only a calculated justification for keeping him by her side.

She stood rigid on the doorstep, her icy gaze now aimed at Garrett. 'How dare you steal my heir away from me?' she said, her accusation quiet and seething. 'Your behaviour is despicable.'

'You are entitled to your opinions,' said Garrett, unperturbed. 'I am comfortable with how I have conducted myself.'

As Patrick stepped up beside him, Garrett placed his hand on his shoulder. Lady Anner's eyes glittered when the boy did not shrug him off.

'You are harming your own reputation as well as mine,' she retorted. 'If the truth is exposed, society will brand us both as deceivers.'

Garrett smiled. 'I am merely assuming my paternal responsibilities after learning of my child's existence. You are the one who knowingly made a false claim about him. And now you must contend with the consequences.' He patted his son's shoulder. 'Are you ready to depart?'

'I am,' said Patrick.

'Wait!' said Emily, her initial relief replaced with sudden panic. 'Our agreement. You will still use your influence to free my father from Newgate?'

Garrett offered her a mocking look of regret. 'That bargain was contingent upon your attendance at the soiree. You will not be coming, so it is now void.' Ignoring her horrified gasp, he went on, 'Our previous bargain shall be reinstated. I will pay you handsomely for your successful completion of the task I assigned you. Take heart—enrolment at Brubaker Art Academy will soon be a reality for you.'

'But my father!'

'He will be convicted and imprisoned or, if the judge is in a generous mood, hanged.' Garrett bared his teeth. 'I look forward to witnessing it.'

That left her speechless. She gripped the folds of her skirts, her fists crushing the red velvet to prevent herself from lunging at him to throttle his neck. He turned from her, gesturing to Patrick to precede him out the front door. Lady Anner was obliged to step aside, her jaw dropping when Patrick went by her without a word. Garrett, however, paused as he passed.

'Please accept my commiserations, Lady Anner,' he said. 'Your sojourn in London this summer has not transpired in the manner you expected. I wish you a safe journey back to Dublin.'

He bowed to her before carrying on down the steps to the street. Sawyer was indeed waiting there with the carriage, ready to convey his passengers to the Swaneset residence where Garrett would formally present Patrick as his long-lost son and heir. Garrett and Patrick climbed in and the coachman urged the horses into motion. As the carriage rattled away, Lady Anner stared after it, white-faced and aghast. Then, without even a glance at Emily, she stormed off down the steps and out of sight.

Tears sprang to Emily's eyes. She stood utterly abandoned in the entrance hall, dressed for an event she was no longer welcome to attend, anguished by the knowledge that she had failed her dear papa. Peter lingered awkwardly by the open door. After a few moments, he started to close it.

'Hold on!' called a voice from the street.

Shock fired through her veins. Peter pulled the door wide again and there was Rory, running up the steps. He halted at the top.

'I held back until all that was over,' he said. 'Thought it best not to interfere.'

Her heart pounded against her ribs. 'Where were you?' she asked, struggling not to reveal how fervently glad she was to see him.

'Newgate Prison,' he replied. 'I've found a way for you to visit your da. D'you want me to take you to him?'

He put out his hand. She didn't even stop to think about changing her clothes. She seized his hand without hesitation and they dashed down the steps, leaving a gawping Peter standing on the threshold behind them.

***

Cormac had swallowed the stale bread and weak broth Roper had brought in for all the prisoners and was now staring up despondently at the high grate. It contained no glass so he imagined that conditions in the cell during winter must be bitterly cold. Even now in the middle of July, the air was dank and the stone wall felt chilly against his back. The light had changed this late in the evening, leaving the whole cell shrouded in gloom.

He fingered the chestnut strands woven through the leather band on his left wrist; it was a comfort to have a sliver of Bridget here with him as he contemplated the bleak end that was coming. His despair had been growing with every passing hour since his arrest. He had no lawyer to defend him and he had no defence in any case – he was guilty of fraud and of many other crimes besides. What evidence could he possibly offer to vindicate himself? He harboured little doubt that either a noose or a prison ship awaited him at the conclusion of his trial.

His chest tightened as he thought of all the people he would fail once the court handed down his conviction. Aside from the emotional upheaval that his death or deportation would bring, Bridget and their three children would struggle to make ends meet. Then there were his two surviving sisters – while Orlaith might be an independent spirit with a husband to look out for her, his search for Bronagh would be cut short and she would never be found. There was a time when he would have counted Tess as a sister too but he couldn't claim an outright responsibility towards her, not anymore. However, Rory would lose his employment at the workshop and that would leave the Careys in financial difficulty. Even Henrietta would be left at the total mercy of Mrs O'Hara if he was no longer able to come to her aid.

Then again, that duty shouldn't fall to him regardless. He shifted his gaze to look across the cell. Munroe had leaned back into the furthest shadows and a sporadic sipping sound indicated that he was rationing his bottle of drink carefully. The rest of the prisoners lounged about in silent lethargy; the only movement came from one fellow striving to find a more comfortable position, his shackles jangling before settling again.

In the quietness, Cormac's low voice carried clearly. 'Do you ever spare a thought for your daughter, Munroe?'

There was a pause. 'Don't have one,' Munroe answered flippantly.

'You're still telling yourself that, are you?' Cormac bit out. 'You and I both know it's a lie. She has your eyes. And your name.'

A deep glug suggested that Munroe had taken a longer swig of his drink. The glass bottle clinked as he set it on the ground.

'What's the point of sparing a thought for the chit?' he said with a grunt. 'Not much I can do for her in here.'

'And what if you secure your release off the back of your testimony against me? Will you go seek her out then? Will that prompt you to take on your paternal responsibilities at last?'

So much time passed that Cormac assumed Munroe had decided to end the conversation right there, but eventually the thug's rough voice emanated from the darkness. 'She won't want to see me.'

'Have you asked her that yourself?'

Before Munroe could respond, footsteps scuffled outside the door. The key turned in the lock and Roper entered carrying a lantern, followed by two other figures.

'Papa!'

A blur of red launched itself towards Cormac and fell into his arms.

'E-Emily?' he stuttered.

She curled herself onto his lap and clung to him. 'Yes, it's me.' Her voice cracked with distress.

Alarm gripped him. 'What in God's name possessed you to come? You shouldn't be here. It's too dangerous.'

Despite this protestation, he couldn't help pulling her closer so that the top of her golden head nestled under his jaw. The fabric of her gown was luxuriously soft beneath his fingers and she smelled like fresh lilacs.

'I think I'm seeing an angel,' mumbled the Ulsterman from his corner.

Cormac couldn't contradict him. Peering around Emily's clinging figure, he recognised Rory standing in the doorway next to Roper.

'Ten minutes,' the guard said, passing over the lantern in exchange for some coins that Rory produced from his pocket. Roper left, locking the door behind him, and Rory's gaze connected with Cormac's, the lantern making his eyes blaze green. Cormac supposed he could berate him for putting Emily in unnecessary danger but instead he chose to accept this precious gift. He would never hold such a treasure in his arms again.

He embraced her as tightly as he could. 'I'm so glad to see you, *a stór*,' he murmured into her hair.

'Oh, Papa!' she said in a muffled wail and even the Irishman in him rejoiced that she had reverted to calling him by that English term of endearment. 'This is all my fault!'

'Hush now, it isn't.'

She pulled back, gaping at him with incredulity. 'Of course it is!'

He shook his head firmly. 'I didn't even know you existed when I met Oliver Davenport,' he said. 'And that crime is why I'm here. I was bound to answer for it sooner or later. This began long before you decided to act on Garrett's letter.'

She lowered her eyes in shame. 'I was so foolish to trust him. I really believed he was telling the truth. But he is just a cruel man full of schemes and lies.'

Tears leaked down her cheeks and he reached out to wipe them away with his thumbs, his shackles brushing against her as he did so. She touched a tentative hand to one iron chain and wept harder. Looking past her shoulder, he beckoned to Rory with a twitch of his head. Rory came over, setting the lantern down on the stone floor as he knelt beside them.

'Do you still have the money I gave you?' Cormac asked in an undertone. The last thing he wanted was for the other prisoners to identify Rory as a target for robbery, even if they were fettered to the walls.

Rory nodded. 'Most of it, apart from what I gave the guard just there. He was willing to let us in to see you for a few minutes but I'm afraid not even the whole amount was enough to tempt him to break you free.' Rory brightened. 'But Patrick's finally agreed to be Garrett's heir so Garrett's promised to pay Emily for helping. Maybe that'll be enough to bribe—'

'Don't waste it on me,' Cormac interrupted. 'No sum will be sufficient, not when there are members of the peerage paying attention to the outcome of my trial. And I don't just mean Garrett. If Lord Bewley learns that I've been apprehended...'

Emily sniffed. 'He has. Or at least, Garrett said he was planning to inform him.'

Cormac's heart plummeted but he kept his countenance composed. 'Well, there you go. Once someone as important as an earl expresses interest in a prisoner, there isn't a hope that any guard could be persuaded to allow that prisoner to escape. Don't squander the money on an impossible endeavour. Use it to leave London immediately.'

'Not without you,' Emily protested.

He swallowed. He had to make her understand the reality of his hopeless situation but, God, it would be hard.

'Yes, without me,' he said. 'We must say goodbye tonight, *a stór*, in a very permanent way.'

Her eyes widened. Horror-struck, she looked from him to Rory and back again. 'No,' she said tremulously. 'I refuse to say anything of the sort.'

'Then let me say it—'

'*No.*' She blinked vigorously. 'I won't listen.'

He took her hands in his and gave them a gentle squeeze. 'I will not be going home with you, *a stór*. That is the bald truth. Rory will see you safely back to America and I'll take great comfort in the fact that you'll be reunited with your mother and brothers there.' He faltered. 'Tell them all how much I love them, won't you? And you know it too?'

With a heart-shattering sob, she flung herself against his chest and he cradled her there, just as he had done when she was seven years old and had gone into hysterics after Mabel went missing. He hung on to these final moments with all his might while her body shuddered and her tears soaked into his shirt, but at last he forced himself to prise her away from him.

'It's time, my baby girl.'

Her head quivered from side to side, denying it. His self-control was splintering. If she didn't leave now, he would never let her go. He glanced at Rory who was gazing at Emily's back with a fierce expression and knew he was placing his daughter in safe hands.

A gruff voice spoke from the other side of the cell. 'I'd agree with you on that, McGovern. Our Ulster friend is getting pretty stirred up by the little angel. I'm starting to guess what got him locked up here in the first place.'

Revolted by the insinuation and keen to remove Emily from the cell as swiftly as possible, Cormac urged her towards Rory. She struggled to hold onto his shirt but Rory grasped her by the elbows and pulled her to her feet; her fingers slipped away and clutched only at the air. Rory dragged her, weeping, over to the door where he thumped his fist until the guard thrust it open. Emily and Rory disappeared through it while Roper came in to retrieve his lantern. As its beam of light swung across the cell, it illuminated the rest of the prisoners; the Ulsterman's hand was engaged in a highly indecent act inside his trousers while Munroe waved his bottle towards Cormac in salutation.

'Daughters are more trouble than they're worth, I reckon,' he said.

Then Roper left, plunging them into darkness, and all Cormac could focus on was the sound of Emily's sobbing receding down the passageway.

CHAPTER 30

Bridget supposed she could spend time wallowing in guilt over the role she had played in facilitating Malachy Kelly to obtain his unearned freedom but, after a night of fitful sleep, she concluded that it would serve nobody, least of all her boys still trapped in the warehouse. Instead, she threw herself into devising a new plan to set them free, one that would not rely on Bronagh's assistance and yet still counted upon her as a crucial factor.

'It's madness,' said Orlaith, her brow furrowed with scepticism. 'It'd never work.'

'On the contrary,' said Bridget. 'This family has availed of such deceptions in the past.'

'Sure, but how did those pan out?'

'With remarkable success, on the whole. Cormac lived for nearly five years under the alias Oliver Davenport and Patrick has grown up most of his life as the fictional Edward Whitmore. In contrast, your ruse would be required for a much shorter time period.'

Orlaith tucked her lips inside her mouth, considering. 'I'm no good at acting. I'm bound to mess it up.'

'You're the only one who can do this,' said Bridget seriously. 'I have faith in you.'

Orlaith hummed and hawed a little longer but in the end she accepted the truth: this plan was the only way and she must be the one to do it.

She would infiltrate the Kelly Greens masquerading as Bronagh.

Following the encounter in the slaughterhouse, they had returned to the brothel on Orange Street in a numb state, staggered by what Bronagh had divulged to them. They had been obliged to admit to Hester that she had been correct the whole time in her assumptions but, rather than crowing about it, she had just said, 'Everyone's got their reasons for doing bad things. Often it's because they can't see any other choices. Let's just get our children back.'

Now she took on the challenge of transforming Orlaith into her sister while Bridget, Tess and Charlie watched with uneasy fascination. She unearthed a large dress from a stockpile of spares she kept for her girls in the brothel and instructed Orlaith to put it on. Orlaith did so and shuffled around the sitting room with the hem dragging at her feet.

'How pregnant is Bronagh at this stage?' Hester asked. 'Seven months? Eight?'

'There or thereabouts, I would say,' Bridget replied, wondering how scared Bronagh was about her baby's impending arrival. There was no guarantee that they would both survive the birth and, even if they did, how likely was it that Malachy would honour his promise to keep the child safe from the gang's activities? Bridget wouldn't trust any bargain made with that fiend but she understood why Bronagh had so desperately wanted to believe him.

Hester eyed a few cushions in her sitting room and selected one, plumping it up before handing it to Orlaith. With a self-conscious grimace, Orlaith tucked it up underneath her dress which raised the hem off the floor. Hester poked and prodded it around her stomach area until she had fashioned a credible semblance of a pregnant belly. Then she stood back and surveyed Orlaith.

'The teeth,' she said and bustled off, returning with a pot of kohl and an ivory stick. 'Sorry, this probably won't taste the best but I think it'll be effective.'

She applied the kohl heavily on several of Orlaith's teeth to blacken them and even used it to make dark circles under her eyes and to create grime beneath her fingernails. Lastly, she collected a cup of ashes from the grate in the brothel's kitchen, dipped her fingers in it and ran them over Orlaith's hair, tangling the strands into messy knots as she turned their dark colour grey.

'Jaysus, you look awful,' Tess said with approval.

Orlaith examined her appearance in a cracked mirror. 'I really do.'

'What about your voice though?' said Charlie. 'You don't sound like your sister at all.'

'Can you try to mimic her?' suggested Bridget. 'Perhaps your Carlow accent is still buried somewhere underneath your Dublin one.'

'It's not just that though,' said Tess. 'Bronagh's a lot hoarser too.'

After much discussion and a number of vain attempts on Orlaith's part to produce a husky voice similar to her sister's, they agreed that it would be best for her to speak as little as possible.

Once Orlaith's physical transformation was complete, they deliberated over how they would execute the rescue. Though they had previously observed the warehouse during daylight hours, Bridget proposed that they wait until dusk that evening to sneak in.

'Chimney sweeping is a daytime profession, even for charlatans, so any men out "working" will surely be back with the boys by that hour,' she said, praying that today would not be the day that Jack, Gus or Willie had a terrible mishap up a narrow flue. 'And doubtless they will have to hold off until full dark before they can make them go out again to thieve.'

Hester herself decided that she would remain behind as she would only draw attention when they needed to be inconspicuous.

'At least most white folk look like other white folk until they open their mouths,' she said dryly.

On that note though, nearly all of their voices would present an issue – Orlaith didn't sound enough like Bronagh to be convincing, while Charlie's American accent and Bridget's English one would both raise suspicion in a building solely occupied by Irish people. In the end, they determined that Tess's red hair and Dublin accent made her the most obviously Irish of them all and so she would do the talking if they encountered any members of the Kelly Greens.

Of course, they did expect to encounter gang members but Bronagh herself had stated that the double doors weren't guarded, so they were hopeful that they would at least manage to get inside the warehouse without being accosted right away. Then, if they ran into anyone who demanded to know their business, Tess would say that they were friends of Bronagh, and Orlaith would nod in confirmation and hurry them along. With any luck, Bronagh's close association with the gang's ruthless leader would be enough to discourage any further queries. Should they stumble into Bronagh herself, they would have to act quickly to convince her to cooperate or, at least, not to interfere.

After that, it would be a matter of locating the room where the children were being held captive. According to Bronagh, it would be guarded, so a measure of improvisation would be required at that point. It was the most imprecise part of the plan and it left Bridget's stomach tied up in knots.

Still, there was one detail on which she was utterly clear: she would not be walking out of that warehouse tonight unless she had her two sons with her.

CHAPTER 31

'We find the defendant guilty as charged, Your Honour.'

Emily wanted to vomit. That was the third conviction in as many trials since she and Rory had sat down in the court gallery that morning. According to the clerk she had pestered when they had arrived, her father's trial had been expedited thanks to the interest of certain elevated personages and hence his name was on the list of prisoners due to appear in court at some point that day. However, no exact time was confirmed so all they could do was wait for his turn to come.

She couldn't imagine how he must be feeling right now. He had kept a tight rein on his emotions the previous night in the cell, but she had felt how fiercely he had clutched her and she had sensed that their parting had been just as difficult for him as it had been for her. Still, it had been vital for them both to share those final precious moments and she was so very grateful to Rory for having orchestrated it on their behalf, and for bringing her back to Wyndham House when she could hardly breathe for crying.

He sat beside her now, wordlessly observing the court proceedings. However, after the latest verdict, he muttered, 'So unjust.'

'What do you mean?' she asked. She didn't need to keep her voice low for there was a good deal of movement and chatter around them as the bailiff removed the condemned prisoner from the courtroom and spectators shuffled in and out of the gallery. The judge left too, although the twelve men of the jury remained seated in their wooden stalls.

'He wasn't guilty,' Rory said with some heat. 'Anyone could see that there wasn't a shred of evidence to place the fella at the house on the night of the theft. But a posh gentleman in fancy clothes stands in the witness box and blackens the fella's character and that's enough to convict him.'

She gulped. If the judge and jury could be so easily swayed, what hope did her papa have?

She shot to her feet and marched out of the gallery, leaving an astonished Rory behind her. Making her way down into the courtroom, she strode right up to the stalls where the jurors sat conversing casually with each other while they waited for the next case to be brought before them.

'Excuse me,' she said loudly. A few of them turned to her in surprise but most of them didn't notice her. She rapped her knuckles on the top of the front stall. That drew the attention of the others and she took a deep breath, looking around at them all with wide eyes. 'I am speaking to you as the loving daughter of an honourable man. Please, I beseech you, *please* do your duty and give each prisoner a fair trial. They are depending on your impartiality for their very lives.'

A man with bushy white eyebrows sitting in the first row gaped at her. 'You are not entitled to address the jury. This is grossly improper.'

Rory appeared at Emily's side. 'Come away, for God's sake,' he murmured. 'Leave them be.'

She paid him no heed. 'I'm imploring you all,' she said, clasping her hands, begging the men to see how earnest she was.

'You must be fair. You must form your opinions without bias, or how will you rest easy at night?'

The man's white brows bristled as he spluttered, 'Is that a threat to our safety, madam?'

She goggled. 'Good gracious, no, I meant—'

He stood and gesticulated at someone behind her. 'Remove her from this courtroom at once.'

She whirled to realise that the bailiff had returned from escorting out the previous prisoner and was now approaching her with a grim expression.

'Oh no!' she exclaimed, swivelling back to the juror. 'You misunderstood me—'

'Such intimidation has no place in a court of law,' he said primly.

Before she could deride the notion that her small person was capable of presenting any form of intimidation, the bailiff had seized her arm and pulled her away from the stalls. She saw Rory's shoulders slump as he followed. She tried to explain the mistake to the bailiff but he ignored her and, panicking, she started to struggle in his grasp. Gripping her more tightly, he practically dragged her towards the entrance of the courtroom. The door swung open as they neared it and three ladies came in. She gasped in recognition: they were her mother's friends...or at least they had been in the past.

'Please!' she cried at them, without quite knowing what she was entreating them to do. What power did they have in this room, after all?

The mousy-featured one pursed her lips and glanced away. The one with the sizeable nose – Emily recognised her as Lady Newby, Angela and Valerie's mother – peered at her with great consternation, while the third sniggered.

'What a diverting spectacle this shall be,' she trilled.

Then the bailiff pushed Emily onwards and out through the door. He deposited her beyond the brick wall that enclosed the area at the front of the Old Bailey and barked, 'Don't you dare come back in, missy!' Squinting in Rory's direction, he added, 'Nor you neither!' and vanished back inside.

Emily stared slack-jawed at Rory. 'I d-didn't mean...' she said faintly.

'I know,' he said. 'But it was still a silly thing to do.' There was no reproach in his tone, only a rueful curve at the corner of his mouth.

'Getting into trouble again, my daughter?' said a silky voice behind Emily.

She spun around. Garrett stood there with a smirk on his face stretching from ear to ear.

'Never *ever* call me that again,' she spat at him. 'You—you—'

'I believe "lousy sod" is the endearment you're searching for,' he said cheerfully. 'Has the miscreant's trial begun yet? I do hope not. I should hate to miss his entrance into the court bound in chains.'

Rory hovered near Emily, ready to intervene if she leapt to attack, but she stayed rooted to the ground, her fists clenched with hatred.

'So after promising to set him free,' she growled, 'you're just going to watch him get convicted instead?'

'Good Lord, I intend to do much more than that. I am going to testify as a witness.' He grinned.

It felt like no air was reaching her lungs. 'You disgust me,' she managed to get out. 'I have such pity for Patrick. What a poison you will be in his life.'

Garrett blinked and an expression of deep hurt filled his countenance. 'He will be a new start for me,' he said softly. 'For the sake of his mother, I will endeavour to become a decent father.'

She scoffed. 'I'll believe that when I see it.' Far more than Miss Lovell had on the *Integrity*, Garrett had severely damaged Emily's inherent trust in people.

Still looking wounded, he said, 'Come to Wyndham House after the trial is over. I will make arrangements for your compensation then. Perhaps it will go some way towards earning your forgiveness.'

She shook her head in disbelief. 'You think every problem can be solved by throwing money at it. I told you before, I won't accept a penny from you. And I will never forgive you for what you have done to my father.'

A vein throbbed at his temple. 'Very well,' he said stiffly. 'I wish you safe passage back to America and all good fortune in your pursuit of artistic eminence.'

With a smooth bow just like the one he had given Lady Anner, he turned away to enter the Old Bailey. Once he had gone, she finally sucked a deep breath into her lungs. Then she choked on it when another familiar figure approached the courthouse, stooped with age and walking with a cane.

Lord Bewley.

He was accompanied by a man she did not recognise. He had a purple birthmark on one cheek and carried a sheaf of papers under his arm. Both of them wore grave expressions.

'Uncle Bewley!' she exclaimed. She knew she had no business calling him that but she was prepared to utilise every instrument at her disposal, including tugging on the heartstrings of an elderly gentleman who had once enjoyed tea parties with her and her imaginary friends on the hearthrug at Raynesworth House, the Bewleys' residence in London.

She ran up to him. 'Please,' she begged, clutching his arm. 'Please don't do this.'

The earl shook her off without a word and, devastated, she watched him and his companion disappear inside the building.

CHAPTER 32

Cormac entered the courtroom escorted by the bailiff and took his place in the prisoner's dock, standing there in his shackles and his humiliation. What would his mother and father say if they could see him now? He had lost count of all the ways he had disgraced them in his life.

His heart hammered as he looked around the court, seeking out faces that he knew. He didn't glimpse any sign of Emily or Rory and was glad for it. While it would have been a comfort to endure the trial in the knowledge that at least two people in the room supported him, there was no need for them to witness his ignominious end. He hoped they were already boarding a ship on the Thames or perhaps a locomotive back to Liverpool.

He discerned other familiar individuals in the crowded courtroom, however, and they did not wear friendly expressions. Alice was present, along with Lucy and Cassandra, displaying shades of resentment, anxiety and anticipation to varying degrees. He spotted Garrett too which came as no surprise whatsoever – of course the bastard would want to be present for his downfall. And there—

Cormac swallowed hard. Lord Bewley had come.

Eight years had taken their toll on the gentleman. Before, his advanced age had never seemed to impinge upon his vigour, whereas now he actually looked old. He was seated on a bench but he leaned forwards, both hands clutching the brass, T-shaped handle of his beechwood cane as though he were relying on it to keep him upright. His face was heavily wrinkled and spotted and he exuded an air of profound weariness. He kept his gaze averted from the prisoner's dock.

The judge entered with a Bible in his hands and the court rose out of respect for the holy book and the dignitary who carried it. All chatter ceased and the spectators in the gallery craned their necks to catch a glimpse of the clerk as he read out the charge against Cormac. Cormac didn't listen; he was wondering whether he had embraced Bridget tightly enough the last time he had held her. Surreptitiously, he touched the leather band to bolster his courage.

Next, a man stood up behind a mahogany table spread with documents and introduced himself to the court as Mr Tyne, the prosecuting lawyer. He had a nasal tone that grated in a spectacularly unpleasant way and Cormac wasn't the only one who winced upon hearing it; even the solemn judge's eye twitched before he got his features under control. Mr Tyne presented the details of the case to the jury, placing a heavy emphasis on the foulness of Cormac's character and the grievous harm he had inflicted upon the parties who had been exposed to his dastardly conduct. At this, he sent an obsequious bow in Lord Bewley's direction but the earl did not react and, flustered, Mr Tyne turned back to the jury.

'I shall be calling upon a number of witnesses to testify in this matter,' he declared, his voice setting Cormac's teeth on edge, 'and I am certain that the court will be persuaded by their honest accounts that this defendant is guilty.'

With that, he called his first witness: Alice Caulfield. She walked up to the witness box with her chin in the air but Cormac noticed the tremble in her gloved hand as she placed it on the Bible and swore to tell the whole truth. Then she took her seat in the witness box which directly faced the prisoner's dock. When she raised her eyes to meet Cormac's gaze, her countenance hardened and she purposefully folded her hands in her lap, concealing any tremor.

Mr Tyne approached and addressed her with exaggerated sympathy which only augmented the annoying quality of his speech. 'Thank you for coming today, Miss Caulfield. It is not easy for a member of the fairer sex to speak of delicate matters. The court appreciates your selflessness in desiring to achieve justice where injustice has festered for too long.'

Alice's eyelashes fluttered in demure acknowledgement of her self-sacrifice.

'Please tell the court of your relationship to the accused,' Mr Tyne said with an inviting wave.

Alice inhaled an unsteady breath. 'I first made his acquaintance eight years ago at a party hosted at the Radcliffe residence. He was introduced to me as Mr Oliver Davenport, the nephew and heir of the Earl of Bewley. I believed myself to be beneath his notice but he took a particular interest in me from the beginning, escorting me into dinner and partnering with me for the first two dances.' Her cheeks turned pink but she persisted in her testimony. 'He continued to bestow his attentions upon me at subsequent gatherings and I felt my own regard grow in return. Our attachment developed to the point that many in our social circle deemed us to be very near to making an announcement.'

Cormac felt sorry that she had misinterpreted his courtesy – borne out of pity, he had to admit – as a conscious effort to single her out in his affections. However, his sympathy rapidly evaporated when she carried on, 'Indeed, he declared his passionate feelings for me in a private discourse between us.

We came to an understanding and it was only a matter of time before we made our engagement public.'

He stared across at her in dismay. The fact that she was willing to perjure herself to secure his conviction spoke volumes about the extent of the pain he had inadvertently caused her.

'And what transpired before that happy event could occur?' Mr Tyne asked gently.

Alice's eyes flashed. 'I received a letter from Lady Wyndham, a former friend of mine who, I must stress, already had a husband and a child. In it, she revealed that she had left London for good and wished me a fond farewell, which was galling when I subsequently discovered that she had absconded with *my* fiancé!'

Scandalised murmurs rippled through the gallery. Alice drew out a handkerchief and dabbed it at the corner of her eye. Mr Tyne clicked his tongue in theatrical compassion.

'So the defendant misled you with amorous intentions before he abandoned his false persona and fled. And, in doing so, he wounded the sensibilities of an incomparable woman whose only error was to fall in love with an impostor.' He shook his head sadly. 'I am truly sorry for the anguish you have suffered, Miss Caulfield, and I thank you for your bravery in coming here and speaking the truth today. I have no further questions for this witness, Your Honour.'

With a humble nod and a loud sniff, Alice stepped down from the witness box and rejoined Lucy and Cassandra on their bench behind the lawyer's table. Lucy gawked at Alice like she was beholding an utter stranger.

'I wish to call upon my second witness,' announced Mr Tyne. He motioned to the bailiff who slipped out of the courtroom and reappeared moments later shepherding Henry Munroe in front of him. Several gasps erupted at the sight of the manacled prisoner. Mr Tyne raised his nasal voice above the noise. 'Let me reassure the court that this man is safely bound and does not present a physical threat. Furthermore, while his past actions have led to his own imprisonment, you will soon hear how his testimony bears both validity and relevance to this case.'

Munroe shambled into the witness box and leered across at Cormac. After taking the oath, he shot an expectant glance at Mr Tyne.

'Do you recognise the defendant, Mr Munroe?' the lawyer asked.

'I do indeed,' Munroe answered smugly.

'Where have you met him before?'

'In Dublin. We both used to work for an upstanding fella by the name of Cunningham.'

Mr Tyne consulted his notes on the table. 'And Mr Cunningham was a money lender by profession?'

'Yes, sir. Until McGovern murdered him.'

Exclamations of shock rang out and this time the judge had to bang his gavel to restore order.

'That is a very serious accusation, Mr Munroe,' said Mr Tyne. 'Did you witness Mr Cunningham's death?'

'I did,' said Munroe, who looked like he was thoroughly enjoying himself. 'Saw McGovern sink a dagger into Cunningham's stomach and stood by the poor fella's bedside when he died two days later.'

'Dear me, dear me,' said Mr Tyne. 'And would you say that this was very out of character for the defendant? Did he act in an isolated incident of violence, provoked perhaps by a fit of passion or rage?'

'No, sir. McGovern had one of the worst reputations in all of Dublin city.' Munroe grinned. 'Just ask him if he's ever held a dagger to a child's neck.'

The outrage in the courtroom was instantaneous and vociferous. By the time the crowd had quietened down, Mr

Tyne could perceive that his objective had been accomplished and Munroe was dismissed. He threw a contemptuous smile at Cormac before the bailiff steered him out of the courtroom.

After that, it was Garrett's turn to paint Cormac's reputation as black as pitch. The accusations rolled off his tongue: 'seduced my innocent wife'...'abducted my darling daughter'...'nothing but a blackguard driven by lust and greed'. The jury paid rapt attention – after all, Lord Wyndham was a viscount and a respected peer of the House of Lords. Mr Tyne was positively brimming with glee when Garrett left the witness box.

'I now call upon the Earl of Bewley,' the lawyer said, bouncing on the spot in anticipation of playing his trump card. 'The primary victim of the defendant's crime.'

Lord Bewley rose laboriously to his feet and his cane tapped on the courtroom floor as he made his way slowly over to the witness box. He swore on the Bible in a thin voice laced with pain and took his seat. Mr Tyne enquired solicitously after the earl's comfort but Lord Bewley waved an impatient hand and, chastened, the lawyer embarked upon his questioning.

'Do you recognise the defendant standing in the dock, my lord?'

'I do,' said Lord Bewley.

'And do you identify him as the perpetrator of this most heinous offence against you?'

A pause.

'I do not.'

Cormac blinked. So did Mr Tyne, his gaze skittering from the judge to the prisoner's dock and back to his witness.

'Y-you d-don't?' he stammered in confusion.

'No,' said Lord Bewley firmly.

A hum of muttering broke out all around the courtroom. 'Order!' cried the judge and the spectators fell silent.

Mr Tyne gaped at Lord Bewley who looked back at him impassively.

'Let me ask again,' Mr Tyne bleated. 'The man who defrauded you—'

'No such man exists,' Lord Bewley interrupted.

'He doesn't?' said Mr Tyne weakly.

'For the fourth time, I must answer you in the negative. Does that satisfy your line of inquiry?'

Mr Tyne could only nod, dumbfounded.

'Do you have any other witnesses you wish to call?' Lord Bewley asked him.

Mr Tyne shook his head.

'Very well,' said Lord Bewley, turning to the judge. 'Your Honour, if you and the jury are ready, my lawyer Mr Carruthers has prepared an argument for the defence. May he summon the witnesses for cross-examining?'

Looking just as astounded as Mr Tyne, the judge said, 'He may.'

Gobsmacked, Cormac watched as a man with a birthmark on his cheek came forwards to the mahogany table while Mr Tyne regained his seat behind it and sank down low. Lord Bewley, too, returned to his bench as Mr Carruthers tapped a few pages together neatly on the table. Then he spoke out in a clear voice.

'The defence calls Miss Alice Caulfield to the witness box.'

Forehead scrunched in bewilderment, Alice resumed her position under the scrutiny of the whole court. Mr Carruthers left his papers on the table when he advanced towards the witness box, his hands clasped behind his back.

'Miss Caulfield,' he began, his manner relaxed, 'you once harboured a deep regard for the defendant, is that correct?'

'Once,' she said tersely. 'Not anymore. Not after I learned that he was a criminal.'

'Alleged criminal,' Mr Carruthers corrected mildly. 'I imagine it must have grieved you terribly when you later learned that his own affections belonged to another woman. You would no doubt have been eager to seek retribution in any form, even if it meant the unjustified incarceration of an innocent man?'

Her lips pinched together. 'I am not here out of a personal vendetta, if that is what you are implying.'

'Come now,' said Mr Carruthers. 'You had believed yourself betrothed to him. Surely you had started to envision the life you would spend by the side of a handsome man due to inherit an earldom. That life was callously snatched away from you. Or,' he suggested pensively as though the idea had just occurred to him, 'it's possible that it had never existed and that the only place it could ever have been a reality was inside your own head. Did you not feel scorned? Did you not feel bitter?'

Cormac didn't like the direction of this interrogation at all and, judging by the ashen shade of her skin, neither did Alice. She couldn't seem to muster any response beyond a tiny quiver of her head but Mr Carruthers had already moved on.

'I understand that the answer to this next question is self-evident, Miss Caulfield,' he said. 'However, for the sake of clarity, would you oblige me by stating your current marital status?'

Her mouth dropped open. After a beat, she said curtly, 'Unmarried.'

'Thank you. And now can you tell me, apart from the alleged conversation that took place between you and the defendant, how many proposals of marriage have you received since you entered society?'

Distress filled her features but she maintained her composure enough to squeeze out, 'None.'

'I see,' said Mr Carruthers. 'Would you agree then that Mr Tyne's assessment of you as an "incomparable woman" was rather generous, given that no suitor ever admired you enough to ask you for your hand?'

'Stop it.'

Cormac's voice rang out through the courtroom. Mr Carruthers turned slowly to face the prisoner's dock.

'That's enough,' Cormac said with forced calm. 'Leave her be.' He didn't care if the lawyer's tactics were helping his case; what he was doing to Alice was unconscionable.

Mr Carruthers inclined his head in acquiescence. 'I have no further questions for this witness, Your Honour.'

Alice had recoiled at his last vicious blow and now, at the judge's nod, she hurried from the witness box like a frightened mouse scurrying back to its hole. When she sat down again next to Lucy and Cassandra, a muffled sob escaped her but she quickly smothered it.

Mr Carruthers dismantled Munroe next, taking no time at all to hang so much scepticism over his credibility that his testimony became worthless. Munroe shuffled back out of the courtroom with the conditions of his negotiated release in tatters.

Garrett, however, would present a much greater challenge. His title commanded esteem and it was evident that he knew this as he sat down in the witness box radiating cavalier self-possession. Mr Carruthers stood in front of him, seemingly undaunted.

'First of all,' he said, 'let me offer you my congratulations, Lord Wyndham. I understand that you have gained a son in the past twenty-four hours.'

Garrett offered a lazy smile. 'Thank you. I'm flattered that my good news has spread with such alacrity.'

'For those of you who are unaware,' Mr Carruthers said, addressing the court at large, 'Lord Wyndham made a public announcement yesterday evening at the home of Lord Swaneset to the effect that he has had a son these past sixteen years. The boy was purportedly begotten within the confines of a valid marriage, although his mother came from a distinctly unprivileged background.'

Garrett's smile didn't alter. 'If you mean to discredit me by exposing that information, allow me to disappoint you. When I introduced my son to the guests at the Swaneset residence, I made no secret of his humble origins. His mother—my first wife—may have been born into lower class circumstances but she was incomparable in countless other ways.' He winced. 'My apologies,' he said with a remorseful nod in Alice's direction. 'That was a poor choice of word.'

She showed no reaction for her face was buried in her handkerchief.

'How touching, my lord,' said Mr Carruthers. 'You were truly fortunate to have met her, though your time together was sadly all too brief. She passed not long after your nuptials, isn't that correct? But you were not cognisant of the fact that she had borne a child before she died?'

The corners of Garrett's mouth turned down. 'I regret to say that I was entirely ignorant of his existence for many years. I will not weary the court with the details of how we came to be reunited but, suffice to say, I am ecstatic to have my son by my side at last.'

'And a legitimate one at that,' said Mr Carruthers. 'Another blessing. Had your union with his mother not taken place within legal parameters, then he would have been nothing more than an inconsequential by-blow to you.'

Garrett folded his arms. 'Happily, we did marry and therefore he is my lawful heir.'

Mr Carruthers delicately cleared his throat. 'And did the written proof of your marriage contract survive across the years?'

Eyes narrowed, Garrett said, 'Alas, it was destroyed in a fire at the church where we wed. But the minister and two witnesses were present at the ceremony, and all three would swear so in any court of law.'

'Indeed. And how much did you bribe them for that pledge?'

'Objection!' Mr Tyne whined.

Before the judge could speak, Mr Carruthers said, 'I retract the question, Your Honour.' He motioned to the clerk. 'It shall be struck from the record.'

Even so, all vestiges of Garrett's amiable expression had slipped away. 'Have you any questions for me in relation to the defendant, sir?' he said in a clipped tone. 'That is, after all, why we are here.'

'None at all,' Mr Carruthers said cheerfully. 'I merely wished to alert the jury to your capacity for concealment. You had a secret bride many years ago, and until yesterday you had a secret son. What other lies are you capable of?' The lawyer spread his palms wide. 'It is my duty to advise caution so that your title does not blind them to your arguable trustworthiness as a witness.'

Judging by the frowns on the faces of the jurors, he had executed that duty admirably. Cormac felt a tiny spark of hope ignite inside him.

'You may step down, Lord Wyndham,' said Mr Carruthers. 'Thank you for your time.'

Looking livid, Garrett vacated the witness box and strode away as Lord Bewley once more came forwards with slow, shaky steps. It saddened Cormac greatly to see him so diminished in vitality. Had his senses dulled as well? Why else would he permit his personal lawyer to defend Cormac's utterly indefensible actions?

He sat down after taking the oath, his cane once again seeming to be the only thing that kept him from pitching forwards over his knees with fatigue. Mr Carruthers gave him a deferential nod.

'My lord,' he said, 'there are several persons present who are under the impression that the defendant is a fraud and that you have been a victim of his deceitful activities. Can you provide any evidence to the contrary?'

'No evidence but my word,' Lord Bewley replied, 'which I hope will be sufficient to counteract the dubious testimonies submitted to the court today. Not, I might add, on the basis of my earldom but on the strength of my good reputation, which is untarnished both in my home county of Bedfordshire and here in London. You will find no crimes or secrets buried in my past.'

He spoke without heat, only a quiet conviction that was just as persuasive. The spectators in the gallery hummed with approval.

'In that case, my lord,' said Mr Carruthers, 'can you please explain the nature of your association with the defendant and enlighten us as to how his past behaviour does not constitute an egregious contravention of the laws of this land?'

Lord Bewley took a few moments before he responded, meditatively rubbing the handle of his cane. He still did not make eye contact with Cormac. At last, he said, 'The defendant lived at Bewley Hall for nearly five years. During that time, my wife and I considered him to be our ward and our responsibility, and that fact remains unchanged, regardless of whatever name he bore then or since. He is accused of fraud which implies that he swindled us. However, the countess and I deem everything he took to be a gift from us, freely given. Consequently, we do not seek any form of compensation or retribution for there was no theft to begin with.'

Mr Carruthers cocked his head as though viewing an intriguing specimen in the zoological gardens. 'So you do not perceive yourselves as victims of the defendant?'

'Categorically not.' Lord Bewley tapped his cane twice on the floor of the witness box as if to reinforce his declaration.

Mr Carruthers bowed, yielding to the earl's assertion of the truth. 'Thank you, my lord, for your candour and for your assistance in this case, particularly during this time of personal distress.' Without expanding on that, the lawyer turned to the judge. 'I have no further questions for this or any other witness, Your Honour. Instead, I must put it to the court: if there is no victim, how can there be a crime?'

Following this dramatic closing statement, Mr Carruthers and Lord Bewley both took their seats again and all eyes in the courtroom swivelled to the judge. Spectators, witnesses, jurors, lawyers and prisoner alike waited with bated breath to hear what he would say. He coughed and swallowed and coughed once more before he addressed the jury.

'I am tasked with summing up this case for your deliberation,' he said, sounding vaguely flummoxed. 'I confess I have not seen one like it for many years, indeed if ever. On the one hand, it appears to be an unambiguous case of fraud and you must bear in mind that just because it has taken eight years to come to light does not mean that any leniency is due.' He coughed yet again. 'On the other hand, the witnesses supplied by the prosecution have proven unreliable at best and, furthermore, the main victim does not consider himself victimised. You are obliged to take all of this into account before you can return your verdict.'

Cormac didn't know what to expect next – would the bailiff remove him from the courtroom, or would the jurors retire to a separate room to discuss the details of the case? But no, the twelve men merely huddled together in their stalls while they muttered to each other, holding his whole future in their hands. A low buzz rose around the room as those watching shared their own opinions with their neighbours.

At length, a man with bushy white eyebrows stood up at the front of the jury. The judge banged his gavel but he needn't have bothered; everyone had fallen silent at once.

'Have you reached a verdict?' the judge asked, genuine curiosity filling his features.

'We have, Your Honour. We find the defendant not guilty.'

***

Outside the Old Bailey, Emily wept inconsolably on Rory's shoulder, his familiar smell her only comfort in her distress. Her poor papa was to be condemned inside that court thanks to her own greed and selfishness. She would never be able to lift her head again with the weight of her shame.

'Emily.'

Her sobs stuttered and she whirled around. Her father stood there with no shackles or guards.

'P-Papa?' she stammered. 'Are you—?'

He spread his hands and smiled. 'Free.'

An inarticulate cry of relief burst from her. She let go of Rory and ran straight into her father's arms, not caring that the odour of two nights in a prison cell still clung to him. He held her close and she relished the ache of being squeezed too tightly. Beyond them, the spectators from the gallery spilled out of the courthouse chattering animatedly but she paid them no mind. Her father was *free*.

At last, she pulled back from his bone-crushing embrace. 'How?' she asked, marvelling up at him.

'Lord Bewley,' he replied. 'He saved me.' He sounded like he could hardly believe it.

Rory approached them. 'I'm thankful to hear it, sir.'

'You and me both,' said her father.

Before Emily could ask what exactly had happened during the trial, three figures emerged behind the last of the straggling spectators: her mother's friends. Two of them kept their distance – the mousy one's face was scarlet, whether from anger or humiliation Emily couldn't tell – but Lady Newby came over, albeit with a noticeable degree of hesitancy.

'I—' she faltered. She looked directly at Emily's father. 'I'm glad her lie didn't result in your conviction. That would have been unjust.'

He nodded warily.

'Tell Bridget,' she began and stopped. She pressed her lips together in a grimace. 'I cannot pretend that I approve of the choices she has made in her life. But please tell her I miss her and that I wish her well.'

'I will,' he said, dipping his head in acknowledgement.

She returned to her companions and the three ladies left the vicinity of the courthouse in a hurry. They had hardly disappeared down the street when Garrett stalked out of the building, looking tremendously peeved. His jaw clenched when he saw Emily's father.

'It appears you have won another round,' he said dryly.

Emily could sense the rage pulsing through her father's body but he somehow kept control of it. He made no move to advance towards Garrett; instead, he stood stock-still with his fists furled.

'Today marks the end of your involvement with this family,' he said through gritted teeth. 'You will instruct your agent to stop following us in Boston and you will cease all forms of communication, be they underhand or otherwise. You will never go near my daughter or the rest of my family again or, so help me God, I won't be held responsible for my actions. Do you hear me?'

Garrett gave a nonchalant shrug. 'That's fine with me. I have what I want now anyway.'

And he strolled away as if he had not been the cause of untold suffering for the McGoverns. Emily wanted to rush after him and express her feelings with physical violence but she was deterred from doing so by the appearance of Lord Bewley at the front of the courthouse.

'Oh, Uncle Bewley!' she exclaimed. 'Thank you for saving my father! I shall be forever grateful to you.'

He made a huffing sound. Taken aback, she realised that he did not seem altogether pleased. Her father stepped forwards.

'You have my gratitude too, my lord,' he said quietly. 'To be reunited with my daughter is a gift beyond that which I deserve. Which begs the question: why did you do it?'

Lord Bewley leaned on his cane and peered from Emily to her father with tired eyes. 'I was...persuaded.' He sighed. 'I'm happy that the trial worked out this way, although I did have an enormous bribe lined up for the guard at Newgate if we had not achieved the desired verdict.' He straightened ever so slightly. 'And now I have a favour to ask in return for my goodwill.'

Emily's father didn't even blink; she supposed he must have expected this. 'Yes, my lord,' he said, without knowing what the earl actually wanted him to do.

'Good.' Lord Bewley's mouth twisted wryly. 'First, however, we shall make arrangements for you to bathe.'

CHAPTER 33

Bridget's heart was in her throat as, under the cover of deep dusk, she approached the double doors of the warehouse with Charlie, Tess and the disguised Orlaith at her side. What if Bronagh had lied and there was a man guarding the doors after all? Or what if she had warned the gang that someone might try to get in and they had bolted the doors for security?

Neither of those things happened. When Charlie reached for the small door set into the double doors, it opened with barely a squeak and no menacing figure lay in wait on the other side. The four of them slipped through the doorway as quickly and as silently as they could and shut it again behind them.

The gloom inside the warehouse was thick but, once Bridget's eyesight had adjusted, she could discern that they were standing at the edge of a large open space with a high ceiling. A balcony ran around its perimeter – a series of vertical poles along it suggested it had previously been bordered by a railing but any remnants of the horizontal bars were gone and a rope strung between them acted as a substitute. The air smelled musty; Bridget could almost taste the mildew on her tongue. All was quiet.

That was worrying.

'Should it be this quiet?' she muttered to Charlie who was nearest to her. She had anticipated some level of noise, perhaps raucous talking or laughter among the gang members as they holed up in a distant corner of their lair.

He chewed on his lip. 'Maybe most of them are out catching a pint in The Gorget before they commence their night-time activities. It was always full each time I went there.'

'Maybe.'

Or maybe Bronagh had betrayed them and an ambush lay ahead. But did that prospect make Bridget want to turn around and reassess their plan? No, she intended to forge onwards even if it meant walking into a trap. She couldn't bear to endure an hour longer without her boys.

Steeling herself, she motioned to the others that they would continue on as planned. She led the way, staying close to the wall as she skulked along the lower floor of the warehouse, eyes peeled for any sort of room or enclosure that could be used to confine the kidnapped children. There were several doors set into the brick walls on this ground level; some were wide open and revealed nothing but empty spaces beyond, while others were closed, generating both caution and hope for what they might conceal. Bridget or Charlie listened carefully at the keyholes of these before easing them ajar but found only bare storerooms, abandoned now that the warehouse was no longer utilised for its original purpose. Meanwhile, Orlaith and Tess hovered at their backs, keeping alert for any movement or sound from the depths of the shadowy building.

They passed a rickety stairs leading to the balcony overhead but it wasn't until they crept towards the back of the warehouse that they came across anything of significance. There, they found two more storerooms, both deserted of human beings like the others. However, upon investigation they discovered that one contained a stack of chimney brushes and several piles of soot-stained sacks, while the second had a hole in its outer brick wall.

'This must be where Blackie Sheedy died,' Bridget murmured.

Leaving Orlaith and Tess guarding the door, she entered the storeroom with Charlie and stared at the gap. It was scarcely three feet in height and even less than that in diameter. Bricks littered the floor in front of it and a length of timber was propped at the edge of its opening, perhaps in an attempt to shore up the wall's questionable structural integrity. It looked like a shoddy job and she pictured the terrified soul who had been obliged to brave Blackie's ghost in order to hastily put it there.

'Do you feel that?' Charlie said, crouching before the hole with his hand out. 'Fresh air. This leads outside.' He tried to peer past the piece of timber. 'I can't see properly.' He leaned further, his head jutting between the timber and the edge of the broken bricks.

'Be careful!' Bridget hissed in alarm, fearful that the wall might collapse around him.

He withdrew and stood, shaking brick dust from his black hair. 'There's another building out there, nearly on top of this one. You couldn't even call the space between an alley but maybe—'

'Charlie!' whispered an urgent voice from the doorway. Orlaith peeked inside. 'Bridget! We heard a noise. It came from above us.'

Bridget and Charlie hurried back out to join Orlaith and Tess in the main space, clinging to the shadows by the wall while footsteps stamped out onto the balcony above them.

'Keep it down or none of you'll eat 'til next week,' a man barked and then a door slammed shut with a bang. There was a creak of wood that sounded like a chair or stool taking a person's weight and the man grumbled to himself before subsiding into silence.

Bridget's pulse pounded. The room, the guard, her two precious boys – they were all right above her head.

'Wait,' Orlaith mouthed at her but Bridget simply couldn't. She darted back the way they had come, seeking out the rickety stairs that led up to the next level. She had just placed her foot on the bottom tread when she peered up and gulped. A man was descending the stairs.

It wasn't Malachy Kelly. Although sixteen years had passed, she could still recall his shoulder-length, greasy hair and shifty expression, and this young fellow looked nothing like him. Rather, he was short-haired and appeared quite fresh-faced for a member of the tough Kelly Greens – a relatively new recruit, perhaps? He noticed Bridget with mild surprise. Then his gaze landed on something behind her and he gawped. She glanced over her shoulder; Orlaith, Charlie and Tess had just caught up to her.

'You,' the young man said in shock.

Charlie froze. Even in the dimness, Bridget could see the colour drain from his features. The young man came down the last few steps and regarded Charlie with astonishment and pleasure.

'You never returned to The Gorget after that night. I wasn't sure if...' He lowered his eyes shyly. 'I'm heading there now if you want to join me.'

Charlie's throat bobbed. When he said nothing, the young man looked back up.

'Or not,' he said awkwardly, blushing. 'Never mind.'

He pushed past them, so embarrassed that it didn't seem to occur to him to ask why they were there. He hastened away into the gloom towards the front of the warehouse and a moment later they heard the door open and close.

Stunned, Bridget turned to Orlaith. Her mouth was slack, her blackened teeth visible between her trembling lips. She stared at Charlie but he couldn't meet her gaze. Bridget's heart was ready to burst with pity; he had been so reluctant to admit what he had done to acquire the information about the Kelly Greens and now she fully perceived why.

Tess emitted a quiet snort of admiration. 'You win, Charlie. You've gone to the most extreme lengths of any single one of us for the sake of this family. Frankly, I'm in awe.'

Charlie looked like he wanted to retch up the contents of his stomach. 'I didn't,' he croaked. 'I didn't go...all that far.'

Tess patted him on the shoulder. 'But you went far enough. Now let's make it worth it. Come on.'

She started up the stairs and Bridget followed because Tess was right – saving Jack and Gus was what would make Charlie's startling self-sacrifice meaningful. After a second or two, she heard Orlaith and Charlie climbing the stairs after her. Both were silent for now, but they would have to deal with this difficult revelation at a later stage.

Once all four of them had reached the balcony, Orlaith went first by unspoken agreement. She led the way along the balcony, her fingers trailing over the fraying rope at its edge, and slunk past more closed doors before rounding the corner towards the back end. A man, scruffy from his hair to the toes of his boots, lounged on a chair outside a barred door with a bored expression. When he saw Orlaith, he jumped to his feet, frowning.

'They're not meant to get any more food 'til morning,' he said.

'I know,' she muttered, coughing a little to mask the difference between her own voice and Bronagh's. 'Open up anyway.'

He squinted at her. 'What for?'

371

Tess sidled forwards. 'So she can watch the lads while I give you a little reward for your hard work.' She tossed her red hair over her shoulder and offered the man a sultry smile.

'But I only started my shift an hour ago,' he said, bemused.

'So?' said Tess.

He licked his lips. 'Who're they?' he asked, pointing at Charlie and Bridget.

Tess gave them a dismissive wave. 'Ciarán's a newcomer, just off the boat from Ireland. He hails from the back arse of Mayo—doesn't have a word of English yet would you believe. And her?' Tess shrugged, scarcely looking in Bridget's direction. 'New meat for the fellas, that's all. Not as tasty as me though,' she added with a suggestive tilt of her head.

Licking his lips again, the man glanced at Orlaith. 'Does himself know about this change of sentry?'

She nodded, staying mute while she rubbed her false pregnancy bump.

'Come with me,' Tess said seductively and the man didn't resist when she tugged him further down the balcony and out of sight. While a very tiny part of Bridget wondered if Tess was acting out of some sort of twisted competitiveness with Charlie, most of her felt overwhelming gratitude towards the woman who had once caused so much havoc in their family's lives.

As soon as Tess and the scruffy man had vanished, Charlie wasted no time in reaching for the bar on the door. He heaved it up and off and Bridget pushed the door open and rushed through it. The room beyond was dark but she could distinguish a number of small forms clustered together on the floor.

'Jack?' she rasped. 'Gus?'

Silence.

Then...

'Ma?'

Her heart hammered as she spun in the direction of the wavering voice, which had issued from the corner of the room. Sidestepping the nearest hunched shapes, she dashed towards the corner and two huddling figures materialised in the gloom.

'Oh, thank the Lord in heaven!' she exclaimed and dropped to her knees in front of her beloved sons.

'Ma!' Gus cried and promptly burst into tears.

She pulled him to her, dragging him into her lap, while simultaneously stretching out her other arm for Jack. He scrambled forwards and pitched himself into her embrace. She held them to her as tightly as she could, clutching their precious little bodies and weeping into their hair. They smelled of soot and filth and their frames were pitifully thinner than when she had last seen them but all of their limbs were intact. She sent up a prayer of fervent thanks to God.

Though she never wanted to let them go, she had to remind herself that they were all still in danger; the threat wouldn't be past until they got out of the warehouse. She drew back to peer into their dirty, tear-streaked faces. Gus blinked up at her.

'Jack lost his other front tooth,' he wheezed.

'How splendid,' she said, not liking the sound of his rattling breathing one bit. 'I know we have lots to tell each other but first we need to leave this place, quickly and very quietly.'

She glanced around as Orlaith approached the other children gathered in the darkness.

'Is one of you called Willie?' Orlaith asked in an undertone.

They cringed away from her, scuttling further back into the shadows.

'Don't worry,' Bridget said reassuringly. 'This is a different woman to the one you've met before. You have nothing to fear from her. We're here to take you home.'

After a beat, a tremulous voice said, 'I'm Willie.'

One of the boys inched forwards from the rest of the group. He had the same coffee-coloured hair as Hester, although his skin looked a few shades lighter than hers beneath the grime. Orlaith smiled at him.

'Your ma's been searching for you for a long time,' she said. 'She's going to be so happy to see you.'

He didn't manage a smile in return but a brighter expression quivered across his face. Bridget shifted her gaze from him to the other children. There had to be nearly a dozen of them, all boys and all crowding forwards now that they grasped that these adults weren't here to hurt them. She looked over her shoulder at Charlie.

'We're taking them all away from here,' she said firmly. 'We can't leave any of them behind.'

'You're right,' he agreed, grim and resolute. 'And I know how we'll do it.' He crouched down in front of the cluster of boys. 'Are you all from Five Points? Do you remember where you live?'

Most of them nodded but one or two seemed unsure.

'Right, here's what's going to happen,' said Charlie. 'First you'll band together in groups of three or four—older boys need to look out for the younger lads. Then, one at a time, I'll show each group how to escape from this building in such a sneaky way that the gang won't even know you're gone until it's too late. But you have to promise to help each other find your homes once you get outside because you're brothers to each other now. Got it?'

'Yes, sir,' several of the bigger boys replied, a glint of hopefulness in their eyes at the prospect of freedom.

Charlie turned to Bridget and Orlaith. 'We'll keep Jack, Gus and Willie with us,' he said, 'but I'll bring the rest downstairs to that hole in the wall. Once they get out through it the Kelly Greens will never be able to follow.'

'Good thinking,' said Orlaith, her tone taut as she addressed his collarbone.

'Just hurry,' said Bridget, stroking Gus's curls as he snuggled into her.

'Are we leaving now, Ma?' he asked, once again sounding breathless.

'Very soon, little miracle, very soon.'

'I amn't a miracle,' he mumbled.

On the contrary, she thought. This very moment was a miracle.

Without delay, Charlie slipped out of the room with the first group of boys. They had been gone less than a minute when a shadow appeared in the doorway. Orlaith let out a gasp.

'It's just me,' the shadow said and Tess entered the room. 'No need to fret,' she added when she saw Bridget and Orlaith's startled expressions. 'The fella's taken care of.'

'"Taken care of"?' Orlaith repeated faintly.

Tess gave her a lopsided smirk. 'We got to a certain point and I threatened to bite it off if he didn't scarper. He scarpered.'

'What does Auntie Tess mean, Ma?' Jack asked. 'Bite what off?'

Bridget coughed. 'His nose,' she replied.

As one, she, Orlaith and Tess began to titter. It wasn't until Willie gave them a knowing stare that they stopped, realising that a boy raised in a brothel would understand exactly what Tess had meant.

Charlie returned shortly after that, confirming with triumphant relief that the first lot of boys had escaped through the hole without mishap. He set forth with the next group but this time he was gone so long that Bridget feared he had been discovered. However, when he came back he told them he'd been obliged to linger in the storeroom until one of the Kelly Greens had finished having a solitary smoke on the bottom step of the stairs. No further calamities occurred on his final trip and soon only Jack, Gus and Willie were left.

'Time to go, my lamb,' Bridget said to Jack, gently shaking him awake for he had become drowsy as he leaned against her. 'Grown-ups are too big to fit through the hole so we'll have to leave by the front entrance.'

They all made their way to the door where Charlie listened intently before beckoning them out onto the balcony. Bridget held Jack and Gus's hands while Tess took Willie's – he still seemed wary of Orlaith, despite having been told that she was not Bronagh. They tiptoed along the balcony towards the stairs and Bridget started to hope that all would be well.

Then a door off the balcony opened right beside them and a person stepped out, stumbling to a surprised stop at the sight of them.

This time it *was* Malachy Kelly.

His greasy hair was longer than ever, tied back in a messy tail at the nape of his neck. He didn't appear to have aged as severely as Bronagh but his teeth were just as bad and his round gut stuck out, speaking of heavy drinking and a sedentary lifestyle. Sleep crusted the corners of his eyes, suggesting that he had only just woken. His gaze travelled over the intruders, widened upon noticing the three boys, and narrowed when he looked at Orlaith. His arm shot out to grab her elbow.

'You're not Bronagh,' he growled.

'Get your hand off her,' Charlie snapped.

Malachy frowned. 'American? What the hell's going on here?'

He didn't loosen his grip on Orlaith so Charlie shoved at his shoulder to make him let go. Snarling, Malachy retaliated with a backhanded blow across Charlie's face; the force nearly knocked Charlie to his knees. Orlaith screamed.

Another door banged open on the balcony at the opposite side of the warehouse and two figures rushed out: Bronagh and a large-breasted woman who had to be Cáit. When they saw what was happening across the way, they both gasped and Bronagh tore along the balcony, both hands supporting her bump. Cáit hurried after her. Meanwhile, Malachy glared at Charlie with flared nostrils.

'I don't care who you are,' he said, jabbing a thumb into his chest, 'but you'd better take your women and piss off before I decide this city needs one less Yankee in it.'

Charlie stood his ground. 'I'd like to see you try.'

Before they could do anything more than square up to each other, Bronagh came dashing around the corner of the balcony towards them, Cáit several steps behind her.

'No!' she cried. She ran up to Malachy and seized his arm. 'Please don't hurt them!'

'Why the hell not?' he spat at her.

'Because...' She glanced at Orlaith. 'They're family.'

He scoffed. 'What're you on about? They just tried to nick three of the boys and now this fella's begging for a hiding. I'm more than happy to oblige.' He strode to the edge of the balcony, leaned over the rope and shouted down into the depths of the warehouse, 'Seamus! We've got trespassers. Get up here with any lads who aren't already out drowning themselves in drink.' He received no immediate reply but he turned back to Charlie with a sneer. 'I hope you're not too fond of your teeth. You won't have any left once we're finished with you.'

Charlie shrugged. 'I'm not worried about my teeth. You look outnumbered to me right now.'

Malachy let out a snort. 'You're not seriously counting the bitches, are you? Or do you think the scrawny brats will back you up? I guarantee they won't be much good to you, not on the scraps we've been feeding them.'

Bridget's rage scalded her throat as she hissed, 'You are the absolute scum of the earth.'

He swivelled to her with a laugh. 'Is that supposed to hurt my feelings or something?'

She pinched her lips together. 'Your grandfather must be turning in his grave.'

His eyebrows shot up. 'My grandfather? How d'you—' He cut himself off, peering at her more closely. 'Jaysus, are you that filly from Oakleigh? I'm right, aren't I? You convinced your ma not to have us transported.'

'And I tell you with the utmost sincerity that my charity in that matter has since become one of the greatest regrets of my life.' She pulled Jack and Gus closer to her. 'Thankfully, I have tonight rectified the consequences of that grave error in judgement, though my sons paid the awful price in the interim.'

He guffawed. 'Those two brats are yours? What a trick of fate.'

'You are repulsive,' she said in as scathing a voice as she could muster. 'You have no regard for anyone or anything, not even the life of your own child.'

He looked sharply from her to Bronagh. 'What've you been telling them?'

She cowered under the beam of his anger. 'J-just the truth. I t-told you, they're family.'

He loomed over her. 'Did you help them sneak in here?' he roared.

He raised his hand but Cáit dragged Bronagh back out of reach and the blow landed on thin air.

'Good God, he's deranged,' said Charlie in disbelief. He started shunting everyone towards the stairs. 'Go on, get out as fast as you can.'

Orlaith, Tess and Willie managed to reach the top of the steps but Bridget, Jack and Gus were further behind. When Bridget cast a fleeting look over her shoulder, she caught a glimpse of Malachy whirling back, incensed at the sight of them all fleeing.

He darted after them with a bellow and reached out to grab Jack and Gus by the scruffs of their necks.

'*No!*' she shrieked at the top of her lungs.

She had just got her boys back and she did not mean to let them be snatched away again. With absolutely conscious intention, she dropped Jack and Gus's hands and pushed Malachy away from them, slapping her palms flat on his chest and shoving him with all her might towards the edge of the balcony. He stumbled but he seemed on the verge of catching his balance...

...until Bronagh appeared at his side. She stretched out her arms and in that moment it was uncertain whether she meant to save him or hasten his demise. Either way, her intervention caused him to lose his footing again and, staggering, he fell against the rope that bordered the balcony. With a creak, it snapped and he lurched out into empty space. His mouth dropped open in a breathless scream as he plunged out of sight. A second later, there came the bone-crunching whack of his body hitting the floor below.

Bronagh clapped her hands over her mouth and moaned.

'Stay back against the wall,' Bridget told Jack and Gus before she herself inched towards the lip of the balcony. When she peeked down, she first spotted the end of the frayed rope swaying gently. Then her gaze landed upon Malachy, his limbs splayed at unnatural angles and a pool of blood spreading out from beneath his skull. She got a fright when she perceived his eyes staring upwards until she realised that they were staring at nothing. Her stomach muscles relaxed.

In the next instant, they clenched again as a figure emerged from below the balcony and moved to stand over Malachy's broken body, studying the corpse with a distinct air of detachment. Bridget heard footsteps close at hand and, glancing sideways, found that Cáit had joined her.

'That's Seamus,' she breathed, her fear palpable in her taut stance.

As though in response to her whisper, Seamus looked up. He regarded Bridget and Cáit for a moment, a smug smile playing around his lips, and then he retreated the way he had come, melting away into the shadows.

Bridget had no energy left to care about him. She returned to Jack and Gus and tucked their small hands securely into her own.

'Let's get the hell out of here,' she said.

CHAPTER 34

Cormac stood in an upstairs corridor at Raynesworth House, freshly washed and dressed in a set of fine clothes which, he knew by their tailored cut, had long ago belonged to him in the guise of Oliver Davenport, though the fit was now a little snugger at his shoulders. He stared nervously at the closed bedchamber door in front of him.

'Go on,' said Lord Bewley behind him. 'She's waiting for you.'

Straightening his posture, Cormac opened the door and entered.

The bedchamber within was bathed in the warm glow of candlelight. Though darkness had fallen outside, the curtains had been left drawn back and the scents of the summer night drifted in through the partly open window, filling the room with balmy air and the sweet fragrance of flowers. These helped to mask the other less pleasant odours that lingered about: perspiring skin, vomit, and corrupted flesh. With a touch of dread, Cormac let his gaze alight upon the figure lying in the bed before him.

Once a substantially plump woman, Lady Bewley now appeared to be no more than a wraith in comparison. She was sitting up in the bed with her arms outside the covers, the fabric of her nightgown swamping her limbs and her greyish skin hanging in fleshless folds beneath her chin. Nonetheless, her kind expression had not altered – her tired eyes managed to twinkle and her lips curved into a genuine smile when she saw Cormac. She let out a long sigh of satisfaction.

'Thank God,' she murmured. She raised a feeble arm. 'Come here to me, my dear.'

Swallowing a lump in his throat, he crossed the room to the side of her bed where a chair had already been placed in readiness for him. He lifted her outstretched hand and pressed a tender kiss to her wasted knuckles.

'My lady,' he said hoarsely.

Her mouth turned down at the address. He regretted disappointing her but naturally he could not call her 'Aunt'.

'Please sit,' she said with sadness in her voice.

He released her hand and lowered himself onto the chair by her bed. Lord Bewley had already entered the bedchamber behind him and shut the door; now, he eased himself into another chair in the far corner of the room, leaning on his ubiquitous cane as he observed Cormac and his wife, present but unobtrusive.

Lady Bewley gazed at Cormac with glistening eyes. 'You were exonerated at the courthouse? You're free?'

'Yes,' he replied and added baldly, 'though we all know I don't deserve to be.'

After a pregnant pause, she said, 'I hope you will indulge the whims of an old lady when I beg to differ.'

He tilted his head, wondering how she had possibly convinced herself otherwise.

She nodded gravely. 'I can comprehend what you are thinking but do not fret—I have not lost my senses during the course of my illness. However, I have had many years to ponder the letter you left us explaining what you had done, and I have also reflected at length upon the period of time that you spent living in our home.' She took a shallow breath. 'And I have concluded that neither is indicative of a wicked man.'

He opened his mouth but she forestalled him with a tremulous finger.

'Desperate? Yes. Reckless? Yes. But wicked?' She shook her head. 'I don't think there is a single evil bone in your body. If there were, you would have taken all you could from us and deserted us at the end without a word of apology or explanation. But you wrote so sincerely about how sorry you were for what had happened with Oliver and for the subsequent choices you made. And, though it took me a while to accept it, now I believe you.'

The lump had leapt back up into his throat, magnified tenfold by the lady's heartfelt declaration. Could it be possible that one of the people he had hurt most grievously in his shady past actually desired to forgive him? She reached for his hand again and he automatically gave it to her, while his mind reeled.

'Cormac,' she said softly, lingering on his name as though experimenting with how it felt on her tongue. 'You lived with us at Bewley Hall for nearly five years. I speak in earnest when I tell you that they were the happiest years of my existence. All I ever yearned for was a child and, although you were an adult when you came to us, you brought that joy into my life.' She glanced over at Lord Bewley. 'Into both of our lives.'

Lord Bewley didn't speak but his eyelids blinked rapidly.

Lady Bewley smiled at Cormac, her countenance full of unadulterated affection. 'You gave us a marvellous gift and so we have gifted you your freedom in return. We know you will use it wisely.'

Cormac's ribs tightened around his lungs. 'Thank you, my lady,' he croaked. 'I can't express...' He truly had no words to articulate the brimming feeling inside him.

He didn't need them. She understood, just as a mother would.

She squeezed his fingers. 'How we have missed you in our family,' she whispered.

With a supreme effort, he prevented his emotion from spilling over. 'And I you.'

She twinkled at him. 'What a scandal you are making of your time on this earth. Furthermore, my husband tells me that your daughter has been walking in your rebellious footsteps, is that true?'

A laugh cracked out of him. 'She has. And I have two sons who will no doubt follow suit.'

'Three children,' she said. 'My, you have been so blessed.' She hesitated. 'Will you...could you tell us what you remember about Oliver? Beyond what you divulged to us in your letter? I have read his book of poetry so many times that I know it by heart, but you are the one who met him in person.'

It was a difficult thing to ask of him but he would grant her an honest answer. He would do anything for this precious, exceptional lady.

So he sat by her bedside and described every detail he could recall of his encounter with Oliver, a young man who had possessed such a tortured soul. She hung onto each word, hungry for any crumb of information he could provide. When he cautiously revealed the name of Oliver's fickle lover to be Victor, Lady Bewley did not blink.

'That makes sense,' she said, keeping her tone neutral. 'His poems...yes, I see.'

Relieved that he could offer enlightenment and that it had been received without outward distress, he carried on with his tale to its gruesome conclusion and at last fell silent, his head bowed.

With remarkable perception, she murmured, 'His death was the source of your nightmares. You poor dear.'

She rested her palm on his bent head and he felt the tide of emotion rise in him again. It only intensified when she said, 'You have my gratitude that I was able to learn of this before I go to meet my maker.'

His whole body jerked in denial and she moved her hand to cup his cheek, encouraging him to look up at her.

'I know you can perceive the truth,' she said gently. 'I am dying. But I have led a blessed life in many ways and here at the end I have my devoted husband at my side and my favourite petunias blooming beneath my window...and I have you, my dear, dear boy. I am so very glad that I got to see you again, that we had this chance to reunite and to bid each other farewell.'

Lady Bewley couldn't realise it but she was bequeathing Cormac a second gift, one no less significant than his freedom. She was giving him the chance to say goodbye to his second mother, to heal the jagged cleft that had existed within him ever since he had lost his first.

This time, he didn't stop the tears when they spilled over.

Afterwards, fatigue conquered Lady Bewley's weakened body and she dozed off with her thin fingers still folded in Cormac's grasp and an expression of contentment sketched across her face.

Lord Bewley gruffly cleared his throat in the corner. 'Come with me,' he said.

Cormac carefully extricated his hand from Lady Bewley's and, wiping his cheeks on his sleeve, followed Lord Bewley from the bedchamber.

They settled themselves downstairs in a study not dissimilar to the one Lord Bewley had always presided over at Bewley Hall. The earl set out a glass of brandy for each of them and then took a seat behind the desk, propping his cane beside him. For a long minute, neither of them spoke.

At length, Lord Bewley said, 'Thank you for doing that.'

Cormac shot him a look of surprise across the desk. 'It is I who owe thanks to you, my lord. Only for your intercession, I might be boarding a prison ship in chains right now. Or perhaps preparing to climb the steps of a gallows.'

Lord Bewley huffed. 'Maybe. But you didn't deserve either of those fates.'

Cormac arched an eyebrow. 'Do I venture to guess that the countess believes that more strongly than you do?'

Lord Bewley breathed in the aroma of his brandy before taking a sip. 'You are correct,' he said after he had swallowed. 'However, our views are more aligned now than they once were.'

Cormac warmed his own brandy glass in his hand while he waited for the earl to continue.

'I have remained in periodic correspondence with Lord Wyndham over the years,' said Lord Bewley. 'I told him that his wife intended to sail west to America, and he subsequently notified me that you had accompanied her. I confess I experienced a measure of relief when I learned that you had survived the ambush in Dublin. What happened in that alley had weighed heavily on my conscience afterwards and I was glad to discover that I had not condemned you to die at the hands of that money lender's thugs.'

Was now an appropriate time for Cormac to inform the earl that he had in fact murdered the money lender? Perhaps not. He sipped his brandy instead.

'Of course, your emigration also meant that you continued to go unpunished for the transgressions you had committed against me and my wife. Still, I am a patient man. I knew I need only wait long enough for you to foolishly return to England, at which point I could exact my vengeance. However, the more time passed, the less I wished to do it.'

'What changed your mind, my lord?'

Lord Bewley glanced at the ceiling. 'She did.' He sighed. 'She wanted so badly to believe that a good man existed beneath your deception. She talked constantly about how you had saved her when she was attacked at the soup kitchen and how you had tended her during her recovery. She reminded me that you had exceeded every one of my expectations with regard to improving your knowledge and acumen in matters related to the estate. She loved to reminisce about the day you resolved the dispute between two farmers by shucking off your riding coat and helping them to build the fence yourself.' He shrugged. 'Those, and countless other things. Your civility to the servants, your gentleness with horses, the way you allowed her to comfort you when you woke from your nightmares. She asserted that all of those moments, be they big or small, were too genuine to have been feigned.'

Cormac's cheeks burned and he hid his face in his glass to conceal his self-consciousness.

Lord Bewley went on, 'Gradually, I came to appreciate what she meant. I, too, could recall the courteous and devoted young man who had augmented the happiness in our home. And when I reread your letter, I recognised the sincerity of your remorse. You had been a victim of your deplorable circumstances just as much as we had. Your behaviour had been abominable and yet, somehow, excusable.'

Cormac could scarcely comprehend the goodness of two elderly people desperately seeking to find decency in the vagabond who had done them wrong. He set his glass down on the desk.

'My lord, you mustn't blind yourselves to the truth. Regardless of my motivations, I am still—'

'I know what you are going to say,' Lord Bewley interrupted him. 'Believe me, I have argued it many times, both with my wife and with myself. Even when I received Lord Wyndham's communication that you were to stand trial for your crime, I vacillated over which outcome I desired most. But the woman I married is a merciful angel—she insisted that you be liberated and that I be the one to ensure it. How could I refuse her, especially in her fragile condition?'

Cormac swallowed. 'Is her condition as critical as she believes?'

'Worse.' Lord Bewley's composed features fractured with grief. 'She is not long for this world. Truth be told, my own time will run out soon too but I shall welcome the end when it comes. I won't have anything left to live for after she is gone.'

Cormac's heart broke to hear the desolation in the gentleman's voice. He knew that he would feel the same way if Bridget were to pass before him, and she in return, but at least their beloved children would be a compelling reason to carry on. Lord Bewley had no such recourse for consolation.

With a subdued sniff, the earl took a moment to gather his composure before speaking again. 'My primary concern ahead of my departure will be to make sure that I leave the Bewley Estate in capable hands. Without a legitimate heir in any branch of the Davenport family, my title will become extinct. However, all of the extensive land belonging to that family name will continue to exist, along with Bewley Hall, Raynesworth House and the rest of my properties and interests. They will need a master, someone who is familiar with the running of the estate and who is willing to uphold the values I have always maintained.'

Cormac nodded. The earl's land agent, Mr Sandler, would be the natural choice, having worked closely with Lord Bewley for nigh on three decades.

'What say you?'

Cormac blinked. 'Pardon?'

'Will you agree to be my successor?' Lord Bewley asked, gazing at him calmly from the other side of the desk.

'Surely you're not in earnest,' Cormac said, barely containing a laugh.

'I am.'

Floored, he gaped at the earl, struggling to grasp the unanticipated direction of their conversation. 'But...that's absurd.'

Lord Bewley flourished a hand in invitation. 'Please list the impediments.'

It was inconceivable that the gentleman needed it to be spelled out for him.

'I'm a criminal!' Cormac spluttered.

'You were acquitted.'

'Even so, I committed the crime and it was against *you*.'

'I have granted my forgiveness.'

Cormac shook his head. 'You don't know what else I've done.'

'I have no need to know,' said Lord Bewley. 'Your other offences are in the past and do not concern me. In my view, all that matters is that your conduct is impeccable from this point onwards.'

Confounded, Cormac changed tack. 'I'm not qualified to take on the management of an estate.'

'Did we not provide you with a full education during the years you spent under our roof? To my recollection, you were a diligent student and cultivated your mind most satisfactorily.'

'My lord, it is nonsensical that we are even debating this!' Cormac burst out. 'You know my origins—I am the son of a stable hand. Setting aside my unlawful endeavours, I have risen no further in social standing than that of a carpenter. I am utterly unsuited to the distinguished position you describe.'

'On the contrary,' said Lord Bewley, unmoved by Cormac's exasperation. 'You are a businessman, and a successful one at that. You have acquired an excellent reputation in Boston.'

'How do you know that?' Cormac asked, taken aback.

Lord Bewley picked up his cane and twisted it contemplatively between his hands. 'Wyndham informed me of your location once his agent discovered where you and your family had settled in America. I didn't intend to do anything with the knowledge but I admit my curiosity eventually got the better of me. I made discreet enquiries from time to time and was thus able to monitor your advancement, from working at the docks to managing your own enterprise. You have displayed a keen sense of awareness when it comes to business matters and such intelligence is highly transferable to the running of an estate.'

That left Cormac speechless. Not only Garrett but also Lord Bewley had been observing their lives in Boston. It was perturbing to realise that he and his family had been under such close scrutiny all this time. He might never sleep easy again.

Oblivious to Cormac's disquiet on that front, Lord Bewley gave him an avuncular smile. 'You cannot deny that you are, in fact, quite an ideal candidate.'

'Far from it, my lord,' Cormac countered. 'No one would tolerate a lowly carpenter being elevated to such a status—not your servants nor the neighbouring estates nor society at large. I would be shunned and the estate would suffer as a result.'

He was certain that this would give Lord Bewley pause but the earl said mildly, 'Other men born to nothing have risen through the ranks and gained the respect of their peers. I am confident you could win the naysayers over. Besides, your lower class background would give you a unique insight into the tenants living under your command. I daresay you could transform many lives.'

'What about the Davenports?' Cormac said, growing desperate. 'There must be someone in the extended family who has an entitlement.'

'There is no entail and no distant relative with a prior claim or fitting résumé. I am at liberty to bestow the estate upon whomever I wish.'

'Mr Sandler, then. He understands the management of the estate better than anybody.'

Lord Bewley's brow puckered. 'Mr Sandler is undoubtedly competent...but no. I would rather bequeath it to an individual who will care about more than its monetary value.'

Cormac grimaced. How was he to convince the gentleman that his faith was misplaced? 'My lord,' he said, his tone quiet and frank. 'You must hear me. I am entirely unworthy of this honour.'

Lord Bewley beamed back at him. 'Can you not see that the opposite is true? The more you protest, the more assured I am of my choice. You are a better man than many aristocrats in my acquaintance. You confirmed that reality yet again today when you censured Carruthers for bullying Miss Caulfield in the witness box. His persecution of her was strengthening the case in your favour—how many men in a hundred would have intervened?'

Cormac's mouth dropped open. 'Was that a test? Did he maltreat her in order to provoke a reaction from me?'

Lord Bewley examined the brass handle of his cane. 'If he did, it proved to be a successful tactic, did it not? You demonstrated to the whole court that you would rather risk your own conviction than see a defenceless woman further humiliated in public.'

Personally, Cormac thought it revealed a lot more about Mr Carruthers's character than his own. He chewed the inside of his cheek.

'I have a family and I must consider them above all else. Bridget—'

'She already possesses a title and an estate,' Lord Bewley said smoothly. 'Her experience would be a tremendous support to you.'

'My children—'

'—would gain an inheritance beyond anything they could ever have dreamed.'

That made Cormac falter. Emily would have the means to attend Brubaker Art Academy – ought he to accept Lord Bewley's offer for her sake? But that was preposterous. He couldn't take on such a huge lifetime responsibility merely to pay for her tuition fees; the impact of this decision had more wide-reaching consequences than that.

'Do you expect me to uproot my whole family from their home?' he asked.

'Do you intend to stay in Boston forever?' Lord Bewley enquired in return.

Cormac hesitated again. He did hope that they would return home someday – and there was another argument to be made: home was Ireland, not England – but they were still tied to America for now.

'One of my sisters is missing in New York,' he said. 'I can't leave America for good until I find her.'

Lord Bewley sat back in his chair. 'How fortunate, then, that the Bewley Estate would provide you with more resources to search for her.'

Cormac rubbed his jaw, nonplussed. 'It's been eight years since you last laid eyes on me. How can you even contemplate putting your estate in my hands when I am virtually a stranger to you?'

Lord Bewley pointed the cane at him. 'You forget that we were keeping track of you during that time. In fact, you were on our minds such a great deal that you do not seem like a stranger sitting opposite me. More like a prodigal son perhaps.' The corners of his mouth curved upwards in wry amusement.

Cormac was silent as he weighed up the matter from all sides. He needed to be certain in his decision. So, for the sake of removing all doubt, he allowed himself to momentarily entertain the possibility: him, a landowner in charge of several properties and hundreds of tenants. He would be responsible for the livelihoods of many, and the prosperity of the entire estate would rest upon his shoulders. How did he feel about bearing such a burden?

To his surprise, a flicker of eagerness stirred in his belly. It was an enormous challenge to undertake, but who was to say he wouldn't relish it? Perhaps he would wholeheartedly embrace the opportunity to manage an estate and to improve the lives of the people who lived and worked upon his land.

His land? For God's sake, the notion was too absurd. He was only a stable hand's son. He had no right to such lofty ambitions.

Despite the tempting prospect that dangled before him, basic common sense prevailed.

'My lord,' he said, 'I am staggered by your proposal but I must regretfully decline. It is not a life I have ever wished for.'

After a beat, Lord Bewley bowed his head in resignation. 'Very well. I am disappointed but I understand.'

Relief coursed through Cormac and he reached for his brandy glass, gulping back a grateful mouthful without any regard for its taste.

Lord Bewley set down his cane again with a sigh. 'In consequence of our failure to come to an accord on this matter, I am visited by a desire to be useful in some other way. May I offer you any financial aid?'

'That is very generous of you,' said Cormac, 'and most welcome, in fact. I was robbed on my journey here so I don't have sufficient funds to cover all the travel costs back to America for myself, Emily and Rory.'

'Then I would be delighted to assist,' said Lord Bewley.

'With the proviso that I remunerate you for it at a future stage,' Cormac added.

The earl nodded with reluctant acquiescence. 'If you insist.'

Cormac pondered Lord Bewley's crestfallen expression and his heart filled with fondness for the elderly man. 'If you really wish to help,' he said with a smile, 'I can think of someone else who might be eager to indulge you...'

***

Emily and Rory sat side by side on the sofa in the drawing room at Raynesworth House, waiting for her father. She was pleased to register the fact that no awkwardness clouded the space between them; though she had thoroughly broken down outside the courthouse, neither of them seemed to retain any embarrassment about the episode. Indeed, all Emily could feel was jubilation. Her father had obtained his freedom – which he now possessed in a much more substantial form than before he had returned to England – and she had been liberated from Garrett's manipulative influence.

'I can't wait to go home,' she said with a contented sigh.

Rory cast her a sidelong glance. 'Aren't you disappointed though? Not to get what you wanted at the end of it all?'

She shook her head. 'I wanted the wrong things. I don't belong in this upper class world.'

He chewed on his lip. 'It seemed to me that you did. Right from that day you curtseyed on the ship, it looked like you were going to fit right in.'

'I understand how to perform the role,' she said, 'but I'm no longer sure that I'm suited to it, or it to me. It feels rather like wearing an ill-fitting pair of gloves and finding relief in the prospect of taking them off.' She clasped her hands in her lap and stared down at them, her elation leaking away. 'I'm so sorry for having embroiled you in this fiasco.'

'Arrah, I invited myself along, to be fair.'

He gave her a teasing nudge with his elbow but she remained serious.

'You wouldn't have needed to if I hadn't been so selfishly determined to chase what I deemed to be my entitlement.' Disgusted with herself, she blew out her breath. 'But I would have been too weak to survive on my own—you were right about that. You proved it even before we left Broad Street, and many times again since.'

He shifted uncomfortably. 'Not weak, just...vulnerable. Women can be strong in lots of other ways. Your da told me that once and you've definitely shown it these past few weeks.'

She scoffed; she couldn't recall any moment where she hadn't been a snivelling, frightened mouse.

'Besides,' he went on, 'if it wasn't for you running away, I wouldn't have learned the truth about my da.'

She gulped. They hadn't spoken directly about Brian Mór since they left Liverpool. 'Oh, um...'

'I'm glad I found out,' he assured her. 'Even though I'm dreading telling my ma, it'll still be better for her to know exactly who he is.' Emily felt his body slump a little. 'And it was a good lesson for me. I never want to let myself become that kind of man.'

She swivelled to him and gazed into his eyes, green as fresh clover. 'You are nothing like your father, Rory. You would never treat a woman the way he has treated Auntie Derval and Maud. I speak with the utmost sincerity when I say that you're as honourable as my own father.'

She could think of no higher praise and, judging by his bashful expression, he interpreted it that way.

'I really couldn't have coped through all this without you,' she confessed and then, realising how maudlin she sounded, added light-heartedly, 'In fact, I believe I am ready to finally forgive you for kidnapping Mabel.'

He stiffened. Indecision flitted across his face before he straightened his shoulders. 'I never took her.'

'What?' she said, confused.

'Una did. When you got so upset, I told her she had to give Mabel back but she was afraid of getting found out so I said I'd do it. And then you caught me red-handed on the stairs.'

'Why on earth didn't you tell me the truth?' Emily exclaimed.

'You didn't give me a chance to explain.' He grimaced. 'And I think it would've hurt you more if you'd known it had been Una.'

Her indignation wilted. Once again, he was right. Learning that her friend had been the kidnapper would have been a monumental betrayal – whereas what else could she have expected from an annoying boy?

Her cheeks flooded with mortification. 'I've blamed you all this time,' she mumbled.

'Doesn't matter,' he said with a shrug. ''Tis behind us now.'

She gave him a cautious look. 'Ought we to establish another truce?'

Equally tentative, he said, 'Maybe we don't need truces anymore?'

After a beat, she smiled at him and he grinned back. Her pulse fluttered and she glanced away, her smile growing even wider.

Then the drawing room door opened and she self-consciously moved several inches further down the sofa from Rory as her father and Lord Bewley entered. She was astonished to discern a faint red tinge around her father's eyes – good gracious, had he been crying? But his expression lifted when he saw her and he strode across the room to plant an affectionate kiss on the top of her head.

'It's been quite an eventful day,' he said, 'but I wonder if you might have enough energy for one more surprise?'

She knitted her brows together. 'What is it?'

He glanced at Lord Bewley who crossed the room more slowly and took a seat opposite the sofa.

'I shall not prevaricate,' he said and she detected the exhaustion in his tone and posture. 'Your father has informed me of your admirable ambition to study at Brubaker Art Academy in New York, and of the costs involved. As a gesture of peace after all the strife that has occurred between our families, I should like to provide the financial support that will enable you to pursue your studies. It would please me to do this for the entire duration of your tuition at Brubaker.'

She stared open-mouthed at him. Had she heard him correctly? She peeked sideways at Rory and he raised his eyebrows at her, amusement dancing in his gaze. She looked up at her father and then back at Lord Bewley.

'My lord,' she said, flummoxed. 'I thank you most sincerely, but...no.'

The blank silence in the drawing room told her that none of the men had expected that response from her.

'I am very conscious of the honour,' she hastened to add. 'I really am so grateful and touched. However, I have learned a great number of difficult lessons this summer and chief among them is that one must earn one's entitlements. I shall only attend Brubaker at a future stage on the basis of my own merit and efforts, regardless of how long I have to wait to achieve it. And that is why I must refuse your kind offer.'

Lord Bewley shook his head, mystified. 'These McGoverns,' he said almost to himself. 'Far too full of integrity for their own good.'

He departed from the drawing room soon after that, citing the weariness in his bones as his reason for retiring. Once he had left them, her father said, 'Are you quite happy with your decision, *a stór*?'

'I am,' she said. 'I'm convinced that this path will be harder but ultimately more worthwhile. I am determined to earn my own way, as I ought to have done all along.'

'I should forewarn you,' he said gingerly as he took the seat the earl had vacated, 'you may not have a job to return to at Marlowe House. The housekeeper was not pleased when you absconded from your duties without a word of notice.'

Emily winced. How she wished she could go back in time and talk some sense into the silly girl who had made all those poor choices.

'A dismissal is nothing more than I deserve,' she said. 'I shall seek employment elsewhere. Perhaps it's for the best anyway, so that I can avoid—' She hastily cut herself off but too many words had already tripped off her tongue.

Her father cast her a shrewd look. 'Who do you want to avoid at Marlowe House?'

She coloured. She supposed she could have refused to answer but she found herself saying glumly, 'Samuel. The Marlowes' son.'

She assumed that she had sealed her fate in that regard – without being the heir to Garrett's title and fortune, she did not possess the advantageous qualities that would make her an eligible match for the son of one of Boston's elite families. She would have to rely on love alone and, now that she could view the situation from a distance and with greater clarity, she didn't think that would be enough. It would be better to find work in a different household where she would not run the risk of bumping into him each day and fantasising over what might have been.

'I see,' said her father and she suspected he saw quite a lot. Next to her, Rory's face was impassive.

Eager to skate past the awkward moment, she asked, 'What happens now? Where will we stay tonight?' Her valise was still at Wyndham House but she had no intention of spending another night under the same roof as Garrett – she and Rory could go back at a later stage to retrieve their belongings.

'Here,' said her father. 'Lord Bewley says we are welcome to stay for as long as we need.'

'Until we can book passage on a ship?'

'Yes,' he replied. 'And on that note, I wanted to ask if the two of you would be open to making a detour on our way back to Boston? If so, I shall write to your mother to let her know that we are all fine but will be delayed.'

Emily only nodded vaguely at this for an awful thought had just struck her: in order to get home, she would have to board a ship again. The mere memory of her seasickness brought a cold sweat to her forehead. Moreover, almost a month had passed since she had first got her courses which meant that she should expect to be visited by them again in the coming days. The idea was daunting but, thanks to Lizzie, at least this time she would know how to react when they arrived.

Her father was still speaking. '—will begin making enquiries tomorrow. We may sail from London but there might be a ship back in Liverpool that will better suit our needs.'

'Anything but the *Integrity*,' Emily and Rory said together.

CHAPTER 35

Bridget knelt by the nest of blankets on the floor of Hester's sitting room and tucked them more snugly around Jack and Gus's shoulders and hips. The boys had bathed after coming back to the brothel and now smelled clean and familiar as she kissed each of their foreheads.

'I hope you both get a good night's rest,' she said, even though dawn had already broken outside.

Gus's anxious dark brown eyes looked up at her. 'Will you stay with us until we fall asleep?' he wheezed.

'I will,' she said, striving to keep her emotion in check. They needed their mother to be a strong presence at their side, not a blubbering mess.

The worry did not leave his features. 'And will there be more food when we wake up?'

'Yes, I promise.'

The poor things had devoured at least a dozen slices of bread and cheese between them before they had washed.

Jack burrowed deeper into their blankets. 'Gus was always hungry in the dark room,' he said. 'I gave him extra from our pail whenever I could.'

It incensed Bridget that the Kelly Greens had fed their captives like animals at a trough but she kept a lid on her anger.

'You're a wonderful big brother,' she said, giving Jack an extra kiss.

He beamed up at her, displaying the gap where his two front teeth were missing. 'I minded him like Da said I should.' In the next instant, his face fell. 'Except sometimes I couldn't. They kept us together in the dark room, but whenever we went outside they split us up and forced us to go to different houses.'

Gus shivered despite the blankets. 'I hated going up the chimneys. It was scary and small and I couldn't see anything.'

'I was afraid Gus would get stuck,' Jack confessed, giving his mother a meaningful look as he glanced from her to his brother, whose body was still plumper than his own, though not as tubby as it had been before they came to New York. 'And the soot made him cough a lot.'

Even though Jack had always been the less domineering of the two boys, it sounded like he had become very protective of his little brother during their ordeal.

Gus piped up, 'And one day Jack's chimney sweep said he did a great job when he snuck a gold brooch out of the house. But the next day he hit him for not stealing anything. That was when his other tooth fell out.'

Consumed with guilt, Bridget felt an obstruction in her throat growing larger by the second. 'You have both been extraordinarily brave,' she choked out. 'I'm so sorry that those men hurt you, but you're safe now. I swear I'll never let anyone harm you ever again. Try to get some sleep if you can.'

She brushed the hair back from their foreheads and waited for their eyelids to flutter closed. Gus dropped off quickly but Jack startled awake twice before he finally drifted off into deeper slumber. Only then did she let the obstruction break apart and the tears fall. They streamed silently down her cheeks as she gazed at her cherished sons and thanked God for his mercy.

After she had composed herself, she left the sitting room, shutting the door softly behind her. She had expressed her desire for the boys to sleep undisturbed so, once the sunrise had chased the brothel's patrons from the premises, everyone else had removed to the parlour. She went there now and found Orlaith, Charlie, Tess, Bronagh and Cáit sitting around on the cushioned chairs, mutely drinking tea from chipped cups and avoiding eye contact with each other. Hester and Willie were nowhere to be seen – following their rapturous reunion, they had retreated to another corner of the brothel where the girls could dote on Willie and Hester could ensure that he stayed well away from Bronagh's presence.

Bronagh was weeping quietly, tears dripping off her nose and splashing into her teacup. Bridget struggled to feel sympathy for her – how could she find it within herself to grieve over Malachy's death? What an unfathomably complicated relationship she had led with that malevolent man. She huddled in on herself as she continued to cry, one hand rubbing her round belly with soothing strokes. At least the baby she carried was no longer in danger from its father.

Orlaith sat two chairs down from Bronagh, her shoulders slumped with fatigue. She had removed the cushion from beneath her dress and its hem pooled on the floor at her feet. Though she had wiped most of the kohl from her teeth, traces of it still remained visible as she chewed on her lower lip. Her gaze flicked covertly between Bronagh and Charlie. Bridget couldn't tell which one was causing her more trepidation.

On the other side of the parlour, Charlie bent over his knees, his face bruised where Malachy had hit him and his hunched form as motionless as a statue. Cáit, too, seemed somewhat frozen by the events of the night. Tess, however, jumped up when Bridget entered the room.

'Good,' she said. 'I want to say something to you.' She put her hands on her hips. 'I'm sorry.'

Bridget stared at her hard. 'You are?'

Tess nodded once. 'I am. I should've said it to you long ago.'

Bridget bit the tip of her tongue. 'I have something to say to you too.' She looked Tess right in the eye. 'Thank you. I wouldn't have got my boys back without your help.'

Tess gazed back solemnly. 'You're welcome. I love them to their bones. We might never be sisters, but I hope I'll always be their auntie.'

'You will,' Bridget said and, although two weeks ago she wouldn't have believed it possible, she meant it.

A hoarse voice spoke up. 'Seeing as it's time for apologies...'

Everyone swivelled towards Bronagh. She set her cup on the empty seat beside her and stood, her cheeks still wet. Her right hand grappled with the fingers on her left and then she held out Bridget's gold ring in the centre of her palm. Bridget took it and slipped it on at once above the thread ring, relief flooding her as another piece of her was restored. Bronagh opened her mouth as if she intended to express her remorse further but a loud sniff from Orlaith forestalled her. Orlaith lifted her shoulders.

'Will you come back to Boston with us?' she asked.

Bronagh gaped at her. 'Why would you want me to?'

'You're family,' Orlaith said simply.

'And this family's very good at forgiveness,' Tess added.

Bridget read the bewilderment in Bronagh's countenance and this time felt her compassion stir. Having spent so many years surrounded by violence and vice, the poor woman couldn't comprehend kindness when it was right in front of her.

'What's left for you in New York?' Orlaith asked.

Bronagh wavered. 'N-nothing.'

'So you'll come with us?'

After a long pause, Bronagh dipped her head. 'I will.' Then she turned to Cáit. 'Will you come too?'

Cáit pressed her lips together. 'I never want to go back to that city,' she said in a low voice. 'It'd only remind me of what happened to Billy.'

'D'you have any notion what you'll do instead?' asked Tess.

Cáit contemplated for a moment. 'You know what? I want to go home to Ireland. I mean, 'tis no paradise but it can't be any worse than here, right?'

'What about Seamus?' Charlie's question came out in a croak; Bridget suspected he had not spoken a word since they had left the warehouse. 'What do you think he'll do?'

Cáit wrinkled her nose. 'He can rot in hell for all I care. He's another good reason to leave this country and never come back.'

A chill ran down Bridget's spine. With no one to challenge him, would Seamus revive the gang as the Sheedy Greens once more? If he did, she could only pray that he would be more like his uncle than Malachy when it came to the recruitment of small boys for their dirty work.

'I need to go find Hester,' Bronagh said suddenly. 'If she'll listen, I have to apologise to her too. She deserves it most of all.'

'I'll come with you,' Bridget said with a nod of encouragement. Part of her considered it prudent for someone else to be present at that meeting, prepared to intervene should Hester not prove ready yet to accept an apology from the woman who had kidnapped her son. But another part of her wished to take the opportunity to ask Hester about trustworthy stagecoach routes out of New York.

The sooner they left the city, the better. She never wanted to set foot there again as long as she lived.

CHAPTER 36

Cormac breathed in the smell of hops from the nearby brewery as he stared across Meath Street at O'Hara's Tobacconist and Lodgings. The sight of the grubby building brought back distressing memories of his search for his family that had led him here eight years ago, and yet he couldn't quell the underlying quiver of exhilaration that had burgeoned in him as soon as he, Emily and Rory had disembarked from the ship in Dublin Port. He was on home soil again at last.

This was the detour he had proposed to Emily and Rory. How could they travel all the way to England and not take advantage of the opportunity to visit Ireland as well? Oakleigh would be their primary destination, of course – however, he could not in all conscience sail back to America without also making an investigation into Henrietta's welfare.

Bracing himself, he led the way across the street, pushed open the stained door of O'Hara's and entered, Emily and Rory trailing after him. The dim front hall was just as he remembered with its high counter and dusty shelves displaying their tobacco wares, although everything seemed to have acquired a few extra layers of grime. A gangly girl was sweeping the floor using a broom missing half its bristles – it left behind a pile of dirt and she swore at it before glancing up at the new arrivals.

'Snuff?' she said curtly. 'Or lodgings?'

Her long black hair and round lips were just like her mother's but she was still only a child of eleven so her body had not yet matured – she held herself awkwardly as though she didn't know what to do with her growing limbs, and pimples spotted her face.

'Hello, Henrietta,' Cormac said, feeling inexplicably nervous.

She frowned. 'It's Henny. No one calls me Henrietta except...' Her eyes widened and she gasped. 'You're him!'

'You remember me?' he asked, surprised. She hadn't even been three and a half years old when they had last met.

'Not your face,' she admitted. 'But I remember' – she scrunched her nose as she struggled to come up with the right word – 'your shape, if that makes sense. You found me and Dolly in that cupboard and took us away.'

'That's right,' he said. 'Do you still have Dolly?'

She blushed, her pimples going redder, and didn't answer. Instead, she looked at Emily and Rory. 'Who're they?' she asked bluntly.

'That's Emily, my daughter, and Rory, my apprentice. We live in America but we're visiting Ireland for a brief time so we wanted to come see you.'

She surveyed Emily with narrowed eyes, which were light brown and flecked with gold like Henry Munroe's. 'Oh,' was all she said, eschewing any word of greeting. Then her gaze shot back to Cormac. 'You write to Auntie Biddy sometimes, don't you?' she blurted. 'She says you ask about me.'

'I do. I ask about how you're faring, especially with regard to your illnesses.'

'Ah, I'm never sick,' she said airily. 'Strong as a bulldog, me.'

What a surprise, he thought wryly.

'Your grandaunt told me you've run away before,' he said. 'Is that true?'

407

Sudden fear shadowed her features.

'You're not in trouble,' he hurried to assure her. 'But I need to know if there's a problem here.'

The hand that wasn't holding her decrepit broom snaked up to her mouth and she started biting at the skin around her nails.

'You can tell me the truth,' he said encouragingly.

She took a breath to speak but then footsteps came thumping up the corridor towards the closed door at the rear of the hall and, alarmed, she shook her head.

'Everything's fine,' she said.

The door opened and a stooped old woman came through with an expression like thunder. 'Henny, you never cleaned out that chamber pot and now the room smells like—'

She halted, the scattered bristles on her chin sticking out as her jaw dropped in astonishment. In the next instant, she plastered an oily leer onto her face.

'Mr McGovern,' she said. 'What an unexpected surprise.'

'Good day, Mrs O'Hara,' he said, keeping his tone civil. 'I'm here to visit Henrietta but I'm afraid I cannot stay long.'

Henrietta's shoulders drooped with palpable disappointment.

He carried on, 'I therefore wish to ask if you can spare her for a few days? I should like to bring her away on a short trip.'

Henrietta lit up like a Fourth of July illumination and she turned her hopeful gaze to her grandaunt. Mrs O'Hara twisted her mouth, perhaps weighing up the inconvenience of her skivvy's temporary absence against the potential of this situation to coerce more money out of Cormac.

'Fine,' she eventually muttered.

Henrietta let out a whoop of delight. 'Just you and me?' she said to Cormac, cheeks glowing.

'Emily and Rory will be coming with us too,' he told her.

408

She visibly deflated at that and cast a sour look at Emily, her attention lingering on Emily's golden curls and flawless skin. 'Fine,' she muttered in the exact same tone as Mrs O'Hara. 'Where are we going?'

'A place called Oakleigh in County Carlow. It's in the countryside, more than sixty miles south of here.'

Her expression lifted. 'I've never been outside of Dublin before!'

That fact subsequently became apparent in many ways. After they departed from Meath Street, Cormac made arrangements to hire a coachman and carriage for their journey down to Oakleigh – it was an extravagance but Lord Bewley had endowed him with more than enough money to cover the expense of their passage back to America and it would be quite a treat for the three youngsters. Once on their way, Henrietta exclaimed continually at everything around her. She marvelled at the freshness of the air after they left the smoky city behind, she gaped at the fields full of cows or sheep or potato crops, she could hardly suppress her excitement at the speed with which they travelled. It was a good thing no railway line had yet been built between Dublin and Carlow – if she had boarded a locomotive, she would probably have fainted in awe.

Cormac observed her delight with pleasure, glad that he had invited her to come with them. She bobbed on the seat beside him, her manner far more childlike than the curt facade she had initially presented in the front hall of O'Hara's. Less than an hour into the first stage of their journey, she began humming happily to herself, only breaking the melody to admire some fascinating new sight through the carriage window. Her pitch was perfect and the timbre of her notes was sweet and stirring.

'You have a lovely voice, Henrietta,' he told her.

She coloured and went silent but looked quietly pleased.

They stayed at an inn for the night and that was another brand new experience for Henrietta, who had never had a meal brought to her or slept in a bed dressed in sheets she hadn't washed herself. She didn't speak much with either Emily or Rory but she stuck close to Cormac like a limpet and took pains to claim the seat next to him when they climbed back into the carriage the next morning. She started humming again as the horses set off and this time he didn't comment so as to avoid triggering another bout of shyness.

Emily and Rory didn't appear to take offence to Henrietta's unsociability towards them and either chatted to each other in low murmurs or sat in companionable silence on the opposite seat of the carriage. At one point, they became absorbed in a nostalgic reminiscence about the passengers they had travelled with across the Atlantic and their distraction seemed to give Henrietta the courage to turn to Cormac and ask, 'D'you remember much about my ma?'

He baulked inwardly. He supposed he should have seen this coming.

'I didn't know her very well,' he said cautiously, 'but I remember a little. Do you have questions about her?'

'What was she like?'

'She was...' Brazen. Flirtatious. Wouldn't take no for an answer. 'Determined. And she was brave—she wanted to make a better life for you. Does Mrs O'Hara ever talk to you about her?'

Henrietta picked absently at a pimple on her chin. 'Not often. She said I look like her though, is that right?'

'You do. You have her hair and her mouth. But you have your father's eyes.'

Henrietta jerked her head towards him, her gaze searing into his face. Into his blue eyes. 'My father?' she muttered with frozen lips.

He winced. 'Yes. Has your grandaunt ever told you about him?'

She gritted her teeth. 'No.'

God, this situation was worsening by the second. 'Do you want me to...shall I tell you?'

She stared down at her lap and shrugged. 'Suppose.'

He swallowed. 'His name is Henry Munroe. He used to live in Dublin but I met him quite recently in London.' He paused. 'I'm sorry to admit that he's in Newgate Prison.'

'What's he in for?' she asked, her tone flat.

'Smuggling.'

She said nothing.

'He's due to go on trial but I'm not sure what his potential sentence might be.'

She remained silent and he did too, not wanting to pursue the topic further when it was clearly upsetting her. He certainly would not be mentioning that her mother had died at her father's hands.

After a long minute, she glanced sideways at him. 'So you're definitely not my da then?'

In that moment, her pitiful tone made him wish that he was. 'I'm afraid I'm not.'

She returned her gaze to her knees and asked no more questions. There was no humming in the carriage for the rest of the journey.

When they finally turned onto Oakleigh Manor's gravelled avenue, Cormac's insides began to churn with anticipation. The last time he had beheld the big house, it had been a burnt ruin. Bridget had tasked the land agent, Laurence Enright, and the stable master, John Corbett, with reviving the manor building and its lands – how much had they been able to accomplish in the intervening eight years?

The carriage rolled to a stop and Emily scooted to the window to peer out.

'Oh, my goodness!' she exclaimed.

She fumbled with the door handle until Rory reached past and opened it for her. She plunged outside, not waiting for a step to be brought around, and Rory followed.

Cormac gesticulated towards the open door. 'After you, Henrietta.'

'It's Henny,' she said with a glower and thumped out of the carriage.

He took a deep breath and stepped out after her. It was nearing the end of July and the afternoon was sunny, but a mild breeze staved off any oppressive heat and the brim of his cap kept the sun out of his eyes as he looked up.

His jaw fell open in amazement. Oakleigh Manor towered above him, its red brick walls bright and welcoming. He blinked and looked again. Yes, the manor stood before him but, although every effort appeared to have been made to model it on the original house, upon closer scrutiny he could discern the differences between it and its predecessor. The red brick was too clean, not yet weathered by natural elements. The front facade featured the same layout of windows but no ivy snaked around them. However, the most glaring alteration was the addition of an extra wing on the western side that had never been there before. Still, apart from that it was remarkably similar. He could scarcely believe it. What an astounding achievement.

'It's magnificent, Papa!' Emily cried, clapping her hands. 'Mama will be so happy. I'm going to commit as much of it as I can to memory and paint it for her when we get home.'

Next to Emily, Rory was speechless as he stared up at the manor. Henrietta, on the other hand, turned her back on it to face Cormac.

'What is this place?' she demanded.

'It's called Oakleigh Manor,' he replied. 'Emily's mother grew up here—that is to say, in the previous house that stood here before it burned down. I used to work for the manor as a stable hand.'

Henrietta squinted towards Emily. 'Her ma's some kind of posh person? Does that make her posh too?'

He grimaced; he was beginning to perceive the flaws in his well-meaning decision to bring Henrietta on this trip. 'In a way. Her mother is a baroness and someday Emily will be one too. Having said that, this estate is technically owned by, ah, another individual so its wealth belongs to him.'

'Oh, Papa, I forgot!' Emily's fingertips pressed to her cheek as she pivoted towards him. 'When Garrett struck his horrible bargain with me, he included Oakleigh in the negotiations. He said that if I succeeded in convincing Edward to become Patrick, he would bequeath Oakleigh's assets to me in his will. Which means the estate could be entirely mine someday.' She pinched her lips together. 'Of course, his word is about as trustworthy as the Devil's.'

Cormac was both stunned by this revelation and regretful that Emily had chosen to impart it in Henrietta's hearing when he saw the resentment swell in the girl's light brown eyes. 'That would be an extraordinary concession on Garrett's part,' he said, 'but I agree that it remains subject to his mercurial whims. There'll be no certainty on the matter until the day his will is read out.'

Though the remark was meant only for Emily, Henrietta's forehead creased as she also tried to grasp its implication. However, before either of them could comment, a wiry figure came around the corner of the manor house and called out a greeting of dumbfounded delight.

'Well, when I heard wheels on the avenue, I never expected this was who I'd find,' John Corbett said, striding up to them.

413

He shook Cormac's hand with vigour. 'Thought you were in America these days, lad.'

'I am,' Cormac replied. 'I just happened to make a recent unplanned voyage back across the ocean' – Emily flushed – 'so when I'd come that far, I couldn't forgo the chance to visit home in the process.'

'There's been a few changes about the place since you were last here,' John said with a grin. 'Want me to show you 'round?'

'I'd very much enjoy a tour.' Cormac turned to his young companions. 'Does that sound appealing to you three?'

Emily's gaze flashed towards Rory. 'Perhaps we could go exploring by ourselves?'

'Very well,' said Cormac. 'What would you prefer to do, Henrietta?'

'It's Henny,' she said. 'And I don't want to go on a boring tour.'

Sensing the distance between them widening with every passing minute, he inclined his head. 'Would you like to accompany Emily and Rory instead?'

'Fine,' she huffed.

With an apprehensive glance at Cormac, Emily said, 'Splendid! Let's set off then.'

She and Rory headed towards the corner of the manor house and Henrietta followed, kicking mulishly at the gravel.

When they had disappeared, John advised the coachman where he could feed and water his horses and then he led Cormac up the broad stone steps of the manor. The steps were unchanged for they had not been affected by the fire, but the front door had been replaced by a pair of black-painted double doors with striking brass embellishments. John pushed them open with a flourish and they entered the expansive entrance hall.

Cormac inhaled in surprise and immediately exhaled with admiration because the manor's interior had been completely rebuilt, leaving not a single trace of charred wood behind. Like the exterior, efforts had been made to replicate it in its previous form and yet several alterations were also evident. The entrance hall's dimensions were just as spacious as before with the walls aligned in the same design, though they bore no paintings. Decorative cornices bordered the high ceiling. A sweeping wooden staircase once again dominated the space but this one wasn't made of mahogany – could it be walnut, perhaps? The most arresting change was the inclusion of a gallery around the upper floor. The staircase rose up towards it and split in two before reaching the top.

Cormac absorbed it all, trying to memorise as much of it as he could so that he, like Emily, could describe it for Bridget when they returned to Boston. He thought she would be pleased; the manor had retained its character while embracing the improvements that a reconstruction could offer. It was rather like meeting an old friend after a very long time apart – age or illness might have altered the body but the person's spirit remained the same. That brought Lady Bewley to his mind with a sad tug of his heart. Swallowing his sorrow, he refocused his attention on what John was saying.

'—done in stages as we wanted to concentrate on reviving the land first. Funds were slim to begin with so our priority had to be giving the tenants the means to feed and clothe their families again. But a little extra income started coming in from the rental of the townhouse in Merrion Square—Webb & Brereton handled all that—which meant Enright and I could hire an architect for the big house and the builders worked on it bit by bit over the years. They've done a terrific job, if I do say so myself. No furnishings yet as you can see, although they won't be needed anyway 'til the place is occupied again.' John paused to give Cormac the opportunity to elaborate on that point but Cormac had no notion what might be a suitable response. Carrying on, John said, 'The drawing room's through there like before and the library's over on that side. Come on this way.'

He ushered Cormac towards the back of the hall and they descended the brand new servants' stairs to the kitchens. These, too, had been restored after being gutted by the fire and now boasted an impressive cast-iron stove. John patted it.

'I tell you, Maura Kavanagh can't wait to resume her reign down here.'

'I'll bet she can't,' said Cormac. 'I must say, I'm extremely impressed with the amount of progress that's been made. But tell me, what's the purpose of that additional wing on the western side?'

John smiled. 'I'll show you.'

They went back up to the entrance hall where John strode past the staircase – yes, it was definitely walnut – and into a passageway in the far corner that Cormac had not noticed before. At the end of the passage loomed an open gap that was clearly missing a door.

'I expect this'll be closed most of the time once it's put in,' said John, tapping the door frame. 'It shouldn't be needed 'cause the wing has external access.'

Powerfully curious, Cormac followed him across the threshold. They emerged into a large hall that was less decorative than the rest of the manor. A plain staircase at the end of the hallway rose up to the next floor while a number of doorways led off it at ground level. These already had their doors attached; John led Cormac up to one, opened it and shepherded him through. He stepped into a room which contained the first piece of furniture he'd seen: a long, wide table that stretched almost from one end of the room to the other. Benches lined both sides of it and a scattering of plates on its surface showed that it was already being utilised. He shot John a questioning look.

'The dining hall,' the former stable master explained with a triumphant bounce of his feet. 'And that stairs out in the hallway leads up to the sleeping quarters—there are rooms of all different sizes depending on how many need to be accommodated at a time.' At Cormac's continued incomprehension, John added proudly, ''Tis for the tenants, those who can't afford their rent or whose homes are in need of repair. Folk who're down on their luck will always have a place to stay on this estate.'

Cormac gaped at him.

John's grin nearly split his face in two. 'Did her ladyship never tell you about it? It was her idea right from the start of the reconstruction. And she said this wing had to be completed first so that we could put it to use as soon as possible.'

'Bridget instructed you to build this?' Cormac said wonderingly, staring around the tenants' dining hall again.

'She sure did. She's got the soul of an angel and a mind as clever as her da's. What a blessed combination.'

Cormac's heart pounded against his ribs and he could feel his whole body glowing with adoration. What an absolutely exceptional woman she was. He had not believed it possible that he could love her even more than he had the second before.

And yet he did.

***

Emily, Rory and Henrietta reached the cobbled courtyard at the back of the manor house where Emily turned to the others and said brightly, 'What shall we explore first? There's the stables and the orchard and—'

'I don't want to explore,' Henrietta said, her forehead wrinkled with a scowl.

'Oh, but...' Emily faltered.

'I want to be on my own.' Henrietta pointed towards a cluster of barns beyond the stables. 'I'm going that way. Yous can go somewhere else.'

She marched off without another word. Emily rocked forwards on her toes but Rory put a hand on her forearm.

'Let her be,' he said. 'I reckon following her will only make things worse.'

She nodded, all of a sudden not thinking about Henrietta as she realised that gooseflesh had risen along her arm. A moment later, Rory dropped his hand but the skin beneath her sleeve still tingled.

She frowned, disconcerted. It wasn't the first time it had happened – at least twice on the journey down from Dublin, she had become conscious of his leg resting so close to hers in the carriage that gooseflesh had erupted on her thigh.

Shaking herself to dispel the unsettling sensation, she said, 'Would you still like to explore the grounds?'

'Sure,' he said, but now he was the one frowning and she couldn't tell why.

Pretending that she hadn't noticed, she crossed the cobblestones to the stables and slipped through the open double doors. Rory joined her and together they wandered past the stalls which housed several horses – not elegant thoroughbreds but sturdy creatures whose tall, muscular bodies suggested that they were accustomed to hard work.

Emily stopped at one stall and, rising on her tiptoes, reached over the half door to stretch her fingers out to the horse within.

'Do you know how to ride?' she asked, turning her head to Rory.

'I don't. Do you?'

'No. But both of my parents are accomplished riders so I wonder if it's in my blood. Perhaps it would come to me natural—ouch!' She hastily withdrew her hand from the stall. 'It bit me!'

The horse gazed out at them, harmless and complacent.

'Are you sure?' said Rory. 'Maybe it just thought you had food.'

'Hmph,' she said crossly, although without any real heat. 'Maybe it thought I *was* the food.'

'Why would it want to eat you?' he said with a straight face. 'There's hardly a pick on you. You wouldn't be worth the effort.'

Not all that long ago, she would have been quite sensitive to a comment like that, especially coming from him, but now her lips quivered as she struggled to restrain a smile. 'Let's move on, shall we?'

When they left the stables, she found herself drawn back across the cobbles towards the walled apple orchard. She knew it held great significance for her parents and she pushed open the green-painted door with more than a little reverence, feeling as though she and Rory were entering a place as sacred as a church.

The apple trees rustled above their heads in the summer breeze, their branches laden with unripe fruit. She gestured towards a path meandering away among the trees and they began to follow it. Her gaze travelled over the peaceful scene, catching on an apple that was ripening a little faster than its fellows, the colour of its skin blending gradually from green to red.

'There are so many images here that I should like to paint,' she said, marvelling at the simple beauty that nature could yield. Her favourite colour green surrounded her on all sides, a variety of shades captured in the leaves and the fruit and the undergrowth...and Rory's eyes, although she didn't allow herself to look there. 'I've missed painting so very much.'

Rory ducked under a low-hanging branch. 'How long d'you think it'll take for you to get to Brubaker under your own steam?'

'It's impossible to say. My first challenge will be to find new employment and I doubt Mrs Coleman will provide me with a character from Marlowe House after my behaviour there.'

She stopped talking abruptly. She wished she hadn't mentioned Marlowe House because it could easily pave the way for a conversation she was reluctant to have. But then perhaps Rory wouldn't want to—

'How come you never mentioned that Samuel fella before?'

She flinched. 'Oh,' she said, striving for airiness and achieving a croak. She cleared her throat. 'He wasn't...um...he wasn't important.'

'He wasn't?' Rory said with a raised eyebrow.

'Not at all.'

'So wanting to become Garrett's heir was all about the money for Brubaker? And not about climbing the social ladder to make yourself more—ah, what's the word?'

Her whole body blazed with mortification. 'Eligible,' she muttered. 'No, it wasn't about that.'

He didn't push the matter any further and, fervently glad, she marched onwards along the winding path.

When they reached the clearing at the centre of the orchard, her embarrassment dissipated. She rushed towards the oak tree, sought out her parents' initials carved into the bark of its trunk, and deferentially traced the weathered letters. What a special place this was. No doubt her father would also come to visit it at some stage. This had been the beginning of everything for him and her mother. It did not matter that they had set down roots halfway across the world; this was where they had first planted them.

With that thought, it occurred to her that there was something very basic she did not know.

'Rory,' she said, turning to look up at him curiously. 'Which county are you from?'

He squinted down at her. 'Kerry. Why?'

'Kerry,' she repeated. 'How did you end up in America?'

'When Da got a regular job on the *Integrity*, he wanted his family to live close to one of its ports. So we moved to Boston.' He twisted his mouth. 'And once he met that Maud woman in Liverpool, he replaced one port with another.'

She cringed, regretting that she had raised the question. 'Do you miss Ireland?' she asked in an attempt to steer him away from the spectre of Brian Mór and Maud Carey.

He shrugged.

'Or do you prefer Boston? Which do you consider to be your true home?'

'I don't know,' he mumbled. 'I reckon 'tis the folk who matter more than the places. Y'know, the ones you could go anywhere with and still feel like you're at home.'

Rory Carey wasn't often eloquent with words but this time she believed he had hit the nail precisely on the head.

Her skin tingled again.

***

By the time they returned to Dublin three days later, Cormac had come to a definite decision. Their trip to Oakleigh had been an entirely pleasant experience, apart from Henrietta's sulky mood which had generated rude retorts and awkward silences on numerous occasions throughout their visit. The more opportunity he had to observe her, the more troubled he grew about her. Ellen and Liam Kirwan had welcomed them into their cottage and he had hoped that their three children, who were closer in age to Henrietta than Emily or Rory, might draw her out of her dour humour. However, she had shunned Liam Óg and Aidan and she had intimidated seven-year-old Bridie to such a degree that the little girl had gone running to her mother in tears. Henrietta didn't know how to interact on civil terms with people of any age nor to be respectful to others even when a situation wasn't favourable in her eyes. All evidence suggested that the circumstances of her upbringing were simply not acceptable.

Thus, when the carriage came to a halt outside O'Hara's on Meath Street, he said to Emily and Rory, 'Would you mind giving me and Henri—Henny a moment alone before we go inside?'

Startled, Emily said, 'Of course. I believe we passed a haberdasher just back there. I should like to call into it.'

He doubted whether she had spotted any such shop nestled among the spirit merchants and pawnbroker establishments that lined the street but he was grateful for her willingness to cooperate without question. She and Rory climbed out of the carriage, leaving him and Henrietta on their own. She slouched in her corner of the seat, surveying him warily.

He chewed the inside of his cheek as he studied her in return. How should he phrase this? 'Thank you for coming with us to Carlow,' he began. 'I hope you enjoyed the overall experience.'

She gave an unenthusiastic nod and nibbled on the skin around her left thumb.

'I have something to ask you,' he said. 'I want to know if you would like to travel on further with us.'

'Further?' she said with her thumb still between her teeth.

422

'Yes, across the ocean. Will you come and live with me and my family in America? We have a house in Boston and we would be very happy for you to share our home with us.' Of course, he didn't yet have Bridget's approval on the matter but he believed her compassion would win out over any residual aversion on her part towards the daughter of the only other woman he had ever bedded.

Henrietta's thumb fell out of her mouth. She sat up and peered at him with sheer astonishment. For the briefest instant, he read the unguarded hope and excitement in her eyes. Then her gaze shuttered and her round lips tightened into a thin line.

'No,' she said.

His stomach sank at her cold refusal. 'If you're hesitant about going on a ship, I can assure—'

'It's not that.'

'I understand that it's a great distance from Ireland. Perhaps you would miss your grandaunt too much?'

She snorted.

'Henrietta, please—' At her glare, he amended himself hurriedly. 'Henny, please know you can confide in me. I suspect you are very unhappy here. All I want is to make your life better.'

'Why?' she said tartly. 'You're not my da, right?'

'That doesn't matter—'

'I don't belong with you!' she burst out. 'Your family is perfect and I don't fit in anywhere.'

She sprang off the seat and dashed out through the carriage door, nearly tripping in her haste to jump down to the street. Then she stuck her head back into the carriage and fixed him with an emotionless look.

'We'll still take your money though. Make sure you give it to Auntie Biddy before you leave.'

Her black hair whipped over her shoulder as she spun around and stalked into O'Hara's.

423

He rubbed his jaw, feeling helpless. His gut told him that it would be a grave mistake to leave her behind; he felt it even more strongly than he had when he had placed her in her grandaunt's care as a small child. And yet he couldn't take her away against her will.

But where would this grim, unpromising life end up leading her?

CHAPTER 37

Bridget opened the kitchen window in Acorn House, letting the humid September air seep inside as the steam from the pot on the stove drifted out. A heavy thumping on the ceiling above indicated that Jack and Gus were engaged in a boisterous tussle in their bedroom but she wouldn't dream of shouting upstairs to berate them. Although they had both suffered recurring bad dreams in the aftermath of their ordeal in New York, these had gradually eased and it was a joy to hear them play freely in the knowledge that they were once again safe. Thankful beyond words, she turned back to the discussion at the kitchen table.

'I still think we should,' Charlie said, tugging on his ear.

'And we will,' Orlaith assured him. 'But replacing my wedding ring can wait. Right now the most important thing we should be doing with our money is saving it.'

She was sitting on the chair next to him; reaching out, she grasped his other hand which rested on the table's surface and squeezed it. After a cautious glimpse at her face, he folded his fingers into hers and squeezed back.

Although Bridget had not been privy to the exchange, she knew that, following their return to Boston, Orlaith and Charlie had talked deeply about what had occurred in New York. Orlaith had told Bridget afterwards that she couldn't view

Charlie's conduct as an act of unfaithfulness because he had not done it willingly, and therefore she did not believe he required forgiveness. Despite that, something had still fractured between them and it would take time for their relationship to heal. Watching them now, however, Bridget did not fear for them; their bond was strong and reconciliation would come in time.

Orlaith cast a furtive glance at the closed door leading into the front room where Tess and Bronagh had retreated when the smell of the cooking pot became too much for Bronagh's sensitive nose.

'We still haven't said anything about Chicago to...' Orlaith said, trailing off.

'Probably best not to bring it up with her just yet,' Bridget said gently. 'Soon she will have a small baby to tend which will occupy her whole attention.'

Not to mention, Bronagh was still dealing with her own trauma from New York. Frequently over the past six weeks, she had withdrawn into herself, her grey eyes glazing over and an expression of pain shadowing her features. They had all learned to leave her be whenever this happened and just wait for her to emerge again once she was ready.

Only for the boys, Bridget might have succumbed to a similar melancholy. The details of that hideous night in the warehouse stood out to her in odd ways – she could remember her anger but not the words she had said, she could remember the sleep crusting the corners of Malachy's eyes but not the feel of his chest beneath her palms. Needless to say, she could not forget the snapping of the rope.

Had she murdered him? Or had Bronagh been the one to seal his fate? Perhaps they had killed him together. She didn't know how to carry the weight of another human being's death on her conscience, no matter how despicable that human being had been. Cormac believed he had been responsible for

426

Cunningham's demise and she desperately wished to ask him how he managed to cope daily with that knowledge.

It was only one of a hundred things she yearned to share with him but she had to remain patient for his return. She had received his letter so at least she knew that he, Emily and Rory were safe and she also understood why they had delayed their journey back to America. The wait was almost unbearable though, and she longed for them to be home already. Furthermore, the lease on Cormac's workshop was due to run out in the next few weeks – she hoped he would be back in time to revive his business before it expired.

Would he be able to afford to retain Rory as an apprentice? Whether he could or not, Una would likely keep her job at the shirt factory, where she had resumed working once she and her siblings had recovered from the scarlet fever. The mood in the Carey family had greatly improved with the passing of the fever and the subsequent good news that Rory was unharmed and on his way home – Derval had wept with joy and relief when Bridget had dashed to Broad Street immediately after collecting Cormac's letter at the post office. The only dark cloud that remained at Broad Street was the sad loss of Mr Lorenzo but a new family had already moved into his room at the top of the building.

Just as Bridget turned back to the stove to check on the pot, the door into the front room flew open and Tess appeared on the threshold.

'Looks like the baby's coming,' she announced.

Bridget and Orlaith rushed from the kitchen; Charlie wisely remained behind with a vow to watch the pot.

Bronagh was sitting on the edge of the sofa in front of the hearth. She leaned forwards with her hands pressed to the small of her back as she groaned.

'We should send for Derval,' said Orlaith, anxiously appraising her sister from head to toe.

'No,' Bronagh said faintly. She had met Derval but was still skittish around people she considered to be strangers. 'I want you to deliver the baby, Orlaith. Please?'

Orlaith only wavered for a moment before saying, 'Right then. We need towels and water and—'

The front door of the house opened wide and they all turned towards it. Cormac, Emily and Rory stood on the doorstep.

'Oh, thank God!' Bridget cried.

She dashed forwards as Cormac strode inside, his countenance full of a fierce gladness. They met in the centre of the room and somehow fell to their knees as they embraced. She buried her face in his neck and savoured the feeling of his arms wrapped around her, fitting exactly where they belonged.

'I missed you, *a rún mo chroí*,' he murmured.

Oh, what a joy it was to hear those words coming from his mouth. She leaned back to beam up at him. Then she looked over his shoulder at Emily who was hovering apprehensively in the background.

'Come here to me, my gooseberry,' she said and, with a sob, Emily also dropped to her knees and folded herself into the space between her parents, her bonnet falling back off her head.

'I'm so sorry for what I did, Mama,' she gushed as they both held her close.

'Hush now,' Bridget soothed, stroking Emily's curls.

Rory still stood on the threshold. Wordlessly, Bridget stretched her arm out to him and he hesitated before approaching the three of them clustered together. When he knelt, she cupped his cheek and whispered, 'God bless you for keeping her safe.'

'Da? It's Da!' came Jack's voice suddenly from the top of the stairs.

'And Emmy!' squawked Gus.

They tore down the stairs to the tune of two squeaks from Barnabas and barrelled into the group on the floor. In the ensuing chaos, Bridget extricated herself so that she could go back over to Bronagh, who was observing the scene with wide, frantic eyes and trying to keep her moans as muted as possible. Bridget suspected that she would have climbed into the fireplace and disappeared if she could.

'You don't need to be worried,' she said, her tone encouraging. 'Will you come meet him?'

Bronagh dithered before wincing and nodding. Orlaith and Tess helped her rise from the sofa and they crossed the room back to the muddled bunch still on their knees.

'Cormac?' Bridget said.

He glanced up with a grin; Jack and Gus were both hanging off him like monkeys. Then his expression froze as his gaze landed on Bronagh.

'We found her,' Bridget said simply. There was so much more to say but now wasn't the time.

He disentangled himself from the boys and scrambled to his feet. 'Bronagh,' he managed to utter and Bridget watched him absorb every aspect of his long-lost sister, from her pregnant belly to the fear in her face. With the same instincts he utilised around nervy horses, he didn't advance any closer, only extended his hand, palm up, in a gentle gesture.

She held back and it seemed at first that she wouldn't do or say anything at all. But then, cautiously, she reached out and touched her fingers to his. He neither tightened his grip nor made any other movement. He just said, 'I'm overjoyed to see you.'

She responded with a whimper of pain and Orlaith interjected, 'I think the baby's going to have to take priority here.'

429

'The pot needs attention too,' came Charlie's guilty voice from the door to the kitchen. 'I let it boil over by accident.'

Amid chuckles and groans, Acorn House became a hive of activity as preparations were made for the birth. A few hours after that, Orlaith helped Bronagh deliver a baby girl, small but robust. Almost immediately, Bronagh named the child Maggie, ostensibly after her grandmother...although Bridget couldn't help noticing that Maggie sounded an awful lot like Malachy.

She put the thought out of her mind. The important, joyful thing was that their family had expanded. Cormac and Orlaith had gained a niece and Emily, Jack and Gus had gained a cousin. Granted, many uncertainties lay ahead for the McGoverns and fragile relationships still needed to be mended, but on this auspicious day the family had so much to be thankful for.

CHAPTER 38

Along every step to Marlowe House, Emily had wondered whether she ought to do this, but she hadn't turned back and now here she was. Bonnet shielding her from the noon sun, she stood in the paved courtyard at the back of the house, a pencil stub and a folded note in one hand and a bundle of papers rolled up under her other arm.

Five days had passed since she had disembarked from the ship with her father and Rory (and declared that she would never again set foot on another vessel unless it was a matter of extreme need). That had been enough time for her to decide upon this course of action, despite her continuing doubt over the wisdom of it.

Inhaling deeply to steady her nerves, she bent down in front of the closed back door and rolled her pencil stub through the gap between the bottom of the door and the sill. Then she retreated to the corner of the courtyard and waited, hoping no one would spot her until the right person saw her pencil.

More than half an hour must have passed but at last the back door opened and a head poked out. Emily recognised the striking cheekbones of her friend Matilda and relief coursed through her. She gesticulated from the corner where she skulked and Matilda's gaze swung over to her, widening in comical disbelief. She glanced behind her, then scuttled out into the courtyard and over to Emily.

'Em!' she exclaimed in an animated whisper. 'It really is you! When I saw the pencil stub, I figured only one person could've put it there.'

Emily smiled. 'I knew you'd remember our trick. It's so lovely to see you, Matilda.'

'I'd say the same about you, only I think you'll get into big trouble if anyone catches you out here. Why have you come? Are you trying to get your job back? But surely you mustn't need it if you're as rich as a queen now?'

Emily halted the barrage of questions with a flapping hand. 'I promise I will tell you every single thing that's happened, and I swear it'll be as good as all the secrets I've told you before. But first of all I have a favour to ask and it's a difficult one so I'll understand if you don't think it's feasible.'

Matilda quivered with curiosity. 'What is it?'

'Can you contrive a way to pass a note from me to Master Samuel?'

Matilda blinked, taken aback. 'What for?'

'I want to ask him to meet me at the Common, if he's willing.'

Matilda's jaw sagged. 'By golly!' she said in awe. 'You've got more gumption than anyone I've ever met.'

'I wouldn't call it gumption,' Emily replied sombrely. 'I'm rather terrified, to be honest. But I believe I must do it. I owe him an explanation and an apology for deceiving him on the night of Miss Knight's ball.'

Matilda nodded. 'I suppose you'd have to clear the air about that before he could fancy you for real.'

'I'm not seeking his affections anymore,' said Emily.

'But aren't you still in love with him?' Matilda said in astonishment.

Emily shrugged noncommittally. 'How I feel is neither here nor there. I comprehend now that a match between us just isn't realistic.'

'But you went all the way to England for him!'

'I did, and I learned a great many hard lessons along the way, although there isn't time for me to regale you with the whole story now. I know you must get back to your work but do you think there's a chance you could bring this note to Samuel's attention at some stage?'

She held out the folded piece of paper.

Matilda's brows knitted together as she took it. 'I reckon I could. Will you tell me what it says?'

Emily bit her lip. 'That I am the girl he met at his cousin's ball back in June and that, if he is open to another meeting between us, I will wait for him near the north entrance of Boston Common at three o'clock every day this week. If he does not appear by the week's end, then I'll know that he has no desire to see me and I'll leave him be.'

Matilda's expression of admiration returned. 'Gumption like I've never seen it,' she murmured before continuing in a brisker tone, 'Right, leave it with me. I'll get it done.'

'You are quite the magnificent friend,' Emily said earnestly.

Matilda grinned. 'I know.'

She started to turn away but Emily put out her free hand to stop her. 'Wait. Before you go, I wanted to ask you...' She paused. How could she put this without making any unwarranted insinuations? 'Um, have you encountered that English coachman again? The one you met at the ball?'

Matilda's countenance turned dreamy. 'No, more's the pity. What a charming accent he had.' She waved dismissively. 'I'd have no time for him anyways. I've been promoted from upper housemaid to head housemaid so I've got plenty on my plate.' She straightened her shoulders proudly. 'And guess what? Mrs

Coleman calls me Matilda now. The butler still says Tilly but I don't care—the people who matter have got it right.'

With a wink, she scurried back to the door and vanished inside. Emily hugged her rolled bundle of papers to her chest, very glad that Garrett's conniving agent had not bothered Matilda again. Sighing with relief, she left the courtyard.

She made her way to Boston Common to linger there until three, even though it was unlikely that Samuel would appear today – after all, Matilda would need time to manoeuvre the note into position. How might she orchestrate it? Would she leave it on Samuel's bedside table? Tuck it into the book he was reading? Or simply drop it on the floor in his vicinity? However she managed it, Emily knew she could trust her to succeed – if not today, then at some point during the coming week.

Although she had no expectation that it would happen swiftly, she still couldn't discount the possibility that her highly efficient friend might accomplish her task that very afternoon and thus, as three o'clock approached, she grew more and more nervous. She eyed the north entrance and imagined how Samuel might react at the sight of her. He would surely be aggrieved for he had become aware that her presence at the ball had taken place by dishonest means – on that score, her mother had apprised her of the circumstances relating to Miss Halliwell's rejection of the blue silk gown.

Shame burned inside her at the harm she had caused her mother, bringing about the loss of her employment at Madame Roche's shop and ruining her good reputation as a seamstress. Her mother had assured her that the disappointment of her dismissal had paled in comparison to her joy at Emily's safe return to Boston but Emily's guilt continued to fester, and she suspected it would persist until such time as she could make some sort of amends.

A movement at the park's entrance drew her focus back to it and, to her shock, Samuel Marlowe strode through it. Thank you, Matilda, she thought with fervour, even as a hiccup of trepidation shook her in anticipation of the coming encounter.

Samuel was just as handsome as she remembered. His bronze waves crowned his beautiful face with those dark eyelashes, and the cleft in his chin simply begged to be admired. He was a perfect specimen for portraiture.

Only her heart did not flutter when she saw him. She understood why, but that would have to wait a little longer.

He advanced along the path, glancing around like he was seeking someone. Clutching her courage and her bundle of papers, she began walking towards him. He came to a standstill when he caught sight of her. She halted a yard or two away. 'Good day, Mr Marlowe.'

A frown shaded his attractive features as he discerned the golden hair peeking from the confines of her bonnet. 'It really is you. I didn't know what to believe when I found that note.'

She dipped into a small curtsey. 'I am grateful you chose to respond to it, sir.'

'I'm not certain that I should have.' His frown deepened. 'You created quite a stir in the wake of that ball. No one could identify you and my mother said you were not on the guest list.' He folded his arms. 'Who are you?'

She gulped. 'To explain that, I must inform you that we actually made our first acquaintance on another occasion prior to Miss Knight's ball.'

He scoffed. 'We didn't. I would have remembered you.'

'Perhaps you could try to picture me wearing a white cap with a pigeon flying above my head.'

He squinted and then his eyelids sprang wide with amazement and unmistakable recognition. 'You're one of the maids?' he exclaimed.

435

'I was.'

'What the—' he spluttered. 'This doesn't make any sense.'

'Will you grant me a few minutes of your time to shed light upon the matter?'

His jaw tightened but, after a moment, he gave a grudging nod.

In the briefest terms, she explained her deception to him, how she had been a servant dressed up in fancy clothing that night and how she had entered the ball via the servants' access within the house. His expression grew darker with every word and she endeavoured not to wilt beneath his accusing gaze as she said, 'You and I shared a very memorable conversation that night. I admit that some elements of our interaction were a fabrication, but not all. I must stress that the most vital parts were authentic: our common interest in the arts, our exchanges of wit, our meeting of minds. If it's not too bold of me to say, I believe we made an instant connection.'

He surveyed her coolly. 'I had believed so too.'

She lowered her eyes. 'I regret that I deceived you, truly I do. And I yearned to make myself worthy of you. In fact, you would not give credit to the lengths that I have gone to since then in an effort to do so.'

'Worthy?' he repeated. 'Did you think a match between us might be possible?'

'I had hoped for it. But I can perceive now that it is an impossibility.'

He gave a reluctant laugh and she looked up to see that his reproach had been overlaid by a gentle humour which shone from his honey brown irises. 'I must say, though I can't condone your methods, I do admire your audacity. Tell me, what has brought you here today? What do you aim to achieve with your disclosure?'

'Nothing, sir, except the opportunity to offer you my heartfelt apology. I behaved abominably and I wounded you, and several others, by my foolish actions. I can't adequately express my remorse for it all.'

He paused to ponder this, a crease forming between his eyes. 'I might be of a mind to accept your apology,' he said at last. 'After all, it takes a lot of pluck to make such a confession. However, you've lied to me in the past. How can I trust that you're being honest now?'

She reddened with embarrassment; what a disgrace it was to be the object of such scepticism. 'All I can do is reiterate that my outright falsehoods that night were few in number. The dress was not mine and I had no invitation to be in attendance, but every word I spoke was truthful. You recall that I never imparted my name so I did not mislead you in that regard. Furthermore, the declarations I made concerning my personal talents were sincere: dancing is no forte of mine, while art is. I did bring some samples of my work to prove that I had not deceived you in every respect, if you wished to verify that.'

She indicated the bundle of papers under her arm. He peered down at them with curiosity.

'All right,' he said. 'Show me.'

She unrolled the bundle and handed the pages to him one at a time. They consisted of a selection of her best landscapes and portraits, some painted in watercolours and others sketched in pencil. Most of them she had created prior to her journey to England, but one she had only worked on in the past few days since her return – it depicted the rays of an ascending sun shimmering over a vast, calm ocean and a riot of private emotions churned behind its tranquil setting.

Samuel's eyebrows rose as he looked at each piece. 'These are all done by your own hand?' he asked, his tone coloured with astonishment.

'Yes, sir.'

He examined them closely, a smile of admiration tugging at the corners of his mouth. 'The subtlety in the strokes is quite extraordinary.'

'That is kind of you to say, sir. I'm glad you like them.'

He passed the pages back to her and she rolled them up again, quietly exultant that at least she could hold her head up proudly in this single aspect. After tucking them under her arm once more, she said, 'Thank you for coming here today, Mr Marlowe. I greatly appreciate it.' She turned to go.

'Wait a moment,' he said. When she looked back, his head was cocked to the side. 'Aren't you going to tell me your name after all this?'

'Oh,' she said. 'I'm Emily McGovern.' How relieved she was to still bear that surname.

'And what do you intend to do with your impressive gift, Miss McGovern? I hope you don't propose to waste it on mere scraps of paper and ignorant eyes such as mine.'

She blushed. 'As a matter of fact, I have recently been offered a place at Brubaker Art Academy in New York City.'

'I'm very pleased to hear that,' he said with genuine approval in his expression. 'Talent such as yours needs to be nurtured and, in due course, conveyed to a wider audience. When do you begin your studies?'

'Oh,' she said again, her embarrassment flooding back. 'Not yet. I need some time to...earn the necessary funds for the fees and accommodation.'

He blinked. 'I see. You surely do not mean to earn those funds under the roof of Marlowe House?'

'Good gracious, no!' she said, horrified. 'I have offended you and your parents enough.'

His arched eyebrow communicated his agreement on that point. 'Then where?'

'I'm not sure yet,' she admitted. 'I left my position at Marlowe House without a character so that might make it difficult to find one in another household. But I'm determined to work hard until I can afford my place at Brubaker, no matter how long it may take.'

He made no response to this at first, only stood there appraising her. Then he said, 'My cousin is newly betrothed.'

Startled by this unexpected turn in the conversation, she said, 'You mean Miss Knight? That...that is happy news.'

He nodded. 'By all accounts, she is overjoyed. There is only one thing that disappoints her: though she has lived in Philadelphia all her life, she will be obliged to set up her household where her future husband resides.' He paused. 'In New York City.'

Emily's breath caught in her throat.

Samuel's lips twitched upwards. 'No doubt she'll need to appoint a number of maids in her new home. It would make a significant difference, would it not, if you only had to earn the money for your fees and not your accommodation as well?'

'S-sir,' she struggled to reply. 'It would be a generosity that I do not deserve.'

'Perhaps,' he said. 'Or perhaps you deserve a second chance.'

Disbelief and hope soared simultaneously in her chest.

'I can't guarantee it,' he cautioned. 'But I'll see what Amelia says and I'll put in a very good word for you.'

She stuttered her thanks so incoherently that he chuckled and advised her to desist. Emitting a weak laugh, she curtseyed instead, her mind reeling from this unforeseen development and the myriad ramifications that could occur because of it.

They parted quite amicably and, still a little disorientated, she left the Common to make for her father's workshop, which he had already reopened since their return. The flutters that had been noticeably absent in Samuel's presence started to build as she walked along Boston's streets, and they were thrumming like a hummingbird's wings against her ribs by the time she reached the workshop. The bell above the door rang merrily as she entered.

Her father was sitting at the table in the front room scanning through some documents. He glanced up in surprise and pleasure at her appearance.

'What brings you here, *a stór*?'

'I'm just looking for Rory. Is he around?' She fully expected him to be for she had overheard her father tell her mother that he would do everything he could to keep Rory on as his apprentice, despite the loss of custom that the workshop's closure had incurred that summer.

'Yes, he's sawing in the back. Shall I fetch him?'

'No, that's fine. I'll go to him. May I leave this here?' At his nod, she deposited her bundle of artwork on the corner of his table. She headed towards the door that led to the back room but paused just before she passed through it. 'By the by, I would appreciate it if you didn't come in here for a few minutes.'

She caught his startled look and then the curve of his smile as she crossed the threshold into the back room.

She found Rory leaning over the bench in the centre of the room, sawing a length of wood. Sawdust coated the bench and floor around him and a generous amount had settled in his hair too. He didn't hear her approach so she sidled around the bench until she stepped into his line of sight. He jerked to a stop.

'What're you doing here?' he said, taken aback. He set down the saw and ran his hands through his shaggy hair, dislodging some of the sawdust which floated away in eddies.

She took a firm grip on her courage; she couldn't let it leak away on her now. 'I came to tell you that I've just been to see Samuel Marlowe.'

Disappointment flitted across his face, followed by resignation. 'Right. How's he doing?'

'He's well. Wait until you hear this—I only meant to explain and apologise to him for my antics this summer, but he saw some samples of my artwork and he was quite impressed. So impressed, in fact, that he has offered to help me secure another maid's position in a household in New York. Nothing has been confirmed yet but, if it were to happen, it would mean that I'd have a place to live in the city. That would allow me to save solely for my tuition fees and perhaps attend Brubaker much sooner than I had anticipated.'

Rory gave her a smile that lit up his green eyes. 'That's great news.'

She edged her way along the side of the bench towards him, trailing an absent-minded fingertip through the sawdust on top of it. 'It is and it isn't, I suppose. On the one hand, I'll be following my dream at long last. On the other...' She stopped only a couple of feet away from him. '...I'll be in New York. It's very far away from Boston, from my family and friends.' She was certain he must be able to hear her heart beating; it sounded extremely loud in her own ears. 'From you.'

His gaze snapped to hers. Colour bloomed in his cheeks as she peeked up at him shyly. The gap closed between them but it was he who took the step. Her skin was tingling again, not just her arm or her thigh but all over – every single inch of her hummed at his nearness. Neither of them said anything. Instead, he seemed to ask her a question with a tilt of his head; she answered with a blink of her lashes.

In the next moment, he bent down to her and she rose up on her tiptoes. Their mouths bumped together, a gentle knock that made her giggle. He exhaled a quick, amused breath which she felt tickle her lips.

'Let's try that again,' she whispered.

More carefully this time, they pressed their mouths together. She snaked her arms around his neck and he enfolded his about her waist as their lips tried this brand new language, touching and tasting, now with a little more bravery, now with a little extra pressure. She opened her mouth and let her tongue graze his lower lip. He reacted at once, meeting her tongue with his own. The sensation was so overwhelming that her legs began to shake. She brushed his tongue with hers one more time before pulling her mouth away. They separated, dropping their arms and exchanging bashful glances. Her knees were still quivering and her whole face felt flushed.

'The timing is poor, isn't it?' she said, her voice a little breathless. 'If circumstances go according to plan, I will likely be gone to New York for quite a while.' She grimaced. 'I suppose it would be selfish of me to ask you to wait.'

'No surprise there,' he joked and she gave him a playful smack on the arm.

'Do you mind?' she asked nervously.

'I do,' he said. Then he grinned. 'But I can wait.'

What's Next

The next book in the series will be A Class Inherited and, as you might expect, it will bring new challenges for the McGovern family! If you're not already a member of the **Susie Murphy Readers' Club**, be sure to join up on www.susiemurphywrites.com so that you will be the first to hear the news when A Class Inherited is ready to be published.

In the meantime, please help other readers discover this series by leaving an honest review about A Class Reunited on Amazon and/or Goodreads. A short review will make a huge difference in spreading the word about A Matter of Class. Thank you so much!

Acknowledgements

I want to start first of all by thanking the triumvirate that makes up my professional team: my editor, Averill Buchanan, my cover designer, Andrew Brown, and my narrator, Gary Furlong. Their talents are, quite simply, unparalleled.

I am so grateful to my early readers who took time out of their busy lives to read the first draft of A Class Reunited and who provided their feedback with such helpful reflection. Deirdre Dore, Bob Murphy, Miriam Bourke, Miriam Lanigan, Noreen Uí Ghríofá and Elizabeth Bell are all rock stars.

Thanks a million to my wonderful advance reader team who read the final version before publication. They gave me the confidence to let this not-so-little one fly the nest.

I'm incredibly lucky to have a growing circle of people around me who are so passionate about my books and extraordinarily kind about sharing news of them with others. These include the nicest book reviewers you could ever hope to meet: Claire Bridle (a truly exceptional lady), Lisa Redmond, Valerie Whitford, Ashley O'Melia and Anne Mendez. Special mention goes to lovely authors Lisa Boyle, Kelsey Gietl, Pam Lecky and Michele Quirke, and in particular Elizabeth Bell, who is always so generous with her advice and friendship. High fives to ER Gurney for her delightful enthusiasm and to Julia JM for her stunning artistic skills. Thanks also to Noel Dundon at the Tipperary Star.

I have nothing but unending gratitude for my fantastic husband, Bob, my parents, my extended family and my friends. Their constant support encourages me to keep writing.

Lastly, thank you, my precious reader. There are so many books out there in the world, and it is an absolute honour when you choose to read one of mine.

Get in Touch

www.susiemurphywrites.com
www.facebook.com/susiemurphywrites
www.twitter.com/susiemwrites
www.instagram.com/susiemurphywrites

Printed by BoD™in Norderstedt, Germany

9 781915 770059